Cassie Miles, a *USA To[day]* [bestselling author, lived in] Colorado for many years [and has recently moved to Oregon]. Her home is an hour from the rugged Pacific Ocean and an hour from the Cascade Mountains—the best of both worlds—not to mention the incredible restaurants in Portland and award-winning wineries in the Willamette Valley. She's looking forward to exploring the Pacific Northwest and finding mysterious new settings for Mills & Boon Heroes romances.

Beth Cornelison began working in public relations before pursuing her love of writing romance. She has won numerous honours for her work, including a nomination for the *RWA RITA*® Award for *The Christmas Stranger*. She enjoys featuring her cats (or friends' pets) in her stories and always has another book in the pipeline! She currently lives in Louisiana with her husband, one son and three spoiled cats. Contact her via her website, bethcornelison.com

Also by Cassie Miles

Lighthouse Mysteries
Fugitive Harbor
The Girl Who Couldn't Forget
The Girl Who Wouldn't Stay Dead
Frozen Memories
Mountain Blizzard
Mountain Shelter
Mountain Bodyguard
Colorado Wildfire
Mountain Retreat

Also by Beth Cornelison

Cameron Glen
Mountain Retreat Murder
Kidnapping in Cameron Glen
Cameron Mountain Rescue
Protecting His Cameron Baby
Cameron Mountain Refuge

The Coltons of Owl Creek
Targeted with a Colton

The Coltons of New York
Colton's Undercover Seduction

Discover more at millsandboon.co.uk

THE LIGHTKEEPER'S CURSE

CASSIE MILES

HER CAMERON DEFENDER

BETH CORNELISON

MILLS & BOON

All rights reserved including the right of reproduction in whole or in part in any form. This edition is published by arrangement with Harlequin Enterprises ULC.

This is a work of fiction. Names, characters, places, locations and incidents are purely fictional and bear no relationship to any real life individuals, living or dead, or to any actual places, business establishments, locations, events or incidents. Any resemblance is entirely coincidental.

This book is sold subject to the condition that it shall not, by way of trade or otherwise, be lent, resold, hired out or otherwise circulated without the prior consent of the publisher in any form of binding or cover other than that in which it is published and without a similar condition including this condition being imposed on the subsequent purchaser.

® and ™ are trademarks owned and used by the trademark owner and/or its licensee. Trademarks marked with ® are registered with the United Kingdom Patent Office and/or the Office for Harmonisation in the Internal Market and in other countries.

First Published in Great Britain 2025
by Mills & Boon, an imprint of HarperCollins*Publishers* Ltd
1 London Bridge Street, London, SE1 9GF

www.harpercollins.co.uk

HarperCollins*Publishers*
Macken House, 39/40 Mayor Street Upper,
Dublin 1, D01 C9W8, Ireland

The Lightkeeper's Curse © 2025 Kay Bergstrom
Her Cameron Defender © 2025 Beth Cornelison

ISBN: 978-0-263-39709-3

0425

This book contains FSC™ certified paper and other controlled sources to ensure responsible forest management.

For more information visit: www.harpercollins.co.uk/green

Printed and Bound in the UK using 100% Renewable Electricity at
CPI Group (UK) Ltd, Croydon, CR0 4YY

THE LIGHTKEEPER'S CURSE

CASSIE MILES

Thanks to Julie Drey, an author who can really sling a curse. And, as always, to Rick.

Hear me, o goddesses,
West, East, North, South.
Scratch out his eyes.
Muzzle his mouth.

Bind his arms.
Heed not his plea.
Death to the Keeper.
So mote it be.

Chapter One

Heavy clouds obscured the moonlight and stars above Cape Meares, west of Tillamook Bay on the Oregon shoreline. Through the darkness, Phoebe Conway crept through tendrils of fog weaving through spruce, hemlock and rugged coastal pines. Her instincts told her to turn around and dash back to her car parked at the scenic viewpoint off Highway 101, but life was about more than mere survival.

She had gold-plated ambition. Whatever happened tonight could be her big break. The instructions told her to come at midnight to the Cape Meares Lighthouse and to come alone. She was willing to take the risk.

Earlier today, a plain white envelope with no return address appeared on her desk at the *Astoria Sun* newspaper. Nobody saw the person who dropped the note with her name in bold above the newspaper's address. She'd read and reread:

> I have new evidence about the Lightkeeper's Curse Murders. You should be the reporter to tell this story, Phoebe. You're a shining star from the Lone Star state but unappreciated. I'll make sure you get what you deserve. Tell no one about this contact. Don't bring a phone or a camera. Cape Meares Lighthouse at midnight.

She wished there had been a signature or an email address—some way to verify the identity of the person who wrote the note. Was it someone who'd been alive in the early 2000s when the serial murders took place? Or a descendant of the Lightkeeper killer? Perhaps the Lightkeeper himself? After all, he'd never been arrested.

Maybe he'd been waiting all this time for the right reporter to come along—waiting for her. The article she'd written about *The Goonies*, a classic movie filmed in Astoria, had been picked up by several major newspapers and had led to three television appearances on the local news in Portland and Seattle. In her vintage letterman's sweater and short white skirt suggesting the costume worn by the female lead, Phoebe had looked fantastic. Camera-ready. Meant to be a star.

If this mysterious note-writer had new information about the infamous Lightkeeper's Curse, she might have the scoop of the century.

Shivering in the October chill, she flipped up the collar on her jacket and followed the downward sloping asphalt path from the parking lot to the lighthouse. A rough wooden railing bordered the seaward side where the trees were spread far enough apart for her to glimpse the churning waves of the Pacific.

The screech of a nighthawk startled her, and she waved her flashlight to chase the bird away. The beam reflected off the fog, giving substance to the wispy shapes. The mossy tree branches looked like claws reaching toward her, trying to grab her blond ponytail and drag her down, down, down. The fog took on terrifying shapes. A humpback monster. A dragon. A ghoul.

She heard a sound behind her and whipped around, dancing on the toes of her sneakers. "Who's there?"

Nothing but darkness and a shredded curtain of mist. The wind droned through the boughs and branches of the nearby wilderness preserve in an eerie hum.

Did she hear an undercurrent of laughter? Again, she pivoted. Her flashlight beam wavered madly. Her pulse raced.

She clenched her jaw and marched onward. This was no time to be scared of the dark.

She rounded the last curve and approached the octagonal, whitewashed brick lighthouse that stood on a rocky promontory at the edge of a two-hundred-foot cliff.

Not a particularly impressive structure, the decommissioned lighthouse was the shortest in Oregon. Only thirty-eight feet high but beautifully maintained by the Park Service, the tower and attached gift shop opened every day from morning until dusk. A porch light hung over the door to the shop, but the bulb must have burned out. Shifting glimmers of moonlight provided the only illumination.

A bit of online research told her the red-and-white flashing Fresnel beacon—when operational—had been visible from twenty-one nautical miles away. Starting in the early 1890s, the Cape Meares Lighthouse guided sailors through the treacherous rocks, shoals and sandbars on the coastal route from southern California to British Columbia. These fraught seas caused an estimated three thousand shipwrecks, including the rusted skeleton of a hull she'd visited on a stretch of beach and a cannon that washed ashore near Haystack Rock.

She stood at the wooden railing, watching the fog and the endless ocean. In the rumble of the surf, she heard echoes of lost souls—the dying screams from sailors calling for help that never came.

Some people saw lighthouses as symbols of hope. Too often, hope wasn't enough.

Phoebe turned her back on the sea and studied the squat tower that stood before her. Where the hell was her mysterious informant? The night was too cold to play games, and she felt the first splash of a raindrop on her forehead.

"Hello?" she called out. "It's me. Phoebe."

No human voice responded. Only the whisper from the wind and the rattle of the surf. Though she appreciated the drama of the ominous setting, which would play well when she wrote her article, enough was enough. "Okay, whoever you are. Show yourself."

"Here."

The deep voice shocked her, and she looked in the direction it seemed to come from. Upward. A person in a black hoodie stood on the circular balcony wrapped around the tower at the same level as the beacon.

Darkness and fog shrouded the figure, but Phoebe had the impression that he was big. "Who are you? Can you give me your name?"

A long arm beckoned to her. "Come."

She hesitated. Something in his voice scared her. They were out here alone. Her hand slipped into her shoulder bag before she remembered that she'd obeyed the note and left her work phone at her office at the *Sun*. Her personal phone was in her car, leaving her unable to call 911.

The figure turned away from her.

"Wait," she called after him. "I did everything you asked." Not one hundred percent true. Though she hadn't spoken to anyone, she'd used her work phone to take a picture of the note he'd delivered. Since he hadn't specifically mentioned weapons, she'd armed herself with a stun gun. If he attacked her, twenty-five thousand volts ought to be enough to slow him down.

He disappeared into the tower.

Reaching into her the pocket of her jacket, she wrapped her fingers around the handle of the stun gun while holding her flashlight with the other hand. She shouted, "I'm coming. Don't leave. I want to hear your story."

She circled around to the gift shop—a small, attached house that had once been used by crews who tended the beacon. The door was unlocked, and she stepped inside just as the raindrops turned into a storm that would turn her long blond hair into a frizzled mess.

The shop displayed books, T-shirts, postcards and tourist

junk. Behind the counter with the cash register stood a row of three-foot-tall replicas of the Cape Meares Lighthouse. Their rotating beacons provided the only light in the shop. The flashes disconcerted her. She blinked and turned away. But then she moved forward. One step at a time.

She left the door ajar so she could make a speedy exit if need be.

When she crossed the shop and entered the actual tower, her gaze traveled around the whitewashed wall to an elegant wrought iron staircase that molded to the octagonal shape of the walls. The glow from moon and stars shone through a narrow window and from the top of the stair. A faint and eerie illumination. Was he up at the top, waiting for her?

She cleared her throat and put some force into her voice. "Hello. Are you here?"

The door to the gift shop slammed. She turned and saw a hooded figure coming at her, vaulting through the racks of T-shirts and shelves of knickknacks.

She froze, unable to believe her eyes. He couldn't have gotten down from the upper level and outside so quickly. "How did you get past me?"

"Climbed down from the outside." He came closer.

"Stay back."

Lightning fast, he grasped her wrists and twisted her arms behind her. Both the stun gun and the flashlight crashed to the floor. Handcuffs clicked into place.

Roughly, he shoved her around to face him. The lower half of his face was masked, but she recognized him immediately.

"I promised new information," he growled. "Here's your scoop, Phoebe."

"Let me go. I don't care."

"There will be more murders to come. Starting with yours."

She heard herself scream. And knew that no one would be coming to her rescue.

Chapter Two

Special Agent Skylar Gambel had paid her dues. After two years working with the prosecuting attorney's office in her hometown of San Francisco, graduation with honors from the FBI Academy in Quantico and four years of desk work as an analyst at the J. Edgar Hoover Building in DC, she had transferred to the Portland FBI field office where she gladly took on the responsibilities of a special agent. Mentally, she underlined *gladly*. It felt like she'd been waiting all her life for this opportunity to be an active investigator.

In addition to her thorough training and education, she had great instincts. Her first impressions of people were nearly as accurate as a computer profile or a lie detector. Ninety-seven times out of a hundred, she could pick the criminal from a lineup. Not a particularly desirable ability for an attorney who ought to presume innocence, even as a prosecutor.

Always look on the bright side of life, right? She struggled to keep an open mind, even when she intuited the truth.

By the end of her third week in Oregon, she felt settled in her new city. Portland offered gourmet dining, fantastic coffee shops, artsy events and Powell's, which was supposed to be the largest independent bookstore in the world. She'd joined a fantastic dojo to practice her karate skills and take new instruction in Krav Maga. She varied the route for her morning run to check out the local gardens, waterfalls and forests.

As far as she was concerned, the only real negative to living in Portland was...bridges. Getting around town almost always meant traversing one or two or more overpasses. Not her favorite thing. She hated the way the prestressed concrete shuddered beneath her tires or the indefinable but frightening sense of dangling in midair. Crossing over rivers and waterways always sparked a twinge of vertigo. A knot in the gut. Accelerated pulse rate. Her reaction was similar to a panic attack.

If she concentrated, she could keep her nasty little phobia under control. If not, she might have a real meltdown. Not a good look for an FBI special agent.

Before lunch on Thursday, she got an important, interesting assignment: an active murder investigation in Astoria at the mouth of the Columbia River. *Finally!*

Though eager to get started, she curbed her enthusiasm. Celebration would be grossly inappropriate, given the gruesome nature of the crime. The victim—twenty-nine years old, the same age as Skylar—died from manual strangulation at the historic lighthouse on Cape Meares.

Though tours of the lighthouse and gift shop ended in September, a Park Service ranger on his morning rounds at the scenic viewpoint noticed the door to the gift shop was open. Inside, he discovered the victim's lifeless body gracefully arranged on the swooping staircase leading to the lighthouse beacon. She'd been blindfolded and gagged with her wrists handcuffed behind her back.

Standing at her desk, Skylar looked over the case notes and the crime scene photos displayed on her computer. The long legs of the dead woman were tucked demurely beneath her on a lower step of the black, wrought iron stairs. Her torso leaned against the railing. Her long blond hair draped across her face, held in place by the bandanna tied over her eyes. A square of duct tape covered her mouth. The dark bruise on her throat could barely be seen under her neatly combed and styled hair, an indication that she hadn't been outside last night in the rain. Also, her sneakers didn't appear to be muddy.

In her work as an analyst, Skylar had seen her share of crime scene photos. Many captured a sense of the untimely death, as if the victim had been interrupted or surprised in the middle of doing something else. Their life was cut short. Expectations erased. That was surely the case with Phoebe Conway, a successful reporter at the *Astoria Sun* newspaper, who had been identified at the scene using the driver's license from her wallet.

Skylar silently promised Phoebe that her killer would be brought to justice. That was her job as a special agent. With a renewed sense of purpose, she holstered her Glock 19 under the jacket of her charcoal gray suit before turning toward her partner. "I'm ready."

The handsome, white-haired senior agent named Harold Crawford—often referred to around the office as the Silver Fox—acted as her supervisor and mentor. He reached into the lower left drawer in his desk, took out a battered nine-by-twelve envelope and dropped it with a thud on his desktop beside the framed photo of his three grandchildren. "First, we're going to Astoria."

"Not the crime scene at Cape Meares?"

"Astoria," he repeated. "Do you have a change of clothes?"

"In my locker." She tucked a strand of dark auburn hair into the low ponytail at her nape and straightened the light blue collar of her blouse.

"We'll be doing some hiking." He stared pointedly at her shoes.

"I'm prepared." Of course, she had alternate footwear. "Unless there's some kind of special dress code for Astoria."

"Don't be a smart-ass. My wife thinks you look and dress

like a recruitment poster for professional women in the FBI, but you're just another newbie in my book."

Growing up with two older brothers had prepared her for teasing. Crawford was like a favorite uncle with a pseudo-grumpy sense of humor. "The boss mentioned that you have a history with this investigation," she said. "The Lightkeeper's Curse Murders?"

His forehead pinched into a frown. "We'll talk on the way. Astoria is about a hundred miles from here, and the ride takes two or two-and-a-half hours, which means we'll get there around three. I asked you about clothes because we'll stay overnight."

"No problem." In addition to the go bag in her locker, she had more clothes, equipment and her bulletproof vest in the trunk of her car, all of which she transferred to the fleet vehicle they signed out for the trip.

Within forty-five minutes of getting their assignment, she and Crawford hit the road in an unmarked black Chevy Suburban. While he navigated Portland traffic and merged onto Route 30 headed northwest toward the coast, she studied printouts of police reports she'd tucked into the extra-large briefcase on the floor between her feet, clad in sensible boots.

The body of Phoebe Conway was found this morning at about half-past nine. The Oregon Park Service employee notified the Tillamook County sheriff's office, who established a crime scene, contacted the coroner and arranged for the deceased to be taken to the Clatsop County medical examiner. They advised them to contact the police chief in Astoria who, in turn, reached out to the Portland FBI field office.

She glanced over at Crawford. "Jurisdiction on this murder has been bouncing around like a pinball. Right now, it looks like the ME in Warrenton passed the ball to the police chief in Astoria."

"Correct. That would be Chief Vivienne Kim. The veteran ME is Dr. Kate Kinski. I'll recommend that she do the autopsy instead of shipping the remains to Portland."

"Tell me why the FBI is involved."

"I might have pulled a few strings," he admitted.

"Because of the serial murders that happened over twenty years ago?"

While keeping his eye on the road, he nodded slowly. "The Lightkeeper Murders. Seven women were killed. All their bodies were found at or near lighthouses in Clatsop County, Tillamook County and across the Columbia River in Washington state at Cape Disappointment."

Cape Disappointment? Well, that's a colorful name. She drew the obvious conclusion. "We were consulted due to the multijurisdictional nature."

"Partially," he said. "Twenty years ago, I was part of the task force. You'll find details in the envelope I took from my desk. I already stuck it into your briefcase."

She dug through the files and found the worn, tattered envelope. Since he still kept that cold case evidence close at hand, she figured SSA Crawford hadn't given up on solving the murders. "Never caught the guy?"

"Never did."

The envelope held extensive reports, depositions, photos and whatever. Digging through it was daunting. "Instead of reading," she said, "I'd rather hear the story from you."

"Straight from the horse's mouth?"

"Talk to me, Seabiscuit."

She leaned back in the passenger seat and prepared to listen. In the distance, she saw the truncated peak of Mount St. Helens across the river in Washington. The snow-covered summit of Mount Hood was in the rearview mirror, still visible in the midafternoon sunlight of a clear autumn day.

In addition to bridges, Oregon was all about trees. Amid conifers, spruce, cedars and pines, a hundred different shades of green surrounded her, starting with the blackberry and chokecherry thickets close to the ground and rising past vines, ferns and boughs to the towering spires of Sitka spruce. The gold and scarlet of autumn appeared in the aspens, larches and maples. Beautiful. Peaceful. Wild.

And dangerous. Wildfires had blackened many of the formerly verdant hillsides, leaving jagged tree stumps and stacks of scrap wood. The skeletons of a small enclave—three dwellings, a garage, outbuildings, fence and a one-story horse barn—spoke of destruction and devastation. The serenity of the forests masked a darker reality.

Crawford continued to speak in a calm tone, more befitting a grandpa telling a bedtime story than a special agent recalling serial murders.

Once upon a time, some twenty years ago, seven women were killed. All died of asphyxiation, either from hanging or by manual strangulation. Their bodies were displayed with wrists in handcuffs, a square of duct tape over the mouth and a bandanna blindfold. All were in or near a lighthouse. The killer sent notes and audio tapes, taunting law enforcement.

She asked, "Have you stayed in touch with other investigators from the case?"

"Occasionally I check in with the former police chief, Jimi Kim, who retired several years ago. He's a third generation native of Astoria. The current chief, Vivienne, is his granddaughter."

"Deep roots."

"Astoria was founded in 1811 and was one of the oldest permanent settlements west of the Rockies. Early residents were mostly sailors and trappers. Now, the coast guard has a base there."

While he filled in details, she noticed the afternoon skies fading from clear to misty gray and then darker as the haze obscured the sunlight. "Fog."

"Get used to it, newbie."

"I know plenty about fog. I grew up in San Francisco."

"Astoria is one of the foggiest towns in North America. That's why there are so many lighthouses in this area."

"Hence the Lightkeeper moniker," she said. "Do you believe the current murder is connected to what happened twenty years ago?"

"Gotta be. Too similar to be a coincidence."

"The work of a copycat."

"That's a possibility, but don't be too quick to make assumptions."

"I understand." She realized that he'd given her the lesson for the day. Her instincts might be useful but were only one piece of an investigation. They needed research, witnesses and evidentiary facts.

The short bridge over the John Day River gave Skylar a shiver, and she closed her eyes for a moment, waiting for her vertigo to dissipate.

"Tired?" Crawford asked.

"A little bit." She'd never told him or anybody else in the FBI about her phobia. Special agents weren't supposed to have psychological issues.

"I've got a warning for you. The people in Astoria, including local law enforcement, don't always follow the rules. We need to be open."

"Got it."

"Flexible."

"I'm as bendy as a yoga guru."

When they entered Astoria, she peered through fog at a port town of steep hillsides, docks, kitschy businesses and an array of Victorian and Edwardian renovations. She stared at the dominant structure.

Massive. Terrifying. The landmark Astoria-Megler Bridge spanned the mighty Columbia River between Oregon and Washington.

Her breath caught in her throat. "Yikes."

"The longest cantilevered truss bridge in the country, it's

more than twice as long as the Golden Gate. Cape Disappointment is on the opposite side." Crawford pulled into a space outside a rectangular, no-frills structure on 30th Street, a few blocks up from the riverfront. He turned toward her and asked, "Did you ever see the movie *The Goonies*?"

"A long time ago."

"Filmed in Astoria. The opening scene took place at the real-life Clatsop County Jail. Years ago, that old-time prison was transformed into a film museum. This less colorful Public Safety Building is home for the APD, the Astoria Police Department."

They left the Suburban in the parking area and walked around a news van, which was *not*—in Skylar's opinion—a welcome sight. Though she'd only been in Portland for a couple of weeks, she'd already had a confrontation with a cranky on-the-scene reporter who thought she was "too big for her britches."

At the corner of the building was a three-foot-tall iron fence surrounding a pink plaster pig with black hoofs. *More local color?* She pointed. "What's this?"

"The pig started as a prank thirty years ago. Now he's a mascot."

Turning her back on the bridge, she went up the sidewalk toward the entrance. The door to the building opened, and a man strode toward them. The first thing she noticed about him was his height, probably six feet six inches—a full twelve inches taller than she was. His clothing—khakis, a dark blue fleece vest and a plaid shirt with sleeves rolled up—was casual but impeccably neat, which caused her to suspect he was former military. When his laser-blue gaze found her, she felt a burst of electricity and a sizzle she hadn't experienced in quite some time.

Large and in charge, he exuded confidence. He reached out and grasped her hand. "I'm Detective Jake Armstrong."

"Pleased to meet you, Detective." She studied his features.

The stubborn set of his square jaw. The dimple centered on his chin. His sharp cheekbones and those amazing blue eyes.

"It's Jake," he said. "I heard the FBI had been summoned. I guess that's you two."

"I'm Skylar," she said. "Special Agent Skylar Gambel."

She felt his gaze sizing her up. Tilting her head back, she did the same to him, continuing her observation and trying to withhold judgment. She guessed his age to be close to thirty. He fit neatly into his environment, and she easily imagined him as a seaman at the helm or a lumberjack. Certainly not an urban transplant like her.

He pushed his dark blond hair off his forehead and zeroed in on her partner. "If I'm not mistaken, you're Special Agent Harold Crawford. You were with the task force that investigated the Lightkeeper twenty years ago."

"Correct."

"We need to talk."

What about me? Skylar wanted to talk with Jake for several reasons. Number one, she wanted information on the prior investigations. Number two, she didn't want to be left out of the loop. And number three...she couldn't explain but wanted to make sense of this attraction to a small-town officer she probably had nothing in common with.

SSA Crawford cleared his throat. "Is Chief Vivienne in the office?"

"Yes, sir. I'm on my way to the crime scene at Cape Meares."

"Perfect." Skylar stepped forward. "I'll ride with you."

Crawford—her supervisor and mentor—gave her a long, thoughtful look. He often encouraged her to make her own decisions and chart her own course. *Somebody* needed to check out the crime scene. Might as well be her. He raised an eyebrow. "Taking the initiative, newbie?"

"I am, sir."

"First, we meet the chief. Then, you and Detective Armstrong head south to Cape Meares." He turned to Jake. "I remember you from twenty years ago. You loved comic books and were about half the size you are now."

"I was ten."

"You've lived here most of your life," Crawford said. "Were you close to Phoebe Conway?"

His brilliant blue eyes dimmed. "I knew her."

"My condolences," Crawford said. "Astoria has my deepest sympathy. I hope we've arrived in time to prevent other tragic murders."

Chapter Three

Though he would have preferred going to the crime scene and starting his investigation into Phoebe Conway's murder, Jake escorted the two FBI agents into the central lobby of the public safety building where the police and the fire department had their offices. Reporters, bloggers and influencers from Astoria, nearby towns and even Portland—including a threesome of pesky little blondes—had taken up residence, hoping for fresh information on the Lightkeeper's Curse.

Without acknowledging any of them, Jake marched toward the entrance for the APD. Following his lead, neither of the special agents paid attention to the shouted questions. Skylar Gambel—who was prettier than any fed had a right to be— shot angry glares at the local press. Her hostility made him think she'd had negative experiences with reporters.

With her low ponytail at her nape and light makeup, she looked too young to be a world-weary fed, and SSA Crawford had referred to her inexperience. *Newbie?* He'd called her newbie.

Jake didn't get it. Even if Skylar had started just yesterday, he wouldn't have picked that nickname. She owned the sort of cool, sophisticated attitude that went along with being the smartest kid in the room.

He didn't recognize any reporters from the *Astoria Sun*, which was where he'd go after the visit to the crime scene. A short while ago, after Phoebe's identity had been confirmed with fingerprints, Jake had called the newspaper where she worked, talked to the editor and told him that Phoebe's desk should be treated as a crime scene. Nobody should touch anything. Not the other reporters. Or the office staff. Or the janitors. Or Phoebe's friends and family.

He doubted his warning would have much effect, and he sent their primary forensic investigator to enforce his instructions. Asking a flock of newsies to stay away from a potential piece of evidence was akin to advising buzzards that roadkill was off-limits. An unfortunate comparison but accurate.

He hustled Crawford and Skylar into the Astoria Police Department, past the front counter, emblazoned with the Astoria Column logo, and down a hall to the central conference room. The large, windowless space had a long table in the middle, several chairs, a podium pushed to the side, whiteboards on easels and the beginnings of a murder board on the wall.

Police Chief Vivienne Kim rose to greet them. "Thanks for your quick response. I hope to take the position of command central for this investigation because my ability to do fieldwork is limited. My doctor advised me to slow down."

Jake pulled a frown to keep from grinning. When the very-pregnant chief turned sideways, the reason for her doctor's advice was evident. A basketball-size bulge puffed out the belly of her dark-blue police uniform jacket. Her badge dangled from a lanyard around her neck. Jake had no idea where she stashed her gun and handcuffs.

She continued, "I suppose I could hand over my responsibilities to somebody else at the APD, but this is the Lightkeeper—the worst, most feared serial killer in our town's history. I need to be involved."

"You're handling the situation well," Crawford said. "Your grandpa would be proud."

She flashed a smile and smoothed her straight, shiny black hair. "Jimi always speaks highly of you."

"Not catching the Lightkeeper was one of the great disappointments of both our lives. I hope he can take part in our investigation, even though he's retired."

"So glad you said that. He's on his way in."

Jake watched Skylar's sea-green eyes for a reaction to the irregular protocol of involving a retired officer in police procedure.

Instead of making a comment, she pointed to an open box of Girl Scout cookies. "Are these for everybody?"

"Help yourself," Chief Vivienne said. "We already ate the fruit and quiche, but there's coffee on the side table and hot water for tea. Mugs are in the break room."

"Much appreciated."

Her attitude remained guarded. She seemed to be taking the measure of the APD, forming opinions about the people she'd be working with before deciding how to proceed. Soon she'd discover that Astoria was a small town with a population of about eleven thousand. They had their own ways of doing business.

Chief Kim introduced two other officers in uniform and a local librarian, Dagmar Burke. The chief explained, "I've asked Dagmar to give us context and reminders of the serial killings. She's an expert on local history and the Lightkeeper's Curse."

In Jake's opinion, Dagmar was also headstrong, smug and irritating as all hell. The tall, broad-shouldered woman with tousled blond hair and a boho fashion sense looked down her nose at them and flipped her wrist, setting dozens of sparkly bangles to clanking. "Before I start, do you have any questions?"

"I do," Skylar said. "How many lighthouses are in this area?"

"A lot. Lighthouses were necessary along this stretch of

coast that was called the graveyard of the Pacific because of the many shipwrecks. There are dozens of replica lighthouses outside restaurants and shops. A mobile one on a coast guard vessel. Cape Meares, of course, and another on an offshore island near Tillamook. Plus, two more on the Washington side of the Columbia on Cape Disappointment."

"How did Cape Disappointment get its name?" Skylar asked.

"The accepted legend focuses on the British trader, John Meares."

"Who gave his name to the cape farther down the coast."

"That's right." Dagmar launched into lecture mode. "In 1788, while returning from Canada, Meares rounded the cape and ventured into the mouth of the Columbia which was so wide and wild that he thought it was a bay and not the legendary river. The knucklehead went back out to sea. Disappointed. He named the bay, too. Deception Bay."

Jake had spent a lifetime watching Dagmar do her thing and appreciated her encyclopedic grasp of local knowledge. Still, he worried about having her involved in a police investigation, especially this one. She was too close.

"I noticed decorations when we drove through town," Crawford said.

"It's only ten days until Halloween," Dagmar said, "and that's a busy season around here."

"Why?" Skylar asked.

"Fog makes everything look spooky. Astoria developed a rep for having ghosts, hidden pirate treasure and mermaids." In her flowing layers of paisley and fringe, she looked like she'd already costumed herself. "But the most important thing, the only important thing, is solving Phoebe's murder."

"So true," Chief Vivienne said.

Dagmar's cheeks flushed. "I knew Phoebe Conway. She was a terrific reporter with a big career ahead of her. Had dreams of someday working at one of the Portland television stations. Her murder is tragic."

Though Jake agreed with what she was saying, he worried about the way Dagmar took her friend's death so personally. The last thing they needed was Dagmar getting too wrapped up in her emotions about the case.

Dagmar tossed an accusing comment at SSA Crawford. "This time, you'd better catch the killer."

"Nice to see you again, Dagmar." Crawford kept his tone easygoing. "It was twenty years ago."

"I've changed, and so have you."

"You grew up, and I grew…" Through the grapevine, Jake heard that Crawford was close to the mandatory retirement age of fifty-seven for a special agent. "I grew old."

Skylar stepped up beside her partner but spoke to Dagmar. "I have another question, if you don't mind."

"Shoot," Dagmar said.

"Unlike most of you, I'm new to this case," Skylar said. "I'd like a brief overview of the Lightkeeper's Curse serial murders from the perspective of the locals."

"Go for it, Dagmar." Jake gave her a nod. "Stick to the facts."

"I always do."

"Or not."

"Here's what we know," Dagmar said. "The women were likely stalked. After they were grabbed by the killer, they were held captive for at least two hours but no longer than a day. They were restrained but not tortured. It's unclear what he was doing with them. Or to them."

"I have analysis and victimology reports from twenty years ago," the chief said. "Their ages ranged from nineteen to thirty-nine, and they were diverse in appearance. We'll know more about Phoebe's death after the autopsy."

Dagmar continued, "The Lightkeeper thought he received instructions from an exalted priestess who despised these women for their wanton ways. It was his job to rid the world of them. With each victim, he made a cassette recording of her last moments, giving her a chance to recant her errors. He didn't blindfold and gag them until after they were dead. The Lightkeeper also sent taunting letters to the *Astoria Sun*."

When Skylar glanced at him, looking for answers, he didn't respond. She turned toward the chief and asked, "Was there a note before the murder of Phoebe Conway?"

"We haven't found anything," Chief Kim said.

"Have you received a recording?"

"Not yet."

"What about the curse?" Skylar asked.

"I'm an expert on this particular subject." Dagmar's voice quavered. "The last woman he killed, number seven, was my mother. Working as a librarian, she studied curses and killers. Once, she told me and my dad that she thought she was being followed. He didn't believe her, but I did. I was only twelve. There wasn't much I could do."

Skylar spoke in a gentle tone. "I'm so sorry, Dagmar."

She shook her head, and her wild hair danced. "Before she died, my mother cursed him, and he recorded her words. Unlike all the other tapes, he spoke on this one and whispered that he was sorry. Mama was his last victim."

Until now?

Chapter Four

After leaving the APD, Skylar walked beside Jake to the parking area where he headed toward a dark gray Ford Explorer with the Astoria police logo on the side. The midafternoon fog was even thicker than when she and Crawford had arrived in town less than an hour ago. She stood at the passenger side of Jake's car and inhaled a gulp of salty harbor air while he unlocked the door and opened it for her.

Seated inside, she tried to center herself as she considered Dagmar's lecture about the twenty-year-old serial murders. The Lightkeeper typified the worst kind of serial killer—an intelligent individual with an organized plan for his assaults, ranging from stalking to staging the bodies while sending written and verbal taunts to the police. Investigating him would be a challenge, for sure. And potentially a failure. He'd escaped before.

Not that they had proof the person who killed Phoebe was the infamous Lightkeeper. The similarity between twenty years ago and the current murder could be coincidence. Or the work of a copycat.

The description of a killer who was on a "mission" and had guidance from a mysterious priestess made her think of the Son of Sam, a serial killer in New York in the seventies who claimed to be taking orders from his neighbor's dog. Hearing voices was symptomatic of several forms of psychosis. Skylar would leave it to the profilers to analyze, but she needed to understand the Lightkeeper's motives.

Thus far, no one had mentioned sexual molestation. Why did the Lightkeeper kill? And why did he quit? She found it hard to believe this brutal murderer was stopped by a curse.

She asked Jake, "How well do you know Dagmar?"

"Why do you ask?"

He didn't answer her question, and she noticed the deflection. His indirect response gave rise to suspicions about him. Not for the first time, she sensed a cover-up in his attitude. Something to do with Dagmar? Their back-and-forth banter had a familiar, teasing edge. She wouldn't have been surprised to discover that they were or had been close, possibly ex-girlfriend and boyfriend. Or something more. He wasn't wearing a wedding ring. "Did you and Dagmar both grow up in Astoria?"

"Yes, but I got out as soon as I turned eighteen."

"Joined the military?" she guessed.

"Marines."

Skylar scored a point for her instincts and returned to the topic at hand. "I'm surprised Dagmar didn't move away. Having her mother murdered by a serial killer must have triggered post-traumatic stress disorder. Tell me again what she does for a living. A historian?"

"Librarian," he said.

"Like her mother," she said. "She's a great storyteller. Not revealing the words to the curse was a master touch. I'm curious. Do you know what it said?"

"Yes."

Of course, he did. "Because the police have the cassette recording of Dagmar's mother's last words. You've gone back and listened to it."

"I heard the tape when the murders took place."

"But you were only a kid, right?"

He turned right onto a street that followed the harbor, and

they passed the historic red-and-yellow trolley that dinged a bell, enticing Halloween tourists to ride. "I shouldn't have heard the recording when I was so young, but the former police chief encouraged my interest."

"Chief Jimi Kim." Crawford had praised this retired officer to the skies. "Surely, he didn't share evidence with you."

"He was too good a cop to break evidentiary protocol or procedure. But I was determined, and I got my sticky little fingers on a copy of the tape."

"You stole it."

"Borrowed," he said. "The audio quality wasn't great. You can hear every word, but voice analysis of the Lightkeeper's whisper was inconclusive when he said he was sorry. Couldn't even tell if it was a man or a woman."

She was about to ask him to repeat the curse when she noticed their route past a marina where fishing boats were docked. "Where are we headed?"

"South. We take Highway 101 all the way to Cape Mcares after we cross the bridge."

The bridge? Panic shot through her. "I thought the bridge went to Washington."

"You're thinking of the Astoria-Megler Bridge—the colossus that looms over Astoria like Godzilla. This is the New Youngs Bay Bridge. In comparison, it's a baby bridge. A two-lane drive, not very high and shorter than a mile."

Peering through the fog, she saw the Explorer approaching the bay as if to dive nose first through the fog and into the water. No time to prepare herself. She couldn't settle her breathing. Or meditate. Or shield herself in any way from her irrational phobia. Not even her mantra—*Nam myoho renge kyo*—could help. Probably she had those syllables twisted and wrong. *Can't do anything right.* Her tension escalated. Her pulse fluttered like a caged bird.

When he drove onto the bridge, she slammed her eyes closed. Less than a mile. She could hold her breath for that long. In her head, she started playing a song with a heavy beat. "Proud Mary" usually distracted her. Again, she couldn't remember the words. "...left a good job in the city..." The rumble of tires on concrete competed with her song. "...rolling, rolling, rolling on the river."

"Skylar?"

She heard concern in his voice and hoped that she hadn't been singing out loud. Her eyelids lifted. *Hallelujah*, the Explorer was on solid ground.

Jake asked, "Are you okay? You look pale."

"A little hungry, that's all." She forced a smile. "What were we talking about?"

"Come to think of it," he said, "I skipped lunch, too. We can make a stop. Grab a burger."

"I'd rather get to the crime scene." She dug into her purse and pulled out a granola bar. "I'll munch on this. Weren't you going to tell me more about the curse?"

He didn't look convinced that an energy bar would put everything right. "I'm stopping at the next drive-through for coffee and a muffin."

"Suit yourself." She managed to inhale a deep, oxygen-rich breath and hoped she'd recovered. "You were going to reveal the magic words of the curse."

"Not magic," he said. "And Dagmar's mom wasn't a witch."

"Okay." This point seemed important to him, and she wondered why.

"Here's what you need to keep in mind. All the victims were blindfolded and gagged with hands cuffed behind their back. All were strangled."

She bit a chunk from the energy bar, chewed slowly and swallowed. "Did Dagmar's mother know about the blindfolds and such?"

"Everybody knew. This is a small town."

"Got it."

He stared through the windshield, looking every bit like a solid, sane, steady detective. A marine. Jake didn't seem like the sort of man who would worry about curses and witches. He recited from memory:

"Hear me, o goddesses,
West, East, North, South.
Scratch out his eyes.
Muzzle his mouth.

Rip off his ears.
Silence his plea.
Death to the Keeper.
So mote it be."

An involuntary shiver rippled down Skylar's spine. Not magic but definitely morbid and creepy. "How did Dagmar's mother come up with this curse?"

"She put it together from various fictions and legends. When she says it on the tape, her words are trembling. Not with fear but with rage. She demands revenge."

And her fierce energy was enough to intimidate the killer. Skylar wanted to believe in the power and strength of Dagmar's mother, but she couldn't help thinking of other possibilities. The Lightkeeper packed up and moved away from Astoria. Or was incarcerated for another crime. Or died.

She turned her head and gazed at a view of the Pacific beyond the sandy beach and roadside shops. The Astoria fog had begun to lift as soon as they left the harbor. Sunlight sparkled on the waves. The offshore rock formations created dramatic vistas. "What do you call those rocks?"

"Sea stacks," he said. "Formed by wave and wind erosion. Many are basalt, volcanic in origin. Some of them are hundreds of feet high—like Haystack Rock, which isn't far from where we're headed. They have their own environments with nesting seabirds and other mammals."

The stacks made her think of guardians protecting the coast and keeping the ships away. "I'm guessing those rocks are part of the reason for the many lighthouses."

"It's a hell of a rugged coast." Though Jake usually didn't waste time and effort on humor, he added, "Living in Oregon ain't for sissies."

Especially when they hate bridges.

When he exited from the highway and drove to the carryout window for a coffee shop, she was grateful for the caffeine and the blueberry muffins. Another factoid she'd learned about her new home state: they made great coffee in the Pacific Northwest.

She snuggled into her seat and watched the fog drift away. The skies weren't totally blue. But not murky gray, either. She felt more optimistic about her first assignment in the field. The drive to the Cape Meares crime scene would take about an hour and a half, which ought to be enough time to recover her equilibrium and focus her attention on the crime scene.

Chapter Five

Jake parked at the scenic overlook off Highway 101 where signage identified important sights and their historical significance as well as pointed the way to the famous Octopus Tree, a Sitka spruce with eight trunks, and the pathway leading to Cape Meares Lighthouse.

The parking spaces were filled with vehicles: another Explorer from the APD, sedans from the Clackamas County sheriff's office and from the Oregon State Police, a few more SUVs from the Oregon Park Service and the Tillamook County sheriff's office, plus three unmarked cars and a van that belonged to the department of the Warrenton medical examiner. Jurisdiction would be a bitch unless Special Agent Skylar Gambel took control right from the start.

She hadn't been chatty on the drive down here, except for a few phone calls, and Jake appreciated the silence. They both had a lot to think about, starting with finding the person who killed Phoebe Conway and making sure the murderer didn't strike again.

Skylar's attack of nervousness on the drive from Astoria worried him, but she had herself completely under control as she exited the Explorer. The lady knew what she was doing. She wore her gray suit and her FBI windbreaker like armor. Allowing himself to appreciate her athletic stride and the confident set of her shoulders, he watched her stalk toward the Tillamook deputy sheriff with his six-pointed star badge visible on his light brown uniform. He stood like a sentinel at the top of an asphalt path, wide enough for a vehicle, that led into the forest.

Skylar displayed her FBI credentials as she introduced herself to the deputy sheriff and a couple of other officers who had gathered.

The deputy scowled, acting tough. "I arrived immediately after the park ranger called. I secured the area, contacted the relevant people and instructed the ME to remove the body."

She glared at the streamers of yellow-and-black crime scene tape draped around the viewing area and pathways like prom decorations. "We received a preliminary packet of info and photos. I didn't see a forensics report on the cars you found here or on tire tracks."

"Nothing to report." The deputy deepened his scowl and puffed out his chest. Arrogant. Antagonistic. Stupid.

"You found no evidence whatsoever," Skylar said in a disbelieving tone.

"It rained last night. Any kind of dusty footprints would be washed away. That blue Subaru Legacy was parked here when we arrived. It belongs to the victim."

"Which you know," she said, "because you forced the locks."

"Didn't have to. The car keys were in her purse."

"Which you removed from the murder scene."

"Yeah, we did," he said defensively. "We needed her ID."

"Did your forensic investigators process the car?"

"I didn't think it was necessary."

"You were wrong," Skylar said. "Attention to detail is how cases get solved. As of now, the FBI has control of this jurisdiction. You may return to your vehicle and stay out of the way unless I need you, which seems unlikely."

"You can't waltz in here and take over."

"I just did." She didn't scoff but her disgust was apparent

as she scanned the four other officers who hovered around. "All of you, step aside until I have further instructions."

When she charged down the asphalt path, the deputy jumped out of her way so quickly that he almost tripped. She didn't spare him a glance. Her focus was directed toward the lighthouse.

Jake walked beside her. He wasn't about to complain about her abrupt attitude with the Tillamook deputy whose sloppy handling of the scene deserved reprimand. He hoped the APD officers who reported to him and were waiting at the lighthouse had done a better job.

A rough wood railing on the downward sloping path held back forest on one side. The other side was at the edge of a high cliff with only occasional trees and shrubs. A spectacular, panoramic view stretched all the way to the horizon. Closer to shore, the surf crashed against sea stacks, sending up plumes of white surf.

Skylar glanced at him and said, "When I talked to Crawford on the phone, he said he'd already given the okay for the FBI forensic team from Portland to document and analyze the crime scene. He also mentioned that Dr. Kate Kinski, the Warrenton ME, had good people working for her who could help."

"I have two officers here," he said. "They've both undergone training sessions and know how to do the basics, like fingerprints and the photos they already sent to APD headquarters. We welcome the opportunity to assist the experts."

"This is an unusual case." They rounded a curve on the path and came into sight of the top of the lighthouse on the rocky promontory below them. "Even without the historic connection to the Lightkeeper, the circumstances are odd."

"You've got that right."

When she met his gaze, he noticed a sparkle in her sea-green eyes. Her full lips quirked in a grin. Not of amusement but satisfaction. He could tell she was looking forward to checking out the scene. Almost like a kid on Christmas Eve. Somewhat ghoulish, but he understood—Jake felt the same way.

The Cape Meares Lighthouse stood only thirty-eight feet tall. The pathway wrapped around the base provided another stunning view at the seaward edge. Skylar asked, "Why is this tower so stubby?"

"It's built on a two-hundred-foot-tall cliff, which makes it visible far out to sea."

They approached the two APD officers—Dub Wagner and Dot Holman—who stood outside the door to the gift shop. Both officers nodded to Skylar and shook her hand when Jake introduced them.

"Who took the crime scene photos?" Skylar asked.

"I did," Dot said. "They were okay, weren't they?"

"Better than okay. The pictures gave an accurate idea of scale and showed several angles. I'm glad you recorded the position of Phoebe's purse before that deputy messed with the scene. Good work, Dot."

"Thank you, ma'am." She was probably the same age as Skylar but gave her a *ma'am* out of respect. A small woman, Dot looked like she was wearing a child-size uniform costume. "I work part-time for the ME, so dead bodies don't bother me."

Not to be outdone, Dub—short for *W* because his first name was Wallace and the last was Wagner, making him a *W* double—spoke up. "First thing we noticed when we got here was the light. Since this lighthouse has been decommissioned, the beacon isn't lit."

Jake encouraged him to say more. "What else?"

"The light over the door doesn't work. There's still a bulb, but we didn't touch it."

"Because there might be fingerprints," Dot added.

"On the inside of the gift shop," Dub said, "none of the overhead lights were turned on, which makes sense now because it's daylight. But we think it was dark in the shop last night."

"What led to that conclusion?" Jake asked, playing along with the gradual reveal of clues.

Dub and Dot led them to the door of the gift shop. Before they entered, Dub produced a box containing Tyvek booties and protective gloves. Jake covered his shoes, proud that his team had paid attention in the forensic classes.

Inside the gift shop, Dub pointed toward the cash register behind the counter where five lighthouse replicas, each three feet tall, lined up in a row.

Dot scampered toward them and activated the battery-operated lights. They all flashed alternating red and white. "These were working when we arrived this morning," she said, "and I'll bet they were on last night."

Jake imagined what it must have been like for Phoebe when she stepped from the darkness outdoors into the shop and was confronted with these touristy strobe lights. Disconcerted. Confused. Phoebe wouldn't have come here by chance. "What was the time of death?"

Dot answered, "According to Dr. Kinski, preliminary estimate of TOD is between midnight and 2:00 a.m."

To Skylar, Jake said, "Phoebe's car is in the lot. She must have driven herself. This late-night rendezvous was prearranged."

"Unless she drove with the killer."

"If she drove, how would he get home?"

"He or she," Skylar said. She was correct. They hadn't determined gender.

"Phoebe must have been concerned about the person she was supposed to meet. She brought a weapon." He pointed to the stun gun on the floor and said to Dot, "You sent photos of the gun and her flashlight. Were these objects moved from their original position?"

"The Tillamook deputy had already removed the purse.

And we turned off the flashing lights to preserve the batteries. But we didn't let anybody touch anything else," Dot said in the no-nonsense tone she probably used with her three preteen kids. "We wanted to preserve the scene for you and Special Agent Gambel."

If Phoebe had seen her attacker coming, Jake figured that she would have reacted. Fight or flight, she would have taken her shot with the stun gun or tried to run...or frozen in place. The deer-in-the-headlights response was not uncommon.

Skylar strolled through the shelves and racks of merchandise, leaving the gift shop and entering the adjoining lighthouse tower, which was set up with educational display photos and posters. She tapped the wall switch, bathing the circular wrought iron staircase in light. "The body was found in here."

"That's right," Dub said. "We didn't want her to be moved, but Dr. Kinski said she'd take full responsibility."

"You handled the situation properly," Jake assured him. Cooperation with the ME was the right thing to do. The doc recognized the references to the Lightkeeper, notified the FBI and recommended that they be brought into the investigation quickly. Obviously, the right call.

His gaze fixed on the first curve where the killer had arranged Phoebe's body. The photos showed her sitting with her legs tucked under her on the lowest step. One of her sneakers had fallen off her foot, revealing a striped sock. Maybe she'd lost her shoe in a struggle. When he squinted, he could imagine seeing her with wrists cuffed, a bandanna blindfold and duct tape over her mouth.

"What else did you notice about Phoebe?" Skylar asked the APD officers.

"Her hair was combed and smooth," Dub said. "She hadn't been out in the rain, which means she was inside before the storm started at eleven minutes past midnight."

"What about cuts or bruises?" Skylar asked. "Were there injuries that didn't show in the photos?"

"Her arms and legs were covered by her clothes so we couldn't see much." Dub cringed at the memory. "Her throat was bruised, probably from being choked to death."

"I doubt she was killed in that artistic position on the staircase." Skylar glanced around the room. "Strangulation could have taken place on the floor in here. Or outside on the path before it rained, which is less likely because her clothes aren't dirty. When the forensic team processes this area, ask them to watch for signs of where she was attacked. The location."

"Yes, ma'am," Dub responded.

"After she was killed, she had to be moved to the staircase." Skylar pantomimed picking up the body and carrying it. "Takes physical strength to do that."

"You bet it does," Dub said. "It's hard to transport dead weight."

"Did Dr. Kinski assign a COD?" Skylar asked.

"Cause of death is homicide," Dot said with a shrug. "The Tillamook County coroner agreed. I expect we'll learn more after the autopsy is done."

"Like if she was drugged," Jake said. In addition to the absence of cuts and bruises, her clothes weren't torn, which led him to suspect she'd been sedated before being strangled.

Skylar gave him a nod. "I'll check with my partner to find out if we're going to transport Phoebe to the Portland medical examiner or leave the body with Dr. Kinski."

"The Lightkeeper murders were before her time," Jake said, "but Kinski has access to all the old files, and she can consult with the guy who did the autopsies twenty years ago."

"She's also close enough that we can go to her facility and observe," Skylar said. "But it's not my call."

Her cool professionalism and awareness of protocol impressed him. He had absolutely no reason to be concerned about her handling of the crime scene or the many and varied law enforcement officers who turned up to help. Their good intentions might lead to sloppy evidence. Like Skylar had said, *Attention to detail is how cases get solved.* He liked her by-the-book approach. Unfortunately, he had a personal issue that might jeopardize the investigation.

He waited until they'd finished up at the Cape Meares Lighthouse, left Dot and Dub to wait for the Portland-based FBI forensic team and returned to his Explorer before he mentioned the potential problem. After he exited the parking area at the scenic overlook and merged onto Highway 101 headed north, he said, "When you first arrived, I mentioned that I needed to talk to Special Agent Crawford. It occurs to me that you are the person I need to speak with."

"Go ahead, I'm listening."

"I have a conflict of interest."

Chapter Six

Skylar swiveled around in the passenger seat of the Explorer so she could give Jake her full attention. Their visit to the crime scene had gone well. The Astoria officers, Dot and Dub, had kept the interior of the lighthouse relatively untouched, despite having to turn Phoebe's body over to the medical examiner. Skylar had been particularly impressed when Dot had insisted they wear the Tyvek booties. Jake's observations had been on point and efficient, so much so that she wondered how many complicated cases this backwoods detective had managed. His logic matched her own.

She didn't want to hear about a problem he was having with the investigation, but she had no choice. "Tell me about this so-called conflict of interest."

"First, I want to give you context," he said. "We've got the time. It's a long drive back to Astoria."

And another crossing of the bridge across the bay. "Still listening."

"Twenty years ago, the Lightkeeper murders interested me. I won't say *obsessed* because I, frankly, didn't know what that word meant when I was ten. Anyway, I liked the idea of fitting pieces together and catching a bad guy. Saving innocent lives appealed to me almost as much as the sci-fi heroes in my comic books. In a way, the Lightkeeper's Curse might have convinced me to become a cop."

"Was this before or after you stole a piece of evidence?"

"I returned the tape. Nobody even noticed it was gone."

"Really?" she said skeptically. "Let's not push former Police Chief Jimi Kim for an answer on that topic."

"After I joined the APD, I decided I wasn't cut out to be a cop who did nothing but give traffic citations. I'm a detective, born to investigate." He glanced across the center console toward her. "I suspect you're the same way."

His perceptions hit close to home. She'd gone through several false starts before she was appointed to field duty as a special agent, which was what she really wanted to do. So far, she'd enjoyed the investigation and found satisfaction uncovering evidence. Being a federal officer with jurisdictional control also appealed to her. She and Jake were more alike than she would have guessed. *A City mouse and a country mouse are still both mice.*

She studied his profile as he kept his eyes on the road. Though the fog had somewhat dissipated, and skies were relatively clear, she didn't need her dark glasses. The late afternoon sun highlighted his high cheekbones and sharp jawline. Staring at his face felt a bit disconcerting. Made her remember the sizzle that zapped through her when they first met. Not that she had any intention of forming a personal relationship with this man.

"Six degrees of separation," he said. "Are you familiar with that concept?"

"Of course. The idea is that all people are separated by a chain of six or fewer social connections."

"In a small town like Astoria, when seven women are murdered, it's a spiderweb of connections. So many people are touched."

"Like Dagmar Burke," she said. "It was a shock to find out her mother was a victim."

"Exactly like Dagmar. She's a good example of what can happen when someone close to the victim gets tangled up in the investigation. In Dagmar's view, her mom was a saint who cursed the Lightkeeper and ended his reign of terror. A lot of people disagreed. Some in town considered her mother to be a witch who whispered secret messages to the Lightkeeper. Others thought Mama Burke was a dangerous crackpot."

She appreciated his insight but recognized his stalling technique. During this drive back to Astoria, cocooned in his Explorer, they could go on forever, tossing theories back and forth. She didn't have the patience. "All right, Armstrong, what exactly is your problem?"

"Victim number seven, Dagmar's mother, was my aunt. After her death, my dad took Dagmar in and raised her as his own. My cousin became the sister I never had."

Skylar swallowed hard. His cousin? That explained their teasing conversation and clearly illustrated why he shouldn't be part of the investigation. A close family relationship was, in fact, a giant conflict of interest. He might be focused on revenge or overwhelmed by survivor's guilt or angry because the killer was never caught. No wonder he hid this relationship from her. "I ought to boot you off this case."

"Do what you need to do," he said. "But I'm not going to quit my investigation. I'll resign from the APD and pursue the investigation on my own. As a private investigator."

"Can you do that?" she asked.

"The state of Oregon requires a license, but I qualify."

Obviously, the investigation was deeply important to him. "You're dedicated," she said.

"That's right."

"Also, annoying."

"Right, again."

When SSA Crawford had told her to expect idiosyncrasies from the Astoria end of the investigation, he hadn't been exaggerating. These people operated in unique, eccentric ways. If they'd been in Portland, she would have been more likely to take Jake off the case. In Astoria, he had an advantage.

He knew everyone in town. His perspective could make a difference. "I hate to lose you as an asset."

"That's pretty much what Chief Vivienne said."

Skylar suspected that SSA Crawford also knew that Jake and Dagmar were part of the same family. And her partner hadn't demanded that Jake step down. Nor would she.

Jake could stay.

"Here's the deal, Armstrong. No more secrets."

"Fair enough." A smile lifted the corner of his mouth. "We'll work together."

"We'll try."

He wasted no time suggesting the direction for their investigation. "Our next stop should be the newspaper where Phoebe Conway worked. The *Astoria Sun*."

"An ironic name for a newspaper in a town that's always foggy."

"We try not to take ourselves too seriously."

During the rest of their drive, they reviewed their observations from the crime scene. Logical conclusions: the killer planned the time and place for the meeting. Phoebe drove herself. She suspected trouble and brought a stun gun for protection. At the gift shop, the killer turned off lights and ambushed Phoebe. Cause of death was strangulation. Her body was posed on the staircase after being blindfolded and having her mouth covered with duct tape.

When they approached the bridge across the bay, Skylar used yogic breathing, closed her eyes and filled her head with her favorite mantra. Apart from the shortness of breath, she did okay. After living in Portland with all the bridges, she'd discovered that after she crossed the same bridge once or twice or more, her phobia lessened. Also, it helped that dusk had begun to settle, and her vision wasn't glaringly clear.

In downtown Astoria, streetlights sliced through the fog and illuminated neon skeleton decorations. Halloween was one of her favorite holidays; it granted people the permission to dress up and become someone else. She happily devoured gobs of chocolate and danced until dawn at wild, macabre parties. Her parents celebrated with elaborate haunted house decorations at their multimillion-dollar home in San Francisco's Nob Hill. Her brothers, both lawyers, usually dressed as bloodsucking vampires, and her mom—a superior court judge—achieved citywide fame with her sexy Morticia Addams costume.

Jake parked the Explorer at the curb down the street from the storefront office of the *Astoria Sun*. His forensic guy claimed to have uncovered important evidence at Phoebe's workplace, and she was eager to learn more.

The office was an open bullpen about the size of a basketball court where several clunky gray desks denoted separate work areas for reporters and salespeople. Overhead, black-and-orange streamers dangled from strings spread like a giant spiderweb on the ceiling. Across the back and down one side, a half wall separated other offices. The upper glass portion of those offices had also been decorated with odd, grotesque drawings.

A skinny, raven-haired young woman dressed all in black perched on a high stool behind the front counter. Halloween had come early for her. She looked like a witch in heavy makeup. Her nameplate read Tabitha Previn. In case the casual observer missed the identification, she wore a necklace with *Tabby* written in silver. At the sight of Detective Armstrong, she clutched a hand with long black fingernails to her breast and nearly swooned.

"Oh my goodness." She bounced to her feet, rushed around the counter and flung herself into his arms. "I can't believe it. Phoebe is dead."

He gently patted her back. "You and Phoebe were close."

"Not besties, but we spent a lot of time together."

"I understand."

"I know you do, Jake. More than anybody, you understand death and murder."

Skylar looked away from the awkward display of one-sided affection and surveyed the office where plastic pumpkins, fanged vampire bats, black cats and witches' cauldrons competed with the yellow crime scene tape draped around a desk to the left of the front counter. Only three other people were in the bullpen, and they gave a wide berth to the designated scene where a guy wearing nitrile gloves tapped keys on a laptop. No doubt, he was the forensic expert assigned by Jake.

The protocol disturbed her. The APD should have waited for the FBI experts to process this scene. Her training as both a lawyer and at Quantico told her they needed to be careful with evidence. Even though she accepted Jake despite his conflict of interest, she wouldn't let the investigation be handled with casual disregard.

Jake introduced her to Alan Quilling, head of APD's forensic department. Like Dot, he also worked as a part-time assistant to the Clatsop County medical examiner in Warrenton. Instead of shaking hands, he flapped his long fingers in a clumsy wave. When he stood, she realized he was another tall guy. Clearly over six feet, he was as long-necked and skinny as the sandhill cranes on the coast. He peeked through circular wire-rimmed glasses. "Special Agent Gambel, you're going to like what I've found. Starting with this. It was locked in her top right drawer." He held up a cell phone.

Instead of taking it, Skylar reached into her purse, found a pair of her own gloves and slipped them on. "Have you checked for fingerprints?"

"First thing," he said. "There are only Phoebe's prints."

Jake stepped up beside her. "Did you figure out the password?"

"Tabitha told me." Quilling cast a shy smile toward the receptionist. "She's very helpful."

Surprised that Phoebe had trusted anyone else with her

password, Skylar glanced at Tabitha who had followed them to Phoebe's workspace and stood close to Jake while reapplying her black lipstick. Skylar asked, "Did Phoebe usually leave her phone in her desk?"

"Sometimes but not often," Tabitha said. "That's her work phone, which is why I have the password. She took her personal phone everywhere."

Jake reminded Skylar, "The personal phone was in Phoebe's car at Cape Meares."

And would be a useful source of leads from people she'd spoken to recently. Contacting the carrier for a listing of her recent calls was standard procedure. "Did you follow up?"

"Chief Kim is taking care of it. Not sure if she has the data yet."

Skylar turned back to Tabitha. "Can you think of a reason she might have left this phone at work?"

"I know why," Quilling said cheerfully. He punched a few buttons on the phone and brought up a photo of an envelope with Phoebe's name and the address of the *Astoria Sun*. The next photo showed a note that had been printed off a computer.

"She was instructed not to bring her phone."

Skylar leaned closer and squinted.

Helpfully, Quilling said, "I can read it for you."

"Please don't." Outraged and appalled to be discussing sensitive evidence in the middle of the *Astoria Sun* newspaper bullpen, she turned to Jake and raised her eyebrows, silently asking why he wasn't taking charge. Quilling shouldn't be waving Phoebe's phone around for everybody to see.

She snapped at Quilling, "Put the phone in an evidence bag and give it to me."

"Okay." He bobbed his head, and his mop of brown hair fell across his forehead.

"Stop your investigation immediately but leave the crime

scene tape in place. Stay right here and wait for the Portland FBI forensic team to arrive."

"Yes, ma'am."

She snatched the clear plastic bag with the phone and steamed toward the exit, barely able to control her frustration and anger. The sloppy handling of evidence merited a serious talking-to, at the very least. On the sidewalk outside the *Sun*, she pivoted and hiked up the incline toward the curb where the Explorer was parked. Jake should have trained Quilling more effectively, should have explained the chain of custody as pertained to evidence.

She came to a halt, belatedly aware that she'd also broken the rules by grabbing the phone and stalking out the door. Losing control. Making mistakes. She needed to settle down before she blew her first assignment as a field agent.

Jake jogged up beside her. "Hang on a minute."

Rather than engaging in an embarrassing chase down the street, she faced him. "Detective, I'm shocked and dismayed by the APD's handling of this case, starting with Chief Kim allowing Dagmar, a civilian, to take part as an expert."

He nodded.

"Involving her grandpa, even if he is a retired police chief, isn't correct procedure." She suspected SSA Crawford would disagree and welcome Jimi into the investigation, but that didn't mean she had to approve. "And then, there's Quilling. There are important procedural reasons for following the rules of evidence. Quilling behaved badly. As his supervisor, you should have stopped him."

He stood silently, waiting for her to continue, but she'd run out of complaints.

She held up the plastic evidence bag—an unspoken admission that she, too, made mistakes. "We need to log this in to evidence."

"First, let's take a closer look at that note on Phoebe's work phone."

"Not here. Not while we're standing on the sidewalk. Didn't I just ream Quilling for being too casual with evidence?"

He gestured toward the Explorer parked at the curb. "Is that private enough?"

"We've been in the car all day." She glanced over her shoulder at a coffee shop on the corner. "And I'm starving."

They ducked inside the shop where Jake knew the woman behind the counter. *Of course, he does.* After placing a quick order for lattes, premade sandwiches and potato chips, they went to a circular table in the corner away from the windows to wait for their coffee. Carefully, she cleared a space, removed the phone from the see-through evidence bag and held it so he could read the message on the screen:

I have new evidence about the Lightkeeper's Curse Murders. You should be the reporter to tell this story, Phoebe. You're a shining star from the Lone Star state but unappreciated. I'll make sure you get what you deserve. Tell no one about this contact. Don't bring a phone or a camera. Cape Meares Lighthouse at midnight.

"It's clever," she said, "the way he praises her abilities as a reporter and promises a scoop on the Lightkeeper."

"Phoebe was ambitious. Doesn't surprise me that she decided to take the risk and follow his rules. The person who sent this note knew her weakness."

She realized that the note was more important than her frustration, Quilling's incompetence and her own imprecise handling of the evidence. "There's more to be found at the newspaper. I'm afraid we're not done there."

"Not by a long shot."

She turned off the phone and returned it to the evidence bag. "First, we try to find out how the note was delivered. Then we check with the editor about possible follow-up messages from the killer. That's how the Lightkeeper operated twenty years ago, right?"

"He left notes or sent letters," Jake said.

"Technology has improved. The present-day Lightkeeper will probably use the contact email for the *Sun*."

"No doubt."

They were back on the same page. Working together to solve Phoebe's murder.

Chapter Seven

Across the tiny, round table, Jake's gaze met hers. In her eyes, he saw an unwavering intelligence that compelled him to look more closely, past the sea green tint and the flecks of gold into their depths. She reached behind her head and unfastened the ponytail at her nape. Thick auburn waves tumbled to her shoulders when she tossed her head.

Pretty but tough as nails, she seemed to like being in charge. The FBI outranked local police, and Skylar was a natural boss lady. When she'd snarled at mild-mannered Quilling, Jake had seen her slender fingers clench into fists. He halfway expected her to bop Quilling on top of his pointy head. Maybe he shouldn't have found her kickass attitude attractive, but he did.

To hide his grin, Jake dropped his gaze and focused on her feet under the table. The ankle boots peeking out from her trousers were stylish and probably had steel toes for kicking butt. She was that type of woman.

She twisted the top off her chocolate chip muffin and took a large bite. Not a dainty eater. Another plus in her favor. She gave a happy moan. "Yummmm."

Though he could have spent hours observing her and imagining what made her tick, there was work to be done. He picked up on what she'd said a moment ago about the Lightkeeper sending notes and recordings to the police. Would the same strategy apply to the person who strangled Phoebe? "Technically, the Cape Meares murder can't be considered a serial killing. It was only one death."

"That's why our case is so interesting. It's not often that investigators have access to the initial crime. Plus, there are parallels with the Lightkeeper."

Things were going to get confusing if they continued to call the long-ago serial killer and the person who killed Phoebe by the same name. He asked, "Do you think it's the same guy?"

"Could be a copycat."

"Or a coincidence."

Her full lips twisted into a frown. "Crawford warned me about making assumptions."

"He's right." A good detective kept an open mind.

The woman who had been at the counter brought a tray to their table and added their to-go coffee cups to the sandwiches. Skylar gave her a thumbs-up and took another bite.

He unwrapped his ham and cheese on rye and bit into the center. More than the taste, he appreciated the caloric fuel to energize his lagging brain power. He hadn't eaten since the drive-through on their way to Cape Meares.

Skylar dabbed her lips with a napkin. "If the Lightkeeper from twenty years ago was a young man—in his twenties—he'd only be in his forties now. I could see him coming out of retirement to kill Phoebe Conway. But if he was forty or fifty when he started..."

"He'd be sixty or older now," Jake said.

"Twenty years ago, there must have been a profile. Was he local? Who were the suspects?" She snapped her fingers. "I know who has that information."

"Crawford."

"I'll check with him. Tell him what we're doing. And ask for his on-the-scene analysis from twenty years ago."

"Until then, we need to figure out a way to refer to Phoebe's killer," he said. "To differentiate him from the Lightkeeper in the past."

"Don't worry. He'll give us a name."

"You think he'll tell us what to call him." He sipped his double-shot latte. The caffeine should get him into gear. "How do you figure?"

"That's an educated guess," she said. "Not an assumption."

He didn't see the difference. "Explain."

"From the smug tone evident in his note and the headline-grabbing nature of the murder, I'm guessing he's a big-time narcissist. He'll gobble up all the credit."

Her reasoning seemed sound. "Seems like you do *not* think this is the Lightkeeper from twenty years ago."

"Not sure. But I tend to make accurate guesses. Call it instinct."

They lit into the food and finished eating in mere minutes. Skylar continued to make those moaning sounds. She licked her fingers when she was done. Sophisticated but not prissy. And sexy as hell.

He was glad to have her on his side.

ON THE SIDEWALK outside the coffee shop, the twilight fog draped over Astoria like a tattered shroud. Through the swirls, Skylar caught terrifying glimpses of the massive bridge over the Columbia River. Downhill below the riverwalk, the deepwater port seemed relatively calm. Well-lit vessels docked at the coast guard base waiting patiently for an emergency summons.

Balancing her to-go latte, she hit the speed dial for Crawford's number on her phone. It rang several times before he answered.

Talking fast, his voice sounded hyper when he told her that his files from the twenty-year-old case had taken up much of the conference room at the APD. Jimi had joined him, and they were putting together details from the past. "We had four viable suspects. Two are still in Oregon. I want to interview these guys as soon as possible. When will you be back here?"

"Soon as possible," she said. "We're going to need more assistance from the FBI forensic resources in Portland."

"Such as?"

She ran through their needs at the crime scene, potential surveillance on lighthouses and cybercrimes to be coordinated with Quilling.

He cleared his throat. "And what will you be doing?"

"Jake and I need to follow up at the *Astoria Sun*," she said. "Speaking of Detective Armstrong, you must have known about his family relationship to Dagmar's mother."

"I knew."

But Crawford hadn't mentioned Jake's inappropriate connection to the victim. She wondered if her mentor had been testing her judgment. She sipped her latte. "I'm still wrapping my head around the fact that he's related to one of the murdered women, but I don't have a problem working with him. His knowledge of the town can help."

"Did he know Phoebe Conway?"

She recalled the hugs and snugs he got from Tabitha. He was a good-looking man. An eligible bachelor. "I have a feeling he knows most of the single women in town."

"I have an idea," Crawford said. "We have a lot of ground to cover in this investigation. How about if you and Jake concentrate on Phoebe's murder by talking to her coworkers at the newspaper and checking out her apartment? Jimi and I will make visits to our two suspects from the past."

She wasn't sure she liked this plan. Though she appreciated the chance to forge ahead with her own investigation, she'd miss Crawford's experienced insights. Not wanting to be perceived as difficult, she accepted. "You're the boss."

"We have rooms at the Captain's Cove B&B. Meet us there in the parlor at ten o'clock."

She ended the call and joined Jake. Crawford had put her

in charge, and she intended to be thorough, starting with the local detective. "How well did you know Phoebe?"

"Enough to say hi."

"Tell me about her. Did she live here all her life?"

He shook his head. "Phoebe moved to Astoria after graduating from University of Oregon three or four years ago. She interned at the *Sun*, working on both the print and online versions. It's a local paper but has been in business since the late 1800s and has a solid reputation. Joseph Rogers, aka Jolly Rogers, is the editor-in-chief. He's been at the paper for as long as I can remember. After her internship, he gave Phoebe a full-time job."

"Getting hired by a legitimate newspaper, even a small operation, is a coup." The outlets for responsible journalism were shrinking all the time. "What were her goals? Did she expect to stay here?"

"Not for long," he said. "Phoebe wrote a couple of articles that drew national attention. One on *The Goonies*. Hard to believe anybody remembers that movie or cares, but she wouldn't stop bragging. She also did an article on one of the kid stars, Ke Huy Quan, after he won his Oscar. I think she saw Astoria as a stepping stone to a bigger and better career."

"Ambitious." She wasn't surprised. In the note, Phoebe Conway had been lavishly praised and promised a scoop. The killer lured her to him by appealing to her ego. She and Jake paused outside the door to the *Sun*.

He grasped the handle but didn't open it. "Tabitha knew her better than I did."

"I'll talk to her," Skylar said, recalling how the Elvira-wannabe had drooled over Jake. She'd be less distracted talking to another woman. "You check with Quilling and make sure he isn't parading evidence in front of reporters. Find out if anybody else in the office saw the person who delivered the note to Phoebe."

"Got it." He yanked the glass door open.

Stepping inside the open bullpen with desks scattered amid Halloween decor, Skylar stared up at the black-and-orange streamers hanging from the ceiling. Tawdry and limp. She checked out the likely places for surveillance and saw no indication of hidden cameras. Under her breath, she said, "No security."

"What are they going to steal at a newspaper?" Jake mumbled back to her. "Words?"

Skylar approached the front counter. Though she'd met Tabitha before, she wanted to establish boundaries. In a practiced move, she flashed her FBI credentials. "Remember me? I'm Special Agent Gambel, and I have a few questions."

Though Tabitha nodded, her heavily lined eyes seemed to follow Jake as he went to the desk behind the yellow crime scene tape and spoke to Alan Quilling. Clearly disappointed, she turned back to Skylar. "Yes, ma'am. How can I help you?"

"I didn't notice any security cams at the front entrance."

"Nope. People just come and go as they please. It's my job to refer them to the right desk for placing ads. Or to a reporter who might cover an event they're hosting. Or an obit writer. They're supposed to sign in with me at the counter. Most of the time, they don't bother."

"That must make you angry."

"Not really. Sometimes, I just have to take a break. Or go to the little girl's room. Or run a quick errand. I figure if it's important, the person will wait for me or come back."

"Very practical," she said. "Did you see the person who left the note for Phoebe?"

Tabitha narrowed her eyes in a futile attempt to remember. Then, she shrugged. "Sorry. When Quilling showed me the address, I remembered Phoebe waving the envelope around after lunch and asking who left it. I didn't remember then. Or now."

"You knew Phoebe better than most people. Tell me about her."

"Well, to start with, she was insanely pretty. Long, streaked blond hair that was always glossy and perfect. Great bod. She knew how to dress, you know, her clothes matched. Everything about her was exactly what my mother would adore." Tabitha hiccupped, a sob catching in her throat. "I can't believe she's dead."

"She must have had a lot of boyfriends."

"She dated a lot. A different guy every day of the week."

"Playing the field. Not ready to settle down. There wasn't anybody special? Had she recently had a breakup?"

"Oh, I get it." Tabitha gave a knowing wink. "You think some guy she was dating attacked her."

"What do you think?"

Tabitha drew her mouth into a small red circle outlined in black. "Maybe."

Skylar wasn't sure how much of Tabitha's info fell into the category of gossip and how much was truth. Didn't matter. She and Jake needed to track down all the boyfriends. At least to run them through NCIC and ViCAP to check for criminal records. "I'd appreciate if you'd write a list with full names, how long she dated them and anything else that might be pertinent."

"Like what?"

"Maybe they took Phoebe on vacation or bought her a special gift. Some guys just stand out from the rest."

"I know what you're saying, Special Agent." Tabitha drawled over Skylar's title. "You have a real badass job. Do you think I can get hired by the FBI?"

"It's a lot of work to get this job."

"Seriously? How hard could it be?"

Skylar didn't appreciate the implied insult. *How hard could it be?* "I have a law degree, worked as an assistant DA, graduated from Quantico and qualified as a Marine-level sharpshooter. I have a brown belt in karate, paramedic training and top-level security clearance." She finished her coffee and dropped the container into a trash can with a resounding thud. "Becoming a special agent isn't easy."

Chastised, Tabitha backed down. "That's not what it looks like on TV."

"Life seldom is."

The door to one of the offices against the back wall flung open with such emphasis that the half-wall-size window shuddered. A gruff, heavy-shouldered man with kinky gray hair and thick black eyebrows stuck his head into the bullpen and barked. "Ahoy, Armstrong. Get your tail over here. Right now."

"Aye, aye." Jake motioned for her to join him. "Let's go meet Jolly Rogers. Managing editor of the *Astoria Sun*."

"Was he working here twenty years ago?'

"You bet. Rogers was a young reporter, probably in his thirties. Back then, he was married, had a seven-year-old kid." At the door to Rogers's office, he gestured for her to enter first, closed the door behind them, introduced her and asked, "What is it, sir?"

"This note came to our open forum for the online *Astoria Sun*. Could be your killer, trying to copycat the Lightkeeper from twenty years ago." Rogers turned his computer screen so they could read.

The first thing Skylar noticed was the signature line:

I rise from the night and the darkness. Call me Shadowkeeper.

As she'd suspected, he had named himself.

Chapter Eight

Shadowkeeper. Jake despised the comic book name. *Shadowkeeper. The Shadow.* It conjured up images of a supervillain in tights and a dark cape. This wasn't a game. The so-called Shadowkeeper wasn't special or clever. Murder should never be celebrated.

In the Shadowkeeper's first note to Phoebe Conway on her cell phone, the killer insinuated that she'd get what she deserved. A sick joke. Ironic. Phoebe surely believed she deserved fame and fortune. The Shadowkeeper—a narcissist like Skylar predicted—had something else in mind.

Jake stood beside Special Agent Gambel, close enough to smell the vanilla and citrus fragrance of her shampoo. When she stretched across the desk in Rogers's office to read the Shadowkeeper's post on the computer screen, the sleeve of her charcoal gray jacket brushed the plaid sleeve of his shirt. Instead of pulling back, he leaned toward her. Gazing down, he saw the black leather belt holster under her jacket. The lethal weapon contrasted her silky, cream-colored blouse. Without even trying, Special Agent Skylar Gambel tapped into dreams and desires he didn't know he had.

Jake read the Shadowkeeper's note on the screen:

Phoebe Conway got what was coming to her. I granted her the honor of being my first victim. She'll go down in history. Thousands of ghouls will read about her online and wonder why I selected her. Too bad she won't be around to write a column for herself.

Some clues for you, Armstrong. I work alone. I hear no voices. And I serve no master.

I rise from the night and the darkness. Call me Shadowkeeper.

Rogers dragged his thick fingers through his curly gray hair. His voice grated like a cement mixer. "I always knew we'd hear from that bastard again."

Jake pointed out the obvious. "You don't think it's a copycat."

"Don't know. But I never believed a curse from a librarian would make him quit killing." Rogers's jaw tensed and his eyes darted beneath his thick black brows. For a long moment, the gruff old man looked scared. His gaze flicked around the incredibly messy office and landed on one of the few photographs on the bookshelves—a picture of a boy in a Little League baseball uniform for the Astoria Otters. Rogers slammed both fists down onto his cluttered desktop, causing the computer screen to jump. "He'll never stop."

Jake understood Rogers's anger and his fear. But not his logic. The Lightkeeper had ended his serial killer spree. For twenty years, there had been no murders attributed to him.

Skylar turned toward Jake with a question in her eyes. "He mentioned you, Detective. Challenged you."

"Could be somebody I've arrested or ticketed. Somebody carrying a grudge." He never claimed to be the most popular guy in town. "Some people just don't like cops."

"Some people are wrong." Her green-eyed gaze studied

him like an X-ray machine, trying to see beneath the surface. "The note says he works alone, doesn't hear voices and serves no master. Why does he think this is a clue?"

"Those characteristics are markedly different from the Lightkeeper," Jake said. "He's telling us that he isn't the same killer from the past."

"Teasing us," Rogers growled. "Pointing us in the wrong direction."

Skylar kept her focus on Jake. "You studied the Lightkeeper."

"When I was ten," he reminded her.

"I'd still like to hear your insights. Give me a quick description."

"A loner, one of those guys who fades into the woodwork. Claimed to be on a mission and believed people would thank him for ridding the world of these flawed women. He referenced a high priestess who whispered in his ear. She demanded sacrifices."

"A contradiction," Skylar said. "He believes his victims deserve punishment. But also thinks they are pure enough to be sacrificial lambs."

"The Lightkeeper never pretended to make rational sense," he said. "I can show you profiles from the FBI and other psychologists. After analyzing his communications, they were pretty sure he suffered from schizophrenia. He experienced hallucinations and heard voices. His condition used to be called split personality."

"DID," she said, "Dissociative Identity Disorder."

His amateur investigations and the opinions of experts had steered him toward that diagnosis. Not that he understood how DID worked. Jake wasn't a psychologist, didn't comprehend brain chemistry. All he could say for certain was that the Lightkeeper was driven to kill and imagined himself to be part of a greater cause. In his head, he heard instructions from a priestess or witch who didn't really exist and, therefore, wasn't—thank God—Dagmar's mom.

"This online note is a trick," Rogers said. "He's trying to confuse Armstrong."

"Doing a damned good job," the detective muttered. He respected the editor's opinion. Rogers's byline topped many of the articles from twenty years ago. At one point, the Lightkeeper sent his follow-up note and cassette to Rogers's home along with a threat to his wife and young son. "But why me? I'm just a cop. Not a brilliant detective. Why would the Shadowkeeper call me out?"

"You're a threat, and he doesn't want to get caught." Rogers threw his arms in the air. "He got away with murder before. Thinks he can do it again. Thinks he's smarter than we are."

"Is he?" Skylar asked.

Rogers glared at her. "Where's your boss? Where's Crawford? He should be here."

"Supervisory Special Agent Crawford is my partner. He's pursuing a different direction in our investigation." She followed up with another question. "Why do you think the Shadowkeeper killed a woman who worked at the *Sun*?"

"To make sure he gets full media coverage. That's what he did the first time around. Kept sending notes and tapes. Scared the hell out of me." He lumbered across his office and stood at the half-glass wall where someone—probably Tabitha—had painted a Halloween vampire. Under lowered brows, Rogers scanned from left to right, trying to see a shadow that wasn't there.

Jake noticed Ty McKenna, a reporter he'd gone to high school with, leaning against his desk and staring back at Rogers's office.

The old man continued, "The Lightkeeper threatened me and my family. I sent my wife and my son, Bradley, to live with her mother in Houston until I was certain the killing spree was finally over. And that, my friends, was the beginning of the end of my marriage."

Even as a kid, Jake remembered the divorce as epic. Rogers's wife, a stunning woman, had taken every opportunity to bash him in furious public arguments while being careful that her rage didn't interfere with her sole custody of their son. Hoping to divert the subject, he asked, "Didn't you write a book about the Lightkeeper?"

"Never finished it." Rogers staggered to the swivel chair behind his desk, sank into it and exhaled heavily. "Maybe it's time for me to do that—write the damn book. Or I could retire, sell my house and cruise up and down the coast on my fishing trawler, the *Jolly Rogers*."

"I didn't know you were a sailor," Jake said.

"Not a sailboat, matey. This old pirate has a twenty-eight-foot trawler with a diesel motor. There's a berth in the hull and a galley in the cabin for cooking fish I catch myself. The boat's nineteen years old but in good shape. A gift to myself because I don't have family to worry about. My ex-wife just got married for the third time and moved to Paris. France, not Texas, her home state."

"What about your son?"

"Bradley and I never really got back together after the divorce. Too bad. I would have been a great dad. We talk on the phone. I send him cash, and he occasionally visits but hasn't lived here since high school. I thought, maybe, after his mom got married again, he'd reach out."

"I'd like to read your notes," Skylar said. "For your book."

He nodded. "I'll email you the file."

Jake watched as she rearranged her features into a no-nonsense expression. "Sir, I need to know where you were last night between eleven and three."

Rogers jolted upright in his chair. His simmering frustration exploded. "What the hell! Am I a damn suspect?"

Jake should have seen the eruption coming and put a lid

on it. Should have done his job, damn it, he should have been the one to ask for an alibi because he had a relationship with Rogers that could have encouraged cooperation.

"I need to know," she said, "for the purpose of eliminating you from our investigation. Where were you?"

"I went to bed at half past eleven after I heard the weather report on the news. Before you ask, I'll tell you that I live alone. No one to verify."

"Home alone with no witness. Correct?"

"You got it." He sank back into his chair, causing the springs to creak. "Are we done?"

Belatedly efficient, Jake stepped up. "We're going to need Phoebe's employment records and any documentation you have on her. Also, we'll track the IP that sent the Shadowkeeper's message to the *Sun*."

Rogers gestured toward the bullpen and front desk. "Tabitha can take care of the background info. Get McKenna to help. He dated Phoebe."

"And if we have more questions—"

"I'll be here. Close the damn door on your way out."

Jake and Skylar stood together outside Rogers's office. When she tucked a strand of hair behind her ear, the overhead lights glistened on her glossy mane. The flush in her cheeks showed the tension from her confrontation. In a low voice, she said, "He's a suspect."

"Yes."

"We should keep him under surveillance tonight."

"I'll arrange for a stakeout."

He turned his gaze away from her and into the cluttered bullpen.

Ty McKenna stood with arms folded across his chest, waiting to be questioned. Jake had always thought McKenna was too eager. During high school track meets, he always jumped the gun.

"As for Quilling," she said, "he needs to wait for the

experts before trying to figure out who sent that email to the newspaper."

"When will they be in touch?"

"Soon," she promised. "The FBI's cybercrimes division is brilliant at manipulating the internet, and they'll keep your forensic guy in the loop, maybe teach him a thing or two about investigating. The cyber-detectives can also scan Phoebe's social media pages and her newspaper articles. She was a public person, which means she probably left a deep, wide, colorful trail."

"With so many paths to research, we're going to need more officers working the case." When Skylar had been questioning Rogers about his alibi, Jake realized they had many other people to interview, including Phoebe's friends, acquaintances and—most important—her enemies. "Chief Kim will have her hands full, coordinating assignments."

"Has she already notified Phoebe's parents?"

"First thing she did. They're flying in from Houston tomorrow."

"That's where Rogers's wife is from. Any connection?"

"We'll see."

She shot a hard-edged glare at McKenna. "Let's get started with the ex-boyfriend. It's your turn to take the lead."

They picked their way through the desks in the bullpen until they stood in front of Ty McKenna—a slim, tall hipster in a flannel vest, a brown pinstriped shirt and a neck scarf in the classic Burberry pattern. His close-cropped black hair matched his carefully cultivated five o'clock shadow. His classy Movado wristwatch screamed money, an accurate description for anybody in the McKenna family.

After Jake introduced Skylar, he directed McKenna toward the break room at the far edge of the bullpen so they could have privacy. When the swinging door closed, the small room went silent except for the hum of a space heater. The smell of old coffee and stale doughnuts hung in the air. The three of them sat around a square table.

Jake asked, "When was the last time you saw Phoebe?"

"Yesterday in the office." With his elbows planted on the plastic tabletop, McKenna hunched over like a praying mantis. "She was all smug and superior. Like she had a secret. Which, I guess, she did. Well, damn, I should have paid more attention."

Jake heard the tension in McKenna's tone and a note of guilt. "You and Phoebe were dating earlier this year."

"Listen, there's something I should tell you—both of you. I've made some mistakes in my life and don't want you to think I'm hiding anything."

When Jake gave him the nod, McKenna blurted, "I have a criminal record. When I was in grad school, I had a drinking problem. I got a DUI and was convicted on two charges of disturbing the peace. Bar fights. Broke a couple of bottles. Threw some weak punches. This girl got a bloody nose."

Jake translated: McKenna hit a woman and now his ex-girlfriend was murdered. Not looking good. He sensed feelings of revulsion coming from Skylar. Her slender fingers knotted together on the tabletop, and he had no doubt that she could effectively punish McKenna if need be. As she'd mentioned, she was Quantico-trained. A brown belt in karate.

"What happened?" Jake asked.

"Nothing. She didn't press charges. I got off with a fine and community service."

"At the time, where were you living?"

"Seattle, going to U-Dub. I was a dumb ass kid, but I got my act together." He lifted his chin and made direct eye contact. "Four years, three months and ten days ago, I joined AA. I've been sober ever since."

"Congratulations," Jake said, and he meant it. Going straight wasn't easy. "Let's get back to Phoebe."

"We were inevitable." McKenna paused for emphasis. "I

was almost forced to date her. We worked together for three years. We were good reporters, competitive in a positive way. She appeared on the Portland TV news four times. I had seven special segments."

"What else can you tell me about your relationship?"

McKenna's head drooped, and he stared down at his hands on the tabletop. "Like I said. Inevitable. Me and Phoebe... We both have apartments in the same house. Made it easy when I said your place or mine. She was just down the hall."

Too close for comfort.

Chapter Nine

Skylar leaned back in the uncomfortable plastic chair in the break room and stretched her legs, watching while Jake conducted his interview with Ty McKenna. The wealthy, cool hipster ticked all the relevant boxes when it came to being a suspect. Number one, he had a record for being drunk and disorderly, even though he was now sober. Two, he had dated Phoebe, and they'd broken up. Three, he and the victim were competitors. Four, they lived in the same building, which was, for a possible stalker, a bonus.

However, McKenna also had a solid alibi. He told Jake that he spent last night at the Sand Bar, a local tavern, where he was the designated driver for four friends. He dropped off the last drinker after the bar closed at two in the morning. Should be easy enough to verify.

Though McKenna sounded confident and showed the aforementioned competitive streak when he talked about beating his drunk buddies in a darts game, Skylar read a different story from his microexpressions and gestures. McKenna repeatedly touched his nose, which made her think of Pinocchio. His gaze flickered. And he stroked the stubble on his chin, hiding his mouth and holding back lies.

She definitely doubted his truthfulness when the topic shifted back to his relationship with Phoebe. According to

McKenna, he dumped her because she was too possessive and demanding. He called her a diva. Self-important. A mean girl.

Skylar suspected the same description applied to Ty McKenna. *A mean girl despite his gender.* Especially when he told them that the renovated mansion where they both lived belonged to his parents. He'd advised them to evict Phoebe when she was late with her rent. A spiteful move. Skylar didn't like this guy or trust him but couldn't be sure he was a killer.

Jake was a smooth interrogator. He did a good job of drawing McKenna out and letting him talk enough to reveal the ugly side of his polished personality. The interview ended with the two men shaking hands and McKenna promising they'd get together and hang out. He didn't notice how Jake wiped the palm of his hand on his khakis, as if to erase the slimy contact.

McKenna disengaged from them, saying he needed to check with Rogers about a piece he wanted to write, then he'd meet them at the six-apartment renovated mansion where he and Phoebe both had lived.

After they left the break room, Tabitha handed Jake a legal-size envelope filled with employment documents and columns written by Phoebe Conway, which Rogers had told her to compile. She leaned close to Jake. Too close. If he wanted, he could have peeked down her low-cut black sweater. Instead, he averted his gaze, which pleased Skylar more than it should. Not only was he great to look at, but he was poised and professional.

She kept her opinions to herself. Working with Jake would be acceptable. Anything more was not.

Before they left the *Sun*, they talked to Quilling who peeked at her with big, round, brown eyes like a naughty puppy. *A mutt who's mishandled evidence.* She stayed aloof, reminding him that she was the boss. Still, she had to admit that Quilling's excitement about working with the FBI cybercrime division endeared him to her and made her want to scratch behind his ears.

Outside, daylight had faded into a gloomy night. Skylar settled into the passenger seat of the SUV and peered through the windshield. Jake had advised her about the fog and clouds causing poor visibility, and the October weather proved him right. The streetlights barely made a difference. The shadows deepened and diffused.

Mysterious and creepy, the Shadowkeeper had chosen an apt name for himself.

Leaving the business district and the docks, they headed toward the residential area of this town built on hillsides. The visit to Phoebe's apartment would help establish a timeline. According to Tabitha—who might not be the most accurate source—Phoebe had left work last night at six. If she arrived at the Cape Meares Lighthouse at midnight and the drive took an hour and a half, that left four and a half hours unaccounted for. Skylar wanted to fill in that blank.

Jake cruised through Astoria with the familiarity of a native who doesn't need street signs to know where he's going. He parked the Explorer at the curb outside a three-story gingerbread-trimmed Victorian mansion, typical of many of the renovated homes dotting the hillsides. Though decently maintained on a corner lot with landscaped hedges, shrubs, a red-leafed maple and a persimmon tree full of plump orange fruits, the mini-mansion showed signs of wear. Could have used a paint job. The roof above the porch was saggy. The house and grounds were poorly illuminated by a corner streetlight swaddled in fog.

An unwarranted sense of foreboding rose up inside her as she studied the face of the building. Light glowed from several windows, including a narrow casement on the third floor.

With a shudder, Skylar recalled ghostly stories about evil creatures locked in the attic and only released at the full moon. Her skin prickled, and her shoulders tensed. She shook off the chill. *Don't be absurd.* This wasn't the home of the Addams family. Her mom, dressed as Morticia Addams, would not step through the front door to welcome them into her lair.

She glanced over at Jake who stood on the sidewalk beside her—tall, protective and intensely masculine. Being with him made her feel safe, and she liked the un-feminist sensation that would have gotten her laughed out of Quantico. No matter how pleasant it might be to snuggle up against that broad chest, she didn't need a bodyguard. In a level tone, she said, "McKenna gave me the master key, but I think we should wait for him before we go inside."

"Can't waste much time," Jake said. "It's eight forty-five, and we're meeting SSA Crawford and Jimi Kim at the B&B at ten. Before that, I need to check in with Chief Kim on the status of our investigation."

"We'll give McKenna five minutes." He was probably pitching Rogers an article about the intimate details of his relationship with the Shadowkeeper's first victim. Nothing like a grand tragedy to draw in readers. Though some reporters were brilliant and even heroic, she saw their breed as the jackals of crime investigation, skulking around to pick the bones of the victims. "He's an annoying person."

"Still, I've got to hand it to the guy. I didn't know about his drinking problem. I respect him for getting sober."

They approached the wrought iron fence surrounding the property. A decorative sign by the gate gave the street number and the name of the mansion: Agate House.

Skylar looked forward to searching Phoebe's apartment. Decor, possessions and housekeeping habits revealed a great deal about people. "I wonder if she was tidy or a hoarder."

"I'm guessing she has quality stuff. Tasteful. Classy. She dressed too fancy for my taste but always looked good. Had a pair of those high heels with the red soles."

"I want to talk to the other people who live here. I'd like

to clarify the timeline, find out when she got home and when she left. If the Shadowkeeper was stalking her, he might have visited."

"We still haven't decided if the Shadowkeeper is a man," he reminded her.

"Obviously, we don't have a description. But we know the Shadowkeeper managed to carry Phoebe to the winding staircase. Whether she was unconscious or struggling like crazy, lifting her required strength. Sure, a woman could have done it. A big, muscular woman."

"Like Dagmar," he interjected.

"We'll keep an open mind, but it's likely that the killer is a man in good physical condition."

"If you don't mind, I'd rather interview the other people living here and leave the search through Phoebe's apartment to you. Pawing through other people's stuff isn't my thing. Makes me feel like a Peeping Tom."

"Not me." She grinned. "Snooping is one of my guilty pleasures. Ever since I was a kid and found my mom's stash of sexy romance novels hidden behind the towels on the lowest shelf of the bathroom linen closet, I've liked poking into other people's secrets."

He held open the gate, and she strolled up the flagstone path to a covered porch with slate blue trim and bannisters. Before she could knock, the heavy front door swung open, framing Ty McKenna in a vintage peacoat. He gasped for breath.

"You're winded," she said. "Have you been running?"

"Drove right here. Parked in back. Came through the rear door." He swept open the door. "Please come in."

Again, she had the impression he was being less than truthful. McKenna might have rushed here ahead of them to slip into Phoebe's apartment and remove an incriminating piece of evidence.

The front vestibule held a row of average-size mailboxes

and two lockers for large packages. Beyond a door that locked was a large hallway with a dining room on one side and a TV room with an extra-large flat-screen on the other. The kitchen was probably in the back.

"No apartments on the first floor," McKenna said. "Upstairs are four singles and two family-size with two bedrooms. No children. No pets."

"Does anyone live on the top floor?" she asked.

"There's one apartment in the attic. The guy who lives there has been at Agate House for thirteen years, ever since he moved to Astoria." McKenna climbed the carved oak staircase that bisected the first floor. "You probably know him, Jake. He teaches science at the high school. Robert Pierce."

"Pyro Pierce," Jake said. "That was his nickname because he was always blowing things up in chem lab."

Another eccentric detail. She paused on the landing. "Which apartment belonged to Phoebe?"

"Number three." He gestured to the right where a mint green door with a gold number three awaited. "It's the second-best suite with two bedrooms, a bathroom, kitchenette and a view of the street."

"Which is the best?"

"Mine, of course." He preened.

"Is this the only door to her apartment?"

"That would be against fire regs," he said. "A French door opens onto the porch roof, and there's a ladder down from there."

"Good to know." She glanced over her shoulder at Jake. "I'll look around in Phoebe's place. You question the other residents."

"I'm on it." He ascended a narrower staircase to the third floor, apparently choosing to start his interrogations with the pyromaniac science teacher.

Skylar crossed the threshold into Phoebe Conway's former residence. The dead woman's home screamed with brilliant colors and patterns. *Look at me. Notice me.* A gold clock in a glass case chimed at the quarter hour. The potpourri scent of lavender mingled with the sweet aroma from a bouquet of fresh red roses. High ceilings and tall windows created a spacious feeling. The feminine living room stretched into a small galley kitchen. An open bottle of red from a Willamette Valley winery stood beside a half-full glass and a carryout container from a bistro. The food and drink filled in a blank on the timeline. Phoebe had picked up dinner last night and brought it home, which probably filled in another hour in the missing four and a half.

"Do I need to stay here while you poke around?" McKenna asked.

She didn't want to give him a chance to return to his apartment until she'd checked it out. "It's best if you stay." She didn't give a reason why. "Does the furniture belong to Phoebe?"

"Yeah, she brought her own stuff. Kind of picky that way."

Having recently moved to Portland, Skylar appreciated Phoebe's taste and orderly decor...until she entered the second bedroom that served as a home office. File folders, printouts, notebooks and reference material scattered across an L-shaped desk that also held a laptop and a computer with an extra-large screen. The color printer had a table all its own.

Skylar slipped on a pair of nitrile gloves before she started shuffling through the papers on the desk. Most of the documents related to the Lightkeeper's Curse Murders from twenty years ago. Obviously, Phoebe had been prepping to write an article after she received the note from the mystery person who summoned her to the lighthouse. How long did this research take? Two hours? Three? The precise time could be verified when the FBI cybercrime experts dumped the memory from her computer. Her electronics would show where she was at the given times. Time-stamped listings from her personal phone would indicate who she'd been talking to and what she'd been doing before her midnight appointment.

Unlike the rest of the apartment where the wall hangings had been selected by color and content, the office featured a cluster of plaques, citations and awards—testimony to Phoebe Conway's success in her field and the pride she took in her accomplishments. Pride or hubris? It could be argued that Phoebe's ambition caused her lack of caution and led to her murder.

Wrong! Skylar knew better than to blame the victim.

The rest of the wall space in the office was chockful of photographs. Some framed and others stuck onto cork bulletin boards. The majority of the pictures featured a smiling, beautiful Phoebe and a male companion.

Scanning slowly, she noticed very few pictures of other women. An indication that she had few female friends. Or maybe she didn't value their friendship enough to take a picture together. With a frown, Skylar once again dismissed her snap judgment. If she'd put together a collage of her own life, there would only be one close girlfriend she'd stayed in touch with since seventh grade. Growing up with two brothers put her in contact with more guys than gals. And her coworkers at the FBI were predominantly male. Nothing wrong with that.

Still, Phoebe's wall of men might have a deeper meaning. She'd posted these pictures near her workspace. Maybe to remind herself of her many conquests… The way a big game hunter hung trophies on his walls.

She spotted several of McKenna. Several others of a familiar-looking face who might be a celebrity. Another photo caught her eye. Phoebe had wrapped both arms around a tall, skinny guy with floppy brown hair and round glasses.

Surprised, Skylar stared at this odd and unexpected clue. The man in the picture with Phoebe was Alan Quilling, the head of APD's forensics unit.

Chapter Ten

Though Jake had to duck under an exposed beam in the third-floor attic apartment at Agate House, the space didn't feel cramped to him. The horizontal square footage of the open floor plan stretched from the front to the back of the building, plenty of room to roam. Vertically? Not so much.

The mansard roof was supported by arched beams, some of which weren't much taller than six feet high at the outer edges. They were too low for him; he stood six feet six inches in his bare feet. The many built-in shelves held books, papers, artwork, plastic models of body parts and weird equipment probably used in experiments by Jake's former high school science teacher, Robert Pierce. Two side-by-side windows at either end were designed to provide light during the day. On the western side of the apartment were long, wide dormers with shelves for dozens of leafy green plants and fragrant herbs.

Jake had taken only one chem class with Pierce, who must have started teaching right after college and was only six or seven years older. He looked much the same as he did back then. Short and solidly built, he wore his dark brown hair—still without a thread of gray—in a long ponytail. Pyro Pierce was known for riding his cross-country bike to school.

"I remember you, Armstrong. Advanced chem, senior year, A-plus student." Pierce pushed up his glasses onto the bridge of his hawklike nose. "You spent a lot of time figuring out the physics behind Batman's gadgets and Iron Man's suit."

Nerdy but true. "My favorite superheroes. They weren't aliens or magically transformed by a laboratory accident."

"Heroes you could identify with." Pierce gestured toward a kitchen table and two chairs at the edge of a kitchenette. "Would you like a cup of herbal tea? I have organic apple blossom. And fresh-baked banana bread to go with."

"Thanks, but no." The bread smelled great. Jake was tempted to sit and chat but needed to stay focused. "Are you aware of Phoebe Conway's murder?"

"She lived downstairs." Pierce cocked his head to one side. "That's why you're here. Am I right? You're a police detective. A whole different breed of hero."

"I wouldn't say that." In his real-life adventures as a cop, he never expected glamor or applause. Jake fumbled for words, couldn't decide exactly what perspective to take. Pierce might be a useful witness but was also a possible suspect. "How well did you know her?"

"Casually. We'd bump into each other on the stairs and say hello. She wasn't a bad neighbor, and I hope you won't think I'm sexist if I say she was *not* unpleasant to look at." He glanced up and to the right, as if conjuring a memory of Skylar's attributes. "Her body was toned but not athletic. Her symmetrical features made her pretty in a conventional way. Fluffy hair like an Afghan hound. And she had a slight but appealing hint of Texas accent."

"Negatives?" Jake asked.

"She was haughty and ambitious, which aren't necessarily bad traits. I'm all for goal setting." He chuckled. "Phoebe was a fan of *The Goonies*. Gotta like that."

"Did you ever ask her out?"

Pierce frowned. "Dating a woman in the building seemed like a bad idea because it could lead to uncomfortable meetings in the hallways after the probable breakup. Besides,

Phoebe never lacked for male companionship, including Ty McKenna. Have you spoken to him?"

"You bet." The telescope near the front window caught Jake's attention. He made the trek across several mismatched throw rugs on the hardwood floor to take a closer look. "What part of the night sky can you see from here?"

"We're facing northwest, so I'm looking at Cassiopeia, Pegasus and the Andromeda galaxy. I prefer taking the telescope to the roof to study astronomy during celestial events like meteor showers or an eclipse of the moon if the fog doesn't get in the way. Some people say we can see the northern lights from Astoria. But I've never found that to be true."

Pierce stepped up beside him and peered through the window glass. When they'd first arrived at Agate House, Jake had seen a silhouette from this upstairs window. "You have a good vantage point to watch the comings and goings of people who live here."

"I certainly do. You showed up twelve minutes ago and were accompanied by an attractive brunette in a conservative suit. I'm guessing she carries a sidearm. A lady cop?"

"An FBI special agent."

"Score one for me," Pierce said. "I'm not a snoop, but I like to figure stuff out."

That characterization sounded right to Jake. A science teacher would naturally be inquisitive. "Did you notice anything unusual about Phoebe's visitors?"

"Like what? Were they obvious ax murderers or drooling psychotics? Honestly, Jake, this interview would move along more quickly if you asked direct questions. There's no point in being subtle."

"What do you mean?"

"I have an alibi," he said.

"Okay."

"From what I've heard, Phoebe was killed on Cape Disappointment at about midnight. At the time, I was...occupied. A friend spent the night." He gestured toward the only enclosed portion of his apartment, which had to be where the bedroom and bathroom were located. "Actually, I think you know my lady."

He knew a lot of people. Astoria was a small town. "Does she have a name?"

"Dagmar Burke."

Jake shook his head. *Cousin Dagmar. Of course. Why not?* They were both single, close to the same age and both a little weird. But trustworthy. Mentally, he crossed Pyro Pierce off the list of suspects. "You and Dagmar, huh?"

"Precisely. Now, tell me what you're looking for. Not general traits, but something more specific."

More scientific. "According to our evidence, the killer knew Phoebe and was familiar with the Lightkeeper's Curse Murders from twenty years ago. He might have been watching her or stalking."

"He? Are you sure the killer is male?"

Jake had to be careful not to divulge specifics about an ongoing investigation. Skylar had gone ballistic when Quilling showed the phone photo of the killer's note. If Jake started sharing conclusions about their murderer or the murder scene, she'd explode. "Let's talk about stalking. Have you noticed a stranger hanging around the neighborhood? Or a vehicle that didn't belong here?"

"Matter of fact, I have. There was a car, a black sedan with tinted windows. It's been parked along the street three or four times in the past few weeks."

A strange car might mean nothing, or it might lead to the killer. The Son of Sam serial killer, David Berkowitz, was apprehended because of a parking ticket near one of the crime scenes. "What else can you tell me about this car?"

"I don't know the make or model."

Of course not. Pierce wasn't a car guy. "Are you still riding your bike everywhere?"

"Keeps me in shape." Pierce bristled. "That doesn't mean I'm opposed to other forms of transportation. I bought a used van for hauling groceries and packing supplies for camping trips, but I prefer my mountain bike for everything else. My Carbonjack is a beauty and cost a whole lot more than the gas-guzzling vehicle."

Jake dragged him back to the topic. "About this black sedan…"

"I know who it belongs to," Pierce said. "The driver wasn't in the vehicle, but I was riding past on my bike and looked in the window. There was a decal with a skull and crossbones on the dashboard."

"The Jolly Roger." The symbol associated with the editor-in-chief of the *Astoria Sun*. Rogers had no alibi. "Anything else?"

"A folded copy of the *Sun* on the passenger seat. And a bumper sticker that says, My Other Car is a Fishing Trawler."

It had to be Rogers. "Thanks, you've been a great help."

"Come back anytime, Armstrong. The world needs more heroes."

In the hallway with the door to Pierce's apartment closed, Jake leaned against the wall and closed his eyes, waiting for his random thoughts to sort themselves into logic. Though he was supposed to interrogate the other residents of Agate House—two couples and a single female—he needed to act on this lead.

Rogers had been stalking Phoebe. He had no alibi for last night, which made him the number one suspect. If he was the murderer, he might be starting a string of serial killings. In his note, the Shadowkeeper said Phoebe was his *first victim*. Obvious conclusion: Jake needed to get Rogers under surveillance as soon as possible.

He charged down the staircase to the second floor where Skylar and McKenna had just exited Phoebe's apartment.

Maintaining calm instead of the urgency churning in his gut, he said, "I need to speak to you immediately, Agent Gambel."

A frown pinched her forehead between her sculpted brows. "Something wrong?"

"We need to talk. Now."

"First, we'll accompany McKenna to his apartment."

He gritted his teeth and fell into step behind her and McKenna. They were wasting time. Another person might be killed.

At the apartment in the rear of the house, McKenna unlocked the door and stepped inside in front of them. He tried to shut it, but Skylar braced her shoulder against the door.

Standing behind her, Jake couldn't see what was happening. Before he could react, she made her move. Faster than a speeding bullet. Equally lethal. She whipped her jacket out of the way, drew her sidearm and dropped into a shooter's stance.

On the other side of a coffee table, McKenna had picked up a gun of his own. He held it away from his body, not aiming but lying flat on the palm of his hand.

"Drop the weapon," Skylar ordered in a voice laced with steel.

"Whatever you say. Don't shoot."

Wisely, he chose not to fight. McKenna lowered his gun to the table, stepped back and raised his hands.

Skylar didn't relax her stance.

"I've got it," Jake said as he picked up the gun—a pricey, compact Springfield Armory. "Got a handgun permit?"

"It belongs to my dad."

"Hold out your arms."

Unwisely, McKenna chose to resist. "What if I don't want to?"

Tired of the whining from this entitled jerk, Jake switched into his military persona. Rough. Tough. And straight as an arrow. They needed to act, to move fast and make sure Rogers was under surveillance. "Do it now."

Surprised, McKenna obeyed.

Quick and aggressive, he frisked McKenna and turned to his partner. "No other weapons."

She holstered her Glock. "I wonder if he's on some kind of extended probation. Prohibited from dealing with other scumbags. Restricted from carrying lethal weapons."

Jake had another concern. "Why is this gun lying around unsecured? It should be put away, locked in a safe."

"I loaned it to Phoebe," McKenna said. "Before I let you into the house, I went into her apartment, grabbed the gun and brought it here."

"You thought Phoebe needed a handgun," Jake said. "Why?"

"She worried that somebody was following her."

She couldn't have been talking about Rogers, her boss. She knew him. "And why did you steal the gun away from her apartment?"

"Appearances," Skylar said. "He didn't want us to know he had a gun. Right?"

"I suppose."

She reached into her purse and pulled out handcuffs. "You have a choice. Cooperate and do exactly as I say. Or I can arrest you for the obstruction of an ongoing murder investigation."

He stamped his foot like an angry hipster toddler. "I haven't done anything wrong."

"Obstruction it is." She nodded to Jake and said, "Turn him around so I can snap on the cuffs."

McKenna dodged around him and got up in Skylar's face. He jabbed his forefinger at her chest. "I've had enough, lady. You can't order me around."

He'd gone from unwise to flat-out stupid. Jake could have warned him not to get pushy with a fed. Or he could have taken McKenna down in a flash. But he waited to see what Skylar would do next.

She didn't disappoint. Skylar grabbed McKenna's wrist, pulled him off balance and kicked his leg out from under him. In seconds, the fashionable jerk was flat on his belly with Skylar looking down at him. "You're lucky you didn't touch me. I would have charged you with assaulting a federal officer. Do you agree to cooperate?"

McKenna forced himself to his knees. Grudgingly, he said, "I'll do what you say."

"Don't go anywhere tonight. Oh, and I'll be taking this pretty little gun."

"Like I told you, it belongs to my father. He's not going to be happy about this."

"Believe me when I say this, McKenna." Her lips curled in a glacial grin. "I don't care."

They descended the staircase and went through the vestibule and onto the porch where she turned to face him. "Lucky for McKenna, he has an alibi."

"So does Pierce, the science teacher in the third-floor apartment." Jake winced. "He spent the night with my cousin Dagmar."

"Madame Librarian?"

"But that's not the important thing. Pierce noticed a strange car outside Agate House. A black sedan had been there several times in the last few weeks."

"A stalker," she said. "Did he get a license plate?"

"Better. He peeked in the car window and saw a Jolly Roger decal. A bumper sticker said, My Other Car is a Fishing Trawler."

"Rogers."

For the first time, she gave him a genuine, natural, spectacular smile. In the glow from the porch light, her long, auburn hair glistened, and her green eyes shimmered. Her lips parted, showing off a row of perfect white teeth.

He swallowed hard and forced himself to speak coherently. "I'll get the surveillance under way."

"Good work, Jake."

This might be the first time she'd used his given name. He'd graduated from the generic *detective* or *Armstrong*. "Thank you, Skylar."

Leaning into the shadows on the porch, she wrapped her arms around his torso for a hug. Her slender body pressed against his chest. He draped his arms over her shoulders and gently squeezed, imagining the sound of their hearts beating in harmony.

Their brief contact—less than five seconds—wasn't strictly professional, but he'd forgotten about his image or credibility. His mind filled with ideas about further intimacy. Maybe a kiss. Maybe more. He wanted Skylar beside him in his bed.

Chapter Eleven

With a name like Captain's Cove B&B, Skylar expected a nautical theme in the renovated Edwardian mansion, and she wasn't disappointed. The wallpaper in her room had an anchor design, and a dark blue fishing net draped artistically on the wall by the window. Kitschy but somewhat charming, not unlike foggy Astoria itself.

She never could have prepared herself for this setting that included twenty-year-old serial killings, curses, Halloween decor, a pregnant police chief and a tall, handsome detective. Her first assignment as a special agent presented a surprising challenge—one she meant to solve.

Her meeting in the downstairs parlor was scheduled for half an hour from now, enough time for a shower. She peeled off her slim leather hip holster, jacket, trousers, underwear and silky blouse, tossing each item onto the pale blue duvet. She'd hustled to arrive earlier than SSA Crawford so she could lay claim to the best bedroom. Her experience with road trips—while working as a lawyer and as an FBI analyst—taught her that the early bird gets the king-size bed, a spacious bathroom and the best view. From her window, she could see the one-hundred-twenty-five-foot-tall Astoria Column atop Coxcomb Hill.

Naked, she carried her Glock 19, still in the holster, into the bathroom and placed the weapon gently on a fluffy blue towel on the tiled countertop. She pulled her hair up on top of her head in a high ponytail and turned on the shower. In renovated homes like this one, the supply of hot water didn't come with a guarantee. The smart move was to grab a shower before Crawford got here. On their first out-of-Portland assignment together, she didn't know whether he was a shower hog or practitioner of the quickie. She suspected the former. His Silver Fox nickname suggested proper grooming.

The spray gushed, and the steam created a pleasantly warm fog as she stepped under the showerhead to rinse away a clammy layer of nervous sweat. Her perspiration hadn't resulted from physical activity. Her only exertion had been to sweep McKenna off his high-top lace-up boots. But her tension had been off the chart.

Luckily, her instincts had been right when she decided to ignore Jake's conflict of interest and partner up with him. He'd proved himself to be an able backup in the confrontation with McKenna and the earlier interrogation. She envied his overwhelming height and size that made him naturally intimidating. Not to mention the growl in his voice when angered. But he was more than a muscular sidekick. Jake was…so much more.

The pellets of hot water rained down and massaged her shoulders. Actually, Jake was nothing like a sidekick. More of a leading man. Smart, intuitive and motivated, his information moved Rogers from a benign position as a former victim and present-day witness to being *numero uno* suspect.

In spite of her unusual skills at reading character, she hadn't considered Rogers to be dangerous when they first met. He was all bluster and no bite. When he spoke of the Lightkeeper, he looked and sounded afraid. Intimidated. Still threatened after all these years.

But Jake had seen another side. She approved of his perceptiveness, his intelligence and…his wide shoulders. Every time she followed him along the sidewalk, she admired the way his upper body tapered to a lean torso and a truly fine bottom. An unintentional moan escaped her lips and echoed behind the shower curtain. Being hugged by Jake on the porch of McKenna's house, being held, even for a few seconds, felt incredible.

It had been a long time since she'd been in a real relationship.

Memory spiraled through her. During her summer vacation before her senior year in college, she was engaged to be married, preoccupied with planning the wedding, finding the perfect dress, selecting colors, flowers, bands and bridesmaids. The girly-girl role wasn't her natural style, but she played the role, dressing up and flashing her diamond ring because she thought she'd found the ideal mate.

She'd been so very wrong. He'd been a cheater who lied about everything, even her engagement ring with the phony diamonds and rubies. Her dreams were severed like a machete slashed through a four-tier wedding cake, and she vowed to keep a protective distance between herself and potential leading men like Jake. She wouldn't get carried away. Never again. Jake Armstrong was a friend and coworker, nothing more.

While she lathered her breasts, she remembered how enthusiastic he'd been about the progress of their case. Eagerly, he assumed the responsibility for communication with Chief Kim who would hand out assignments to the police staff, including the interviews with the other residents of Agate House.

She and Jake had discussed how to handle Rogers. For tonight, they decided not to arrest him. Parking on the street outside Phoebe's apartment didn't rise to the level of crime. But Jake arranged to keep Rogers's home under surveillance. The idea of standard police procedure seemed to please him. The Astoria cops didn't often handle stakeouts.

When she mentioned finding the photo of Alan Quilling

and Phoebe in a steamy embrace, Jake had been disappointed but hadn't dismissed her suspicions. Similar to their plan for Rogers, they decided not to confront Quilling immediately. Instead, they curtailed his forensic activities and arranged for him to be on paid leave-of-absence.

Leaving the shower, Skylar felt renewed and energized. She dressed in skinny jeans and a T-shirt with an oatmeal-colored cable-knit cardigan covering her holster. With her hair brushed and hanging loose past her shoulders, she appeared tidy enough for a meeting with Crawford and his old buddy, Jimi. After a glance in the mirror above the bathroom sink, she dabbed on blush and lipstick. Jake would also be downstairs, and she didn't want to be pasty-faced and tired-looking. It was barely ten o'clock. Plenty of time to make progress on the case.

She heard a knock. Through the closed door, Jake said, "It's me, Detective Armstrong."

So formal. She wondered if he was embarrassed about visiting the room of an unmarried federal officer after dark. When she opened the door and confronted the large man who filled the doorframe, she saw nothing self-conscious in his manner. His intense blue-eyed gaze slid from the top of her head and her unbound hair to her lipstick to her sweater and jeans. He gave an appreciative nod. "You clean up good."

"That doesn't make sense. I'm not cleaning *up*. I changed out of my suit, which means I'm dressing *down*."

"I like this better."

When he entered, she realized the clothes she'd discarded when she stripped were still strewn across the duvet where she tossed them. With a swoop of her arm, she gathered her jacket, blouse and silky underwear, flung the garments into the closet and snapped the door closed.

Nonchalantly, she flipped her hair out of her eyes. "What's on your mind?"

"Here's the update." His brazen grin told her that he'd seen the undies and noticed the lacy trim. "Chief Kim deployed and deputized every individual who's ever worked as an officer. She gave them 'profiles' to fill out when they talked to potential witnesses and/or suspects."

Skylar wasn't sure she liked the idea of half-trained cops conducting interviews. "I'm impressed by her ability to respond so fast. Tell me about these profiles."

"Nothing that requires analysis. It's a questionnaire. Name, address, phone number and how did you know Phoebe. Anything that stands out is highlighted for future follow-up."

"Then we can run them through the FBI criminal database. And verify alibis."

"So far, we haven't got much," he said. "The ex-boyfriends on Tabitha's list don't like Phoebe but none sound homicidal. The other residents of Agate House barely knew her. Two of McKenna's friends and the bartender confirmed his alibi."

"And the stakeout?"

"Officer Dub Wagner finished up at the crime scene and volunteered. Nothing has happened yet, but Chief Kim thinks Dub has got to be tired. She wants me to assign someone else to take his place in a couple of hours."

So far, so good. But she wanted to solve this case before the Shadowkeeper struck again. "What's going on with Crawford and Jimi Kim?"

"They're up to their eyebrows in data from twenty years ago. They've got boxes of files. Also, charts, maps and game plans. Though they claim to be keeping open minds, their investigation is rooted in the past."

Not a surprise. From the moment she saw her partner pull the battered old file for the Lightkeeper's Curse from his bottom desk drawer in the Portland office, she recognized his obsession with the serial killer he failed to apprehend twenty years ago. Crawford needed closure almost as much as the victims. His current theory posited that the Lightkeeper had come out of retirement with a new moniker. *Shadowkeeper.*

Though unusual for serial killers to take a break once they started, it had happened before. "Are you familiar with the BTK murderer in Kansas?"

"I don't know much. BTK stands for bind, torture and kill."

"Correct." She suppressed a shudder. "He stopped killing and took a thirteen-year hiatus before he started up again."

Jake stroked the line of his jaw, drawing her attention to the interesting dimple on his clean-shaven chin. No stubble. Though still not wearing a uniform, he was well-groomed. "I've got a hunch that it's *not* the same guy. The Lightkeeper took orders from a high priestess and thought he was ridding the world of evil. The Shadowkeeper—as you pointed out—is a narcissist and doesn't give a damn about the rest of the world."

"You don't think we're wasting our time by following up on clues about Phoebe?"

"I don't," he said. "The Shadowkeeper targeted her for a reason."

"Too bad we don't know why." As she reached for the doorknob, her stomach growled. "I don't suppose we'll be lucky enough to find snacks downstairs."

"Oh, there's food. Chief Kim is here. One of the perks of working for a pregnant boss is the parade of munchies."

Before leaving her room, Skylar grabbed her briefcase packed with files, crime-scene photos and her handy-dandy laptop for taking notes. There hadn't been time to transcribe her interviews with McKenna and Rogers, but she'd downloaded the parts she'd recorded on her phone. The required paperwork would come later.

The carpeting on the wide landing had a seashell pattern that extended to the magnificent oak staircase. She descended and followed the sound of her partner's voice from down the hall on the first floor.

SSA Crawford sounded excited and energetic. Unusual for

him. In addition to his rep for being as handsome as the next Golden Bachelor, he was known for being laid-back and cool.

Another voice joined his. This speaker had clear enunciation but talked a mile a minute.

She entered a large parlor with a mix of Victorian furniture and more practical styles. The main feature was a four-foot-tall freestanding antique mahogany helm wheel, fully appropriate for the captain of a sailing vessel. A long, rectangular table provided a space for meetings. At the closer end of the table, Chief Vivienne Kim presided over an array of hummus, pita chips, samosas filled with kimchi, deep-fried eggrolls, doughnuts, pickles and Girl Scout cookies. Skylar's grumbling stomach drew her toward the feast. "This looks wonderful."

"I had to skip dinner," the chief said, "and I can't do that when I'm eating for two."

Her grandpa, Jimi Kim, introduced himself with a vigorous handshake and an explanation. "I called my wife, and Nana insisted on feeding Viv and the rest of the crew. We have bottled water and juice to drink. No coffee. No booze."

"Much appreciated." Skylar took an immediate liking to Jimi, a wiry man with neatly trimmed black hair turning gray at the temples. A wispy goatee encircled his mouth. His gentle smile didn't show his teeth.

"Come," he said, gesturing to the table. "Eat."

"Not yet," said Crawford. The senior agent stood at the helm, appropriate for the captain of this venture. "We have a lot to explain."

Jimi waggled a finger in his direction. "Not on an empty stomach."

Skylar helped herself to a plateful of food, grabbed a water bottle and found a seat near the other end of the table where Crawford and Jimi had arranged three standing easels. One held a map with markings, another showed the results of their meetings with two former suspects, and the third was a whiteboard covered with Crawford's scrawl.

"We'll start with the map," he said while she ate. "I've marked the locations of the seven Lightkeeper murders with red X's. You can see there are no repeats."

She swallowed a savory bite from a samosa. "Are all the locations lighthouses?"

"There were two actual lighthouses," he said. "North Head on Cape Disappointment and Cape Meares, which was where Phoebe was found. He didn't use the other two lighthouses in the area. Another is near the one on Cape Disappointment. Then, there's Terrible Tilly."

"Tell me about Tilly."

"It's on a one-acre basalt island about a mile offshore from where the Tillamook River merges with the Pacific. Iconic and impractical, the tower is battered by fierce winds and high surf that crashes as high as the beacon. Lightkeepers have died at that place. It was decommissioned as a lighthouse many years ago. Once it was used as a columbarium, but no more. Actually, I think it's for sale."

"Not my dream home," she said, scooping hummus onto a pita. "What about the other one on Cape Disappointment?"

"It's more difficult to get to. These other X's are for a light boat used by the coast guard, a miniature golf lighthouse, a motel and two restaurants with lighthouse themes."

The red marks on the map covered an area along several miles of coastal property, ranging from the Washington side of the Columbia River to Cannon Beach. Most of the murders had been in the vicinity of Astoria or Warrenton.

Skylar paused in her feeding frenzy to ask, "What's your takeaway on the map?"

"If the Shadowkeeper kills again, he might use one of these locations. Establishing physical surveillance on all of them is nearly impossible."

"I thought you arranged with FBI forensics team to set up virtual surveillance at all the possible sites."

"First thing tomorrow morning," SSA Crawford said. "We'll arrange for them to place cameras that feed into a closed-circuit system at APD headquarters, but this is a wide territory. We can't post enough trained officers to respond quickly."

"We have to try," Chief Kim said. "The cameras will provide more surveillance than guards at each place."

"It's a start." Jimi crossed the room and stood beside Crawford. "I may be an old man, but I am all in favor of modern technology. Things have changed for the better."

Crawford nudged his arm. "Think of what we could have done twenty years ago with the current improvements in DNA analysis and computer info in CODIS."

"Nowadays, crimes nearly solve themselves," Jimi said.

His granddaughter nibbled on a doughnut with rainbow sprinkles. "Are you admitting that the good old days weren't really so good?"

"Change is good. The Buddha says nothing is permanent, except change."

Skylar glanced toward Jake who was talking on his phone. When he pushed away from the table and left the room, she turned back to Crawford. "What else can we do?"

"I'm not totally convinced that the Shadowkeeper and the Lightkeeper are the same person. However, the Shadowkeeper has chosen to follow the patterns of the earlier murders." He pointed to the middle whiteboard. "The first heading: Warnings and Clues. The Lightkeeper left notes or sent messages that hinted at his next victim or the next location."

Not the first time SSA Crawford had mentioned these clues from the past. In his files, he'd copied these sometimes taunting and sometimes haunting comments.

Skylar asked, "Have we uncovered any other communication from the Shadowkeeper about his next victim? Or his next location? The cybercrime techies in Portland are usually able to track email addresses and give us a name. Surely they've come up with something."

"They haven't unraveled the computer routings." Crawford twisted the mahogany helm as though changing course. "That doesn't fit the pattern."

She asked, "How so?"

"The Shadowkeeper is clever enough to outwit the FBI's highly trained, sophisticated computer experts. That's very unlike the Lightkeeper. Twenty years ago, he made his audio recordings on cassettes, which was an outdated technology even then."

"A different profile." Though she believed they were dealing with two different killers, she also thought they'd learn something from the past. She stole a quick glance at the notes Crawford and Jimi had made about the two former suspects.

Before she could comment, Jake came back into the room and spoke for a moment with the chief who nodded her agreement. Swiftly, he approached Skylar and said, "Dub Wagner needs backup on his stakeout. Jolly Rogers is on the move."

Crawford shooed her toward the exit. "Go."

Chapter Twelve

Jake respected the investigative wisdom of SSA Crawford and former police chief Jimi Kim. Between them, the two lawmen had nearly fifty years' experience, and they were brilliant when it came to evaluating and reexamining the Lightkeeper evidence. More than expertise, they shared a fierce dedication. This was probably their last chance to revisit the serial murders from twenty years ago and finally nab the killer.

The procedure Jake and Skylar pursued was more simple and straightforward. *Who killed Phoebe Conway and why?* He was happy to leave the theoretical meeting behind and get back to basic police work.

Outside the Captain's Cove, he dashed down the stairs from the veranda to the street. Looking over his shoulder, he saw Skylar following. She paused on the sidewalk by his Explorer. With an eggroll in one hand and cookies in the other, she somehow managed to open the passenger door and climb inside. Breathless, she asked, "What's the problem with the stakeout?"

"The suspect is on the move, and Dub isn't sure what to do. Apart from Quilling, he's the youngest officer on the force. This is his first stakeout." Jake switched his phone to hands-free. "I have to call him to communicate. He didn't take his police car. So, no radio."

"That was smart procedure," she said. "Rogers would have noticed a cop car."

"So far, it seems like Dub has done everything right. He told me that he found a great place to park for surveillance. Far enough away to not arouse suspicion. Close enough to see if Rogers left."

"And then he did."

He nodded. "And Dub panicked. He's afraid he can't tail Rogers without being noticed, and he doesn't want to screw up."

Listening through earbuds, Jake followed Wagner's directions. To Skylar, he reported, "Rogers stopped at Billy's 24-Hour Trading Post where he apparently bought a pack of Marlboro cigarettes. As soon as he was outside, he lit up."

"Maybe that's why he left his house." She swallowed the last bite of eggroll. "Is he a regular smoker?"

"He quit several years ago."

"We must have stressed him out."

They were almost in sight of the Trading Post when Wagner gave new directions. Not wanting Rogers to see his Explorer with the Astoria Police logo, Jake pulled over to the curb. "Sounds like he's headed toward Highway 101."

She used a paper napkin with Halloween designs to dab at her lips. "This is the best meal I've had in quite a while. Nana Kim is a great cook."

And Skylar was a great eater—the kind of woman who enjoyed and appreciated food. When she'd changed out of her FBI suit into jeans, her personality had changed. Her features relaxed. She seemed more approachable. Her glossy auburn hair tumbled around her shoulders. He'd never seen anybody chow down with so much gusto, which made him eager to find out about her other appetites. "I'll let Nana Kim know you approve."

"Why the Girl Scout cookies?"

"The chief's oldest daughter is a Brownie and gets a prize for selling the most boxes."

"I should have guessed." She craned her neck and peered through the windshield at the swirling mists of fog. "We drove on Highway 101 to Cape Meares. Rogers could be going back there."

He never understood why criminals returned to the scene of the crime. Guilt. Pride. Fear that they'd left a clue. Didn't make logical sense, and Rogers wasn't that stupid. "We're not going to the highway. Rogers turned onto a side road and is driving to the west marina. We'll meet Dub there."

Jake took familiar shortcuts. He'd never owned a boat but had friends who did and knew his way around the piers, docks and marinas. Growing up in a harbor town, he'd spent a lot of time on the water and still enjoyed lazy afternoons, fishing on the river. He bypassed the turnoff to the Astoria-Megler Bridge and drove to a parking area on a hill above the marina where he easily located Officer Wagner's silver Subaru station wagon. Dub stood beside his front fender with a pair of binoculars raised to his eyes.

Jake greeted him with a compliment. "I thought you might be too tired to handle the stakeout after spending most of the day at the crime scene, but you're doing good."

"And I can use the overtime." He nodded to Skylar. "My wife is pregnant with our first. All the baby stuff costs a bundle."

"Congratulations." She pointed toward the marina. "Is the suspect alone?"

"I didn't see anybody in the car with him."

"May I use your binoculars? Nikon?"

"Yes, ma'am." He handed them over. "I've been itching to try these out, wondering if I should get infrared like the scope on my hunting rifle."

In this marina—one of several along the waterfront—

boats of varying size, shape and horsepower parked in the slips at either side of several interlocking docks.

She asked, "What's that little hut in the middle, the one with the light through the windows?"

"The harbormaster's shack. He's not usually available this late on a weeknight, but it looks like he's there."

"I wonder if he has surveillance cameras focused on the marina." She turned to Jake and passed the binoculars to him. "I spotted Rogers's trawler. The *Jolly Rogers*. Gotta be the one with the skull-and-crossbones flag."

He saw it immediately. In addition to streetlights along the dock, the small, enclosed cabin of Rogers's boat poured light onto the deck. "I'm not sure whether we should continue our stakeout from a distance or confront him directly."

"If we approach," she said, "he'll know we're suspicious."

"You already made that clear at the *Sun*. When he didn't have an alibi."

She appeared to be taken aback. "I didn't accuse him or arrest him."

"You've got that fed attitude that says don't-mess-with-me. You can be intimidating."

"Said the six-and-a-half-foot former marine," she scoffed.

"No such animal," he said. "Once a marine, always a marine."

"Got it."

"And I want to know why he came to the marina." Though the evidence against Rogers seemed to keep piling up, he couldn't bring himself to believe the newspaper man was guilty of stalking his employee and brutally murdering her. "If we don't question him, there's not much chance we'll find out what he's doing. We don't have enough evidence for a search warrant."

"Not nearly," she said, "and we need to be careful about exerting undue pressure on a member of the press who can make us look bad."

His thinking took a different direction. "What if he's preparing his boat to make an escape? Remember how he talked about retirement and cruising up and down the coast?"

Skylar met his gaze, and he saw determination in her sea-green eyes as she came to a decision. "You're right. We can't stand here watching while he heads off into parts unknown."

He returned the binoculars to their owner. "Dub, I want you to stay here and keep an eye on Rogers. If he leaves, follow his car and continue your stakeout."

"Yes, sir."

Together, he and Skylar walked down to the marina, unlatched the gate and walked side by side on a long wooden pier. A narrow branch led them to the slip where the *Jolly Rogers* was docked. The trawler, with a black hull and white cabin, showed signs of its nearly twenty-year age as they got closer. Though Jake couldn't imagine shooting a man he'd known since he was a kid, he pushed aside his jacket for easy access to the Beretta in his holster. He noticed that Skylar had left her FBI windbreaker open. He saw the outline of her Glock and recalled her quick draw when facing Ty McKenna. He hoped she wouldn't need that skill.

"Something about this is all wrong."

"You're the one who wanted to approach the suspect," Skylar said.

"But Mr. Rogers?" In the back of his mind, the lyrics to "It's a Beautiful Day in the Neighborhood" played. "Mr. Rogers?"

Jake went first on the narrow dock beside the trawler. As soon as he and Skylar stood where the boat was moored, Rogers stuck his head out of the cabin and yelled, "What the hell are you doing here?"

Skylar didn't draw her weapon, but her head-on confrontation showed solid FBI aggressiveness. She was calling the shots, as she usually did. "Step out of the cabin and onto the deck," she snapped. "Show me your hands."

"Damn it, Armstrong," Rogers appealed to him. "What's her problem?"

"You'd better do what Special Agent Gambel says." *Always back up your partner.* "Our investigation has turned up evidence we need to ask you about."

"It's past my bedtime," Rogers complained. "Too damn late to play stupid games."

"Out on deck," Skylar repeated. "Now."

Instead of obeying her order, he hesitated, stuck an unlit cigarette between his lips and glared. "What are you going to do? Arrest me?"

Her voice went low and dangerous. "You asked for it, Rogers."

Before she could whip out her Glock, and before the newspaperman could toss out another dumb unedited comment, Jake climbed aboard the *Jolly Rogers*. After taking a moment to get his balance, he stood equidistant between the two adversaries.

"Hey!" The old man emerged from the cabin, stepped onto the deck and waved his hands in the air. Instead of his usual attire of a shirt and necktie with a loose knot, he wore an over-large black hoodie that flapped around his arms like bat wings. "I damn well didn't give you permission to come aboard."

Without preface or explanation, Jake asked, "How often, in the past couple of weeks, was your vehicle parked near Phoebe's apartment house?"

"Why the hell would my car be there?"

"We have a witness who saw your black sedan with the skull-and-crossbones decal."

"They're lying," Rogers said. "It's his or her word against mine."

"A credible witness." Jake made direct eye contact. "Consider carefully before you speak. Was your car parked outside Agate House where Phoebe lived?"

Rogers reached into the pocket of his sweatshirt and took a Zippo lighter. The wind through the marina made it difficult to light his Marlboro, and he took his time. An effective ploy to irritate both Jake and Skylar. When he had a glow at the tip, Rogers said, "I was there. I had to talk to her about an assignment for the paper."

When Skylar stepped onto the deck beside him, Jake noticed—thankfully—that her Glock stayed in the holster. She asked, "What was your relationship with Phoebe?"

"None of your business," he said defiantly.

Jake cringed inside, not wanting to think of Rogers chasing Phoebe. Not that there was anything wrong with an older man dating a younger woman. The small town of Astoria couldn't claim to be immune to the cliché of an employee sleeping his or her way to the top. And the ick factor was nothing compared to cold-blooded murder. He prompted, "You were her boss."

"Goes without saying. She was my employee and a damn good reporter. Her articles on *The Goonies* upped our circulation."

"How many times did you visit her?" Skylar asked.

"I don't know. Maybe twice."

"Our witness saw your vehicle several times, enough that it attracted his attention."

"So what?" His thick eyebrows lowered in a scowl. "It's not illegal to park on the street. Did you think of that? Maybe I just happened to be in her area."

Skylar scowled. "I don't believe in coincidence."

"Lawyer," he shouted.

"One more question." Jake wanted to get as much info as possible. "Why did you come to the marina tonight?"

He inhaled deeply and blew his cigarette smoke into the fog. "I was looking for somebody and thought they might be here. But they aren't."

Trying to find a person who wasn't there? That excuse was just weird enough to be true. "Who?"

"I want my damn lawyer. You can't ask me any more questions."

Jake pushed again. "This person isn't here. Why can't you tell us about him or her?"

"Her," Rogers snapped. "It's a *her*."

"Tell me about her. Hypothetically."

"She might be my alibi for the night when Phoebe was killed. Maybe I wasn't alone in bed. Maybe I won't give you her name because she's married to somebody else." He straightened his shoulders. "That's all I'm going to say. Now, get your sorry ass off my boat."

"While we're here," Jake said, "we could do a quick search."

"Don't push your luck, Armstrong. You're trespassing on my boat, and you have no right to be here unless you have a warrant."

"We have what we came for." Skylar climbed off the deck onto the pier. "Don't leave town, Mr. Rogers, not without telling me."

Jake followed her without a backward glance at the newspaper man. On the pier, he walked beside her. "What did you mean when you said we had what we came for?"

"He gave us an alibi for the time Phoebe was killed, which I suspect we can verify through the local gossip you're privy to. And he claimed his car had a work-related reason to be in Phoebe's neighborhood."

"Right."

"I don't believe either of those statements," she said, "but that's what we wanted to know."

Jake agreed with everything she said, especially about local gossip. If he put out a couple of feelers, he'd have the name, address and occupation of Rogers's lover in no time flat. The reason for visiting Phoebe presented more of a problem. "He's not telling the whole truth."

"I don't think he's the Shadowkeeper," she said.

"I agree."

"But I was right about him," she said. "The man definitely has something to hide."

Chapter Thirteen

Just past dawn the next morning—a few minutes after seven—Skylar stood at the street corner outside the Astoria Police Department. She hadn't gone to sleep last night until after two in the morning when she'd concluded her update for SSA Crawford and Jimi, filed the required reports, requested search warrants for Rogers's property and launched plans for this morning.

Those plans had been blown to hell. One untraceable text message on her phone shattered their investigation.

Hello Agent Skylar. The princess is in the tower. Such a pretty girl, she looks a bit like you, my dear. She wasn't a Disappointment. At the North Head Lighthouse. Phoebe would have written a full column about this little songbird and her silence. —The Shadowkeeper

The repeated ping from the text had wakened her less than an hour ago. The clues were blatant. Cape Disappointment. North Head Lighthouse.

Skylar bolted from the bed, notified Crawford and Jake, who said he'd contact Chief Kim. The chief would follow up on the message and try to track the phone that had placed the text. Confirmation of the text message came through before

Skylar was fully dressed in her standard FBI outfit: gray suit, cotton shirt and black leather belt holster. On top, she wore a rain jacket, standard clothing for damp, foggy Astoria.

The chief had notified the Washington State Parks service, who established a crime scene and sent photos of a dark-haired woman hanging by her neck from the high lighthouse tower below the beacon while fog swirled around her body and night began to lift. Further investigation would wait until members of the task force in Astoria arrived. No identification had been made.

An hour earlier, she and Crawford had driven to the Astoria Police Department. He dropped her off to check in with Chief Kim while he drove to the crime scene. In the pre-dawn, every light had been lit at the APD and every parking space filled. Officers—some in uniforms and some in plainclothes—had been working the phones from their desks or dashing through the corridors, seeking more information.

The investigation was in full swing. But they were too late. The Shadowkeeper had already struck again.

In the conference room, Chief Kim had offered doughnuts and coffee while she brought Skylar and Jake up to speed on other aspects of the investigation. Rogers's house had been under surveillance all night. After his trip to the marina, the suspect hadn't gone anywhere else.

Arrangements had been made with the FBI forensic and surveillance teams to set up cameras at likely spots for the Shadowkeeper to strike, which included the seven red *X*'s on the map that marked lighthouses and lighthouse replicas. One less now. The North Head Lighthouse.

Though hungry, Skylar had only nibbled the edge of a plain doughnut and sipped a mild tea. No coffee. Not yet. She needed to pamper her stomach in case of potential queasiness. Today, she had her own secret trial. Her own phobia.

On the street corner in Astoria, she slowly lifted her chin, turned northwest and confronted the monster that stood between her and the crime scene.

Today, Skylar would cross that bridge.

Random facts blasted through her mind, providing zero consolation. The Astoria-Megler Bridge over the Columbia River was over four miles, the longest cantilevered truss bridge in the country. *Anybody would be scared, right?* Clearance above the water was over two hundred feet—high enough for container ships and Carnival cruise vessels to pass through on their way to Portland. The trusses and towering framework resembling the backbone of a T. rex hunched over the two-lane traffic.

Clear skies this morning showed the monster in all its glory. She inhaled through her nose and exhaled in a whoosh through her mouth. Over the years, she'd learned that meditation also soothed, but there wasn't time to drop into a mindful session. Taking a sedative was out of the question. She had to be alert while working the crime scene.

She'd make it across the damn bridge. She had to.

Jake hiked toward her on the sidewalk with long, fast strides. Occasionally, he glanced over his shoulder as if he were being chased. Errant rays of sunshine glistened in his blond hair. He looked angry. He stalked toward his Explorer in the parking lot, and she fell into step beside him. Trying to match her stride with his very long legs, she was almost jogging.

Before they reached his vehicle, the threat he'd been avoiding on the sidewalk caught up to them. Three young women, aggressively snapping photos of Jake with their phones, surrounded them and shouted questions about the investigation. They represented Astoria's media coverage. Blond. Bright-eyed. Enthusiastic.

"No comment," Jake said coldly.

"Somebody else got murdered, huh?"

"Who is it? Come on, Detective Armstrong, tell us. My

older sister, Juliet, didn't come home last night. She's blond like Phoebe. Is it her?"

Skylar silently vetoed Juliet. The Shadowkeeper said that the victim looked like her, which meant dark or auburn hair color. But she knew better than to say anything to the press. One response would lead to another to another.

Undeterred, the trio trailed behind them.

At Jake's car, another individual appeared. She was tall and solid. When she moved, her scarves swirled, and her bangle bracelets jingled. Dagmar. Jake's cousin and the daughter of the Lightkeeper's final victim. Dagmar, the alibi for Pyro Pierce.

In most instances, Skylar would have been annoyed at further interference, but she approved when Dagmar snarled at the blondies and told them to bug off. The ladies of the press took a step back while she and Jake entered the SUV. Before they could stop her, Dagmar leaped into the back.

Skylar snapped. "We can't give you a ride."

"I'll be gone in a minute," Dagmar said. "I have info."

Driving carefully to avoid crashing into one of the reporter/blogger/influencer gang, Jake merged into Astoria's meager imitation of the seven-to-nine rush hour. Instead of thanking his cousin, he threw out an accusation. "You're dating my old science teacher, Pyro Pierce."

"Have you got a problem with that?"

"The opposite. He's a great guy."

"Stop calling him Pyro. He's only had six major explosions in the chem lab. And I think he's cute without eyebrows." She shifted in the back seat. "Anyway, I have information for you. About Joe Rogers's gal pal."

Skylar swiveled her head so she could see Dagmar. "How did you hear about that? We only found out last night."

"I'm a librarian." Dagmar shrugged. "I know things."

"Her name?" Jake asked.

"Delilah Miller. She runs a beauty salon."

Skylar took a moment to digest the fact that Delilah—the Biblical seductress known for cutting Samson's hair—ran a salon. Astoria had to be the quirkiest place she'd ever worked. "This Delilah. Is she married?"

"Separated," Dagmar said. "Attractive. Curvy. Has magenta hair. Surprisingly age-appropriate for Rogers. They've been dating for over a year. If you ask me, she's using the 'married' excuse to avoid getting too close to Jolly Rogers."

"Or vice versa," Skylar said.

"Drop me off at Toast-To-Go," Dagmar said. "Don't suppose you'll tell me the name of the victim."

Jake scoffed. "Listen, Dagmar, you've got to back off. Let us do our job."

"Sure thing, cuz. Let the cops handle it? Sure, that worked really well twenty years ago."

He pulled up outside the corner coffee shop, let his cousin out and watched her enter. "I sure as hell hope she doesn't get herself into trouble. Dagmar looks fierce, but—in some ways—she's fragile."

Oddly enough, Skylar could identify. Like Dagmar, she cultivated a tough exterior. "Her mother's murder must have been devastating."

"When her mom died, her father didn't want to be saddled with a kid. He took off. She had no family, except for my dad and me." Remembering, he frowned and stroked his clean-shaven chin. "Probably wasn't the best thing for Dagmar to be raised by a high school football coach. There was nobody in her life to add a feminine touch."

"I grew up with two brothers." Her mother had always participated in her life, but Mom was a judge, not exactly someone who encouraged her to collect dolls. Though she and Jake had been together almost nonstop since she arrived in Astoria, they really hadn't talked much about their families or hobbies or private life. If she knew him better, she might have mentioned her phobia. Or not...probably not. "Did you play football?"

"When I was seventeen, I was my full height. Six feet, six inches. And my dad was the coach. So, yeah, I played. Wasn't very good. Kept tripping over my own big feet. Dad said it'd take a while for me to grow into my body. When I did, I joined the marines. *Semper fi.*"

Before Skylar had a chance to prepare herself for what was to come, he swerved onto the circular approach to the Highway 101 bridge. The curve gradually climbed to the full elevation above the wide Columbia. She looked down at treetops and houses as they ascended higher and higher. Acrophobia wasn't her problem. She didn't love heights but could handle them. It was bridges...always bridges. *Gephyrophobia.*

Eyes open. Eyes closed. Her pulse accelerated to a staccato drumbeat. Quietly, she hummed the lyrics. "Left a good job in the city..." Her blood surged. A high-pitched squeal overwhelmed "Proud Mary" and echoed against her eardrums.

Eyes open, her gaze darted across the clear blue sky, seeking an escape from the torturous noise. A terrible whine. It thinned and faded but didn't go silent. The high note competed with the rumble of tires on pavement.

She trembled, knotted her fingers together to keep from showing her lack of control. Her gaze flicked downward, and she was struck with paralyzing vertigo. The inside of her head whirled fast and faster on a whirling carousel.

Eyes closed, closed, closed. She barely constrained her nausea. A sour taste crawled up the back of her throat.

She heard Jake speaking. "Are you okay, Skylar?"

"Fine. I'm fine."

Her eyes stayed closed. She felt rather than saw their descent to a level closer to the water, but there were still miles to go before they reached the Washington side. Fireworks went off inside her head. With each explosion, pop and sizzle, the pressure increased. A vice grip encircled her head and squeezed from either side. Tighter and tighter. One more turn of the screw, and her skull would be crushed.

She heard Jake calling to her. "Skylar, open your eyes. Look at me. You're not okay."

"Fine."

"I can't stop here. I have to keep moving until we're off the bridge."

"Don't stop."

Behind her closed eyes, she saw the darkest shade of black. Ebony. Not a trace of light.

She couldn't breathe. Couldn't move. Falling, overwhelmed by inky blackness. *Losing control.* She plunged headfirst into unconsciousness.

TIME LOST ALL form and meaning. She felt like only a minute had lapsed, but she might have been knocked out for hours. Still seated in the Explorer, the upholstered seat supported her back. Her feet rested on the floor mat. She heard the passenger door open, felt the latch on her seat belt snap.

Strong arms wrapped around her, and he pulled her out of the car. A fresh breeze caressed her cheek. Half awake, standing, she leaned against the front fender. Her eyelids fluttered open. She saw Jake.

"W-where are we?" she stammered.

"On the Washington side of the bridge. I parked on the shoulder." Gently, he held her upper arms and supported her so she wouldn't collapse onto the pavement. "No matter how many times you tell me you're fine, I don't believe you. Something happened on the bridge."

"Yes." She couldn't explain. If she admitted to having a debilitating phobia, she worried she'd lose her job as a special agent and be assigned to a desk. "But it's over."

He didn't argue with her or demand that she come clean. Instead, he offered warmth and a comforting embrace. She rested her cheek against his chest. The big, brawny marine held her with the softest touch imaginable.

For a moment, she snuggled into the folds of his merino wool vest and inhaled his clean scent. Cedarwood and pine. He smelled like a forest at sunrise when the dew had evaporated. She could have stayed there for hours.

But the lighthouse and the crime scene were on the road ahead. There was work to be done.

"We should get going," she said.

"You were singing 'Proud Mary.' Why?"

"I'm a big Tina Turner fan."

"Me, too."

With her head tilted back, she gazed past the dimple on his chin to his mouth. "I'm really okay. It must have been something I ate. A mild case of food poisoning."

"Yeah, sure."

"Sometimes, I get really tired." She wanted to talk about her phobia but wouldn't. Not yet. "There's no rational explanation for why I passed out."

"It's okay. You don't have to tell me."

"I'm not afraid."

"I didn't say you were." He leaned closer. Close enough to kiss. Close enough that she felt the warmth of his breath on her forehead. "You're a trained federal agent, Skylar. A brown belt in karate. A trained markswoman. You have all the tools to take care of yourself."

But how could she do battle with a bridge? She peered into the depths of his dark blue eyes. "It's irrational. The closest I can come to explaining is that I'm overwhelmed by a sense of vulnerability."

"Nothing wrong with that," Jake said. "Vulnerable is another word for sensitive. Sympathetic. You're open."

A one-word explanation. One syllable. "Weak."

"Never," he said.

She wanted desperately to believe he was right.

Chapter Fourteen

Tucked back into the passenger seat of the Explorer, Skylar concentrated on regulating her breathing and centering her thoughts. After a few miles on Highway 101 following the course of the Columbia and heading toward Cape Disappointment, she felt more in control and had stopped shivering.

On the way back to normal, she was hungry again and wished for a venti-size French roast. Her meltdown on the monster bridge had been one of the most extreme phobic reactions she'd ever had, possibly due to the stress of the investigation. It was a relief that she'd been with Jake instead of SSA Crawford.

If she'd been riding with her supervisor, there would have been consequences. Though Crawford respected her level of experience and gave her a lot of leeway, she was still on probationary status as a special agent in a field investigation. Hyperventilating and fainting were most definitely not acceptable behaviors. Sometime soon, she'd need to give Jake a better explanation than food poisoning or lack of sleep. The truth. She'd have to tell him the truth.

That surprising conclusion caused her to gasp. A shudder rattled down her spine, and her fingers twitched as if losing her grasp. Though she'd had gephyrophobia for as long as she could remember, she'd never told anyone. Not her parents or her brothers or her best friends. She never wanted to be seen as a person who had problems she couldn't handle. Even her name stood for strength. Skylar was mighty, a warrior in battle and a leader in peace. Yet, she found herself seriously thinking about confiding in Jake, a man she'd known for only a day.

In his calm, conversational baritone, Jake said, "If we'd turned right instead of left when we got off the bridge, we'd be headed to Dismal Nitch."

The area around Astoria contained a boatload of weird history, some of which she was beginning to actually enjoy. "I'm sure there's a story behind that name."

"Lewis and Clark had almost reached the Pacific, the end of the trail, when their expedition was stopped from further progress by wind, rain and—you guessed it—fog. They hunkered down near the river. Starving and soaked to the skin, they were miserable. In his journal, Clark referred to the campsite as Dismal Nitch. Little did he know, they were only a couple of miles away from the ocean."

"I guess that proves what you said earlier." She smiled. "The Pacific Northwest ain't for sissies."

"Guess so."

When he shot her a glance, his gaze showed concern. He must be questioning her breakdown, but he didn't make verbal accusations or ask if she was okay. Instead, he seemed willing to accept her panic attack and move forward, which was fine with her. *No muss, no fuss, don't look at us.* "How far are we from the lighthouse?" she asked.

"Half an hour or so. Your partner is already at the scene, right?"

"You bet he is." SSA Crawford had been anxious. He told her that he hoped Phoebe's murder hadn't been a harbinger of other deaths. The discovery of a second victim meant this crime should be investigated as the beginning of serial killings—part of the Lightkeeper's Curse. "I'm guessing he picked up former Chief Kim on the way."

"Smart move. Everybody in this part of the world knows and loves Jimi Kim."

"And his wife's cooking."

"I'm guessing that you're hungry again," he said. "No problem. We'll stop in Ilwaco and pick up coffee and a bite."

Though she felt guilty about not rushing directly to the scene, she really needed a boost of caffeine and calories to charge her system.

Being slow to report for duty didn't compare to the regret she felt about not preventing the second murder. She and Crawford had literally been in the vicinity when the Shadowkeeper killed again. She should have stressed the urgency for the FBI forensics teams to set up their surveillance. They hadn't baited the trap. She exhaled a sigh. "You know, if we'd had the cameras in place, we might have caught a glimpse of the killer."

"We might have a sighting, anyway. Chief Kim assigned a team to review footage from the traffic cams on the bridge."

"I never thought of that," she admitted. The damn bridge might be useful, after all.

They stopped at a roadside convenience store and gas station to grab coffee and packaged burritos that were surprisingly tasty after being heated in a microwave. In minutes, her energy and confidence returned. She was back to the investigation with her faculties fully intact. No time for second-guessing. She had to find the Shadowkeeper wherever he was lurking.

While Jake drove through a thickly forested wildlife preserve, he devoured his burrito. "I can't help but wonder… Why did the Shadowkeeper send that text to your phone? How did he get the number?"

"Chief Kim said the caller's phone was untraceable. My contact numbers are no secret. I often write them on business cards I hand out to witnesses."

"He said the victim looked like you. How would he know unless he's stalking you?"

"Everybody knows everything in Astoria," she reminded him.

"There could be deeper reasons."

"The behavioral analysis people would probably draw all sorts of psychological inferences from the text, but I think it's something less complex. The Shadowkeeper is childish, as many narcissists are, and he's teasing us."

"That's what Rogers said when he read the message that mentioned me."

"His messages have been snarky," she said. "And he's playing a game. Giving us a series of clues to prove he's smarter than we are."

When Jake turned into the parking lot for the North Head Lighthouse, he had to show his badge to a Washington officer who monitored the entrance and advised people that this area had been designated as a crime scene. Similar to Cape Meares, law enforcement from many jurisdictions had responded. Skylar thanked her lucky stars that she wasn't the special agent in charge of this chaos. SSA Crawford won that prize.

Instead of leaping from the Explorer, Jake parked and turned toward her. "Let's see what we can figure out."

"Okay."

"In addition to the location, the main point in his text seems to be about the songbird. Not sure what that means."

"When we have a victim identification, we'll know more."

He studied her with a bit of concern. "Are you good to go?"

"Ready as I'll ever be."

They left the Explorer and walked side by side down a curving asphalt path through a forest of pine, cedar, scarlet maple, golden aspen and hemlock. There was a chill in the October air. Fog dimmed the morning sunrise, and the wind hummed through the branches and boughs in a haunting melody interrupted by the cries of gulls and terns. In a clearing to their right, she saw a couple of two-story residences offering overnight lodging for tourists. Smoke spiraled from the chimneys, adding the scent of burnt firewood to the salty ocean air.

When they came out of the forest and stepped onto the rocky promontory above the Pacific, they saw the whitewashed lighthouse tower, sixty-five feet tall. Similar to the setup at Cape Meares, a small house adjoined the tower. The automated beacon continued to flash, two bursts of light every thirty seconds.

She caught her breath. "This is way more impressive than the other one."

"The tower had to be taller," Jake said, "because the cliff isn't as high."

From the crime-scene photos she'd received, Skylar knew what to expect and wasn't looking forward to viewing the body. From where they stood, she and Jake couldn't see the woman dangling at the end of a noose. The forensic investigators wearing gloves and Tyvek booties had congregated on the seaward side of the tower. Several markers on the ground indicated evidence that might help solve the case.

She straightened her posture and went forward on the path that encircled the lighthouse. The victim gradually came into view.

She'd been hung by the neck from an iron gallery encircling the tower at the level of the beacon. Death by hanging made a horrific display, especially since the victim wore a skimpy outfit for this time of year—a sleeveless burgundy tank top and short, cutoff jeans. The heels of her red, pointed-toe cowboy boots clunked against the tower when the wind tossed her in one direction and another. The victim's wrists were cuffed in front. A bandanna blindfold covered the upper half of her face and a rectangle of silver masking tape had been slapped across her mouth. Except for her nose, her features could neither be seen nor identified. And yet her hair was pulled back and the bruising on her throat was visible.

Officer Dot Holman—in a pressed uniform with an APD jacket—joined them. Her elfin face wore a mask of sorrow. "I knew her. Lucille Dixon."

Surprised, Skylar asked, "How can you tell who she is?"

Without turning to confront the gruesome sight, Dot said, "I'd recognize those boots anywhere. Plus, she has a tattoo on her upper right arm. A yellow rose with a long stem that goes all the way to her elbow."

"As in 'The Yellow Rose of Texas,'" Jake said. "She always wore that kind of outfit with her trademark boots when she sang at the Sand Bar."

The name of the tavern sounded familiar. Then Skylar remembered. The Sand Bar was where Ty McKenna established his alibi with his drunk friends.

The connection between the victim and a suspect bore further examination. Or maybe not. So many people in this area knew each other that it would be strange if the victim, Lucille Dixon, didn't have friends in the inner circle of her investigation.

Both Dot and Jake were solemn. Lucille must have been someone worth knowing.

When Skylar looked up again, she saw a thin ray of sunlight gleaming off SSA Crawford's white hair. He stood at the railing above the noose and appeared to be studying the knot in a heavy-duty rope similar to those used in boating. Crawford looked down, saw her and gave a nod before entering a door into the lighthouse. While Jake stayed to talk with Dot, Skylar headed toward the entrance into the North Head Lighthouse where she waited for Crawford.

In minutes, he stepped through the door and approached her. "Glad you're here. We have a lot of ground to cover. And I want to move fast."

He didn't need to warn her that the killer might attack another woman tonight. Skylar was already counting down the hours until nightfall in her head. "I can help gather information here at the scene."

"Our FBI forensic team is already on the job," he said. "As soon as they arrived from Portland, I pulled them away from setting up surveillance cameras and told them to process the lighthouse. I'm sure they'll find prints and trace evidence, but this little house is a tourist site. Strangers are tromping in and out all day."

"We'll learn more from the ME," she said.

"Dr. Kinski and her people will be here soon to remove the body and transport her to the autopsy suite where she'll join Phoebe Conway."

Two for the price of one. She kept that irreverent comment to herself. "We have a tentative identification. Lucille Dixon, a singer at a local tavern. Her occupation syncs with the Shadow's mention of a songbird."

"I've heard her name."

"Do you have a theory about how the murder happened?"

"I always do." Seeking privacy, he directed her to the outer edge of the path and spoke in quiet tones that no one else could hear. "The Shadowkeeper either enticed the songbird to meet him here, or he brought her here in his own vehicle."

"You think she came willingly, like on a date."

"It's possible. The traffic cams on the bridge can give us more information. Once they were here, he needed to get her to the upper level using the winding staircase."

She thought of three possibilities. "He could have convinced her to make the climb herself. Or forced her to climb using a gun or some other weapon. Or he might have drugged her and carried her up the staircase."

Crawford nodded. "Dr. Kinski will run a tox screen for drugs and can tell us if cause of death was strangulation by hanging or being choked with his hands."

She nodded. "The forensic team might be able to determine where she was strangled. From prints, fibers and scuff marks at Cape Meares, they suspect Phoebe was unconscious, then strangled and finally posed on the staircase."

"Could be what happened here," Crawford said. "If she was convinced to meet him on her own—like a date—I'd think the Shadowkeeper was a younger man."

"You know better than that," she said with a grin. Crawford wasn't called the Silver Fox for nothing. "Plenty of young women are attracted to older men."

"I didn't say that Jimi and I were giving up on proving that the Shadowkeeper and the Lightkeeper are one and the same. Which reminds me…" He raised an eyebrow. "Even with the stakeout at his house, are you certain Rogers didn't sneak out last night?"

"It's possible." The stakeout was being handled by inexperienced officers, and Rogers might be more clever than they gave him credit for. "This morning, we learned the name of the woman who was his supposed alibi for the night of Phoebe's murder."

"Follow up on that this morning. Then, you and Jake need to go to the Sand Bar and find out who Lucille was dating. Guys who were interested in her and so on. You know the drill."

"Yes, sir." She heard what he was saying, but her mind filled with images of the bridge, and her gut wrenched. She'd have to cross again.

He patted her shoulder. "I'll stay here at the scene. You and Jake have made significant inroads among the locals regarding Phoebe's murder. That's where I want you to focus."

"Yes, sir."

She had her marching orders. Though she would have liked to observe the forensics at the crime scene and avoid the bridge for as long as possible, she understood the need to gather information and talk to witnesses. They needed answers, needed to shine a spotlight on the Shadowkeeper before he killed another victim.

Chapter Fifteen

Outside the North Head Lighthouse, Jake watched two muscular guys in FBI T-shirts rig a pulley system on the wrought iron gallery wrapped around the upper level of lighthouse tower outside the beacon. They attached the pulley to the rope and severed the original rope below the knot. The railing where the rope had been tied was about fifty feet above the asphalt path. The noose around Lucille's throat hung down another ten feet, which meant her cowboy boots dangled thirty to thirty-five feet overhead. The discussion about whether to lower her body from inside or out had been fierce, but Dr. Kate Kinski prevailed. She convinced everybody, including Jake, that the interior option would cause more postmortem contusions and contamination of potential evidence. Hence, the pulley system.

The two husky FBI forensic techs—nobody had bulging pecs and biceps like those without regular bodybuilding workouts—removed the portion of rope that had been tied to the railing and bagged the knots as evidence for further forensic study. Slowly and carefully, they used the pulley to lower the victim to Kinski and her assistants from the ME's office, who stood below, waiting with a gurney. They all wore protective Tyvek suits and booties as well as nitrile gloves.

Since Kinski couldn't get close enough to study the bruise

pattern on the victim's throat, she refused to speculate on whether death came from manual strangulation or from hanging from the noose. Any supposition would be pure guesswork until the autopsy this afternoon, but Jake couldn't imagine the Shadowkeeper being dumb enough to drag a victim who was alert to the top of the interior staircase, much less fling her over the edge. Seemed logical that Lucille was already dead or unconscious when she was hanged.

Skylar peered down from the gallery, watching as the body descended inch by inch. Then she looked away, raised her head and gazed out to sea. A gust of wind brushed her auburn hair off her forehead, and she tucked a strand behind her ear. If they hadn't been investigating a murder, he wondered if she would have waved and called out to him. The unusually sunny day with a light breeze contrasted the aura of tragedy that hung over the grotesque crime scene.

A second victim. Though he didn't know her well, Jake would never forget Lucille Dixon. The songbird was a tiny woman who made a lot of noise. She had a big, raucous laugh and loved to dance the Texas two-step. Now she was gone. Brutally, senselessly murdered. Others would die…unless he and Skylar stopped the Shadowkeeper.

He watched the assistants in their Tyvek bunny suits maneuver the body onto the gurney while Dr. Kinski shouted instructions about how they shouldn't disturb the knots in the noose. Jake was too far away to get a clear look at her face. Not that he wanted to.

Looking up, he saw Skylar again. She pointed to her black titanium field watch, shook her head and shrugged. Probably meaning she wasn't quite ready to go. She seemed to have recovered from her earlier meltdown on the bridge.

Yeah, the bridge. He'd noticed the timing. Yesterday, she'd been struck by a similar tension when they crossed the less imposing bridge over Youngs Bay. He worried about when the next incident would occur. She sure as hell wasn't weak, but she had a flaw—an irrational reaction triggered by bridges. During his tours of duty in the marines, he'd seen similar attacks suffered by combat veterans. Overwhelming panic. A waking nightmare. PTSD.

He knew better than to suggest that she get a grip and ignore it. The nature of her disorder didn't make sense and couldn't be controlled. But he had an idea about how he might help her. He took out his phone and placed a call.

No sooner had he made the necessary arrangements and disconnected than his phone rang. Chief Vivienne Kim was calling with an update.

"A new email message just came through," she said. "It was sent to the *Astoria Sun* page for comments from readers. Hasn't been posted yet."

Not unexpected, but damn. He hated this. The killer wanted his chance to gloat, to let them know they were no match for him. "Does he say anything about the victim?"

"He does not."

"We have reason to believe it's Lucille Dixon."

"I know. Dot texted me." She sighed loudly. "I hate this."

Me, too. "Send the message to my cell phone and to Skylar's. Make sure Crawford and your grandpa have a copy."

"When you leave Cape Disappointment," she said, "you and SA Skylar are going to the autopsy, correct?"

"First, we need to check in with a potential witness at Delilah's Hair Salon and others at the Sand Bar where Lucille worked. Then the autopsy. But don't worry, I'll stay in touch."

He scrolled down his phone screen and read:

All the pretty princesses should form a club for the popular people. Ty McKenna would be invited. And you, Agent Skylar, would be their queen. A winner. A star. A hole-in-one. Too bad Phoebe isn't here to write about the true fate of beauty in her column. It never lasts for long.

He signed off as Shadowkeeper. Bitter and hostile.

Skylar stepped up beside him. She'd shed her rain jacket and adjusted her suit jacket to hide her holster. "I'm ready to go."

"Let's wait for these guys to move on." He pointed to the team of ME bunnies who were rattling along the asphalt path with the gurney. He handed her his phone. "I just got this from Chief Vivienne. It was emailed to the *Sun* reader comments page. They had the good sense not to post it."

She read and cursed under her breath. "Mentioning me, again. And McKenna."

"I'm beginning to think we let the hippest guy in town off the hook too soon."

"The hole-in-one reference seems obvious," she said. "And he also mentions a club. A golf club, perhaps. There's a lighthouse at a miniature golf course, right?"

"We'll go there if we have time. Our most important job today is the autopsy in Warrenton. On the other side of Youngs Bay. Across the bridge."

He watched her for a reaction. As she trekked up the pathway to the parking area, her shoulders stiffened, and she winced—an indication of her discomfort at the mention of a bridge.

"First, we go to Warrenton," she said, "although I have no idea why your county medical examiner is based there instead of Astoria. Warrenton is even smaller."

"The population is a little over six thousand," he said as he approached the Explorer and used his fob to unlock the doors. "The town marks the last campsite of the Lewis and Clark expedition and was home to Fort Stevens."

She fired a sharp glance in his direction. "How do you know all this stuff?"

"I worked as a tour guide in high school and then again when I got out of the marines."

"Really?" Her eyes narrowed as she absorbed this shred of

trivia about his life. "I would have expected you to do something more...physical."

"Why? Because I'm extra large?" he scoffed. "Do they teach stereotyping in the FBI?"

"As something to avoid."

"You're a pretty woman," he said. "Does that mean you should be a model?"

"Okay, I got the point."

"I'm into learning stuff, like my cousin Dagmar. It's satisfying." She was about to discover the value of his tour guide experience. "There's something I want to talk to you about before we get back to town."

They settled into the Explorer and exited the parking area. He drove behind the ME's van back toward Astoria. Neither of them were using flashers or sirens to race through traffic. Not an emergency situation. Autopsies and interrogations accounted for their regular business on a Thursday morning.

He was about to explain his plan when her phone buzzed and she answered.

"It's Crawford," she whispered to him.

Her end of the conversation consisted mainly of "yessir" and "no sir." Clearly, she was getting her orders for the day. When she ended the call, she turned to him.

"You have new information," he said.

"They did an on-scene fingerprint analysis on the victim. Lucille Anne Dixon wasn't a saint. Her prints popped in AFIS. She has a criminal record."

He wasn't shocked. Lucille worked as singer in a tavern, not in a nunnery. "Let me guess. Drunk and disorderly? Speeding tickets?"

"She was acquitted on felony theft charges when she apparently robbed an ex-boyfriend, and she was twice convicted of vandalism."

He shook his head. "I might have been the arresting officer on one of those vandalism charges. It had something to do with graffiti. Once again, an ex-boyfriend was involved."

"This doesn't give us a motive for why the Shadowkeeper went after her," Skylar said. "But Lucille had the habit of associating with dangerous people."

"Don't blame the victim," he said.

"I'm not. I'm just saying that she wasn't cautious."

"Like Garth Brooks said, she had 'Friends in Low Places.' Nothing wrong with that." He remembered watching Lucille perform. "She sang a lot of the country-western classics. Her sign-off was always the same. 'Your Cheatin' Heart.'"

"Could be a motive," she said. "We should pay close attention to her boyfriends."

He drove into Ilwaco behind the ME's ambulance van but turned onto a different route. There hadn't been time to explain his reasoning to her, but he believed he was doing the right thing. "We're taking a detour."

Suspicious, she asked, "Where are we going?"

"I'm asking you to trust me."

"The most dangerous words in the English language. Trust me."

"Hear me out." He parked outside the harbor where dozens of boats—all shapes and sizes—were docked. Exiting the Explorer, he came around to open her door.

When she stepped out and faced him, her hazel-green eyes held a million questions, and her full lips stretched in a stern, unbending line. Obviously, Skylar wasn't a woman who liked surprises. She growled. "We can't be wasting time. There's a lot to do."

"Right."

"You've got five minutes, Armstrong."

"Remember how I told you that I used to work as a tour guide? Well, here's another bit of trivia. From 1921 until 1966 when the Astoria-Megler Bridge opened, this stretch of the

Columbia was regularly serviced by a three-ferry system. After the bridge was built, they sold the boats."

"Talk faster." She tapped her wristwatch. "Three minutes left."

"Nautical traffic in this part of the river is regulated," he said, calmly and slowly. Not to be rushed by her self-imposed deadline, he guided her toward the boats bobbing in the light waves. Circling gulls squawked a greeting while they walked. "The giant cargo ships and cruise vessels have to be guided through the bridge by port pilots. The man I worked for, Two-Toes Tucker, was a port pilot—"

"Wait! His name was Two-Toes?"

"Nickname. He lost two toes on his left foot in some kind of boating accident. He claims it was a shark attack. Anyway, he ran a sightseeing business—Tucker's Tug Tours—cruising from Astoria to the coast and along the Pacific from Ilwaco to Tillamook."

Her hostility began to thaw, and she looked away from her watch. "A tugboat?"

"Seaworthy and cute."

"I like tugs," she said. "A small boat with a powerful engine to move huge obstacles."

Like her. At the edge of a pier, he stepped aside and gestured toward the red-and-white boat trimmed with gold and emblazoned with the logo for Tug Tours. "Here's your ride across the Columbia. I told you she was cute."

"You shouldn't have gone to all this trouble."

But he could tell she was pleased. Her radiant smile made him want to go to even greater lengths. He'd swim the harbor with her on his back to keep her away from that damn bridge. When their gazes met, a lightning bolt crashed into the center of his chest and reverberated through his entire body. "It only took a phone call. Tucker was happy to help out. He knows my dad, and the two of them are conspiring to get me married and settled down. So, please ignore any of his attempts at matchmaking."

He felt like he'd said too much, but he couldn't help adding, "You don't have to tell me why you don't like bridges. I'm not judging or complaining. You're my partner, and I care about you."

With determined strides, she came closer to him. Less than a foot away, she rose up on her tiptoes and wrapped her arms around his neck. Her slender body molded to his. Her breasts crushed against his torso. Though he hadn't expected a reward like this, he adapted. Wrapping her in a firm embrace, he adjusted his position and intensified their contact.

Tentatively, her mouth joined with his, tasting his lips. He wanted a lot more from her. He hadn't expected this kind of spectacular contact when he arranged for her tugboat ride. Not on a conscious level. Of course, he'd been attracted to her from the first moment he saw her. But he never planned to put the moves on a fed.

She kissed like she meant it. Full contact. Full pressure. Nothing gentle about it. Her kiss held a whisper of desire, and he responded with a full-bodied roar of lust.

As suddenly as the kiss had started, they broke contact and separated. Breathing heavily, both of them stared at each other as if in a trance.

Then, she spoke. "Thank you, partner."

Chapter Sixteen

The midsize tugboat with a bright red hull and a white wheelhouse painted with gold trim met Skylar's expectations for a friendly sightseeing ride. The roof of the wheelhouse had been modified for sunbathing, and the front deck had been expanded and enclosed by sturdy but decorative railings.

Standing at the bow, she waved goodbye to Jake who went ashore after he introduced her to the business owner, Two-Toes Tucker. She managed to maintain her poise, even though the incredible sensations unleashed when Jake kissed her still lingered on her lips. Her legs were still weak at the knees. Her pulse chugged more furiously than the powerful motor of the tugboat, which Tucker told her was capable of pulling eight tons or more.

"Jake's a good man," Tucker said. The white-haired gent with a full beard gave a signal to a salty redheaded woman who was visible through the window of the on-deck wheelhouse, and the boat lurched forward. "That's my niece. I'm teaching her how to run the sightseeing biz. Wish I could get Jake to come back."

"He seems happy being a detective."

"How long have you been friends with him?"

"Not that long," she admitted. Tucker had probably seen their kiss and was sizing her up as a potential mate who would make Jake settle down. That opinion might be preferable to being labeled unprofessional.

"I don't rightly know much about you, young lady, but I'm guessing you're new in town. Are you here about the murders?"

"I'm with the FBI," she said. "You might know my partner, Supervisory Special Agent Harold Crawford."

"Damn right, I do. He's friends with Chief Jimi Kim."

She hadn't done much boating, and the sounds of the harbor played a maritime symphony in her head. The rhythmic lap of waves. The whistling winds. Cries from terns and gull. And the rumble of boat motors. When they cruised past a coast guard cutter, Tucker's niece tooted a spunky little foghorn and the guard responded.

Being on the water didn't bother Skylar, not like the bridges. But when the tug chugged under the giant bridge and she looked up at the towering structure, her gut clenched. Her phobia would have made more sense if she'd experienced some sort of terrible trauma involving a bridge. But there was nothing she could recall. She'd tried using a therapist who specialized in hypnotism to dig into her buried memories. Again, *nada*.

Beside her, Tucker exhaled a sigh. "She's a beaut, ain't she?"

"The bridge?"

"A marvel of engineering, you betcha. She takes my breath away." His gaze turned misty as he stared upward. "A couple of weeks ago, we had the annual Great Columbia Crossing, which is the only day in the year when the bridge is closed to vehicles and opened to pedestrians. My wife and I used to cross every year, holding hands and grinning like a couple of tourists."

She looked toward the short, round man who leaned heavily on his cane. He was adorable. A charmer. As cute as his tugboat. "You're an expert on the history of this area."

"You betcha."

"What do you remember about the Lightkeeper?"

"When those murders were happening, that was all anybody could talk about. Some people blamed it on the supernatural, like sea monsters coming ashore or the ghosts of drowned sailors. Others claimed to have seen aliens. Since I'm into landmarks, I tried to figure out why he went to lighthouses."

"And why do you think he did?"

"A symbolic thing. A lighthouse is a good place to hide. Or a fortress to give tactical advantage over an enemy attack. Maybe the Lightkeeper wanted to keep a flame burning to commemorate his evil deeds." Tucker shrugged. "I can't explain how Dagmar's mama found the right curse to make him stop. I don't want to think she was a witch."

"There are good witches."

"I suppose."

She remembered Jake's hostile reaction to the idea that his aunt had been a witch. "Did Jake ever talk about it?"

"He sure did. Got all tangled up in the mystery when he was a kid. We used to call him Boy Detective." Tucker barked a laugh. "None of us—not even his dad—thought he'd join the police when he grew up."

As they drew closer to the Astoria shoreline, Tucker the tour guide automatically pointed out various sights, ranging from the coast guard station to the waterfront trolley. When his redheaded niece carefully guided the tug into the marina, Skylar saw Jake waiting for her on the pier, and her heart took a little jump. Bringing herself under control, she did some deep breathing and employed the compartmentalizing techniques she learned at Quantico when practicing with firearms or attending an autopsy. *Concentrate.* She knew how to turn her attention away from one problem and focus on another.

It worked on everything except her phobia.

And Jake.

"Are you okay?" Tucker asked.

She realized that her nostrils had flared. And she was probably blushing. *This won't do.* She smiled at the old sailor. "Thanks for the ride."

"Anytime. I don't have a regular schedule this time of year, so my tug can always respond." He tilted his head to the side. "I think you're going to be good for Jake. He needs someone special."

And so do I.

"I'M NOT GOING in there by myself." Jake looked beyond Skylar in the passenger seat to see the front window of Delilah's Beauty Salon, decorated with hanging baskets of fake foliage—vines and pink azaleas. "We should start at the Sand Bar, questioning witnesses about Lucille Dixon."

"We're already here, and it's not even eleven o'clock. The bar might not be open." Her mouth twitched as though holding back laughter. "Don't worry, Samson. She won't cut your hair and zap your strength."

"Why me and not you?"

"Because you know everybody in town, and the ladies will talk to you."

If Skylar hadn't been so cute, he would have flat-out refused. But she seemed like a different woman after their kiss and her ride on the tug. Gone was the kickass special agent. This version of Skylar wore a smile. For the first time since they met, she actually seemed happy.

"Okay, I'll go in there," he said. "But you owe me."

"Fine with me. How should I pay you back?"

The unwanted but very much appreciated image of Skylar lying naked in his bed with her glossy auburn hair spread across the pillow popped up in his mind. "I'll think of something."

He shut down his imagination before entering the salon, not wanting to project his lust for Skylar at the five women who fluttered around the adjustable-height barber chairs and studied themselves in the wall-to-wall mirrors. The scent of perfumed shampoo and fancy products mingled with the chemical smell of the disinfectant used to sanitize combs and such. The colors on the walls and countertops were pink, black, white and pinker.

He approached the bleached blonde at the front counter who presided over a glass case filled with lotions and potions and fancy barrettes.

"I'm looking for Delilah," he said. Dagmar had mentioned the salon owner's magenta hair, and he didn't see anyone matching that description. "Is she in today?"

His deep baritone echoed through the salon and silenced the *snip-snip* and the background music of Taylor Swift on the radio. All the women stopped what they were doing and stared. He was a dab of testosterone in a sea of estrogen. A fish out of water. A bull in a—

"Jake Armstrong!" A blonde stylist with a Mohawk whirled away from the head of hair she'd been clipping and stalked toward him. "You remember me, don't you?"

Not really. He took a stab in the dark. "From high school?"

"We were in the same chem class with Pyro Pierce. I'm Chloe."

He couldn't avoid her snuggle without being rude. And the hug wasn't all bad. She had standout breasts. "Chloe O'Connor. Coco." He stepped away from her. "I'd like to chat, but I'm here on police business."

"I know," she gushed. "The Shadowkeeper. Gawd, so awful."

"I need to talk to Delilah."

"She's out for the rest of the morning," Coco said. "Over at her boyfriend's house."

"Joe Rogers?"

"Yep." Coco bobbed her head, which somehow caused her

cleavage to bounce. "They've been going out for a couple of years, and I don't know why she doesn't marry the guy."

A stylist with short, spiky turquoise hair piped up. "Could be because she's already married."

"Separated," Coco corrected. "Her almost ex-husband is also dating."

"Whatever. I heard that Delilah's son hates Rogers."

Much as Jake disliked gossip, it was a good way to pick up info. "What's her son's name? How old is he?"

"Trevor Miller," said Coco. "Kind of a hottie, but too young for me. Just eighteen."

Not too young to be the Shadowkeeper. Jake didn't know how this detail fit into the investigation, but he'd keep young Trevor in mind.

"If you ask me," said the woman at the receptionist's desk, "it's not Delilah who's avoiding marriage. Did you ever see photos of Rogers's first wife? She was a fashion model from Houston. Tall and gorgeous and totally out of Delilah's league."

"I heard she married some millionaire rancher after she dumped Rogers," Coco said. "A real cowboy who rides horses and shoots six-guns. Do you know how to ride, Jake?"

He steered back to the main topic, recalling something Rogers had told them. "She divorced the rancher and married again. Moved to Paris, France."

Coco rolled her eyes. "Some women have all the luck."

"She's supposed to be a designer," said a gray-haired woman who sat in one of the barber chairs. "I remember her swooping around town in leopard prints and blouses cut down to her belly button."

"Did her son go with her to Paris?" he asked.

"Don't think so," Coco said.

Turquoise Hair spoke up. "Joe Rogers's son, Bradley, split his time between here and Texas when he was in school. I went out with him in high school. Only once, but that still counts."

"Tell me about him," he said.

"Nerdy but kind of macho at the same time, always talking about how women need to be treated like princesses. Hah!"

Jake's ears pricked up. "Did he use that word? Princess?"

She wiggled her fingers in front of his face, showing off her lavender manicure. "Called me his Purple Princess. Because it's one of my fave colors."

"Have you heard from Bradley recently? Is he in town?"

"We lost touch."

Jake would make finding Bradley Rogers's current address and phone number a priority. After a few more moments, he extricated himself from the salon, rushed across the sidewalk and dove into the driver's seat of the Explorer. He pulled away from the curb before the ladies in Delilah's could peek out the window and wonder about Skylar in the passenger seat.

She ended her phone call and turned to him. "How did it go?"

"I hate rumors."

"Me, too."

"Everybody has a story. Most aren't verifiable."

"Much like questioning witnesses," she said. "We hear biased opinions more than facts."

"I never saw Delilah," he said. "She's supposed to be at Rogers's place, which is where we're going right now. But I did get a couple of ideas. Delilah has a son—a hottie according to Coco, a woman I knew in high school—and he doesn't like Rogers."

"I'm not following," she said. "How does that apply to the Shadowkeeper?"

"Her son—his name is Trevor—might be trying to frame Rogers by taking his car and leaving it outside Phoebe's apartment. Making it look like Rogers was the stalker."

"Flimsy," she decreed. "What else did you find out?"

"Bradley, Rogers's son, divided his time between his parents. His mom had custody, and he mostly lived with her in Houston. But he came for long visits, enough that he was enrolled in the Astoria high school. One of the women in the salon dated him and said he called women princesses."

Her green eyes widened like a snowy owl, and she leaned across the console to give his arm a tap. "Good job, Gossip Girl."

"The way I figure, Bradley is twenty-seven or twenty-eight. His childhood was disrupted by the Lightkeeper who threatened him and his mom, causing his mother to move him away from Astoria. Plus, he could have known both victims in Texas."

"And he thinks of women as princesses. A significant clue. Our best chance at solving this thing is breaking down the Shadowkeeper's messages. He's telling more than he realizes."

His downfall. "He needs to be stopped before tonight."

She waggled her phone at him. "I heard from Crawford about the traffic cams on either end of the bridge. They show license plates and a glimpse of the driver, but last night was too foggy to make an identification."

"Did Lucille's car cross last night?"

"A red Kia. At 1:17 in the morning, which was probably after she left the Sand Bar, her Kia entered the Astoria side of the bridge. The camera never showed her car returning."

He drew a logical conclusion. "Which means the Kia is still on the Washington side."

"Crawford already put out a BOLO and sent a team to look for it."

Considering the camera footage, he tried to picture the sequence of events. Either Lucille drove herself across the bridge and met her killer, or he rode with her in the Kia. Or he waited for her at the lighthouse in his own vehicle, killed her and then moved both cars. "Something doesn't add up."

"It gets worse. I'm sorry, Jake."

"Were any of our other suspects on the bridge last night?"

"Actually, yes." She turned her head, avoiding his gaze. "There's not much traffic late at night, and the camera guys analyzed speeds, patterns and timing from the footage. A fifteen-year-old Toyota crossed from Astoria at 12:22 and returned at 3:45, which would place the driver at the lighthouse at the right time."

"Who was it?"

"Alan Quilling."

Jake had almost forgotten about his forensic tech as a suspect. Not a smart investigative tactic. They were *all* under suspicion, and Quilling had just moved to the front of the line.

Chapter Seventeen

On the street where Rogers lived, the Explorer parked in front of an unmarked car with a person in the driver's seat. While Jake checked in with the officer on stakeout, Skylar got out of the car and looked toward the newspaper editor's house.

The unusually sunny day showed a well-maintained Craftsman home in pale yellow with white trim and a porch across the front. In the side yard, a neglected wooden swing set with a plastic slide hadn't fared so well. The weathered crossbars showed damage from years of exposure in the damp climate. The slide tilted at an awkward angle. And the chains on the swing were rusted. An eyesore. A painful reminder that children no longer played here. Rogers's son hadn't lived with his dad for a very long time.

Jake returned to her side. "The officer on stakeout says Rogers's purple-haired girlfriend came over a couple of hours ago for breakfast."

"Magenta, not purple. Is he certain Rogers didn't leave the house?"

"Not on his watch. He's been here since 3:15 a.m., and the guy before him swears nobody left or entered. They're inexperienced and could be mistaken, but…" The police stakeout gave Rogers a decent alibi for last night. "Do we really need to talk to him again?"

Even if he wasn't the Shadowkeeper, she wasn't about to

let Rogers off the hook. Not when she sensed that he was up to something. He'd initially lied about his alibi and gave flimsy excuses for why his car was parked outside Phoebe's house. "I want to get his son's contact information."

"Okay." He shuffled from foot to foot. "Let's not stay long. I'm anxious to talk to Quilling and find out why he drove across the bridge last night."

She and Jake approached the front porch as Rogers and an attractive, middle-aged woman with bobbed magenta hair exited. Her frank grin and straightforward attitude made a positive first impression on Skylar who stuck out her hand. "You must be Delilah Miller."

"And you must be that female fed everybody is yakking about." Graciously, Delilah accepted the handshake. "Come by my salon, honey, and I'll touch up those highlights."

"We've already been to your shop," she said. "And my hair color is natural."

"Well, aren't you the lucky one."

"Can we come in?" Jake asked.

"Buzz off," Rogers said rudely. "I'm leaving."

Jake centered his considerable bulk in the middle of the sidewalk, blocking access to the driveway where Rogers's black sedan was parked. "We're getting a search warrant."

The newsman's heavy eyebrows lowered into a scowl. His outthrust jaw locked, and his complexion flushed red in a burst of anger. "When are you going to catch on, Armstrong? We're on the same damn side. I need to get to the *Sun* and make sure everything is running smoothly. The Shadowkeeper sent another email."

"We're aware," Jake said.

"We don't have time for another damn interrogation. As for the search warrant, I'd advise against it and so would my lawyer. I'm not letting you in my house when I'm not here."

"I'll stay." Delilah volunteered.

"Thank you for your cooperation," Skylar said.

Delilah gave a pleasant smile. "The important thing is finding this horrible Shadow person who is killing young women. We'll do anything we can to help."

Rogers's hostility faded as he gazed at her. "You're a good woman, Delilah, but you don't understand. These two idiots suspect me."

"And a search will prove you did nothing wrong. That way they can get back to the real business of solving these crimes." She kissed him on the cheek. "Go to work, Joe. I'll lock up when I leave."

Their casual interaction seemed average and innocent to Skylar. They came across as a normal couple in their prime. Likewise, the interior of his home was neatly decorated with pottery, wood carvings and house plants. Nothing spectacular. Nothing suspicious. The scent of coffee and bacon hung in the air.

"Might as well get this over with," Jake said to Delilah. "Where were you the night before last?"

Delilah pointed down the hall. "In the bedroom. Joe and I watched the late news to check the weather forecast, which was—no surprise—cloudy and wet. Then we rolled over and went to sleep."

"That gives Rogers an alibi," he said.

"If you're serious about searching, I expect you'll want to take a gander at Joe's files and paperwork," she said. "His office is the first door on the left."

"Thank you, ma'am."

"It's Delilah," she said. "I'm not sure we've met, but I know you, Jake Armstrong."

"How's that... Delilah?"

"Astoria is a small town, and you're hard to miss."

Jake disappeared into the office, but Skylar stayed put. Still curious about the alibi, she asked, "Why didn't Rogers want to tell us that you spent the night?"

"He's old-fashioned." Her laughter sounded like something between a giggle and a snort. "That old goofball worries about my reputation, even though I've been separated for five years and live in my own house with my son. He's the real reason I haven't married Joe."

"Your son," Skylar said, watching for a reaction. "Trevor."

Delilah showed the first signs of real alarm. "Why does the FBI know his name? He's not in trouble, is he?"

Purposefully, Skylar didn't directly answer the question, allowing the other woman's worries to fester. "You said Trevor was the real reason you haven't married Joe. Why?"

"He's a teenage boy." Delilah's lower lip trembled. Her fear hadn't receded. "I guess I should start calling him a man. Has he done something wrong, broken the law?"

"We heard his name from the stylists in the shop." Skylar cocked her head to one side. "Does he often get into trouble?"

"Not a bit." Delilah fluttered her hand, showing off a gorgeous manicure that matched her hair. "Anyway, he disliked Joe from the minute we started dating. Not because of anything Joe did, mind you. It's about me. Trevor is jealous of my attention. Know what I mean?"

Though she had no children of her own, Skylar recognized the pattern. Young men often became overly attached to their mothers. "Must be difficult for you."

"If I married Joe, my son would be super upset. Right now, he's being a good kid, taking classes at the local college and working before he decides what he wants to do with his life. After that, he'll probably move out." She blinked away a tear. "I'll miss him."

"Is he friendly with Bradley Rogers?"

"Joe's son?" Delilah shook her head. "I've only seen him a handful of times. A good-looking kid, real tall. Not as big as Jake, but much taller than his daddy. Probably gets it from his mom who used to be a model. She's almost six feet."

"What does Trevor think of him?"

"First time they met, a couple of years ago, he looked

Bradley up online. Found out that his mom upgraded with her second husband. A Texas rancher with gobs of money. Trevor was impressed, but not me. That cowboy isn't cool. In every photo, he's packing a gun."

Skylar would have been more concerned if their victims had been shot. "The second husband was different from Joe Rogers."

"I'll say. My Joe is grumpy but has a heart of gold. He's thoughtful and funny. He'd never hurt a flea. The cowboy looks like a badass." Delilah fluffed her hair. "Trevor mentioned Bradley's scars from supposed 'accidents.' I think he was abused."

Skylar made a mental note to follow up on this accusation. Many a serial killer had a background of childhood abuse. "Is Bradley living here in Astoria?"

"Wish I could tell you, honey, but I don't know. Joe hasn't mentioned it."

"He went to high school here," Skylar said, recalling what Jake had told her. "At least part of the time when his parents were sharing custody."

"That must have been eight or nine years ago. Well before Joe and I were a thing."

"Do you have a phone number and address for Bradley?"

Delilah took her phone from her purse and scrolled. "This is the most recent. Used it to send him an online gift card for his birthday a couple of weeks ago, so it's probably current."

After Skylar downloaded the information—which included a Houston, Texas, address—she looked up and saw Jake coming down the hall. His timing couldn't have been more perfect if he'd been listening through the open door for the moment when she had the addy and phone. Probably, he had been eavesdropping. He was itching to talk with Quilling.

"I'm done," he announced. "You've been real helpful, Delilah."

"Anytime, cutie pie."

She ushered them to the door. While Delilah locked up, Jake bounded down the two steps from the porch and hurried toward the Explorer. Skylar understood his eagerness to deal with Quilling. The tall, skinny head of APD's forensic department was part of the team, and—as a marine—Jake would follow the code of loyalty: never leave one of your soldiers behind.

As soon as she fastened her seat belt, he said, "We need a forensic person to process Quilling's Toyota for trace evidence, and I can't use someone who works with him. Will you arrange for an FBI tech who is in town putting up cameras to meet us at Quilling's apartment?"

She bobbed her head. "I can do that."

"Forensics can tell us if Lucille was in the car with him." He winced. "Or in the trunk."

She wished she could reassure him, but Quilling had twice popped up in compromising circumstances. He had to be considered a suspect. She pulled out her phone and started making calls to find a tech.

By the time she made plans with a team of FBI forensic experts who had just installed closed-circuit cameras outside a restaurant with a twelve-foot-tall lighthouse replica, the Explorer arrived at a rectangular, three-story apartment building with all the charm of a shoebox. In the parking lot, she saw a beat-up, gray, late model Toyota sedan. "Is that Quilling's car?"

"He's not into vehicles."

She figured as much. Though trying not to stereotype, she suspected the nerdy guy in round eyeglasses spent all his extra cash on computers and electronic equipment. Before getting out of the car, she said, "I'll stay here and wait for the FBI tech. If you bring me Quilling's car keys, we can get started with the processing right away."

"I appreciate the chance to talk to him alone," Jake said. "I want you to know that I agreed with your reprimand about the sloppy way he handled evidence. If you hadn't sent him home, I would have."

She believed him. Still, she recognized his concern for a guy he had trusted and worked with. "What would you have done if I hadn't found that photo of him with Phoebe?"

He exhaled in a whoosh. "I probably would have put him back to work. This investigation is testing the limits of the APD. We just don't have all that many officers."

She reached across the console and rested her hand on his arm. "I hope Quilling has a good explanation for why he went to Cape Disappointment last night."

He caught her hand and brought it to his lips for a quick kiss. "I'm hoping the same thing."

AT THE FRONT ENTRANCE, Jake followed another resident into the building, so he didn't need to use the buzzer before he hiked up to apartment 306 at the rear.

Though he and Quilling were friendly, he'd never been here. When people got together after work, they usually came to Jake's bungalow at the edge of the forest—a fixer-upper he bought when he left the marines. His first project was to add a huge cedar deck with a grill for cooking meat outside.

He tapped his knuckles against the door. "It's Jake Armstrong. Open up."

In seconds, the door swung wide. Dressed in grungy, baggy, mismatched sweats from head to toe with his hair uncombed and splotches of stubble on his pointed chin, Quilling looked like he'd just crawled out of bed. "Good morning, Armstrong."

"It's almost noon."

Jake pushed the door aside and entered the typical bachelor pad furnished with a worn sofa and two matching chairs, probably from his parents' house, unopened mail on the desk, lots of clutter, a fifty-five-inch flat-screen TV and an impressive computer setup for gaming. A pile of empty pizza boxes and beer bottles attested to Quilling's less-than-healthy diet. On the computer screen was a video game with flying dragons blowing fire down upon a medieval village.

Quilling darkened the screen and muted the sound. "Would you like a beer?"

Jake squinted at the label. "Is that a lighthouse?"

"What? No, it's brewed here in Astoria, and that's supposed to be the historic column at the top of Coxcomb Hill—our famous landmark."

Jake cut to the chase. "What the hell were you doing on the bridge last night?"

"I wasn't on the bridge."

"Don't lie to me. We have footage from the traffic cams that show your car crossing to Cape Disappointment at 12:22 and returning at 3:45."

"I swear, I was here. Had a few beers. Played my video game and went to bed."

"What time?"

"I don't remember. After one or one-thirty, for sure."

"Did anyone see you? Maybe a clerk at the store where you bought your beer. Does your computer have a system to show what time you're playing?"

Quilling took a long chug from the beer. "You're asking me for an alibi."

Damn right. "Give me your car keys so I can give them to Agent Gambel. We need to process your vehicle for trace evidence."

"Evidence of what?"

"There was a second victim last night." Quilling was probably the only person in town who didn't know. "Killed at the North Head Lighthouse."

The blood drained from his face. He swallowed hard, pushed his glasses up on his nose and staggered toward a shelf by the door. Not saying a word, he held out his key ring.

Jake grabbed it and went to the window overlooking the

parking lot. He spotted Skylar in her official-looking suit. She'd been joined by the two musclebound techs who lowered the body at the North Head Lighthouse. He unlocked the apartment window, then shoved the glass and the screen open. Waving to Skylar, he dangled the car keys. Before she could refuse, he tossed the key chain down to her.

She easily made the catch, which somehow satisfied him. Then she gave a thumbs-up.

He swung around and focused on Quilling who had collapsed into an indented place on the sofa which had to be where he usually sat. The guy was pathetic. Hard to picture him as the brazen Shadowkeeper—a narcissist who posed his victims and sent taunting notes to the police.

Jake stalked into the adjoining kitchen. "I'm making coffee."

"You don't have to do that."

"It's for you, Quilling. You need to get sober fast because I want you to use your brain." Taking him into custody would be embarrassing. "I don't want to arrest you."

Quilling bolted to his feet. Apparently, the thought of being on the wrong side of the jail bars galvanized him into action. He picked his way through the clutter into the kitchen and took over the process of making coffee in one of those machines with the pods. Clearing his throat, he spun around to face Jake. "Go ahead, Detective. Ask me anything."

"Let's start with Phoebe Conway. Tell me about your relationship with her."

"One-sided." Quilling pushed his floppy brown hair off his forehead. "She asked me to take some publicity photos of her. Even though it was an obvious ruse to get inside information from me for an article about the burglar who hit seven houses in a week, I agreed. She was friendly and so pretty. Way out of my league."

"You must have been tempted to tell her about the leads we had on the robberies."

"Tempted, yes." Quilling took his full coffee cup, carried it to a kitchen table piled high with clutter and sat in a straight-backed chair. "But I didn't say a word. I know better than to talk to a reporter. Coffee for you?"

"I'm fine."

"Why are you asking me about Phoebe? It was only a couple of hours."

"When Special Agent Gambel searched Phoebe's apartment, she found a photo of you in an embrace with her. Explain."

He slurped his coffee as though it was the magic elixir he needed to win his imaginary battle with the dragons. "She wanted me to show her how to set the camera to take a photo five seconds after she posed for it. Her equipment didn't have that feature, but mine did. So, I illustrated. When I got into position, I didn't expect for her to hug me like that."

"But you didn't mind," Jake said.

"I won't lie. It was nice."

"Do you have an alibi for the night she was killed?"

"Wasting time with Phoebe put me behind in my regular duties. I had to work late at the forensic lab. Didn't leave until after midnight." Behind his glasses, his eyes teared up. "Who was killed last night?"

"Lucille Dixon."

"The cowgirl who sang at the Sand Bar? The 'Your Cheatin' Heart' girl? Damn." Quilling seemed genuinely upset.

For a few minutes, they talked about their memories of Lucille. When Quilling mentioned the note he'd found on Phoebe's phone, Jake refused to discuss the case with him. His phone buzzed in his pocket. It was Skylar.

"You can stop interrogating Quilling," she said.

Relief spread through him. "That's good news."

"The techs found evidence. A hair."

Jake didn't understand. Typically, a hair would be run

through all kinds of tests to determine DNA and all the rest of the forensic stuff. "How do you know who it belongs to?"

"It's magenta. Not purple, magenta. And it was in the passenger seat."

Jake drew the logical conclusion. Delilah had been riding in Quilling's car, and her fiancé was the driver.

Quilling was off the hook.

Chapter Eighteen

After reassuring Quilling and ordering him not to leave his apartment, Jake joined Skylar and the forensic techs in the parking lot. Given Quilling's position in the APD, the techs agreed to transport the aged Toyota to Portland for further tests. Though the dashboard and steering wheel had been wiped down, four different sets of fingerprints, including Quilling's, had been collected. Three magenta hairs had been found.

Leaving them to do their jobs, Jake got back into the Explorer with Skylar. She tapped the face of the black titanium field watch she always wore. "It's almost two o'clock. If we hope to make it to the autopsy in Warrenton by three, we should leave now."

"Our time is better spent here," he said. "We need to talk to people at the Sand Bar. To come up with a timeline for last night and find out who Lucille was talking to. Not to mention, who she'd been dating."

"When we get a list of suspects," she said, "we'll compare Lucille's boyfriends with Tabitha's list for Phoebe."

He started the car and pulled out of the parking area. Unanswered questions rattled around in his brain. He started with the most perplexing. "What the hell was Delilah doing in Quilling's car?"

"In the passenger seat," she reminded him.

"Which probably means Rogers was driving." The newspaper editor might have needed a different car to cross the bridge last night because his little black sedan was already compromised. But why Quilling? They didn't live in the same neighborhood. "There's got to be a connection."

"And we'd better find it," she said. "We'll skip the autopsy. I spoke to Crawford a few minutes ago. He and Jimi Kim will be with the medical examiner, and they'll give us the conclusions. He said it wasn't necessary for us to attend in person."

"We can start at the Sand Bar. Get lunch."

"Yes," said the woman who loved to eat.

He did a celebratory fist pump. "Food *and* interviewing witnesses. Two birds, one stone. Sand Bar makes a decent clam chowder."

"Back to the main topic. Delilah in Quilling's car. She might have been riding with Quilling. But I can't imagine they're friends. I doubt he goes to her salon. His hair doesn't look like it gets special attention from a stylist."

Jake raked his fingers through his own short hair. Most of the APD officers, including Dot, used a barber shop around the corner from headquarters. "Quilling is too old to have gone to high school with Delilah's son. He's more like Bradley Rogers's age."

"And we don't even know if Bradley is in town." She looked down at her phone screen. "I could call the phone number Delilah gave me. But I'd rather figure out where he lives and visit him unannounced."

"An ambush."

"Exactly."

"Finding out if he's in Astoria and where he's staying sounds like a job for Chief Kim. Give her a call."

While she contacted the APD command central, he considered questions that should be asked at the Sand Bar. The bartenders tended to keep watch over the inebriated patrons to prevent fights from breaking out. Had they noticed anyone suspicious? Anyone approaching Lucille? Yesterday, he'd spoken to a couple of the regular employees about Ty McKenna's alibi, and they'd been cooperative.

Skylar finished up her phone call at about the same time as he made a right turn into the parking lot for the waterfront tavern and restaurant. Not a place he'd ordinarily go to get a meal. Apart from the chowder, their menu was burgers and anything deep fried. The Sand Bar was—as it said in the name—a bar. With an impressive selection of craft beers.

Before they left the Explorer, she briefed him. "Chief Kim is doing a search for Bradley Rogers's local address. Most of the surveillance cameras have been placed near lighthouses and are sending their simultaneous broadcasts to a big-screen computer at APD. The chief compared it to one of those online meeting places with locations instead of faces. The sites are also available on many phone screens—including yours and mine—through a special app." She shook her head. "I'm always amazed at what the electronics guys can do."

"Which lighthouses aren't covered?"

"Terrible Tilly on the offshore island isn't, because getting there is too complicated. And not Cape Meares, which is farthest away in the opposite direction from Cape Disappointment."

"And has already been used." He leaned across the console toward her and inhaled the vanilla and citrus fragrance he'd come to associate with Skylar. She smelled like the Dreamsicle ice cream bars he'd loved as a kid. "Show me the app."

On her phone, she tapped an icon and brought up a picture of the lighthouse replica at the miniature golf course where a worker in a dark green polo shirt was hosing down sidewalks. "When we leave the bar, we should go there. The Shadowkeeper pointed us in that direction with his clues."

He didn't like the idea of taking directions from a serial killer, but the communication from the Shadowkeeper couldn't be ignored. He had clearly indicated the North Head

Lighthouse in his text to Skylar. "From his messages, it seems like he knows something about the women he kills. He stalks them. What's his trigger? Why did he select Phoebe and Lucille?"

When he left the Explorer, she walked beside him through the pleasantly sunlit day. "Victimology," she said. "One of my fave topics."

"But you're not one of those people who tries to get inside the killer's head, are you?"

She shuddered. "Can't think of a more repulsive place to be. But I like to speculate about what comes next. Both Phoebe and Lucille are attractive women in highly visible professions. Local celebrities."

A simple but accurate description. "He keeps mentioning Phoebe and her column. And I expect we'll see more comments about the songbird, which has to be Lucille. And maybe about you, Skylar. You're pretty. And everybody in town knows who you are now."

"I certainly don't think of myself as a celebrity, but the Shadowkeeper has targeted me. He's sent a text directly to my phone. Makes me wonder if I could be used as bait to draw him out."

"Not exactly regulation FBI protocol."

"Protocol," she said, "is whatever works."

THE ENTRANCE TO the Sand Bar featured rough, unvarnished wood siding and two porthole-shaped windows with brass fittings. The theme, Skylar guessed, was a shipwreck in the bay.

Only a handful of patrons were scattered at the dark wood tables. Later in the evening, she supposed, a full band would take the stage, and the dance floor would be hopping. The interior lighting came from dim, flickering lantern fixtures, but several large windows lined the wall overlooking the harbor. The atmosphere tried for a cool vibe, but the mood today was decidedly somber.

A blond waitress with red-rimmed eyes gestured to the tables. "Sit wherever you want."

As soon as they settled at a window, a dark, bearded guy built like a fireplug pulled up a chair and made it a threesome. "We got to catch this bastard, Jake. For Lucille."

"Sam Henderson is the owner. Sam, this is Special Agent Skylar Gambel. We're investigating."

He gave her a nod. "Order anything you want. Both of you. It's on the house."

After deciding on chowder and a cheeseburger, she mentioned Ty McKenna. "He was here on Tuesday night until closing time."

"Ty's sober, but I appreciate him being designated driver for his hard-drinking friends. Tuesday is usually quiet. Not a big night for us." His face crumpled, and he looked down at his stubby fingers as they twisted in his lap. "Lucille was singing. Early in the evening, McKenna did his best to pick her up, but she wasn't interested."

"Had he dated her before?" Skylar asked.

Henderson frowned and stroked his beard, trying to remember. "I don't think so. Lucille might have been a world-class flirt and would let anybody buy her a beer, but she didn't actually date many guys."

The shorter the list, the fewer suspects they had to check out. "Tell me about her current boyfriend. Or boyfriends. Has she recently broken up with anybody?"

"To hear her tell it, Lucille never ended a relationship until she had a good reason. You know, it was always 'Your Cheatin' Heart' with her boyfriends." He tapped the tabletop to emphasize his point. "She's been dating the guitar player who works here on Thursday and the weekend. He'll be in at four and plays until eight. He and Lucille were making a demo tape."

Skylar jotted down his name and phone number, just in case the guitarist didn't show. While she'd been talking to

Henderson, Jake was fielding questions from others on the staff and the sad-eyed waitress. Though they might be more inclined to talk in a group setting, Skylar didn't like to conduct interviews with more than one person at a time. She separated the waitress, Jillian, from the herd and went outside with her.

Jillian, dressed in snug jeans, a tiny apron and a Sand Bar T-shirt, lit up a cigarette and strolled to the edge of the walkway above the Columbia. The smell of freshly caught fish from the docks mixed with the oily, mechanical stink from motorized vessels. Casual waves splashed against the pier while terns and gulls made their own racket. Low, drifting clouds hadn't yet masked the glare from the sun.

In the daylight, the wrinkles around Jillian's big, blue eyes were more visible. At one time, Skylar guessed, the waitress had been as cute as a Kewpie doll, and she was still an attractive woman.

Jillian exhaled a cloud of smoke and said, "Lucille and I used to come out here a couple of times every night. To get away from the loud, handsy jerks in the bar. She was a sweet kid. I'll miss her."

"Henderson mentioned a boyfriend," Skylar prompted.

"Xander the guitar player." She combed her fingers through her shoulder-length blond hair. "A nice-looking dude, if you like them tall and skinny."

"Was that her type?"

"You bet. Soulful eyes and messy hair."

Skylar knew who fit that description. "Did she date Alan Quilling?"

"The nerd who works for the APD in forensics? Lucille didn't date him, but he's somebody she might find interesting."

On a hunch, Skylar asked, "What about Bradley Rogers?"

"In his dreams." Jillian inhaled and exhaled quickly. "He's been in here a couple of times recently, shooting off his mouth about how everything's bigger and better in Texas. And comparing the size of his cowboy boots with Lucille's. He'd dance the two-step with her, and accidentally-on-purpose grab her bottom. She slapped him."

Though Skylar hadn't come face-to-face with Bradley, he was beginning to look better and better as a suspect. "Did Henderson throw him out?"

"He said he was sorry, and we cut him some slack because his dad is the guy who runs the *Sun*. Joe Rogers has always been good to the Sand Bar. We advertise with him." Her gasp sounded like the beginning of a sob. "A shame about that reporter who worked for him. Phoebe."

"Did she know Lucille?"

"Know her? She wrote a whole article with photographs about how talented she was. Called her a songbird."

That must have been where the *songbird* label got started. Figuring she was on a roll, Skylar asked, "Did Lucille ever date Trevor Miller?"

"Delilah's son. Gawd, no. He's not even old enough to drink. Dyed his buzz cut hair in a red-and-blue checkerboard pattern. He's cute but not for dating." She put out her cigarette and tucked it into a little pouch to dispose of later. "I adore his mom. She's the genius behind my highlights that totally cover the gray."

"Anything else you can tell me about Bradley Rogers? Do you know where he lives? I want to get ahold of him."

"After he tried making the moves on Lucille, he started in on me. He's a major, major jerkwad. Of course, I shut him down. But before I did, he told me we could spend the night in the best hotel in Astoria, soak in a hot tub and have a spa treatment."

"I'm new in town. Which hotel is that?"

"The Pierpoint—a crazy expensive, gorgeous place. Every room has a balcony and a view. I'd love to stay there and wallow in luxury." Jillian pivoted to face the Sand Bar, which would never be defined as luxurious. "But not if it means spending time with that creep."

"You've been a help," Skylar said. "Thanks for talking to me."

"I'll do anything to help catch the monster who killed Lucille." Jillian cringed. "You don't think it was Bradley, do you?"

"He's a person of interest."

Back inside the Sand Bar, Skylar stood at the horseshoe bar and took out her phone to call Crawford. He had given her a great deal of leeway during this investigation, but she still wanted her mentor's expert judgment.

Her wristwatch showed 3:07. Too early for the autopsy to be over. She left Crawford a message to call her. The time was 3:11. Minutes dragged like hours, but time passed too quickly. They needed results. She feared the Shadowkeeper would strike again in spite of the surveillance cameras. Her ride on the tugboat—though a wonderful relief—had been a time waste. And here she and Jake were at the Sand Bar eating dinner.

A burst of laughter from the table where Jake and three other guys sat caught her attention. Two of them held pool cues. An adjoining room had three tables. A glance told Skylar that none of these men would have appealed to Lucille. Not her type at all.

Do I have a type? She returned Jake's wave but didn't rush across the restaurant to join him. Most of the guys she dated were athletic. All of them were smart. Twice, she'd lived with men. Both were dark-haired, professional and fit well into any setting or situation. They blended. Not like Jake.

He stood out. Clearly, she would notice this tall, muscular Viking with the slow, sexy smile and blazing blue eyes. A near-perfect physical specimen. Of course, she was drawn to him. Evolutionary theory indicated that women sought males who would produce strong, healthy babies. But the ripple of excitement flowing through her veins felt like more than natural selection or hormones, more than pure animal attraction...or maybe not. Maybe lust was enough.

She didn't really have time to consider her romantic prospects. First order of business: find Bradley Rogers. She called Chief Kim to see if she'd discovered where he lived. His permanent address was in Houston, but he was having mail forwarded to a box at a postal service center in town. That was where her trail ended. No trace of Bradley in Astoria or any of the other nearby towns.

Skylar said, "I heard that he might be staying at the Pierpoint Hotel."

"How very bougie," the chief said. "I didn't know he had that kind of money. I'll check with the front desk and get back to you."

When she turned away from the bar, Skylar came face-to-face with Dagmar and a man with a long ponytail who had to be Pyro Pierce, the science teacher. With all of Dagmar's flowing scarves and Pierce's Sasquatch T-shirt and denim jacket, they reminded her of pictures of hippies from the 1960s. Their height difference—with Dagmar in platform heels that gave her a good six inches on him—was endearing.

"We've come to help," Dagmar said.

Their offer was wrong on so many different levels. They were citizens. Untrained and untested. If they were hurt—God forbid—Skylar and the FBI would be liable. Jake wanted his cousin kept apart from the investigation. Crawford certainly wouldn't approve. Still...

"Cool," Skylar said.

Chapter Nineteen

Dagmar introduced her beau in a fond drawl that sounded like slow motion, which was probably because Skylar was so driven. Everything needed to sped up. She recalled what Jake had said about Pierce. "You're a science teacher."

"Guilty." He had a nice smile and a healthy glow. A bicycle rider, Pierce had given them their first clue when he noticed Rogers's black sedan parked outside the apartment house where Phoebe lived.

"You might be able to help me. Did you ever have Joe Rogers's son, Bradley, in class?"

"I did." His eyebrows pulled together over his glasses. "Bradley wasn't a pleasant kid. Not an atypical personality for an adolescent with raging hormones, but Bradley was worse than most. I think the technical term is…creepy."

Jillian had called him a jerkwad. Apparently, he hadn't mellowed since high school. "How so?"

"In chemistry class, he showed intense interest in how to rig a bomb for maximum casualties. In biology, he loved dissecting the frogs and earthworms. Kept asking if we could get a human cadaver and promised his rich stepfather would pay for it."

"Dark," Dagmar said. "I'd probably like him."

"No, luv. You have nothing in common with him." When

he looked at her, his face lit up. "You study the macabre as a learning experience. Bradley wanted to hurt other people."

An interesting perspective. Before she could say more, Skylar's phone buzzed, and she excused herself to answer.

The usually even-tempered Chief Kim sounded irritated. "Sorry, Skylar, I couldn't get much info from that snobby woman at the Pierpoint front desk. Leah Fairchild, not so fair in my opinion. All she'd tell me was that no person named Bradley Rogers was currently registered. And then she refused to answer any other questions."

"What did you ask?" Skylar asked.

"If she knew Bradley from when he was growing up. Or if he'd used a different name." She huffed a sigh of pure exasperation. "If you go over there and flash your FBI badge, that snooty woman might cooperate. She likes authority figures."

"But that applies to you as well," Skylar pointed out. "You have clout. You're the police chief."

"I'm also little Viv, Jimi's granddaughter. And I'm massively pregnant, which undermines my status as a kickass chick."

"Checking out the fancy hotel…" Following up on the lead from Jillian was worth the trip. "I'll give it a shot."

"Thanks so much."

Skylar noted the time—3:42. She didn't want to waste another minute. Turning her attention back to Dagmar and Pierce, she asked, "Could up drive me to the Pierpoint?"

"Sure," Dagmar said. "But why?"

"I'm looking for Rogers's son and might need someone to identify him. Would you recognize him, Pierce?"

"I believe so."

The buxom, wild-haired librarian linked her arm with Pierce's and beamed a smile down at him. "We're in."

THE PIERPOINT HOTEL and Spa in Astoria thrust into the harbor on its own pier, close enough to the monster bridge that

Skylar had to tilt her head back to see the high arch. The lines of the hotel were sleek and modern. The entrance combined transparent plexiglass walls with an outdoor display of native species of the Pacific Northwest, including sea otters and sea lions who greeted the guests with growls and barks.

"Love the otters," Dagmar said after she parked her battered station wagon and moved to the railing that enclosed the display. "The rest of this isn't my cup of chai. I prefer something that's natural and wild."

"Like me," Pierce said.

"Still," Dagmar continued, "the patrons are willing to pay exorbitant sums to stay here and get massaged."

"And I'm happy to do it for free, luv." Pierce turned to Skylar when they gathered outside the station wagon. "What's the plan?"

She explained. "The woman at the front desk told Chief Kim that Bradley wasn't registered here. Then she refused to take steps to search for him."

"Got it," Dagmar said. "Are we going to beat the truth out of her? Smack her around? Get out the rubber hoses? I always carry pepper spray in my purse. A special formula that Pierce makes for me."

"You're here as backup," Skylar said. "Don't say or do anything unless you see Bradley walking around in the lobby."

The next step in her plan depended on whether or not they found a room number for Bradley. Smoothing the lapels of her jacket, she stalked across the marble floor of the lobby to the front desk made of frosted glass and etched with the sights of Astoria, including the bridge, the historic column atop the hill, a row of pines and seagoing sailing vessels.

The woman standing behind the desk wore a salmon-colored uniform jacket with a gold-plated name tag: Leah Fairchild.

Skylar stormed the desk and thrust her badge into Leah's smug face. She introduced herself loudly enough for others in the area to overhear. "Special Agent Skylar Gambel of the FBI. I have questions for you regarding the current serial killings."

"Hush." Leah placed her index finger across her lips as if talking to a toddler at nappy time. "We don't want you frightening the customers, do we?"

"They should be scared." Skylar made eye contact with a few well-dressed guests of the hotel. "The situation is dangerous, dire, fraught."

Leah scowled. "What do you want from me, Special Agent?"

"Earlier today, APD Chief Kim asked if Bradley Rogers was staying here."

"He's not registered here. That's all I'll tell you."

"You can do more," Skylar said.

"How about a warrant? Why are you bothering me?" Leah's voice got shrill. "What's your problem, lady?

Skylar calmly explained, "I want to look at your records for the past week. Then, I would like to show Bradley's photo to your staff and interview them. I advise you to cooperate."

"Are you threatening me?"

"Certainly not." Skylar held her impatience in check. "I will obtain search warrants and go through all proper procedures."

"That's better," Leah said.

"May I remind you that time is of the essence. The Shadowkeeper has already killed twice. Other lives may be at stake."

Pierce stepped up beside her at the counter. "May I make a suggestion?"

Skylar turned to him, hoping he had an answer for this largely unproductive conversation. "Go ahead."

"Back in high school, Bradley sometimes used the surname of his rich Texan stepfather. Knox."

Skylar glared across the counter at Leah. "Do you have someone named Knox registered?"

"I do," Leah admitted grudgingly. "J. B. Knox in room 460."

On her phone, Skylar pulled up a recent photo of Joseph Bradley Rogers and showed it to Leah. "Is this Knox?"

She nodded. "Is he the killer?"

"Thanks so much for your cooperation," Skylar said.

She pivoted and went toward the elevator. In moments, they stood outside his door, ready to knock. They'd found him, at last.

THE LONG DAY faded into dusk, and the Sand Bar filled with people who had come to talk about the murder of Lucille Dixon, aka the songbird. Jake's private conversation with Xander was cut short again and again by mourners who wanted to hear her favorite tune or offer condolences. The guitarist's comments touched lightly on evidence and heavily on emotion. He missed her. His heart was shattered. His future, dim.

At Jake's urging, Xander focused on those who might have wanted to do her harm. Lucille had known several men but only had problems with a few. A couple of guys cheated on her, but there wasn't a special enemy. People liked her. Xander gestured to the growing crowd. "See them. They had a connection that went deeper than just liking her music."

"Tell me about grudges," Jake said. "Bitter rivals. Someone looking for revenge."

"Everybody loved her." Xander dabbed at the corner of his soulful brown eyes. He sang mostly folk songs and looked like the part with long, glossy black hair and thick stubble. "Lucille was something else. Stomping around in her brave red boots and making people grin. She was one of a kind."

A young woman with a long braid poked her nose into

their talk. "Excuse me, Xander, would you play 'Leavin' on a Jet Plane'? I loved the way Lucille sang that tune."

Jake waved her off. "We're talking, ma'am."

"Just one song. Please."

Jake stood, took the guitar and motioned for Xander to follow him to the backstage area beyond the bathrooms. A small storage room, packed with broken tables and cardboard boxes, had been turned into a dressing room for the musical performers. Though it was aboveground, the area smelled like a musty basement. Two makeup mirrors encircled by lights hung over a scarred wooden table where bits of makeup, used tissue and hand lotion were scattered. Four rickety chairs waited at the table. Jake closed the door and directed Lucille's boyfriend to sit.

"In the past week or so," Jake said, "did you notice anything unusual about Lucille?"

"Her Texas accent got thicker. Lots of y'all and howdy and such."

"I don't understand. Why is that important?"

Xander tapped on the side of his head as though jump-starting his brain. "When she was around other people from Texas, she picked it up."

"Who was she with?" Jake thought of Bradley who'd spent half his life in Texas and had a Houston address, but he didn't want to lead Xander to a false memory. "Give me a name."

"Sorry. I can't think of a particular person."

Jake switched to a new direction. "Did she tell you why she hopped into her little red Kia and drove to the North Head Lighthouse last night? Did she have a friend who lived there? Was she meeting someone?"

"It was an appointment," he said.

Now they were getting somewhere. "Odd location for a meeting."

"Lucille wrote a ballad about Cape Disappointment and broken dreams." His eyes misted, and he blinked to keep the tears from falling. "Gentle melody. Beautiful lyrics. She wanted to evoke loneliness and the hope for a brighter horizon. The top of the lighthouse seemed like a good place to take promo photos."

"In the dark?"

"The photographer had some kind of special lens that gave sharp focus, even at night in the fog. They planned to climb to the beacon and take the pictures there."

In one quick statement, so much was explained. Lucille went to the lighthouse after dark when it was closed to the general public. And she climbed to the upper level for the dramatic photo, which meant there was no need for the killer to drag her up the winding staircase. Only one question, the most important one, remained. "Who was the photographer?"

"I don't know. She said he wanted to be anonymous."

Jake's gut clenched. He didn't want to think it was Quilling, but the prior evidence had pointed toward him. Quilling had taken photos of Phoebe. Had he applied the same method to get close to Lucille? His vehicle had been caught by traffic cams on the bridge, proof that his battered old Toyota had made the round trip to Cape Disappointment. Even if Delilah had been in the car, Quilling could have been the driver. "Was it someone local?"

"I didn't recognize him."

"You saw him?" Pulling information from Xander was like peeling layers from an onion. "Describe him."

"Brown hair. Pale skin. A fussy dresser, the kind of guy who wants starch in his shirt and a crease in his jeans."

That didn't sound like Quilling. "Did he wear glasses?"

"Nope, and I couldn't see his eye color from across the room."

"What else?"

"Not too husky. He was tall." Xander chuckled. "Made himself look even taller by wearing cowboy boots."

So far, Jake and Skylar had only discovered one suspect

who dressed like a Texan—the elusive Bradley Rogers. He hoped Skylar had tracked him down at the Pierpoint, and they could take him into custody. Maybe tonight there would be no murder.

He wrapped up his interview with Xander with a few more basic questions and advice for him to call or text if he remembered anything more. Jake released the guitarist at the same time Skylar came into the tiny backstage room. The fresh citrus scent of her shampoo cut through the dismal stink. The makeup lights brightened.

She closed the door and turned toward him. "I found Bradley. He used the surname of his stepfather in Texas. Registered at the Pierpoint as J. B. Knox."

"A fake name?"

"Actually, no. He has an innocent excuse because his credit card is in the Knox name, which he must have used when he lived in Texas."

"A spare identity," he said. "Handy."

"Anyway, we went to his room and convinced the snobby front desk woman to let us in. His bed was made, his suitcase gone, and there was no sign of him."

"Had he checked out?"

"Not yet." She shook her head, and her dark curls bounced around her shoulders. Her cheeks were rosy from being outdoors in the wind. "I left a voicemail for Bradley on the phone number Delilah gave me. Asking him to call me. As if? Also, a text. I wish there was something else we could do to find him."

"You could always eat." Jake held up a doggie bag from the restaurant. "Your burger."

"Thoughtful." She snatched it from him, extracted a limp, soggy French fry and dropped it back into the sack. Belated burgers and fries didn't make good leftovers. "I talked to Crawford, and he has information from the autopsy. Wants us to meet him and Jimi at the APD."

Jillian burst through the door. "Skylar, you have to come with me. Right now. Right this minute. He's here."

"Bradley Rogers?"

"He's here," she said breathlessly. "Brought a huge bouquet of flowers in remembrance of Lucille."

Jake dashed down the corridor, passed the bathrooms and charged into the Sand Bar, which was now almost full.

A giant display of yellow roses stood on the bar like a shrine to Lucille Dixon.

Chapter Twenty

Skylar read the printed ribbon draped across the flower basket: *In Memory of Lucille Dixon, Our Yellow Rose from Texas*.

The customers and crew surged around the bar. Some wept. Others raised their craft beer bottles in a toast. When a woman sang an alto version of "Your Cheatin' Heart," others joined in.

Skylar searched their faces, looking for a brown-haired man in his late twenties who matched the photos she had of Bradley. She recognized Ty McKenna with his short, black hair and a hipster-style vest decorated with a pewter watch chain. Tabitha, the goth girl from the *Sun* office, was also there. The three short blond bloggers in their pink-on-pink outfits tried to maintain funereal composure without giggling.

From his taller vantage point, Jake also scanned the crowd that had swelled to over fifty, which she supposed was a lot for early evening. Lucille Dixon must have been well-liked and well-known—a profile that also applied to Phoebe Conway.

If the Shadowkeeper targeted this type of woman, Skylar wondered about his motivation. Lucille and Phoebe might have both embarrassed him in a personal encounter. Or he might have been magnetically drawn to these attractive women. He'd appealed to their vanity to lure them into a dangerous situation. Then he'd attacked. In anger. Or revenge. Or seeking notoriety.

Jillian waved frantically, and Skylar rushed to where she was standing near the exit. Jake was right behind her. Jillian pulled them out the door and pointed into the depths of the jam-packed parking lot. "Bradley is over there. Driving away in a silver BMW. I wrote down the license number."

Skylar took the scrap of paper torn from the waitress's order pad and squinted toward the parking lot exit in time to see the Bimmer merge into traffic. If they hoped to catch him, they needed to move fast.

Jake dashed toward the Explorer only to find it penned in by other cars. With no time to maneuver, he looked for another way out. As if on cue, Dagmar's station wagon chugged to a stop beside them.

"Need a lift?" Dagmar asked.

Skylar watched an array of emotions flicker behind Jake's eyes. He didn't want his cousin involved in the investigation because of the danger. But her offer was the quickest solution to their problem. He desperately wanted to catch up with Bradley, but calling on Dagmar freaked him out. She was the very definition of a loose cannon.

Skylar took charge. Turning to Jillian, she snapped, "Get the area around Jake's Explorer cleared. We'll pick it up later." She shoved him toward the open rear door of Dagmar's car. "Get in." To Dagmar, she said, "Follow that Bimmer."

With a wild grin, Dagmar punched the accelerator, and they took off. "Yeehaw!"

In the passenger seat beside her, Pierce leaned forward as far as his seat belt would allow and fixated on the distant view through the windshield. "Stay on the riverfront road until the traffic clears. Then we'll have a better visual on the silver car."

Skylar was surprised by his sharp analysis. "I thought you didn't like driving."

"Doesn't mean I can't find my way around," he said. "On my bicycle, I think ahead so I can access the most efficient routes. It's all about math and percentages. Bradley is *not* headed to the Pierpoint, which is north of our location. Most of the local businesses are in the opposite direction. Unless he's planning to stop in town, I figure the odds are that he's headed toward the main thoroughfare. Highway 101."

And the highway meant they'd have to cross the bridge. It took a moment for her to remember that the towering Astoria-Megler Bridge was in the rearview mirror. Ahead was the bridge across Youngs Bay that she'd already managed to cross twice without a massive phobic reaction. Only a bit of nausea. And hyperventilation. Racing pulse and—

Jake tapped her arm. "Are we sure that's Bradley's car?"

"He signed in at the hotel with that make and model." Skylar took the note from Jillian out of her pocket and compared it with her data from the Pierpoint. "The license plates match. I already checked with the rental place at the Portland airport."

"When did he pick up the Bimmer?"

"Ten days ago."

He slid across the back seat until he was right beside her. The warmth of his body soothed her momentary panic about the approaching bridge, and she wondered if he had also been concerned about her phobia. With no tugboat in sight, he might be offering himself as a security blanket. But when she glanced up and read his expression, she could see that he'd wanted to be near her for a less drastic reason: he wanted to be close. She understood. After a few hours apart, she was glad to reciprocate.

She snuggled against him but didn't attempt to wrap her arm around his shoulders—a move that Dagmar or Pierce would notice. Though not embracing, their upper bodies touched, and she matched the length of her thigh with his longer, more muscular leg.

For him to get close like this meant he wasn't wearing his seat belt. Breaking the rules, but she didn't mind. Her hand glided from his knee to his upper thigh.

He rested his hand atop hers. "Bradley has been in town for ten days."

"Uh-huh."

"And never visited his dad. Do you believe that?"

Skylar mumbled her assent. Forcing herself to be coherent, she tossed out another piece of data. "He used the Knox credit card for the rental car."

"Hey, you two." Dagmar darted her station wagon through traffic. On the bridge, she wouldn't be able to change lanes. "He's crossing Youngs Bay, headed for Warrenton."

Skylar stared into Jake's blue, blue eyes. And she sang, "Rolling, rolling, rolling on the river."

Though it didn't make sense, he joined in on the "Proud Mary" chorus. Of course, Pierce sang harmony.

She felt the jolt as the tires bounced onto the paved surface of the two-lane bridge. Not a long drive. Less than a mile. Completely distracted by the rhythmic beat and the intoxicating nearness of Jake's body, she experienced a very mild phobic reaction. She had this. She was under control. *What could go wrong?*

"Damn it!" Dagmar yelled as she slowed drastically. The traffic ahead of them was a stream of red brake lights. "The bridge is lifting."

"What do you mean?" Skylar demanded.

Pierce explained. "Midway across the bridge is a vertical lift section that can be raised to accommodate tall ships and sailboats. There's nothing we can do but wait."

Stuck on the bridge. A nightmare scenario. She gripped Jake's hand, clinging to him. In her rational mind, she knew nothing terrible would strike them down. No trolls or kraken lived beneath the bridge.

But her panic wasn't rational. Her pulse raced. Her throat closed. She gasped for breath.

Dagmar rolled to a complete stop.

Traffic going in the opposite direction passed them, one car at a time. The last rays of sunlight before dusk glinted off the silver BMW as it drove toward them.

Skylar thrust her arm between the two front seats and pointed. "It's him."

Bradley had doubled back from the Warrenton side and was returning to Astoria. He'd returned quickly enough to get past the vertical lift. As his car came closer, she imagined she could see him peering through the windshield, laughing at them.

Without really being aware of her actions, Skylar realized her hand was on the butt of her Glock, ready to draw and shoot. Not a smart move. Not safe at all. She ordered herself to stand down.

Dagmar lacked her self-control. There was a break in the oncoming traffic after Bradley's car, and she flipped her station wagon into Drive. With aggressive maneuvering, she managed to make a U-turn in the middle of the bridge. She headed to Astoria, two cars back from the BMW.

Talk about breaking the rules! Dagmar's actions would have earned her a half-dozen traffic citations if the entire APD hadn't been preoccupied with chasing the Shadowkeeper. She would have been in big trouble. And yet, she'd pulled it off.

Skylar bounced on the seat, cheering Dagmar on. She could tell that neither Jake nor Pierce were thrilled, but she didn't give a damn. All that mattered was catching up to Bradley.

Her bridge panic morphed into a manic phase. Something she'd never experienced before. A state of euphoria. An extreme grin stretched her mouth. Her heartbeat whirred like a hummingbird inside her rib cage.

Dagmar was forced to stop at the light at the end of the bridge. The Bimmer, two cars ahead, made it through and turned right into the hills rising above the marina and the waterfront shops. Once again, Bradley Rogers, aka Knox, was getting away.

Her spirits crashed, and she slumped back against the seat. Too embarrassed to gaze directly at Jake, she focused on her fingers as they twisted into a knot on her lap. "Sorry. I got carried away."

"It's okay." He leaned close and whispered, "I like this better than the last time we crossed a bridge."

"I almost pulled my gun."

"But you didn't." He lightly kissed her cheek. "Sit up so you can watch for Bradley's car along the street."

They made a search, following a grid set out by Pierce, and finally decided they'd lost him. Dagmar drove them back to the Sand Bar where Jake's Explorer had been extricated from the clogged parking lot. From there, they proceeded to the APD where they would meet with Crawford, Jimi and Chief Vivianne.

"I'm hungry," she said.

"Not interested in the cold cheeseburger?"

"I've got a fairly simple appetite, but there are some things I won't touch. Soggy fries and cold burgers drenched in mustard and pickle chips are inedible."

The daylight had rapidly faded into foggy darkness. She could feel the danger closing in. When her phone made the subtle ping announcing the arrival of a new text, she groaned. The message was probably from him.

She read:

Tick tock. Time running out, Skylar. The game is between you and me. Poker players. All in, betting all the marbles.

Warning: I never lose. Tonight, I give the bloggers something to write their columns about. The Shadowkeeper

The mention of bloggers was a warning. Thinking of the three blond influencers she'd just seen in the Sand Bar, Skylar called Chief Kim and asked her to have someone warn them and advise them not to go out tonight.

Chapter Twenty-One

The direct focus of the Shadowkeeper's latest text was Skylar, which worried Jake a lot. Phrases like *the game is between you and me* and *I never lose* made his message clear. The Shadowkeeper had challenged her to a showdown and had no intention of failing.

Driving to the APD, Jake looked over at her in the passenger seat and said, "That text is meant to be personal."

"Well, yeah. It's addressed to me and came through on my phone."

"It's not about your job. It's about you. The Shadowkeeper wants you for his next victim." In their talk about victimology, they'd sketched the rough outlines of a profile. Both Phoebe and Lucille were young and beautiful—local celebrities who worked in visible professions. People recognized them and talked about them. "You have a lot in common with the victims."

"Not really," she said. "I'm not a hometown gal."

"Lucille came from Texas. Phoebe, too. She grew up in Houston."

"Exactly." She dropped her index finger on the console to make her point. "The Texas connection is one of the reasons we suspect Bradley. His mom took him there after they were threatened by the Lightkeeper. She married Knox the rancher who, for all practical purposes, became Bradley's stepfather."

He heard a pensive note in her voice and knew her mind had wandered. "What else?"

"I was thinking about that rusted swing set in the yard beside Rogers's house. He could have trashed it long ago, but he keeps it there as if he's expecting to look out the window and see his son going down the slide. And he has a Little League photo of young Bradley in his office. I think he loves his son."

Jake had sensed the same thing. "Maybe Bradley feels the same way about his dad, and that's why he came back to Astoria."

"To show his love by killing young women?" She shook her head. "I took my thinking in a different direction, concentrating on the stepfather. Based on inference and hearsay without a shred of tangible evidence, I'm guessing that the gun-toting Knox abused Bradley. Physically and verbally. His mother's second husband seems like somebody who'd tell a kid that he had to kick butt to prove he was a man. And some women like men who take charge."

He agreed with all she'd said. "As you pointed out, we have no proof. Nothing to go on."

"And no time to go deep." She looked at her watch again. "If we could interview Bradley or have a team from the Behavioral Analysis Unit interview him, we could make a case."

Again, he agreed, but he wouldn't let her drag him off track. "We were talking about why the Shadowkeeper threw down that challenge. Like you, both of the victims were headstrong, intelligent and talented. Phoebe was a journalist. Lucille was a singer."

"And what's my talent?"

He shot her a glance. "My guess is martial arts."

"You've never seen me in action."

"They don't hand out brown belts to just anybody." He'd looked up her background information on the internet and discovered that she was something of a legend in San Francisco martial arts tournaments. "Do I need to track down somebody at your dojo to find out how many awards you've won?"

"I do okay," she said.

"Most important, both of our victims were competitive, driven to succeed. Like you. The Shadowkeeper used their ambition to lure them into danger."

Skylar couldn't deny that similarity. She'd told him how hard she worked to earn her position as a special agent. She'd dedicated herself to investigating and solving crimes, starting with the apprehension of the Shadowkeeper. "You might be onto something," she admitted. "If he was going to hook me into doing something stupid, he'd appeal to my need to apprehend him."

He imagined a text the Shadow might send. "He'd start with something about how you're a brilliant investigator and deserve to make this arrest. Playing to your ambition. Then he'd invite you to a dark, lonely lighthouse."

"We can use his challenge to set a trap."

This was the second time she'd suggested something like this, and he still wasn't interested in risking her life. He knew exactly what he intended to do. From now on, he'd be with her all day and all night. She'd never admit to needing a protector, but she did. "We've got to be hyperaware. Watch for him to make the first move."

"And find him tonight. Right now. Before he kills again."

At APD command central, Jake delivered a point-by-point briefing on their findings. They would continue to monitor Rogers the editor, Delilah the magenta-haired girlfriend, Quilling and Ty McKenna, but they focused on Bradley Rogers as their primary suspect.

Crawford and Jimi Kim had researched and interrogated the two suspects from twenty years ago and their families. Though disappointed, the two investigators agreed that neither of these two bad guys warranted further surveillance. In spite of prior involvement in petty crimes and misdemeanors, these men and their families lived unremarkable lives and had valid alibis.

Chief Vivienne Kim waddled to the front of the room and took a position with her pregnant belly obscuring the lower frames of a wide-screen feed set up by the FBI techs. "We have ten camera positions at possible locations. Officers are standing by, ready to respond."

"Impressive," Skylar said. She filled a plate with Nana's homemade Italian dinner, featuring lasagna, pizza, caprese, bowls of Caesar salad and Girl Scout cookies. "Who do you have stationed near the miniature golf course?"

"Since you and Jake seem to think the seventh hole with the lighthouse replica is our next target, I put our best team on it. Dot and Dub."

Jake studied the camera feed, watching as a foursome of young teens lined up their shots. The surveillance screens were set to mute, but reading the giggles and teasing from the golfers wasn't difficult. The limited range of vision showed several people on the course, which featured mastheads, bridges, a shark with an open mouth and an octopus with arms that blocked the path of the ball to the hole. "Too many witnesses," he said. "When does it close?"

"Eleven o'clock on a weeknight. By midnight, everybody should be gone."

Skylar checked her wristwatch, a timekeeping gesture he was beginning to find annoying. "It's 8:47," she said. "Gets dark early here. Something to do with the fog?"

"Actually," Jimi said wryly. "It's because the sun goes down."

Jake never knew when to take the wiry old gent seriously. Jimi's enigmatic interrogation technique had fascinated him since he was a kid spying on the local police. After Jimi asked his series of questions, the person being interrogated was often too confused to do anything but confess. Jake trusted the former chief of police completely. "Tell us what you learned from the autopsy."

"Both victims were administered a drug by syringe. The final toxicology report is pending, and Dr. Kinski doesn't like to make guesses. But her initial analysis indicates the presence of ketamine and points to a fast-acting anesthetic." To illustrate, he held up his hand with fingers splayed to countdown. "Going backward from one hundred, you will reach ninety-nine, ninety-eight and then be out cold. Contusions indicate that the victims were already handcuffed when drugged. No other signs of premortem injuries."

Crawford added. "He knocked them out, then killed them, then posed them."

"Cause of death?" Jake asked.

Jimi responded, "Asphyxiation. Broken hyoid bones on each victim. Phoebe was garroted with a thin cord which was not found at the crime scene. Lucille was manually strangled before being hung from a noose."

"Were they raped?" Skylar asked.

"Not Phoebe." Jimi pursed his lips and shook his head. "For Lucille, the evidence is pending. She engaged in sexual intercourse shortly before her death, but there were no signs of violence. The act may have been consensual."

"Or she was unconscious." Apparently, that thought disturbed Skylar so much that she set down her fork and stopped eating. "Unable to struggle."

Jimi said, "Traces of semen were left behind. Dr. Kinski will run DNA tests."

Jake remembered his conversation with Xander, Lucille's boyfriend, who told him they were together before she left for Cape Disappointment. The folk singer never mentioned having sex, but Jake hadn't specifically asked. He needed to go back to the Sand Bar for verification from Xander. Also, one of the bartenders hinted that Ty McKenna was known for his grandiose lies and practical jokes—possible indications that his alibi wasn't rock-solid.

Jake listened while Crawford tweaked a few more threads of evidence. The knots on the noose around Lucille's throat were typical of those used in boating. Not much of a lead in a harbor town like Astoria where boats were as common as taxis.

"And Lucille's car has been located," Crawford said. "It went off a cliff near the North Head Lighthouse and crashed on the rocks. As far as we can tell, there was no driver or passengers. Someone must have put it in Neutral and shoved. Forensics will study the waterlogged wreckage, but the chances of extracting any viable evidence are slim to none."

"We need a new plan," Jimi announced. "Skylar and Jake, how can we contribute to your investigation?"

"Find Bradley Rogers, who also uses the last name of Knox," Skylar said. "We put out a BOLO on his silver BMW but haven't gotten any hits."

"We're usually more efficient," Chief Kim said with a scowl. "My people are stretched thin. Some are keeping watch over the likely spots for the Shadowkeeper to strike. Others are staking out suspects."

Jake exhaled a long sigh. He wished they could have activated Quilling. His expertise would be helpful. He turned to Skylar. "Show them the latest text."

She pulled up the message on her phone. "I received this just before we came here."

Crawford read quickly, then looked up with worried eyes. "Is this untraceable?"

"I'll check," Chief Kim, "but I suspect he's using the same process as before. He makes the initial contact using a disposable burner, which is not equipped with GPS or tracking. Then he sends the text, dumps the phone and walks away."

"What happens if we find the discarded phone?"

"It's nothing more than a piece of plastic and wires."

"Not if he left fingerprints," Jimi said. "Not likely, but possible."

"Here's my thought," Jake said. "The Shadowkeeper enjoys outsmarting us. In his messages, he keeps leaving clues and Easter eggs."

Jimi shook his head. "What does this mean? An Easter egg?"

"A reference to something hidden in plain sight. Like on an Easter egg hunt." Jake offered an example. "When the Shadowkeeper sent us to Cape Disappointment, that was a clue. Mentioning a hole-in-one might be an Easter egg pointing to the miniature golf course."

"He likes puzzles," Crawford said. "We should break down all his messages and see what might be significant. I seem to recall that he consistently mentions Phoebe's columns. Do we have copies?"

Chief Kim shuffled through stacks of paperwork from the *Sun*, searching for relevant documents while Crawford and Jimi laid out the various messages from the Shadowkeeper and attempted to decipher his meaning.

In the meantime, Jake and Skylar would return to the Sand Bar to find Xander.

ON A THURSDAY NIGHT, the street outside the police department was relatively quiet, broken only by the occasional cries of gulls, a foghorn and the hiss of tires against pavement.

Skylar squinted through the swirling mist outside the windshield. She took a sip from a container of pomegranate juice from the spread laid out in command central. "I'm glad we're able to follow our instincts. SSA Crawford trusts us. He's still encouraging me to investigate in the field."

"He'd switch directions in a minute if I mentioned your idea to use yourself as bait."

"Nobody likes a tattletale, Jake."

The quiet of the night shattered into a wild cacophony that spilled into the night when they drove close to the Sand Bar. Apparently, the disorganized wake for Lucille Dixon that started with a yellow rose bouquet had escalated into high gear.

Jake parked across the street outside a closed dry cleaner shop to avoid getting trapped in the parking lot again. "Do you think Bradley came back here after he dropped off the flowers?"

"Wouldn't that be a stroke of luck," she said. "When we're done here, we should pay his father a visit. Now that we have proof that Bradley is in Astoria, his dad might be willing to tell us why he returned to his hometown."

"Also, we need to hit the miniature golf course," he reminded her.

A dozen small projects called for their attention, but their priority was to interpret the messages the Shadowkeeper had sent. Skylar hated to imagine his glee, thinking he'd outsmarted them, tossing out clues and laughing when they charged off in the wrong direction.

As soon as she and Jake stepped through the door, she saw that the single display of yellow roses had been augmented by several other floral tributes to Lucille. "Red Roses for a Blue Lady" and "Sunflower" and "Daisies" celebrated her music. Squawks from the stage signaled a country-western band getting ready to perform. Conversations bloomed with memories and then faded into quiet sorrow.

Skylar felt a prickling across her shoulders—a feeling that someone was watching her.

Jillian raced through the bar with a trayful of beer. Pausing on her route through the tables, she spoke to Skylar. "Haven't seen him again."

"If you do..."

"I'll let you know." She pivoted back toward the table she

was serving and informed them that if they wanted mixed drinks or wine, they needed to go to the bar.

Jake tagged Xander and pulled him aside. "Thought you were scheduled to sing tonight."

"It's too loud and too crazy for my kind of music," he said. "I just want to go home and sit with my memories of Lucille."

Clearly, this wasn't the most sensitive time to pose uncomfortable questions. Still, Jake pushed forward. "Last night before Lucille left for her photo session, did you make love to her?"

"I did." Xander's soulful brown eyes shone with tears. A single droplet slipped down his cheek into the thick stubble that outlined his high cheekbones. "I'll miss her."

Unable to gaze directly at his pain, Skylar looked away. Again, she sensed someone watching. She looked toward the flowers, then to the black-clad mourners mingling with brightly dressed drinkers in Hawaiian shirts. People were laughing. And crying. And cursing. The place was a madhouse. On the stage, the standing cymbals fell to the floor with a discordant crash. When she turned toward the noise, she saw him.

They had never met in person, but the tall man with narrow shoulders resembled the photos she'd seen of Bradley Rogers. Nicely dressed and well-groomed with a light trace of stubble on his chin. His pleasant, unremarkable features and calm attitude allowed him to fade into the crowd. He didn't look like a serial killer. *Neither did Ted Bundy.* She studied him more closely, trying to decide if she was wrong.

His dark-eyed gaze latched on to hers and held her captive. He was the person who had been watching. Her instincts screamed in warning. He meant to do her harm. Cruelty brewed in his gut. Rage and hatred rolled off him in waves.

Even more terrifying was his smile. He was enjoying himself, smirking and licking his upper lip as though savoring a rare rib-eye steak dripping with juice. Casually, he raised his hand and pointed directly at her.

"Jake," she said as she grasped his arm. "Come with me. Now."

"Wait." He was in the middle of his own conversation. "You've got to hear this."

She refused to allow herself to be distracted. Picking her way through the crowd, she moved across the floor. A surge of line dancers arranged themselves in front of her, making it impossible to see Bradley. While she searched, Jake followed. He had Ty McKenna in tow. Finally, they came to a stop.

"Tell her, McKenna."

"Fine," he snapped. "Phoebe wasn't as important as she thought. You asked me about her columns. And I informed you that she never had a column. She wasn't good enough."

Skylar had lost track of Bradley in the crowd. He was escaping from her again. Desperately, she shoved her way to the corner where he'd been standing. *Gone!*

"Did you hear that?" Jake asked. "Phoebe had a byline that she used for articles like *The Goonies* story and the piece she did on Lucille Dixon. But no column."

Frustrated, she whipped around to face him. "So what?"

"It's the Easter egg, Skylar. He mentions the column in almost every message."

"Something hiding in plain sight."

"The Astoria Column," Jake said in his tour-guide voice, "was dedicated in 1926 by the Astors and the people who ran the Great Northern Railway. It stands on Coxcomb Hill overlooking the mouth of the Columbia. The tower is one hundred twenty-five feet high, and it looks like…the grandest lighthouse on the coast."

The site of the next murder.

Chapter Twenty-Two

Back in the Explorer, Skylar put through a call to SSA Crawford while Jake contacted Chief Kim using his two-way radio earbud. The Astoria Column was less than ten minutes away from the Sand Bar, using a shortcut Jake had learned years ago when he was a tour guide. The gates into the five-acre park surrounding the monument weren't locked until ten. A few sightseers might still be parked there, watching the hourly display when the spotlights against the column cycled through every shade in the rainbow.

"Contact the park service and tell the rangers to stand down," he said to Chief Kim. "Skylar and I will be at the scene in a couple of minutes, making a final approach on foot. Other officers should be ready for backup if we need assistance. Tell them not to move until you give the word."

"Do you think he's there right now?"

"If he is, I don't want him to escape."

"I'll coordinate timing with the others," Chief Kim said. "The last thing I want is a bunch of armed, excitable cops blundering around without direction."

"Copy that. I'll be in touch."

Relying on memory, Jake took a narrow backroad to a little-used gate where he parked. Completely hidden by forest on the lower slope of Coxcomb Hill, he peered through the fog to glimpse the spectacular structure with the history of the Columbia River depicted in carved, painted scenes encircling the column. He glanced toward Skylar, who leaned so far forward that her nose almost touched the windshield. "Can you see it?"

"It's mostly hidden by the trees," she said, "but impressive, nonetheless. Why was it built?"

"As a tribute to the people of the Northwest. The artwork starts after the first contact with Chinook and Clatsop tribes and extends to the opening of the railroad. My Norwegian great-great-grandpa Gunderson on my mom's side could trace his roots to the early days. Jimi Kim's family was here earlier than that. They came as fishermen from the part of Asia now known as South Korea." And he didn't need to be giving her a history lesson. Not while they were so close to catching the Shadowkeeper. "I'll turn off the light over the dashboard so nobody will notice when we get out of the Explorer."

"He's not here," she said firmly. "I saw Bradley at the Sand Bar. He vanished before I could talk to him."

"Why didn't you say anything?"

"I had to talk to Crawford, and I wasn't totally sure what was happening. He just vanished. The place was crowded, chaotic and too loud to even think. But I really think it was him. He stared at me. His eyes were like tractor beams. Then he cocked and pointed his index finger."

"Like aiming a gun?" Jake hated the threat. He wished he could take her back to the Captain's Cove where she'd be safe. "Maybe we should wait for backup."

"The two of us should be able to handle one creepy, narcissistic, psychopathic serial killer."

He knew she intended to make a joke, but he wasn't laughing. "Not funny."

"I'd rather maintain the element of surprise."

"You're right." But the Shadowkeeper had already killed twice. He didn't want Skylar to be the next trophy on his mantel. If she knew how much he feared for her safety and how much she meant to him, she'd be furious. She'd tell him in no uncertain terms how qualified she was to take care of herself with her brown belt in karate and top ranking as a sharpshooter.

"By the way," she said, "Crawford was impressed with your insight about the difference between a newspaper column and the Astoria Column."

He turned off the overhead light and eased open the car door. "Stick close to me. The entrance is on the opposite side."

"Are rangers manning the building?"

"Right now, nobody is on-site. The gift shop is closed. The front gate will be locked at ten, about a half hour from now." He led the way from the trees to their first unobstructed view of the one-hundred-twenty-five-foot-tall column. "It's almost a hundred years old. When they first erected it, the Astoria Column was supposed to rival the Eiffel Tower. Unfortunately, they didn't consider the effects of constant wind and rain against the artistic carvings. The column has undergone several repairs and renovations, including a seismic upgrade."

She paused beside him. "It's a good thing you're cute."

"Why is that?"

"In spite of your height, muscles and background in the US Marines, you're kind of a history nerd."

"Guilty." Now was probably not the best time to brag about his comic book collection. He unholstered his Beretta and crossed the mowed grass surrounding the concrete patio and walkway outside the column. In the parking lot on the opposite side of the structure, he saw only one vehicle. A sporty blue Toyota SUV. Not the silver Bimmer driven by Bradley.

"I hope we're wrong," she whispered. "I don't want to find another victim."

"From the number of times he mentioned 'columns,' it's obvious that he planned to use this place from the start. He might also have preselected his victims. We know he stalked Phoebe."

"Did he?" she asked. "Joe Rogers's car was parked outside her apartment, but we have no evidence against Bradley. And we don't know why Delilah's hair was found in Quilling's car."

They reached the edge of the concrete patio, complete with walkway and benches. Nothing seemed unusual or out of place. He led her to the entrance of a small building at the base of the column. A numerical keypad beside the door unlocked the monument. Years ago, he had the right combination to do an open-sesame, but when he tried the series of six digits, nothing happened. "I'll get the code from Chief Kim."

With her back to him and her Glock 19 held at the ready, she stayed alert and scanned the grounds. "I don't see the driver of the SUV. Is there anywhere else a tourist might go?"

"Not that I know."

Chief Kim got back to him quickly, and he punched in the code. The door opened, and overhead lights came on automatically. Inside, he glanced at the display cases, sepia photographs from the early 1900s and historical artifacts. His attention was immediately drawn to the inner area where a wrought iron spiral staircase rose to the upper observation deck that encircled the cupola.

Jake recognized the third victim. Chief Kim was supposed to reach out to her but must have been too late. This young, blond woman was one of those who blogged about true crime, and her name was…something Shakespearean, like her sister Juliet. He snapped his fingers. "Portia. Her name is Portia. A high school senior."

Portia was arranged in a pose similar to the photos he'd seen of the crime scene at Cape Meares. With her long, denim-clad legs tucked under her, she sat on the third step from the floor. A forest green bandanna blindfolded her eyes and pulled her curly hair back behind her ears. Silver duct tape covered her mouth. Zip ties fastened her wrists to the railing on the staircase.

Skylar felt for a pulse. Excited, she said, "She's still breathing."

Immediately, he alerted Chief Kim. "Call an ambulance. We found an unconscious woman inside the column."

With the ambulance on the way, he took out his Leatherman pocketknife and sliced through the zip ties. Portia's limp body fell into Skylar's arms. Together, they lowered her to the floor. When Skylar tore the tape from her mouth, they heard the welcome sound of a gasp. But her eyelids remained closed. Portia was alive but unconscious.

Cradling the young woman in her arms, Skylar gently unwound a long knitted scarf from around her throat. All the while, she spoke softly and offered reassurances. When the scarf was removed, Portia's neck showed signs of bruising.

A jolt of anger went through Jake. The Shadowkeeper had attacked this young woman, a high schooler. Why? And why had he stopped choking her before she was dead?

"Ask her who did this. Did she see him?" He was anxious to gather as much information as possible. Based on the tox screen from the ME, the Shadowkeeper used a ketamine-based anesthetic, fast-acting and available from many sources including thrill-seekers and veterinarians. A small dose shouldn't be life-threatening, but he didn't know for sure. "Ask her."

Skylar shot him an annoyed glance and continued her one-sided conversation. "Portia, can you tell me what happened? Is that your sporty blue SUV parked in front?"

Portia gave no response.

It occurred to Jake that the Shadowkeeper might still be in this building. There weren't many places to hide in the concrete tower, but he needed to check the place out. With his Beretta in hand, he circled the lower two floors, entering every closet, bathroom and office. In the small women's bathroom on the second floor, he found splatters of water and muddy footprints. The Shadowkeeper might have hidden in here with Portia, waiting for the rangers to lock the column for the night.

When he returned to the central area where Skylar was still comforting the victim, Jake looked up at the spiral staircase. From his tour guide days, he knew there were one hundred and sixty-four steps. Not a trek he wanted to make unless he had to.

As the distant squeal of the ambulance grew louder, Skylar waved him over. She held up a postcard with the column on the front and said, "I found this tucked into Portia's bra."

He read the note written on the back:

Hi Skye. Thought I'd give you a break with this one. Pretty little Portia looked lonely. Do you ever feel that way? All alone without a crew or a partner or a husband? It's your curse.

You're next, Special Agent. When you die, wait for me.
The Shadowkeeper

The threat couldn't have been more direct or personal. No way would Jake leave her alone until the Shadowkeeper was behind bars.

Chapter Twenty-Three

At 3:23 a.m., Skylar dragged her feet up the sidewalk and across the veranda at the Captain's Cove. Jake had insisted on seeing her home after a long night at the hospital with Portia's family and then at APD command central. They worked with SSA Crawford and Jimi Kim to dissect and analyze evidence while keeping tabs on the surveillance cameras placed throughout the area. *A long night.*

Jake waited patiently for her to unlock the front door to the B&B. Then he followed her inside. Before she could thank him and send him on his way, he strode across the entryway to the carved oak staircase. "I'm coming up to your room," he said.

Ever since he'd read the Shadowkeeper's threat, he'd been extra attentive. Several times, she'd caught him staring at her when he thought she didn't notice. And he'd constantly patrolled up and down the hallways, checking windows and doors. Though she'd told him that she wasn't a delicate little buttercup and could take care of herself, Skylar had to admit she liked his attentions. His gentle touches on her shoulder, back or arm—as if to remind himself she was all right—comforted her in a primal way that didn't sync with her feminist attitude but felt good, damned good.

In her bedroom at the top of the stairs, she unlocked and he entered first with his weapon drawn. Following tried-and-true police procedure, he searched and cleared the bedroom, bathroom and closet. He peered under the bed and assessed the view from the windows to be sure she wasn't in a sniper's line of fire.

"I can see the column from here," he said as he closed the curtains. "Great room."

Too tired to comment, she collapsed onto the pale blue duvet. The firm mattress supported her back and shoulders, encouraging her to grab a few hours of sleep, but as soon as she closed her eyes, her brain awakened.

Their investigation had reached a tipping point. The postcard left on Portia's body had produced a clear thumbprint that matched Bradley Rogers's print from a high school arrest. Until now, he'd been careful not to leave clues, which made her wonder if the card had been planted for them to find. If not, Bradley was the killer. They decided to back off on other suspects and persons-of-interest from twenty years ago. Though their surveillance on lighthouses in the area continued, more effort concentrated on finding Bradley and his BMW.

The quiet in her room told her Jake had completed his search, but she hadn't heard the door close. Peeking through half-opened eyes, she turned her head and saw him standing at the window. He came toward her, lifted her right foot and removed her boot, and then he did the left.

She moaned with pleasure. Relief nearly overwhelmed her. Those boots were comfortable, but she needed to wiggle her toes. "Thanks."

He sat on the bed beside her. His large hand rested on her thigh just above her kneecap. "Is there anything else you want me to help you take off? A jacket? A shirt? A bra?"

Though his tone was playful, her imagination leaped from exhaustion to lust in a single bound. She recalled the moment when she'd impulsively kissed him at Cape Disappointment. *Disappointment? Hah!* There was nothing unsatisfying about the erotic sensation of his rock-hard body pressing against hers.

Using Tucker's tugboat, he had rescued her. Jake had sensed her need to cross the Columbia without a bridge, and he made it happen. He was both a proactive alpha and a sensitive beta. His hand inched higher on her thigh, and she brushed it away before she succumbed to his suggestion, threw away her self-control and begged him to remove every stitch of her clothing.

"Stop," she said in an unconvincing tone.

"In case you're wondering, I'm spending the night in your room."

He didn't ask her permission, and she liked his assertiveness whether she agreed to his plan or not. Acting as her protector made logical sense because the Shadowkeeper had made direct threats against her and preferred to act at night.

Still, she objected. "I don't need a bodyguard."

"We'll see about that." He kicked off his own boots, stood and stretched with his arms over his head. His knuckles brushed the ceiling. From his backpack, he took out a few pieces of electronic equipment that he placed on the table beside his Beretta. "I'm going to scan the room for hidden cameras and bugs. The Shadowkeeper likes stalking, and I want to make sure he's not spying on you."

"Good thinking."

"I have my moments."

She rolled onto her side and propped her chin on her hand to watch him as he swept the bug detector in logical places. He reached high to the crown molding near the ceiling and ducked low to poke beneath the dresser. For a big man, he moved gracefully. His long legs and arms were proportional to his torso and muscular shoulders.

To distract herself from ogling him, she said, "Seems to me that the Shadowkeeper is dissembling, starting with the obvious fact that he didn't kill Portia."

"When she's conscious and able to talk, she might be able to give us an identification."

"I hope so."

He'd told Skylar about the signs of someone hiding in the bathroom at the column, which was a risk. If he'd kept Portia there, he would have needed to keep her drugged for at least three hours. Her level of intoxication would be difficult to balance without triggering an overdose.

Jake must have been thinking along the same lines, because he asked, "Have you heard anything more about her condition?"

"Her parents are with her. She's expected to have a full recovery, but the doctors won't let us question her until morning."

"In another sign of his increasing carelessness," Jake said, "he left a fingerprint."

"Not only the print, but he handed over a sample of his handwriting. His other communications came through untraceable phones and computer links. Even his first note to Phoebe was printed, not written."

"He was equally cautious at the other crime scenes. Our forensic experts haven't turned up enough evidence to identify him. No fibers, hairs or bloodstains."

"On the other hand," she said, "if Bradley is the Shadowkeeper, he didn't bother to hide his credit card in the name of J. B. Knox when he registered at the Pierpoint."

"A sign of inexperience." He shrugged. "Even an intelligent sociopath makes mistakes."

"The FBI cybercrime team in Portland have been tracking his purchases. He hasn't used the card since he checked into the hotel."

"He almost made physical contact with you at the Sand Bar. But then he ran away."

She appreciated this type of analytical discussion almost as much as she enjoyed the opportunity to observe Jake in action. He had turned out to be a great partner when it came to investigating, and she wondered if they'd be compatible in other areas.

"These changes have significance," she said, "but I don't know what it means."

"He's playing a game, and he's getting bored. Murder doesn't give him as much of a thrill as he expected. Like a poker player, he makes the game more interesting and more important by raising the stakes." He replaced his tools in his backpack and approached her bed. "By naming you as his next victim, he escalates to a different level."

"A direct challenge."

"Like a duel." His laser-blue eyes made fiery contact with hers, and they exchanged an unspoken but eloquent message. They were playing for high stakes, indeed. He illustrated by holding out his hand toward her. Resting on his palm were two tiny listening devices that actually did resemble insects. "Gifts from the Shadowkeeper. Should I crush them or keep them?"

She chose another option. "Flush them."

After a quick detour to the bathroom, he returned to her bed and stretched out beside her. His body radiated a pleasant warmth, and she caught a whiff of the outdoorsy scent she'd come to associate with him. "You'll be glad to know that I didn't locate any teeny-tiny cameras."

"Oh, good." She turned toward him. "Then nobody will be able to see me do this."

She glided into his horizontal embrace, tilting her head to snuggle into the curve of his throat. Blazing a trail, she kissed from the dimple on his chin to his jaw and ultimately to his ear where she caught his lobe in her teeth and gently tugged.

He inhaled a ragged breath. "I like that."

She pulled back and gazed into his handsome, chiseled face. "You mentioned something about taking off clothes."

He didn't need a second invitation to unbutton her blouse

that had started the day looking fresh and professional. Not anymore. Her clothing was a rumpled mess.

Before he unfastened her bra, she insisted on taking her turn. She unzipped and unbuttoned him. After a slightly frenzied moment, they were both nude from the waist up.

Though she'd imagined being intimate with him, she hadn't planned for what might happen. Or what it meant. Or what sort of relationship they might have. An FBI special agent based in Portland and a police detective from Astoria could certainly be friends. More than that was problematic.

Right now, she'd settle for friends with benefits. And enjoy the ride.

His arm encircled her and pulled her close, matching their naked flesh together and making them as one. Hearts beating in unison. Her breasts rubbed against his chest, and the friction sparked a nascent flame that became a wildfire when she threw her leg over his thighs and wriggled the softest part of her body against the hardest of his.

Passion churned through her and exploded in an incredible kiss. The pressure of their lips alternated between hard and soft, demanding and yielding. His tongue thrust into her mouth and engaged with hers. Teasing. Tasting.

Though she wasn't sexually inexperienced, she'd never felt anything like this before. Amazing sensations quivered across the surface of her skin, and she abandoned herself to these feelings Jake created in her. Like the karate moves called katas that she'd practiced until they were rooted in her memory, she danced in harmony with him. He seemed to anticipate her every pose, and she did the same for him.

Not that they were totally synchronized. There were delightful surprises. She wasn't sure how they got out of their pants and between the sheets but knew their moves didn't follow an elegant choreography. Their passion was directed by feral need and instinct.

Cocooned under the pale blue duvet with the bedside lamp

turned low, she gazed into his eyes. Her fingers traced the structure of his face, then slid down to his shoulders and lower. She traced the line of hair from his chest to his groin.

He fondled her breasts, flicking his thumb across her taut nipple and sending shock waves deep into her body.

Between spasms of pleasure, she gasped a single word. "Condom."

He replied, "Yes."

When he rolled away from her to pick his jeans off the floor and find his wallet, she felt bereft, which was ridiculous. She'd only known him for a few days, not long enough for him to become an integral part of her. And yet, she couldn't imagine being apart. A dangerous thought for a woman who had just attained her goal of becoming a special agent.

When he returned to her, she clung tightly to him. "I missed you," she whispered.

"Me, too."

He showed her how much her absence had affected him with an all-consuming kiss. An earthquake so powerful that she felt the aftershocks all the way down to her toes. She had truly come undone. At the same time, she knew exactly what she wanted. When he sheathed himself and penetrated her with hard, strong thrusts, she was driven to climax, again and again and…again. And then…she was complete. Fulfilled. Satisfied.

Lying beside him, looking up at the anchor-patterned wallpaper and the decorative fisherman's net draped in the corner by the window, she smiled. Not just with her lips but with her whole body. Oh yes, this was going to happen again. As soon as possible. Maybe in the morning.

"Tomorrow," she said.

"Yes."

"I really need to take a shower. At least run a comb through my hair or brush my teeth." She couldn't believe she'd let him see her like this. "Actually, I clean up well."

He laced his fingers with hers. "You're perfect."
"But I—"
"Perfect," he said.
She knew it wasn't true. Still, nice to hear.

Chapter Twenty-Four

The next morning at half past seven, Jake wakened to a dull sunrise blanketed in fog. After he stumbled from the bed to the window and opened the curtain, he stood staring and wondering why the weather didn't reflect the glow that radiated from his chest and warmed his entire body.

When he looked at Skylar, still in bed, he saw a reflection of that light in her beautiful smile. For a moment, the clouds outside the window parted, and a ray of sunshine lit the skies. Last night, he'd been more than a friend, more than a bodyguard. He'd taken their partnership to a different level that surprised him and yet felt inevitable.

He was anxious to get started on the day. They needed to find the Shadowkeeper, to end these murders and bring him to justice. Then Jake could move forward to the more important issue of convincing Skylar to fall in love with him.

"Before you start making plans," she said as she rose from the bed, naked and unembarrassed, "you should know that I'm not leaving this room until I wash my hair and take a shower."

"I'll join you."

"Fine by me."

They stood together under steaming jets of water. They kissed, fondled and soaped each other, but there couldn't be a final consummation because he had no more condoms. Picking up a six-pack or a twelve-pack or an entire crate would be the first priority on his to-do list.

When they got to the police station, he planned to change into the fresh clothes he kept in his locker, but Skylar dressed now, selecting another conservative suit and a rose-colored shirt.

He asked, "Do you always wear suits?"

"It's my work uniform. Looks neat, and the jacket is long enough to cover my holster." She scrunched her dark auburn hair to let it air-dry in wavy curls. "Crawford says I dress like a recruitment poster for women in the FBI. Actually, his wife says that. Crawford doesn't notice what I wear."

"Today, I want you to add a bulletproof vest." Thus far, the Shadowkeeper hadn't used a gun, but there was always a first time.

"Fine. I have lightweight flexible body armor that's custom fitted. The color is camo green. Matches my eyes. Very fashionable."

"Is it weird that I'm getting turned on?"

She grinned and lowered her voice to a breathy, sexy level. "The vest has a sheath for my Ka-Bar knife. And extra magazines for my Glock 19."

He cupped his hands over his ears, pretending he couldn't hear. "Stop."

"And then, of course, I have my ankle holster, a pocket switchblade and a razor-edged hairclip for when I fasten my ponytail."

In his opinion, she still needed his protection to watch her six and make sure the Shadowkeeper didn't sneak up behind her. "Let's go."

When they checked in at APD for a briefing from Chief Kim about what happened last night after Portia was rescued, they scarfed down coffee, apple juice, a couple of doughnuts and egg rolls with kimchi and bacon. Last night, the surveillance teams discovered nothing. The officers who staked out suspects' homes saw zero activity. The biggest event was when Officer Dot's nine-year-old daughter got a hole-in-one at the miniature golf course. The Shadowkeeper was AWOL.

Crawford and Jimi Kim showed up with more food and no further leads. The next step for Jake and Skylar would be visiting the hospital to interview Portia. After that, they'd retrace their steps, hoping to find a new direction to search for Bradley.

At 10:45, they heard back from the doctor at Columbia Memorial, a small facility with a heliport and a level-four trauma center. Portia was wide awake and anxious to talk to them. Finally, they might get a definite identification of Bradley as the Shadowkeeper.

On the short drive to the hospital, Jake laid out a strategy. "We need to split up. One of us talks to Portia. The other deals with her parents and friends."

"I'll take Portia," Skylar said. "I'm not good with family."

"Doesn't the FBI train you for interpersonal stuff?"

"We've got classes on interrogation, hostage negotiation, suicide prevention and active shooter situations. Not so much on dealing with an angry parent or pushy friend."

"It's not my favorite thing, either." He shrugged. "Flip a coin. Heads I talk to Portia."

He won the toss. When they got to the hospital, they found her room occupied by a rotating group of parents, sister and friends, including a young man who called himself her fiancé over her sister's objection. Grumbling, Skylar took charge, herding Portia's people into the waiting area with all the warmhearted friendliness of an FBI-trained hostage negotiator.

Jake saw Portia tucked into a bed in a private ICU room, the petite blonde looking vulnerable, afraid and very young. Her vitals were monitored while saline solution dripped into her bloodstream through an IV and a cannula delivered oxygen to her nostrils. Her complexion had paled beneath her tan.

She'd covered the dark circles under her eyes with concealer but had done nothing to hide the purplish bruises around her throat and ligature marks on her wrists.

In a hoarse voice, she thanked him for clearing the room. "My parents are so mad. They've told me a million times not to go off by myself. I was stupid, stupid, stupid."

"You made a mistake," he said. "Doesn't mean you're a moron or a failure. Everyone—your family and friends and the people who listen to your podcast—will eventually forget to be angry and will celebrate the fact that you're still alive."

"Thanks, Jake."

"Tell me why you went to the column."

She inhaled a deep breath and the story spilled out. She'd started getting text messages on her phone from someone who said they knew the Shadowkeeper and would give her an exclusive interview. Unfortunately, she couldn't show him the texts because her phone was missing. "He must have taken it."

"What happened when you got there?"

Again, she gave a long-winded explanation which essentially told him that she'd been following directions in the texts that led her to the bathroom on the second floor near the offices which was, apparently, where he held her after the building closed to the public. "At the upstairs bathroom, I pushed the door and went inside. And then..." She went silent.

He prodded. "Did you see him?"

She touched her neck and winced. "I felt a pinprick, like getting stung by a bee. Then I passed out. I don't remember anything else until you and Skylar were standing over me."

Though he reassured her and told her she was brave and everything would be all right, there was nothing left to say. Her experience with the Shadowkeeper hadn't produced new evidence.

"One more thing," she said. "In the back of my mind, I keep hearing a man's voice saying the curse. You know the one. 'Hear me, o goddesses. West, East, North, South.'"

"Did he change the words?"

"I don't know. It was like he was singing. Like a lullaby."

Before he allowed her family and friends back into her room, he reminded them that they should never blame the victim. Portia escaped with her life, and no serious physical damage was done. They should be grateful. And supportive. Then, he fled with Skylar.

On the way to Rogers's house, he reported Portia's story to her. "He used much the same model that worked with Phoebe, another reporter who was so hungry for a story that she disregarded her own safety."

"But Portia's assault is different," she said. "He attacked her during the day when there might have been witnesses. Might be a sign that he's becoming overconfident. And he didn't kill her. If you hadn't figured out that the column would be the next site, Portia would have been tied up all night and discovered in the morning when people came to work."

"According to the doctor, she had ketamine in her system, but she was never in real danger. It wasn't a lethal dose."

She shook her head. "Why was he singing the curse to her? It's a gruesome verse about scratching out eyes and muzzling his mouth. I think he's coming unglued."

Jake parked in the driveway behind Rogers's black sedan, making it impossible for him to leave. Together, he and Skylar walked to the front of the pleasant yellow house with white trim. Before he could knock, Rogers opened the door.

Scowling, he said, "This has got to stop, Armstrong."

"I don't know what the hell you're talking about."

"Harassment," he said. "Okay, maybe I wasn't completely forthcoming, but you people have to stop pestering me. There were cops watching my house all night. And somebody came by this morning and demanded a hair sample from Delilah, as if there are dozens of women with magenta hair running around town."

"May we come in?" Skylar asked.

He stepped aside and gestured for them to sit in the living room on the plaid sofa while he took the overstuffed chair facing the television. "Tell me why you need to test Delilah's hair."

"You admitted that you weren't forthcoming," Skylar said. "Please explain."

"Okay, I get it." He leaned back in his chair and lowered his heavy eyebrows in a squint. "If I tell you something, you'll tell me. *Quid pro quo.* Am I right?"

Without agreeing to anything, she said, "Let's start with why your black sedan was seen near Phoebe's apartment. Your excuse was something about stopping by to talk to her about newspaper business."

"Are you calling me a stalker?"

"If it wasn't you in the car, then who?"

His fists clenched, and he cursed. Jake could see that Rogers was barely holding himself together. "Can we move on? Please."

"Who was driving your car?" She continued, "Was it your son?"

Losing energy, his shoulders hunched. He rested his elbows on his knees and splayed his fingers, gesturing nervously. "I was trying to protect him. I haven't always been a good dad. When I found out he'd been taking my car, it seemed like a harmless little lie."

This conclusion had crossed Jake's mind, but he hadn't given it serious consideration. Not until now. That harmless lie had kept them from finding the Shadowkeeper. "You lied about your car to protect Bradley."

"I owe it to him for all the years I couldn't be with him. Not that it was my choice to be an absent father. I didn't want the divorce and tried to fight his mother's move to Houston." He shook his head as if he could dislodge memories. "She was a beautiful woman. Still is. Didn't take her long to find a new husband in Texas."

"Knox," Skylar said. "The wealthy rancher. Did he abuse your son?"

For a moment, Rogers looked shocked. "How dare you—"

"Did he?"

"I never knew for sure. Didn't want to know. When Bradley came back to Astoria to attend school for part of the year, he had bruises. But he told me it was because he lived the outdoor life on the ranch. Riding horses and hiking and hunting. Damn, I hated that he was hunting. And he spouted a bunch of macho baloney about how a 'real' man is tough, aggressive and doesn't take sass. Especially not from womenfolk."

"How long has your son been back in town?" she asked.

With a groan, Rogers climbed out of his chair, too uncomfortable to sit, and paced toward the dining room. He didn't need to state the obvious. Bradley had been here before Phoebe's murder because he took his father's car to spy on her.

Jake asked, "Did Bradley meet Phoebe when he was in Houston?"

"Knew her and didn't like her. She dumped him." He held up his hand to stop their line of questioning. "*Quid pro quo.* Before I say anything else, there's something I want to know."

Jake nodded.

"It's about Delilah," Rogers said. "Why are you so concerned about her hair?"

"Magenta hairs were found in a car that crossed the bridge to Cape Disappointment on the night when Lucille was murdered."

"Whose car?"

"It belonged to another suspect." Jake worked the math in his head. Quilling and Bradley were roughly the same age. They might have been in high school at the same time. By framing him, Bradley could have been hitting two birds with one stone, implicating Delilah and Quilling at the same time. "Do you know Alan Quilling?"

"Nice kid. He and Bradley were friends."

Or enemies. "Someone might have deliberately placed Delilah's hairs in Quilling's car, then used his vehicle to cross the bridge."

Rogers sank into a chair at the dining room table and fell forward, dropping his head into his arms. "I don't want to believe any of this. My son isn't a murderer."

Jake's phone vibrated in his pocket. The caller ID showed Pyro Pierce. When Jake answered, his former science teacher talked fast. "Have you seen Dagmar?"

"What's wrong?"

"She said she was going to investigate. Now I can't get ahold of her."

Jake had a bad feeling about where his cousin might be. Like mother, like daughter.

Chapter Twenty-Five

Skylar stepped onto the porch behind Jake. The fog had thickened. She could barely see the house across the street.

Jake switched his phone call to Speaker so she could hear the worry in Pierce's voice when he talked about Dagmar trying to find the Shadowkeeper. She hadn't said where she was headed but promised to stay in touch. "That was two hours ago," Pierce said. "She's not answering calls or texts."

"I'll help you find her," Jake promised.

When he disconnected the call, his indecision and tension were evident. He didn't want to leave Skylar unguarded but needed to track down his cousin and make sure she hadn't made an impulsive, risky move.

"Go," she said. "Find Dagmar."

"You and I need to stay together."

"I'm not letting Rogers off the hook. He still has questions to answer." Like telling them where to find Bradley. "I'll call Crawford and have him join me. He's at APD, ten minutes away from here."

He slipped his arm around her waist, pulled her close and planted a firm kiss on her mouth. "I'll be back."

She watched him disappear behind a curtain of fog when he went to his car. Back in the house, she stalked directly toward Rogers who sat stiffly at the dining room table. He'd used the few minutes of privacy to pull himself together. No more talk of *quid pro quo*. He'd made his decision. "I want my attorney."

"You have every right to contact your lawyer. I have only one question." She paused for emphasis. "Where is he?"

"I don't know."

She believed him. There was no point in badgering Rogers. All she could do was sit here at the dining room table and wait, figuring that sooner or later Bradley would contact his father again.

A heavy silence spread across the room and settled over them. Minutes ticked slowly by. Then, the back door slammed. The sound of cowboy boots thudded across the kitchen tiles, and Bradley appeared in the doorway to the dining room. He held a SIG Sauer 9mm Luger in his hand. "Nice to finally meet you, Special Agent Gambel. I think I'll call you Skylar. Or Sky. Or Honeybunch. Would you like that, Special Agent Honeybunch?"

She rose from her chair and took a long step to her left to put herself in a position where the dining room table wouldn't be in her way. Skylar had no intention of making this a shootout, even though she was probably faster and more accurate with a firearm, but she wanted to take him alive, which meant hand-to-hand combat. Instantly, she was ready. A warrior. Her mindset shifted. Her body went on high alert, prepared for battle by years and years of karate training.

"I'm curious." She reached into her pocket and activated the recording function. "Why did you wait for Jake to leave before making your presence known?"

"Have you seen the size of that guy? He's Sasquatch."

But I'm more vicious, little old me. She took a jab at his oversize ego. "Poor Bradley, you were scared."

"I was smart," he said with a sneer. "I tricked you and your boss and everybody in the Astoria Police Department. Losers, all of them."

In her mind, she measured the distance she needed to

launch a flying kick at his gun hand. Her martial arts training made her fast, powerful and accurate. Once the gun was out of the way, she could easily take him down.

"This is my fault," Rogers said. He pushed back his chair and stood, planting himself between Skylar and Bradley, getting in the way of her plan. "I need to tell you that I'm sorry, son."

"Yeah, great. Who cares?"

"The first time the Lightkeeper killer came around, twenty years ago, and threatened us, I should have gone with you and your mother to Texas. But I chose to stay here and report on the story. I put my career above my family."

"Your career?" Bradley scoffed. "You're a small-time editor of a small-town newspaper. Don't pretend you're Rupert Murdoch."

"I lost you both," Rogers said. "You and your mom."

"Mom already had one foot out the door. You could never give her what she wanted. You'd never be as rich as Knox. Or the new husband—the French guy who took her to Paris."

"Did that cowboy hurt you? Were you abused?"

"Knox taught me how to be a man. How to take what I wanted and move on. We hunted. He taught me how to kill without regret. He was good for me."

He stuck out his scrawny chest. He was taller than Skylar had expected, probably six feet two inches in his cowboy boots. But he was neither imposing nor intimidating. His wild, curly black hair was similar to his father's. His dark eyes, nearly ebony, stared at her, unblinking like a snake. Though not the type of man who stood out in a crowd, he had the uncanny ability to capture and hold her attention.

He pressed the barrel of his SIG into his father's chest. "Take a seat, Dad. This isn't your show. Today is about me and Skylar. She's going to do everything I say, and so are you."

He held up his phone. The screen showed a picture of Dagmar from the waist up. She appeared to be sitting on the floor and leaning against a dark wall. Her wrists were fastened together with zip ties. A silver square of duct tape covered her mouth. Her eyes were closed.

"You drugged her." Skylar braced herself for action. "Tell me where she is."

"Settle down, Special Agent Honeybunch." Bradley tucked the phone into his pocket and pointed to the dining room chair. "Sit down, Dad. I'm not going to ask again."

His father obeyed. Before he could object, Bradley plunged a hypodermic needle into the back of his neck. "Go to sleep, old man. When you wake up, everybody is going to know that your son is a genius serial killer who outwitted the dumb cops and got away with murder. Damn right, it's your fault. They're going to blame you for being a bad father."

While he watched his father drift into unconsciousness, he spoke to Skylar. "If you want to see Dagmar alive again, you'll do exactly as I say."

"What if I don't?"

"In about an hour, it'll be high tide. Dagmar could be underwater. Do you want to take that risk? Isn't it your job to offer your own sweet FBI body as a substitute hostage?"

She didn't have much choice. If she delayed or went too slowly, Dagmar might suffer. Bradley might have rigged something to drown her at high tide. "I'll do what you want," she said. "Take me to her."

"Disarm yourself. The Glock and the piece in your ankle holster. Any knives or Tasers or sprays. Oh yes, and your phone. Can't have you calling your boyfriend."

She stacked her weapons on the table. When she pulled the lethal Ka-Bar knife from her vest, he whistled his appreciation. "By the way, if you fail to follow my instructions, you'll be punished. I need for you to be able to walk, so I won't injure your legs. I'll start with a bullet in your left hand."

He sounded like he'd enjoy hurting her. She asked, "Where are we going?"

"Venture a guess?"

"No more games," she said. "Just tell me."

"You're tired of losing to me." He tossed several zip ties onto the table. "Fasten his arms and ankles to the chair. Then slap duct tape over his mouth. By the way, we're going someplace cheesy."

Her first thought was Tillamook, where the world-famous cheese factory and creamery were located. She turned off the recording function on her phone and placed it on the table. "Someplace cheesy?"

"Leave the phone here," he said. "I don't want to be tracked by some GPS device."

When she'd finished securing Rogers to the chair, Bradley tossed her a set of car keys. "You'll drive Dad's car. I'll be in the passenger seat with my SIG."

Standing at the dining room table, she analyzed the situation. Bradley had the upper hand because he knew where Dagmar was and she didn't. He'd taken away her most effective weapons, but she'd managed to keep her switchblade pocketknife and was still wearing her bulletproof vest. Most important, she'd left her phone with the recorded conversation. When Jake came looking for her, he'd have a starting place. "I'm ready," she said with a confidence she didn't truly feel.

"You know," he said, "Dagmar is obsessed with her mother's murder. I only needed one text message to lure her to me."

Much as she hated to acknowledge his cleverness, she asked, "What was the text?"

"'Hear me, o goddesses. Meet me at the marina. The Shadowkeeper.'" He laughed. "She couldn't stay away."

Jake would hear the phone recording. She had to believe he'd find them.

Chapter Twenty-Six

When Jake couldn't reach Skylar by phone, he rushed back to Rogers's house with Pierce. The black sedan was gone. So was Skylar. They found Rogers in the dining room.

Pierce removed the duct tape from Rogers's mouth and used Skylar's Ka-Bar knife to cut the zip ties. When Rogers toppled forward, still unconscious, Pierce caught him. "We need to take care of this guy."

Using his phone, Jake contacted Chief Kim at APD and told her to send an ambulance and an officer to accompany Rogers to the hospital. Then he played the recording on Skylar's phone, listening for clues. Bradley told Skylar she'd need to walk a distance. He never actually described the threat to Dagmar, but Skylar said she looked drugged.

Worried, Pierce tried to make sense of what they'd heard. "The location is cheesy. That points to Tillamook."

"Too obvious?"

"Occam's razor," said the science teacher. "The most obvious solution is usually correct. We have to accept that Dagmar is in imminent danger of drowning at high tide. We have to find her."

"We'll find both of them." Regarding the weapons on the table, Jake cringed. "Skylar is totally disarmed. I never should have left her alone."

"All for the best, Sasquatch. Bradley had to find Skylar

so he could use Dagmar as a hostage. Where do we go next? The cheese factory?"

"The marina. *Jolly Rogers* is a boat the editor keeps there. Bradley had access to his father's car, so it stands to reason that he also has keys to the boat."

Pierce finished the train of thought. "He can use the boat to go to Tillamook."

Jake remembered the night they followed Rogers to the marina. He must have been looking for Bradley. Didn't tell them because he was still protecting his son. "We start there."

They handed off Rogers to the paramedics in the ambulance and instructed the officer accompanying him to ask questions about Skylar and Dagmar as soon as he was awake.

Outside, heavy fog obscured the trees and the rusted swing set. Though Jake knew the temperature was in the sixties, a damp cold penetrated his windbreaker and whistled down his spine. His fear expanded exponentially, bigger than when he engaged in firefights, faced IEDs and fought armed combatants in the marine corps. Skylar was being manipulated by a serial killer who wished her dead.

I can't lose her. In a few short days, she'd become everything to him.

Behind the steering wheel of his Explorer, he went in Reverse. Rogers's black sedan was no longer in the driveway. "Cheesy Tillamook. How can we narrow down the location?"

"Think outside the box," Pierce said. "There's Tillamook the town and the river and Tillamook Bay on the coast."

"And an Indigenous Salish tribe," he said. "What else?"

Think. Think. Think.

Together, they said, "Terrible Tilly. A lighthouse."

Jake knew exactly what to do. He hit a speed-dial number on his phone.

SKYLAR HUDDLED ON the double bed in the belowdecks cabin of the *Jolly Rogers*. Dagmar sprawled beside her—still out cold but showing signs of coming around. Skylar had removed the duct tape from her mouth, making it easier to breathe, and it was encouraging to hear Dagmar cough.

The interior of the old trawler needed patching and painting, but the only way Dagmar could have drowned in here was if a torpedo had blasted through the hull.

Bradley led her to believe Dagmar was trapped in a cave or some other enclosure where high tide would put her under water. He'd lied, which shouldn't have come as a huge surprise. The man was, after all, a serial killer with a badly skewed moral compass. To him, a lie was nothing.

While he piloted the boat from the helm, she looked for ways she could take advantage in hand-to-hand combat. The small, belowdecks area favored the larger, heavier opponent—all he needed to do was pin her to the mattress, and she'd be helpless. Bradley had the edge unless she could get him outside where she had room to maneuver. When they arrived at their destination, she had the additional benefit of having her pocket switchblade which she would use to cut the zip ties fastening her wrists when the time was right. The element of surprise could not be overestimated.

She heard the rumble of the twin engines change rhythm and felt the boat slowing. It hadn't been a long ride from Astoria. Where were they?

Bradley swaggered into the cabin and leaned over Dagmar. "I see you took off the gag."

"She was choking." Ironic, since that might be his plan for her.

"Just as well. I'd like for her to be awake enough to walk up the path to the lighthouse. Between the two of us, we can guide her, but it'll be easier if she's mobile."

"Where are we?"

"Terrible Tilly. The most famous lighthouse on the Oregon coast."

She shrugged. "If you say so."

"I keep forgetting that you're not from this area." He actually smiled, and his knife-edge features softened. His enthusiasm about the next phase in his plan apparently gave him pleasure. "We've landed on a solitary rock about a mile offshore from the Tillamook River. It's isolated. And small with a surface slightly more than an acre. Over the constant roar of the wind and pounding surf, you can hear the cries of gulls and cormorants and sea lions."

"You like this place," she said.

"Terrible Tilly is always where I wanted the Oregon part of my story to end. Standing on an iconic symbol of loneliness, facing all the pressures nature could generate and coming out on top, unshakeable and dominant. It suits you to be here with me. Your last sight will be the harsh Pacific crashing through the fog, dragging you to your doom."

"What about Dagmar?"

"I don't really care about her. You're the one I want. The high-achieving FBI special agent. I always knew there would be three women. Phoebe the bitch would be the first to go as payback for her hubris—she used men, then threw them away. Not me, though. Lucille the songbird was less evil but equally blind, disregarding my advances, giggling and blabbing in that annoying Texas twang. Portia didn't fit. She was too young. But you, Special Agent Honeybunch, are the epitome of a woman who thinks she's better than everybody else."

Like your mother? "If you didn't care for the Texas accent, why did you stay there so long? Your dad would have welcomed you home."

"I don't want to be the son of a loser," Bradley said. "I have my own pride. My own accomplishments. Mom never understood. When she took off with Frenchie to live in Paris, I knew it was time for me to show her what I could do."

Skylar saw a classic pattern playing out. Bradley rejected his father for not living up to some impossible masculine ideal. And he felt abandoned by his mother who found one wealthy mate after another and dragged her son along behind her. Without caring for his needs. Without consulting him. *Without getting him into therapy.* Her second husband after Rogers was Knox, an abuser. Her marriage to the Parisian might have been the trigger for Bradley to take on the role of the Lightkeeper—a serial killer he blamed for destroying his family twenty years ago.

Somehow, Skylar had gotten caught up in his fantasies. Just at the moment when she discovered something special with Jake. Skylar wasn't going to give up. Not yet.

Bradley reached around her and shook Dagmar by the shoulder. "Wake up, you wicked witch. You need to come with me. Now."

JAKE MIGHT HAVE contacted the US Coast Guard unit based in Astoria. Or he could have arranged a ride to Terrible Tilly with the harbor patrol. The best course would be to take a helicopter. Landing a helo on that desolate rock would be safer than approaching by sea, and he got Chief Kim working on it. Even with a sanction from SSA Crawford of the FBI, the red tape would slow him down. He and Pierce needed to move fast, and Jake knew another way: Tucker's Tug Tours.

They boarded the brightly painted tugboat in Astoria and chugged south to the solid basalt rock a mile offshore—the home of the Terrible Tilly lighthouse. The location had never been very successful. The weather was too severe. In high tides and storms, waves crashed against the west-facing side and splashed plumes of white surf higher than the beam that shone across the sea from the two-story tower atop a larger house. Ferocious winds threw heavy stones against the tower. Workmen and lightkeepers had perished on the one-acre rock. And there were supposed to be ghosts. From the tours he'd led, Jake knew the history.

After Tilly lost functionality as a lighthouse, it sold as private property. From what Jake heard, Tilly was for sale again with an asking price in the millions.

He and Pierce clung to the railing at the front of the tugboat, watching for the rock to come into view through the fog.

"When this is over," Pierce said, "I'm going to ask Dagmar to marry me."

"Funny," Jake said. "I was thinking much the same thing. Not about Dagmar. But...you know what I'm saying."

"You've only known Skylar a few days."

"It's long enough."

He'd never been in love before. Not like this. He knew Skylar wasn't perfect. Her beautiful face and athletic body counted as a plus, but he'd heard people call her bossy or brusque. Others didn't like her sense of humor. And her thing with bridges needed to be faced and dealt with. But she was perfect for him.

The fog thinned for a moment, and he saw Tilly. He gave the signal to Tucker who was at the helm, and the old man honked the spunky foghorn. Once. Twice.

We're coming, Skylar. Hang on.

HER HEAD TURNED when she heard the sound of the horn. She'd heard that blast before when Two-Toes Tucker's tugboat ferried her across the Columbia. Jake was on his way!

"Keep moving," Bradley snarled. "This isn't a sightseeing tour."

Leading the way, she climbed the rocky stairs chiseled from the natural basalt while he helped Dagmar. Skylar had already taken advantage of her position where Bradley couldn't see what she was doing with her hands. She'd maneuvered the pocket switchblade out of her pocket and cut through the zip ties, freeing her hands. Then she'd hidden the knife in the sleeve of her jacket. She wouldn't try an attack until she was certain that Dagmar was safe.

Still feeling the effects of the drug, Dagmar appeared to be woozy and weak, barely to climb.

Finally, they entered the large house below the tower. Faint glimmers of light spilled through the boarded-up windows. The filth and the stench of guano from nesting seabirds nearly overcame her.

Bradley released his hold on Dagmar, and she stood in the semidarkness, weaving and unsteady on her feet. He gestured with his gun. "That way. Take the stairs. We're going to the roof."

"Dagmar can stay here," Skylar said. "It's me you want."

But Dagmar lurched toward the stairs. "Stinks in here."

Skylar inserted herself between Bradley and Dagmar, still not revealing that she'd escaped the bonds of her zip ties. She hadn't really been able to see the rooftop but hoped there would be enough room to make her move. First, she needed to disarm Bradley. Then they could square off and fight. Her years of karate training and the recent addition of Krav Maga made her a worthy opponent. Was it enough to handle Bradley?

Gulping down breaths of the relative freshness of the outdoors gave her hope. The rooftop below the tower provided a wide, flat surface nearly the size of a football field. Skylar believed she could work with this, especially when she saw the tugboat bobbing in the waves at the foot of the rock.

Bradley stepped up beside her. "They'll never get up here," he said. "I put in a lot of work making a place for my boat to dock. Tilly isn't accessible."

But as they watched, Jake peeled off his windbreaker, zipped his vest, climbed off the tugboat and dropped into the water. She took an involuntary step forward, terrified for him. That water had to be freezing cold.

Dagmar had broken away from them. She took a position, leaning against the tower and raising her wrists, still bound together, toward the heavens. In a husky voice, she shouted, "'Hear me, o goddesses, West, East, North, South...'"

Bradley gaped. "Does she think she can curse me?"

Skylar took advantage of his momentary distraction to lash out with her switchblade. She stabbed at his gun hand, slicing the sleeve of his jacket. He dropped the weapon.

Dagmar continued. "'Scratch out his eyes. Muzzle his mouth.'"

Skylar made a dive for the SIG, but Bradley managed to kick it out of reach. Her well-trained body assumed a lethal pose with her weight balanced and her arms in position to strike. Instead of slashing with her open palm, she unleashed a fury of kicks. Bradley was driven back, nearly to the edge of the roof.

"'Bind his arms,'" Dagmar wailed. "'Heed not his plea.'"

Looking over the edge, Skylar saw Jake charging up the stairs. There was another man behind him. Surely not Two-Toes.

Bradley had darted back toward the gun. She caught up to him just in time, throwing him off balance. He fell onto his back. Glared up at her with pure hatred in his eyes.

Dagmar finished her verse. "'Death to the Keeper. So mote it be.'"

Skylar picked up the gun and aimed at Bradley. "Stay down. I'll shoot your left hand first."

She didn't want to kill him. Yes, he was a serial murderer who had taken the promising lives of two young women. On some level, she felt sorry for him. Mostly, she thought, he'd make an outstanding subject for the psychologists to study. And wouldn't he love all those hours of talking about himself.

Dripping wet, Jake staggered onto the rooftop. He straightened his posture as he walked toward her. "I see you've got everything under control."

"Was there ever any doubt?" She heard the *thwap-thwap*

of helicopter blades. "I'm so glad we're not going to have to walk down those stairs."

The other man stumbled onto the roof and went to Dagmar. Pierce embraced her and kissed her. Over the rumble of the aircraft, he yelled, "Marry me, Dagmar."

"Yes." She looped her arms around him.

"Show off," Jake said. He took a pair of soggy handcuffs from his vest pocket and ordered Bradley to roll onto his stomach. When he was cuffed, he returned to Skylar's side.

She lowered the gun and embraced him, even though the helicopter crew was watching. She'd shocked herself. Could be a consequence of nearly being killed. It was unlike her to make a public display of affection.

Even more unusual, she said, "I love you, Jake Armstrong."

"And I love you."

She beamed. "I know."

"In approximately one year, you'll marry me," he said. "During the annual Great Columbia Crossing when the Astoria-Meglar Bridge is open to the public. At the peak, we will exchange vows."

"And live happily ever after."

She could hardly wait.

* * * * *

HER CAMERON DEFENDER

BETH CORNELISON

For Jeffery and Kelly as they begin their
Happily Ever After. Much love to you both!

Prologue

"I should be dead by now. Dinna know why I'm not."

Eric Harkney winced internally at the older woman's blunt comment. Other members of the Cameron family gathered around the long, crowded table also groaned or chuckled at their grandmother's proclamation.

"Nanna, don't say that!" Isla Cameron cried in dismay. "You'll jinx yourself, and we want you here for years to come."

Flora Cameron, or Nanna as she was called by Camerons young and old, lifted her chin to a jaunty angle. "Dinna fash, *m'eudail*. I've no mind to go anywhere. I'm that glad to be here with so many of my kin celebrating ninety-three years on earth."

But even as the rest of his extended family moved on from Nanna's wry comment, a jangling uneasiness, never far from Eric's mind in recent weeks, filtered through him and left his heart racing.

"Blow out the candles! The wax is getting on the cake!" six-year-old Lexi Turner said, bouncing on her toes.

Eric eased away from the table and out of the room. He needed a moment. Needed air. Needed... *Damn*. What did he need? Absolution?

He pushed through the squeaky screen door to the backyard of his grandparents' house in Valley Haven, North Carolina. Step-grandparents, technically, but since he'd never known his mother's parents and wasn't close to his father's, the warm way his dad's in-laws had welcomed Eric into the fold of the Cameron family made it easy to drop the "step" and just think of the entire clan as blood relations.

He ambled to the wrought-iron bench in the garden and sank heavily onto it. He exhaled harshly, trying to cleanse his body of the roiling feeling that gripped him when he remembered that dark day last summer. The day his world shifted on its axis.

He bent his head and pinched the bridge of his nose, trying hard to dispel the haunting sights and sounds. The guilt.

"Hey, man. You all right?" a male voice asked.

Eric snapped his head up. He'd been so embroiled in his morose thoughts, he hadn't heard Daryl's approach. Eric shrugged. "Yeah. Just not in the mood for celebrating, I guess."

The Black eighteen-year-old joined him on the bench and bumped him with his shoulder. "You sure that's all?" A teasing grin twisted Daryl's mouth. "C'mon. Tell Uncle Daryl what's bothering you."

Eric gave a humored snort. The fact that Daryl, who was two years younger than Eric, was his stepmother's adopted brother, and thus his "uncle," had long been a source of amusement and jesting between the two.

"It's nothing," Eric said.

"Okay," Daryl said. "But if you change your mind…" He spread his hands in a gesture that offered a listening ear without getting too sappy.

Nodding, Eric said, "Thanks."

Both young men glanced to the back door when its hinges squeaked again, heralding another family member joining them. Fenn Turner, their contemporary in the large multigenerational family, backed through the door carrying three plates and forks as ably as any diner waitress. "Cake, gentlemen? I saved you guys a piece before Brody and my dad ate it all. Aunt Cait made it with that extra creamy chocolate icing everybody loves."

"Bring it on," Daryl said, holding out his hand to take a plate. "Thanks."

Eric took a plate, despite his lack of appetite, simply because Fenn handed it to him, and he appreciated her thoughtfulness.

"So what are you dorks doing out here? I mean, I know our parents' parties can be lame, but it's *Nanna*." Her tone said what her words didn't. Their great-grandmother was a treasure, full of stories and traditions from her native Scotland and prone to spoiling the Cameron children. Witty, blunt and full of love, she held a special place in her family's hearts.

"I just came out here to check on him," Daryl said around a big bite of cake.

Fenn's gaze shifted to Eric in silent question.

"I'll be back inside soon," he said, poking at the cake without eating any. "I just needed a minute." He hesitated before adding, "When Nanna talked about dying, my head went to...dark places."

Daryl grunted. "Yeah. But, you know, she's ninety-three. We all die sometime. We're lucky to have had her around this long."

Eric made a low hum of agreement in his throat, not bothering to correct Daryl about the dark places where his mind had traveled.

Fenn, who'd always been more in tune with him and had her own past shadows to cope with, continued to hold him in her penetrating stare. "But that's not what this is about, is it?"

Eric glanced away, toward the dappled shade of the woods behind his step-grandparents' house.

"Huh?" Daryl said, his last bite of cake suspended halfway to his mouth. "What...? Oh." He put his fork down on the plate and turned on the bench, angling his body toward

Eric. "You're still beating yourself up over what happened with that jerk who tried to kill your mom?"

Fenn nudged Daryl's shin with her toe. "D, don't. Recovering from trauma doesn't happen overnight. Everybody heals at their own pace, and it looks different from one person to the next."

Eric lifted a corner of his mouth. "You sound like my counselor. I'm guessing that's what your shrink's been telling you, too, huh?"

She grinned and shrugged. "Yeah, well, it's true. I mean, I still have bad days, but I've learned how to refocus my negative thoughts and express my emotions in healthy ways."

"Hey, I wasn't dismissing what happened or how you're dealing with it," Daryl said, putting a hand on Eric's shoulder. "I just meant I wish you wouldn't blame yourself for anything that happened—to your mom or to Henry what's-his-name."

"Cavendal," Eric supplied. The name was engraved on his brain in deep bloodred strokes.

Daryl sat straighter, his chest puffing out a little. "In your place, I'd have done the same thing without a second thought."

Eric frowned. That was part of what bothered him. In the same dire circumstances, even knowing how guilty and troubled he'd felt over his actions in the months since that awful day, he knew he'd do the same thing again. What did that say about him? Was that dark instinct a part of who he was?

"And so would I."

All three of the young adults turned at the sound of the new voice. Nanna sat in her wheelchair on the back porch, somehow having gotten through the squeaky back door without Eric noticing.

"Fenn, Daryl, will you give me a moment with Eric, please?"

The two quickly complied with the older woman's request, but as he left, Daryl gave Eric's shoulder a squeeze. Fenn nudged his toe with her own and shot him an understanding grin.

Nanna motioned to one of the rocking chairs on the back porch. "Come sit with me, *m'eudail*."

Her oft-used Scottish endearment stirred a warmth in his chest. When he took the chair beside her, she reached a frail hand toward him, and he gripped it. Her blue eyes sparkled as she regarded him and sighed contentedly.

"Have I told you recently how blessed I feel to have you and your father as part of our family?"

He flashed a polite grin in response. "Thanks."

"And your mother and Gage, as well. You can't have too many loved ones, so we are glad to call them family." She gave his hand a small squeeze.

"We're the lucky ones. You've all been so good to us, so welcoming. I love being a part of this fam—" he hesitated a beat, then said, "Clan," with a lopsided grin.

Nanna laughed. "Aye! I'll make you a Scot yet, lad." Her expression sobered a bit as she pressed her other hand to his, as well. "And because I love you like family, it grieves me no end to see you hurting. I heard you just now telling Fenn and Daryl how your heart is still troubled o'er Mr. Cavendal."

His smile fell, and he averted his eyes.

Nanna tugged his hand. "Listen to me, *mo ghràidh*. It speaks well of your character that you don't dismiss your actions or his demise easily. I am proud of you, that you value another man's life this way. Even one who wished to harm your mother."

"I'm okay. Really." He tried to retract his hand from between hers. "And I don't want to talk about—"

"Fine," she said, gripping his fingers tighter. "We won't speak of it." She lifted one thin shoulder in dismissal. "I'm sure you talk about it all you want and more with Dr. Bivens. All I want to add is that I love you. I'm proud of you and your plans to become a doctor. I predict you will do great things and save many lives. Life has a way of balancing the scales. You contributed to the death of one man, but you will go on to heal many more." She gave a satisfied sighed. "And even if I'm not still here to see it, know that I will be watching from beyond and rooting for you every day."

He snorted wryly. "There you go getting morbid again. If you're trying to cheer me up, talking about your dying doesn't help."

She chuckled. "I suppose that's true. But don't miss my point. Eric Harkney, my dear lad, do *not* let the events of that terrible day last summer keep you from all the good things your future holds. You saved your mother's life, your stepfather's life. Let *that* be your takeaway, and forgive yourself for the rest. Please."

He'd heard as much from so many people over the past several months, and he gave her the stock answer. "I'll try."

But how did he forgive himself for taking a man's life? The police called it justifiable, but his conscience still wrestled with the fact that he'd killed someone. For that, he'd spend his whole life trying to make amends.

Chapter One

Ten years later

A biting winter wind whipped around Eric's legs as he climbed into his Honda Civic at the end of his work day and turned the key to start the engine. The engine sputtered and strained, and Eric muttered encouragement to his old car. "I know it's cold, but you can do it. C'mon!"

His hands were raw from working in the freezing conditions most of the day, but he still preferred icy hands to the quagmire of guilt that plagued him as a medical resident. His parents, both sets, were vocally worried about his recent career choice—working construction for his step-uncle's company instead of finishing his medical residency and starting a surgical practice of his own. But he'd felt like a fraud tending the sick and aiding in saving the lives of the patients who crossed the surgical table on his rotation.

Finally, his car's engine caught, and he fed it more gas before backing out of his space on the Turner Construction lot. He headed down the road toward the small cabin he was renting from his stepfamily at Cameron Glen as the snow accumulated on the pavement. The roads were becoming icy, the key reason his boss and step-uncle, Jake Turner, had sent his work crew home early.

As Eric navigated the city street to the twisty two-lane

state highway that would take him home, he contemplated the pale gray sky and the January-bare trees. A sense of despair washed through him. He recalled a day just like this one last January when a traffic accident caused by slick winter roads had landed a young father in surgery. Eric and the surgical team had lost that patient, and the wailing cry of the man's wife upon receiving the news still rang in his ears on days like this.

But while the patients he'd lost haunted him, even more disconcerting were the times the family of his patients called him a hero and thanked him for the medical miracles he performed, giving ailing loved ones back to them. They wouldn't hail him a hero if they knew his past, knew his secret shame. He knew it though, and he'd reached a point where he couldn't continue living a lie.

The guilt ate at him. The hypocrisy had become more than he could stand. And on a Tuesday in July, just seven months ago, he'd left the hospital room of a little boy whose infected appendix he and his attending physician had removed and whose mother had been tearfully grateful to him for saving her child's life, and he'd gone to his old Honda and not returned the next day. Or the next. He'd called his attending physician and given notice of his resignation. Then he'd called his parents and broken the news to them.

His choice had not gone over well, to put it mildly. But after his parents' shock and frustration had faded, they'd moved on to the worry and hovering that made him grind his teeth. "I'm fine," he'd told them time and again. He was happier doing construction. He was sure about his choice and had no regrets, which was at least partly true.

Not facing life-and-death decisions and the results of his skills, good or bad, allowed him to push the darkness that had lived with him the past eleven years to a back corner of his brain. He could temporarily quiet the demons that stalked him. He could pretend he hadn't made a fatal choice, no matter the reasons for his actions.

He shook his head now and blinked hard, trying to shake the gloom that clung to him. That part of his life was behind him, and he—

Eric cut his deliberations short when he spotted a flash of color amid the swirling white and bleak grays of the day. Red.

He slowed, driving carefully past the pedestrian walking on the side of the road. A young, blond-haired woman. Carrying a baby. Without proper winter clothing.

And covered in something red. His heart jolted. He'd seen enough blood in his life to recognize what he was seeing. Instinct took over, and he pulled to the side of the road, turning on his Civic's warning flashers as he climbed from the car.

"Ma'am? Excuse me, are you hurt? Do you need help?"

The young blonde woman's head snapped up, a look of sheer panic flooding her expression as she gaped at Eric.

He took a step toward her. "Are you hu—"

She matched his forward step by backing away. Shaking her head, she sucked in short, frightened breaths and clutched the baby closer to her chest.

Eric raised a hand to calm her, visually assessing her for injuries. "I want to help. Are you bleeding?"

In answer, she pivoted and tried to run. When her feet slipped on the icy pavement, she dropped awkwardly to her knees, giving an anguished cry.

He darted forward to help, and the young woman cringed away from him.

"No! Stay away!"

"Hey, hey, hey," he said softly, holding his hands up for her to see. "I'm not going to hurt you. I want to help." Seeing the shiver that racked her small body, he took off his own coat and draped it around her shoulders. She wore only a generic-looking uniform like a waitress in a diner might wear. "Where's your coat? Is your baby okay?"

He tried to catch a glimpse of the whimpering infant in her arms, but a thin blanket, the name *Rachel* stitched on the edge, was wrapped around the child, largely hiding the baby. But two bare feet, bright red from the cold, poked out from the loose blanket, and deep concern over frostbite sawed in Eric's gut. He swiped off his knit cap as well. "Here. Put this on your baby's head, and let's rewrap her so her feet are covered."

The blonde narrowed a wary look on him before glancing down at the baby as if confused why she was holding an infant. Her obvious confusion prodded notions of a concussion. He saw no signs of head injury with a cursory visual examination, but blows to the head didn't always present externally.

"Hey, my car is warm, and I can take you to the emergency room—"

Before he could finish, she was shaking her head again, muttering, "No. I have to… I—save Rachel. S-save her."

He quickly changed tack, considering what he'd learned about a mother's protective and overriding concern for her child's well-being. "Your baby should be checked for frostbite. I'm not going to hurt you. I'm—" he took a deep breath, defaulting to a title he'd rejected months ago "—I'm a doctor, and I want to help. Rachel's feet are quite red, and little toes could be damaged if we don't get her warmed up quickly."

The woman stiffened and furrowed her brow. "You know her name?"

He tugged up a corner of his mouth. "You just said it. And it's on her blanket." He aimed a finger at the bright purple stitching. "I'm Eric, by the way. What's your name?"

She shivered again, despite his coat around her. Blinking, her expression grew blank. Her mouth tightened, and her eyes narrowed. Something dark passed over her face.

"It's okay. You don't have to tell me. But we really should get—"

Her hiccupping whimper stopped him, and she angled panicked eyes to him. "I… I don't know. I can't…remember."

"Excuse me?"

Her breathing became fast and shallow again, and she made a low moaning sound. "I don't know! How could I not know my own name?"

Eric took a slow breath and gently touched her arm. "Try not to panic. There could be a simple reason for a brief blank in your memory."

Or a much more complicated and serious one. But he certainly wasn't going to frighten her further with that information.

"Right now, our priority is getting you and little Rachel somewhere warm and safe and making sure you're not hurt." He hesitated, not wanting to upset her further but needing to know. "Do you know where this blood came from?" He indicated the blood smeared on her face, her uniform top, the baby's blanket.

She looked down at the crimson stains, and horror washed over her face, as if she were just seeing the blood for the first time. Small, choked noises wrenched from her chest, and she wavered as if she was about to faint.

"Okay, take slow, deep breaths." He moved his hands toward her slowly. "I'm just going to help support you as we go to the car." He put his hand under her elbow, and she tucked the baby close to her chest again. As he helped steady her, his coat slipped from her shoulder, and he glimpsed a plastic name tag pinned to her uniform over her collarbone. It read simply, *Lisa*.

"Look at that," he said, smiling. "A clue. Does *Lisa* ring any bells for you?"

She blinked and looked down at the tag. "I…don't. Maybe. If I'm wearing it, then… I guess it must be." She didn't sound convinced. More confused and dazed.

Wanting her to stay calm and warm to his help, he nodded, giving her another friendly grin. "Good point. All right then, Lisa. Let's get you and Rachel warmed up and checked by a doctor. Okay?" He tried to steer her toward his car, but she balked again.

"I c-can't." She blinked as tears formed in her eyes and spilled onto her chapped cheeks.

"Why can't you? Lisa, what's wrong? Why are you out here alone?"

Her tears came harder, and she shook her head in frustration. "I don't know! But I... I think...something happened. Something bad. I have to...save Rachel." She frowned, her expression puzzled and frightened and frustrated at the same time.

"We're going to take good care of Rachel. But we have to—"

She shook her head hard. "N-no. I'm scared. I... I have to hide. I have to...to stay safe."

Eric narrowed his eyes, his pulse kicking up. "Hide from what? From who?"

She squeezed her eyes shut, and tears spilled on her cheeks. "I don't know. I just feel...so scared. I have to...save the baby."

He clenched his teeth, considering the scenario. The blood covering Lisa and her baby, her frightened and confused state of mind, and her circumstances, wandering the side of the road without proper winter clothing, all pointed to some sort of dire domestic situation. Was she fleeing an abusive husband? Afraid to give her last name in fear of her abuser finding her? Or did she genuinely not remember what had happened to her or who she was?

Whatever was going on, Eric wouldn't solve it or help Lisa's situation by standing here in the increasingly brutal snowstorm. With a hand at the small of her back, he nudged her toward his car. "We'll sort this out, Lisa. And I promise, I will not let anyone hurt you or Rachel."

SHE HADN'T REALIZED how cold she was—numb, really—until the man who'd stopped—Eric, he'd called himself—put her in the front seat of his car and turned the heater on full blast. Her body shivered as the hot air poured from the vent.

Eric climbed in the driver's seat, and, instead of pulling onto the road, he reached for the baby.

Lisa gasped and shrank back, pulling Rachel closer to her body.

Rachel? Lisa? Why didn't either of those names trigger any certainty or memories? Her heart raced as she realized her mind was a complete void. Nothing felt familiar. She couldn't form any clear memory. Blank. Her mind was completely blank.

She couldn't even say how she'd ended up on the side of the road with this baby. Her baby?

Save Rachel...

She swallowed hard over the lump in her throat. The baby must be hers. Why else would she have the child in her arms? And the imperative that echoed in her head spurred a protectiveness, a deep bond with the child. That had to mean something, didn't it?

Save Rachel...

Eric stilled and angled a calm glance toward her, his dark brown eyes gentle and compassionate. "I need to warm Rachel's feet, and my hands are warmer than yours." He reached again and uncovered the infant's feet, pressing one foot, then the other, between his palms. Rachel squirmed and cried, and her rescuer cooed softly to her. "I know. It hurts. Doesn't it, sweetheart? You're going to be okay."

"Will she?" Lisa asked.

Eric turned his gaze back to Lisa. His mouth tightened, and he hesitated before answering, triggering alarms in her. "I have every reason to believe so. I don't think she's sustained any frostbite damage to her feet."

"What aren't you saying? Why did you pause before answering?" she asked, a fierceness rising in her that surprised her. Where had the fire that prompted her doubt come from?

And why couldn't she remember anything before five minutes ago when Eric stopped and confronted her?

Eric's eyebrows lifted. "I was only deciding what you were really asking and how to be as honest as I could."

"What other question would I be asking?" A shudder raced through her as the car's heat began to thaw her icy limbs.

"I thought you might have been asking about the long term. I know you're scared. Something or someone has frightened you. Something has happened that you either can't remember or won't tell me about. It's clear you're in a bad position, and it's understandable you'd be worried about what's going to happen to you and Rachel."

Lisa released a long tremulous breath. *Dang.* When he put it that way, she *did* worry about the future. Before, she'd just been putting one foot in front of the other, trying to survive the next few minutes, shivering and numb and lost. Now, new issues of survival and difficult decisions crept to mind.

Panic swelled in her. A great overwhelming wave that swallowed and suffocated her. Her breathing grew shallow and quick, and her ears buzzed. Her head spun, and the car seemed to move under her.

A firm hand gripped her shoulder, and she flinched.

"Lisa, you're hyperventilating. Take slow, deep breaths. I promise you are safe now. No one is going to hurt you on my watch."

She blinked hard and refocused on the man beside her. Kind expression. Steady gaze. Calm demeanor. But did she dare trust him? And if not, what was the alternative? Step back out on the roadside, putting herself and Rachel in the blustery, freezing storm again? In harm's way?

In harm's way. Her gut rolled, and acid climbed her throat. Why was she so sure there was danger lurking out there for her? Whose blood was on her clothes, her hands, her hair?

Swallowing hard, she curled her fingers in the thin blanket wrapped around the baby, inhaled slowly. Exhaled a juddering breath. Nothing could stop her body from trembling, though, shaking from the inside out as her frozen limbs thawed.

"That's better," Eric said, lifting a corner of his mouth in a smile that shone through his eyes, as well. He was handsome, her rescuer, though the instant she realized that, a second voice in her head shut down the track of her thoughts. *Men are trouble.*

She frowned at the thought, an impulse that flickered through her mind. Maybe she shouldn't trust Eric. Maybe—

"That's it. Slow breaths. That's better," he said. "Before we go, I'd like to check your head for cuts or swelling. And I want to do a cursory scan of both the baby and of your torso and thighs to be sure you don't have wounds that need immediate attention. I know you said you weren't hurt, but shock, adrenaline and numbing cold can mask the pain of injuries."

She frowned at him, newly skeptical of his intentions.

"Can you lean your head toward me?" he asked, turning on the overhead light in the car's cabin.

After an initial hesitation, she complied, and he probed her skull gently and parted her hair in a few places to examine her scalp.

"Look straight at me," he said, shining the flashlight from his phone in her eyes, his own gaze shifting back and forth as he stared at her. "Pupils reactive and even. That's good."

Next he unwrapped Rachel briefly, lifting her little bunny-print shirt and pushing up the legs of her pants to assure himself she had no bleeding wounds.

Raising his gaze to Lisa, he said, "Your turn. Can you lift your shirt to here?" He indicated mid-chest with his hand to his own chest.

She glared at him for a moment, deciding whether to comply. She ached all over but didn't think she had an open wound. And yet…there was blood on her. On Rachel.

When she hesitated, he added, "I just want to be completely sure you aren't bleeding. All this—" he motioned to the stains on her shirt and the baby's blanket "—came from somewhere."

With a sigh, she raised her uniform shirt to just under her bra. Seeing his frown, she glanced down at herself. Large red welts and purpling bruises glared on her pale skin like warning beacons. Lisa's heartbeat scampered, and she shot him a startled look.

"Any idea how you got those bruises?" he asked, his voice soft and deep with concern.

She shook her head, more tears puddling in her eyes. What *had* happened to her? The notion that she'd experienced some sort of violence frightened her as much as the fact that she couldn't remember anything. "I...d-don't know."

Eric tugged the edges of his coat closed around her and leaned back in his seat. "Well..." He released his own frustrated sigh and fastened his seat belt. "Let's get you to the ER before the roads get any worse."

He steered the car from the shoulder onto the road where snow was accumulating. He cast side-glances at her as he navigated the highway. He opened his mouth a few times as if to speak, then clamped his lips tight again. He clearly had questions for her, and she was relieved he didn't ask them. She didn't have any answers. Not for Eric...or for herself.

Chapter Two

Eric placed a hand at the small of Lisa's back, feeling strangely protective of her as he guided her inside the emergency room. Both her obvious fear and unexplained amnesia spoke to something inside him that had always championed the underdog, the vulnerable. That she had a young baby with her only heightened that instinct.

The admitting desk wanted a host of information, from her address to her insurance policy details. A stricken look crossed Lisa's face when she realized she had none of this information, down to her last name.

"I'll take care of her expenses," he said, surprising himself. Bringing her to the hospital was one thing, absorbing possibly several thousand dollars of medical bills was another. But one look at her wide, frightened eyes and trembling chin slashed through his sense of what was practical.

Lisa turned her pale blue eyes on him, shaking her head. "I can't let you do that."

"Why not?"

"I don't know you. You don't know me. Why...why would you?" Her voice cracked, and she cuddled Rachel closer to her as the baby began whimpering.

At that moment, one of the emergency room nurses stuck her head in the admitting office, and the question on her lips died when she spotted Eric.

"Eric? What are you doing here? Are you all right?" The beautiful South Asian nurse hustled into the office and to Eric's side, casting a concerned glance to Lisa and the baby. "What's happened?"

Eric raised a hand to calm the nurse, his step-uncle Brody's wife, Anya. "I'm fine. I brought Lisa and her baby in. She has amnesia, and the blood on her clothes seems to indicate she's been involved in an accident or altercation of some kind. She and the baby are a bit hypothermic, but I don't think they've suffered frostbite."

Anya arched a manicured black eyebrow. "Amnesia? What *can* you remember?"

Lisa glanced from Anya to Eric, then back to Anya. "Nothing. Not even my name. This is my only clue." She touched the name tag pinned to her waitress uniform.

"She can't provide any insurance or billing information, and since she doesn't appear to have life threatening injuries..." the admitting clerk started.

"Hang on." Anya chewed her bottom lip. "At a minimum, we should do a CT of her head to check for an injury that would have caused the amnesia."

"I've agreed to cover her expenses," Eric said, adding silently, *somehow*. That would prove a challenge on his construction worker's salary, but he wouldn't renege on his offer, having seen Lisa's need.

Anya divided a glance between Lisa and Eric, then nodded once as if she'd made a decision. "Lisa, bring the baby and follow me. Eric, I don't think your paying will be necessary, but give Sharon your contact information."

He nodded his understanding and thanks.

"When you finish out here," Anya added, "you can join Lisa in the exam room if she says it's okay. Otherwise, you'll have to wait in the lobby. Sharon—" she turned to the admitting clerk "—I'd originally come to tell you I could cover for you while you took your break, but..." She wrinkled her nose in apology. "Can you wait about fifteen or twenty minutes while I check these two out and call radiology about the CT?"

Sharon nodded, and Lisa stood, clutching Rachel close to her chest. At the office door, Lisa turned and gave Eric a lingering look, as if remiss to leave his presence. She opened her mouth as if to say something, then bit her lip and furrowed her brow before whispering, "Thank you."

A fist of emotion squeezed his chest, and he nodded to her.

Lisa slipped through the door, and as Anya followed, she said, "I'll take good care of them."

Ninety minutes later, Eric was leafing through a year-old *Field & Stream* magazine in the lobby waiting area when Anya pushed through the swinging doors to the patient screening area. "Lisa has had her CT scan, and she's asking for you, if you want to come back with me."

He stood and crossed to Anya quickly. "Is she okay? What about the baby?"

"You know I'm not allowed to talk to you about it. A little thing called HIPPA? Remember that law, Dr. Harkney? I'm sure she'll tell you what we've found, if she wants you to know." Anya jerked her head toward the back and led him to one of the exam rooms.

He found Lisa sitting propped up on the gurney, wearing a set of disposable scrubs with Rachel asleep in her arms. Lisa's expression reflected a sense of relief when he came in. "You're still here. I thought maybe you'd have left. It was taking so long, and…you really have no reason to stay."

He lifted a shoulder. "Not true. You're my reason to stay. The both of you." He heard Anya close the door behind him, and he moved closer to the side of the small bed. "What did the doctor say?"

"We're gonna live." She gave a weak smile, which he returned.

"Whew!" He wiped his brow with an exaggerated motion. "That's good news." He raised his eyebrows and inclined his head, inviting her to continue. Instead, she said, "Why did you tell me you were a doctor?"

"Huh? 'Cause I am." He frowned. "What did Anya tell you?"

"That you're currently employed by someone in the family, working construction. You don't have the money to pay for a new car, much less my medical expenses."

"That's...technically true, but I—"

"You lied to me?"

"No! I am a doctor! I have a degree and was about six-months short of finishing my residency when I—" *Quit.* He shied from the word, not wanting to destroy her faith in him. "I took leave to clear my head and get a handle on what direction I wanted to go with my life."

"You quit?"

And yet, there was that word, regardless of his best dodge. "Um."

"With just six months left?" She sounded appalled. "After all that work?"

"It's a long story. Not so black and white. Meantime, will you tell me what *your* doctor said? What tests have they run, other than the CT?"

Lisa hesitated, still studying him dubiously. After a moment, she glanced down at the baby in her arms and spoke quietly. "We both got a warm saline IV, and they found some formula for Rachel. She was really hungry." Lisa paused, her face darkening before she continued. "You saw the bruising on my stomach. There doesn't seem to be internal damage beyond contusions. The doctor said I'll be really sore for several days but nothing more. They're still waiting on the CT scan, although the doctor didn't find any sign of a blow to the head."

Eric scratched his chin, processing that information. "So did he say why he thought you couldn't remember anything? What caused your amnesia?"

He had his own diagnosis, but he wasn't the doctor on record and would defer to the ER physician's experience and opinion.

"He's waiting on the CT results to confirm, but he had a fancy name for what he thought had caused it." Lisa swallowed hard. "Especially in light of the blood on my clothes." She dropped her gaze to Rachel. "Also...the hospital called the police. Because of my bruises and the blood on me."

Eric stiffened his spine. "Oh." He cleared his throat. "Yeah, that's the law. They have to report suspected abuse or violent crime."

"I couldn't tell them anything." Forehead furrowed, she moistened her cracked lips with her tongue, taking a moment before adding, "Because of my amnesia, they checked current missing person reports, but said there were none that matched my description or Rachel's." She sighed, and her frown deepened. "They took my clothes with them to try to identify the blood on me. It doesn't seem to be mine or Rachel's. Neither of us has an open wound." She lifted a stricken gaze to his. "But the police told me not to leave the county until they have a better idea of what happened to me. Or what I may have done."

What I may have done.

Eric's stomach flipped. Clenching his hands, he moved to the chair beside the gurney and sat down slowly. He'd not let himself consider the possibility that Lisa had been the one to have done something illegal, something violent. He scrubbed both hands over his face and raised his eyes to hers again. Tears hovered on her lower lashes and dripped onto her cheeks.

"What did I do, Eric? What if I hurt someone?" She squeezed her eyes shut and lowered her face to the top of Rachel's head. "Why can't I remember anything?"

He had no answer for her. No answer for himself about how he was going to help her. But he *was* going to help her.

He knew that to his core. From the moment he'd discovered the vulnerable pair wandering the side of the road in the snowstorm, he'd known he was committed until the end. Seeing Lisa through her predicament was just going to take a bit more time and effort than he'd imagined.

"Eric," she said, her voice soft and broken. "I'm scared. I'm so scared! I hate not knowing what happened or who I am."

"I can understand that." He laid a calming hand on her arm, knowing the healing power of human touch. "But I promise not to let anything happen to you. I'm going to help you figure things out and keep you safe until your memory returns."

Her breath stuttered as she cocked her head to an angle. "Why would you do that?"

Eric took a moment before answering. She'd asked the same question earlier, and a distraction had spared him from answering. The question deserved an answer, if only to ease her qualms with the whole unusual situation. He opened his mouth, and a craggy "uh" was all that came out. *Way to build her confidence, Harkney.*

He thought back to advice he'd been given while in medical school and performing rounds with one of the most demanding doctors at the teaching hospital. *Even if in doubt, always project confidence on rounds. The patient will take their cues from you.*

Lisa needed to feel that Eric had a handle on the situation, had good motivation for assisting her and had a plan going forward. He squared his shoulders and met her gaze evenly. "Because I can. Because I need to know you're all right, and I can't justify turning my back on you when I have the means and willingness to see you through this..." He paused, deciding what word to use. He didn't want to characterize her circumstances as a crisis, though it surely could be considered one. He wanted his words to set a tone that would help Lisa rather than heighten her anxiety. "This situation."

Anya arrived then, documents in hand. "Okey dokey. CT results confirm no head injury. That's good news. The doctor will be back to talk with you soon. He's prepared to release you but wanted to be sure you had a place to go, considering your memory loss. He doesn't want you out in this weather without warm clothes, either."

Lisa gave a wry laugh. "Did he have any suggestion where I was to get these clothes? I don't remember where I live, and I have no money with me."

Anya cleared her throat quietly, drawing Eric's attention. "I think she's about the same size as Lexi, wouldn't you say? And I still have baby clothes in storage from when Nicole was little that would work for Rachel."

Eric pictured his boss's younger daughter. Sixteen-year-old Lexi was slim and about the same height as Lisa, who was petite and thin. He nodded his agreement. "I can pick up the baby supplies on the way to Cameron Glen. I'm hoping Grandma and Grandpa will let Lisa stay with them. They have the empty bedroom, and I can even pay extra rent if they want until Lisa is back on her feet."

Lisa divided a scowl between Anya and Eric. "Whoa, whoa, whoa! Wait a minute. First, you're talking about me and making plans for me as if I'm not right here in the room. Were you even going to ask if staying with Grandma and Grandpa is what I wanted?" She pitched her voice to a harsh whisper when Rachel stirred and whined. "Second, I can't accept charity. How can I just—" she waved a hand gesturing her sense of imposition "—move in with people I don't know and expect them to take care of me, even for one night?"

She focused a dubious gaze on Eric. "Burdening someone for a room, much less until I get back on my feet, is too much. I have a job. Or, at least, I was wearing a uniform. And I must have a house or apartment somewhere. Probably a car too, but—" She stopped abruptly, giving a soft gasp.

"Lisa?" Anya stepped closer to her patient, narrowing a curious look at her. "What is it?"

The blonde blinked and shook her head. "But if I had a car, why was I walking with the baby? It doesn't make sense."

Eric sat forward. "Can you remember a car?"

She shook her head slowly, though her expression seemed confused. Lisa rubbed the back of her neck, massaging the muscles with one hand while cradling Rachel with the other. "I don't...think so. I'm just trying to make sense of things. Hoping I can find even a flicker of feeling or memory that will tell me where I belong, and—" She looked down at her hands, where blood still lined her fingernails. Her expression darkened. "And what h-happened?"

"Do you have any sense of how long you were walking? If we can establish a radius from where you started walking, we might find your car. Then we can have the police run your license plates to get an address and last name."

Lisa's mouth pinched, and her brow furrowed. "No. Nothing like that. I only remember you waking me from a sort of stupor. Why would I have been out there without a coat? That's...crazy!" She raised her chin. "I *know* that. And if I know going out without a coat is stupid *now*, why would I have done it *then*?"

"I'm sure you had a good reason," Anya said, her tone soft and soothing. "Or, considering the blood on your clothes, the evidence something bad happened, you may not have had time to get a coat."

Lisa's nose crumpled, and her shoulders shook as she began crying again. "Why can't I remember? You said I don't have a head injury, so why is my whole life a blank?"

"You want to explain it to her since she's officially your patient?" Eric asked Anya.

Lisa peeked up with teary eyes. "Explain what? What aren't you telling me?"

Anya propped her hip on the edge of the bed and laid a

hand on Lisa's knee. "Did the doctor use the term 'dissociative' or 'psychogenic amnesia' with you?"

"Maybe. He said a lot of things, but mainly he wanted the CT scan results before he made his diagnosis."

"Yeah. The doctor is supposed to be in to discuss this with you in a bit, but he's busy with another patient at the moment. It could be a while."

Lisa's eyes widened. "What is that disso—whatever thing you said? Am I sick? Am I going to die?"

"No, no. Nothing like that." Anya flashed a calming smile and squeezed Lisa's forearm. "Psychogenic or dissociative amnesia, and more specifically, in your case, a dissociative fugue, means your brain has, at least temporarily, erased your memories. Likely because of some trauma or highly emotional event that was too much for you to deal with. Something so frightening or shocking or sad that you shut down rather than face the memory of the event."

Lisa's golden eyebrows shot up, her breath quickening and growing shallow. "Something horrible."

Eric moved closer, too, rubbing a hand on her back and whispering, "You're safe now. Take a deep breath."

Once Lisa had complied and seemed calmer, Anya continued. "The amnesia is a defense mechanism of the brain. We've classified your case as a fugue, because, as you put it, you were in a stupor. Because you were wandering the side of the road with no idea how you got there."

Lisa shuddered. "Because something really bad happened to me." She blinked and scowled. "Or because *I did* something awful." Her throat convulsed as she swallowed. "All that blood... I—"

Anya patted Lisa's knee. "Yes. It's likely the blood is related to why you can't remember. Sometimes, with this sort of amnesia, it will just be the traumatic event that is erased. Other times, as with your case, the brain wipes the slate clean with complete memory loss. Your brain blocks access to your history to protect you from the upsetting information. We see psychogenic amnesia sometimes from soldiers returning from war. Or survivors of child abuse."

"Will I get my memory back? And if so—" she drew a trembling breath as she sent a wary look to Eric, then to Anya "—will the memory of the horrible thing come back, too?"

"I can't make promises, but quite often patients recover their memory, given time. Occasionally a picture or smell or music or another person will trigger the recall. And it's quite possible that through therapy with a trained mental health counselor, you might regain the memories of the bad thing in a safe environment and have help processing and coping with the blocked memory."

"What if I don't *want* the blocked memory back? What if it's something best forgotten?" Lisa's voiced cracked, and her expression spoke for her fear.

Anya gave Lisa a regretful frown. "Repressed memories and feelings have a way of resurfacing eventually. Better that you work with a counselor to recover it in a safe space than let the negative emotions cause physical illness or potentially return in some devastating manner." Anya pressed her lips in a taut line before adding, "I can recommend someone if you'd like to set up an appointment."

Lisa's shoulders drooped. "I'm not against seeing a counselor, but…how do I pay for it?"

Eric cleared his throat. "Let's, um…cross one bridge at a time. We don't have to figure everything out tonight. And, who knows? By morning you may have remembered parts of your history." He spread his hands. "Will you accept my offer of lodging, at least temporarily…for Rachel's sake?"

Tipping her head to the side, she gave him a narrow look that said she knew he was playing on her maternal instincts to win her compliance. Her sigh said it worked. "All right. Temporarily."

Anya passed her a clipboard. "These are your discharge

papers. Just sign the bottom, and once you've talked to the doctor again, you're free to go."

Shifting Rachel to one arm, Lisa took the clipboard and pen, frowning. "All I know is my first name."

"Good enough for now." Anya waved away her concern. "Some patients just mark an X."

Eric stood and lifted Rachel into his arms so Lisa could scribble her name on the form. The baby's peach fuzz brushed softly on his chin as he cuddled her close, and a pleasant contentment buzzed through him. When Lisa reached to take the baby back, he regretted needing to hand her over so soon. Someone had given her a bath, and she smelled sweet, her tiny hands so soft and delicate.

The doctor came soon after and confirmed to Lisa everything Anya had told her, signed the discharge papers and wished Lisa well.

"Wait in the warm lobby until I get the car," Eric said as they headed out of the ER. "We'll stop on the way home to buy more formula and diapers for Rachel."

She nodded, and he tucked his head down against the blowing snow as he crossed the parking lot. But his stride held a purpose and determination he hadn't known in months. Helping Lisa felt good.

Chapter Three

"Oh my gracious! Isn't she just the sweetest thing?" Grace Cameron, the matriarch of the family Eric's father had married into, cooed as she took Rachel into her arms for a snuggle. "Despite your trouble today, she doesn't look too much worse for wear. Chapped cheeks, perhaps, but I think we have a lotion that will help that."

"Are you sure you don't mind us staying the night? Eric sort of volunteered your home without any warning." Lisa opened a can of ready-made formula and poured it into the just-purchased bottle. A couple pacifiers, feeding spoons and teething toys had all been put through the sterilizing cycle in the dishwasher, and new clothes, blankets and stuffed animals were in the Camerons' washing machine, readying them for Rachel's use.

Eric had paid for it all, and Lisa had saved the receipt with full intentions of repaying him...eventually. She'd need to get a new job if she couldn't remember where she worked—soon. But how did she find her old job? Did she go from one restaurant to another, check at each retail store asking, "Do you know me?" And how did she get around to the diners without a car?

The weight of the stumbling blocks she had to surmount made it hard for her to breathe. Whether she liked the idea of accepting charity or not, she needed Eric and his family's help.

"Of course you're welcome. Any friend of Eric's is a friend of ours," Eric's grandmother—step-grandmother—said. Lisa didn't bother to explain to the attractive older woman that she wasn't a friend of Eric's. Except...he had been kind to her. She liked what she knew of him. Didn't that make him a friend of sorts?

"Nanna's room has been vacant and waiting for someone like you since she died," Neil Cameron, Grace's husband, added. "We're happy to have you stay with us."

Lisa blinked. Someone had died? Another grandmother from the sound of it. She knitted her eyebrows and divided a sympathetic look between the senior Camerons. "Oh, I'm so sorry for your loss."

Grace stroked Rachel's back, swaying from side to side in a comforting gesture that mothers just seemed to do naturally when holding a child. "Thank you, dear. But her passing was serene and painless, and she'd enjoyed 101 happy years on earth. While we miss her, we know she's at peace."

Lisa cast an inquisitive glance to Eric, seeking what, she couldn't say. Confirmation that her presence wasn't infringing on the memory of the couple's loved one? His reading on the older couple's sincerity in the welcome? Reassurance that this was really her best option?

He met her eyes and gave her a warm smile that glowed as much from his dark brown eyes as his lips. He bore little physical similarity to the blue-eyed Cameron couple, but then he'd said they were his stepfamily, right? A tingle chased through her as she studied his cut jaw and well-shaped lips.

Curling her fingers into a ball, she shoved the small trill of attraction aside. *You're in danger, running from who-knows-what and stranded with a baby. You have* no *business noticing anything more about this man than his trustworthiness and determining his ability to help or potential to hurt you. Cut jaw and sexy eyes be damned...*

Lisa refocused her attention on the Camerons. What Eric *did* share with the older couple was a generous and kind spirit that drew her in and wrapped her in warmth like a homemade quilt. *Quilt*...the word reverberated oddly in her skull. Lisa made a note of the odd sense, promising to return to it later. For now, she focused her attention to what Grace Cameron was saying.

"I have a pot of soup that I started earlier when I saw the first snow flurries. Nothing like homemade vegetable soup and cornbread on a cold day. Am I right?" Grace skillfully cradled Rachel with one arm while she began gathering bowls from the cabinet and spoons from a drawer. "Eric dear, will you get the cornbread from the oven and the butter from the refrigerator?" Turning to Lisa, she said, "I'll give the baby her bottle while you eat, sweetheart. You look ready to blow over." Grace hitched her head toward the pot on the stove. "Come on. Help yourself."

Lisa's stomach rumbled at the thought of a hot meal, and after only a moment's hesitation—Rachel was her responsibility, and it felt a little scary to hand off any duty to a stranger—she passed the bottle to Grace.

"So, how old is little Miss Rachel?" Grace asked as she rearranged the infant so Rachel could suck on the bottle.

"Um," Lisa said, racking her brain for an answer. Surely she knew *that* much! But she drew a blank, and tears prickled her eyes again. "I'm n-not sure." Lisa bit the inside of her cheek, fighting not to sob with frustration. How could she *not* know how old her own baby was?

Eric moved closer, putting a hand on her arm. "It's all right. I'm sure as you rest and begin to feel safe again, things like Rachel's age will come back to you. Don't beat yourself up."

She drew a shuddering breath. "What kind of mother can't

remember her child's birthday?" Then she gave a wry, hiccupping laugh. "Or her own birthday for that matter?"

Eric's grip tightened. "The kind who has likely suffered a trauma or tragedy that's blocking her memories. It's not your fault."

He pitched his voice low, his tone as smooth and comforting as a lullaby. His compassion sparked an even deeper gratitude in her that made the tears fall. She forced a wobbly grin, trying to reassure him she was fine. Then, hurrying to the stove, she served herself some soup, if only as an excuse to pull away from the awkward moment and distract herself from her tumbling emotions.

"Based on my experience with my own children and several grandbabies, I'd guess Miss Priss here is about six or seven months old." Grace used a clean kitchen towel to wipe the dribbles from Rachel's chin. "We can see how she does sitting up and if she can manage small bites of soft food like banana later. Meanwhile, the jars you bought will be fine."

A loud knock sounded on the back door, and even as Neil shouted, "Enter!" a woman and teenage girl bustled into the house, chased in by a cold breeze and shaking snow from their heads and sleeves.

"Brrr!" the teen said, adding a full-body shiver. She flipped her long caramel-colored hair out from her coat collar with one hand and set a large plastic sack on the table with her other. "Love the snow. Hate the cold. Irony, I know!"

The brunette woman with the teenager appeared to be in her forties but had smooth facial skin that could have been much younger. "Evening, all. We brought some of Lexi's clothes as requested." The woman smiled at Lisa and added, "Hi! You must be Lisa. I'm Emma Cameron Turner, and this is my youngest, Lexi. Welcome to Cameron Glen."

Eric leaned close to Lisa with a lopsided grin. "Be nice to them. Emma's husband is my boss at Turner Construction."

Lisa sobered in order to present a pleasant smile to the newcomers. "Hi. Thank you for loaning me the clothes."

"No problem. In fact, if they fit, keep them. Lexi has outgrown them. She gets taller every time I turn around!" Emma sniffed the air. "Oh, wow. What smells so good?"

"Vegetable soup," Grace said, angling her cheek to receive a kiss from Lexi. "Grab a bowl, both of you. There's plenty."

"Thanks, but I have a lasagna in the oven. Just wanted to deliver the clothes and see if there was anything else we could do to help Lisa." Emma faced Lisa now, spreading her hands. "Toiletries? Diapers?"

"Mom, look how cute the baby is!" Lexi said with a coo in her voice. "Can I hold her?"

Lisa glanced from one face to another, feeling a tad overwhelmed. The Camerons had swooped in to help her with no holds barred, and she had no way to repay them. On top of her memory loss and the body aches and bruises she was suffering, she felt rather in over her head.

Her face must have reflected what she was feeling because Eric sidled between the family and Lisa, his hands lifted in a "stand down" gesture. "Thank you for the clothes and offers of assistance, but what I think Lisa needs right now is a quick meal and lots of rest. Let's not deluge her with questions and visitors until she's had a chance to settle in, huh?"

Emma nodded. "Understood. Lexi, you heard Eric. You can hold the baby later." She leaned to peer past Eric. "In fact, she's a great babysitter if you need her in the days to come."

Lisa nodded, although she wasn't sure what she'd need in five minutes, much less tomorrow or the day after. "Thanks."

Emma and Lexi waved as they left, letting in another arctic blast from outside.

Lisa shivered, although not entirely from the cold draft from the open door. She was surrounded by kind people in a loving home, yet without any sense of who she was or where she belonged, she felt completely alone. And terrified.

Eric sat across from Lisa as they ate large bowls of soup and buttery chunks of cornbread. He knew Lisa was awkward with the attention and outpouring of assistance the family was offering. He could understand that. She didn't know them and had to be scared. The simple fact that her amnesia was likely the result of a terrible event or dark history only heightened his concern for her.

"So, the Camerons…they're a big family, huh?" she asked, her tone holding a wary edge.

"Yeah. Grace and Neil have five kids with four spouses and something like ten grandkids. I've lost count. They can be a lot, I know."

The first thing he could do for her was serve as a buffer, holding the well-meaning but sometimes overzealous Camerons at bay for a day or two. Lisa and the baby needed sleep, quiet, calm. A chance to decompress. He didn't need his medical degree to tell him that much.

What he couldn't explain was why he felt an inexorable pull toward her, a hounding need to be the one who took care of her and Rachel. To be her protector and provider. Maybe the urgency came from the fact that he'd been the one to find her and rescue her. An imperative called from deep inside him, a responsibility toward her, as if she were a project he'd started and didn't want to leave unfinished or unsuccessful.

Except she wasn't a *project*. She was a human being. A frightened and vulnerable woman with an even more vulnerable baby. She spoke to his every impulse to champion the underdog, care for the sick or hurting and defend the weak. All the instincts that had led him into medicine once upon a time.

"It's okay. They're all really nice." She hesitated, then asked, "But didn't you say they're your stepfamily?"

"Yeah. My dad married into the family about twelve years ago, and they sort of absorbed us into the big happy tribe. I usually don't even use the term 'step' when I talk about them anymore. They are more family to me than my extended blood relatives."

"I like them. They've been so good to me already."

Eric crumbled some of his cornbread into his bowl. "I remember when my dad and I first met them all. I was sixteen, and my dad brought us here for the summer for father-son bonding time and to give him a retreat where he could finish writing his novel."

Her head came up. "Your dad is a writer?"

Eric nodded and slurped a spoonful of soup.

Her face brightened a bit as she latched on to the new topic. "That's cool. What kind of books does he write?"

"Military thrillers mostly. He was an MP in the Army until his medical discharge. But that's a story for another time."

"Will I meet him? Does he live nearby?" she asked.

He wiped his mouth on his napkin, nodding. "You can count on it. He and his wife, Cait, and my half sister, Erin, live on the property. They built a house across the lake and up the west ridge a couple years ago." He aimed a finger in the general direction of his dad's home. "I'm sure the grapevine has told him and Cait about your arrival, and they'll be here, eager to meet you, bright and early tomorrow."

Lisa stared into her soup bowl for a moment, a wrinkle in her brow as if considering the prospect of meeting more of his family, before lifting a strained smile. "That will be nice."

They continued eating in silence for a moment, while Eric cast covert glances at Lisa, deciding what else he might say to help put her more at ease. He wanted to do more to calm her obvious awkwardness and erase the understandable dark shadows of fear and vulnerability that haunted her expression.

As he scooped up another spoonful of soup, he smothered a chuckle. He could imagine her reaction to being called weak or vulnerable. Though she was clearly frightened by her circumstances, he also saw a defiance and core of strength that sparked in her eyes when her situation was discussed.

Her pride, her reluctance to accept what she deemed charity, spoke to her self-sufficiency and moxie.

Lisa raised a curious look toward him, her brow furrowed. "Something funny?"

He waved his empty spoon. "No. I mean, I just had a random, sort of ironic thought."

"I could use a laugh, and I can appreciate irony. Want to share?" She broke off a corner of her cornbread and popped it in her mouth. *Her full-lipped, wide and seductive mouth.*

Eric quickly dropped his gaze to his soup, startled by the lustful analysis that had popped into his brain. He cleared his throat and dug for the professional detachment he'd learned to employ with his patients.

"Well?" Lisa prompted when he didn't answer.

"It was nothing, really." Hoping to change the subject, he added, "Listen, for the last few months, since I started with Turner Construction, I've been renting a cabin here on the grounds of Cameron Glen, but I'll ask Grandma Grace if I can use my uncle's old bedroom for a few days." He hesitated. "The one next to where she's putting you. You know, to…be closer to you if you need anything."

One golden eyebrow sketched up. "I don't need a babysitter. For myself or Rachel."

He raised a hand and offered a conciliatory grin. "I don't mean to imply you do. But… I want to be on hand in case anything comes up. I'd prefer to be your go-to if you need anything or if…"

When he let his sentence trail off, her second eyebrow joined the first. "If…?"

"Well, it is possible that your memories could return anytime. If you do remember something…frightening or concerning—" He debated how blunt to be. The last thing he wanted to do was add to her stress levels. Clearing his throat, he finished with, "I feel like, with my medical training, I'm better prepared to help you than my grandparents are. They're kind and well-meaning, but we don't know what you'll remember or how you'll respond to the memories or—"

"Are you trying to scare me?" She gave a short harsh laugh. "Because you're doing a pretty good job of it."

"I'm actually trying *not* to scare you, believe it or not. And failing, clearly." His cheeks puffed out as he exhaled his frustration. "All I'm saying is, I want to say close by. I want to be helpful in any way you might need me, up to and including feeding Rachel or changing her diaper in the middle of the night—"

Lisa's mouth opened, refusal clearly on her tongue.

"—if she needs it," he rushed to finish, "so you can get the sleep you need, undisturbed."

Her expression shifted, a reflection of skepticism. "Do you even know how to change a diaper? I can't believe that is part of your medical training."

He chuckled. "Not in medical school, no. But I like kids, and for a while, I considered pediatric medicine for my specialty. My diaper training came from the family. My younger sister was born when I was in college, and I was drafted to change diapers for her and for various other infant cousins who were born around the same time when I was home on breaks. This place has been busting at the seams with babies for about ten years. The youngest is Aunt Isla's son, Joey. He's three now."

Lisa pushed her bowl away and set her spoon beside it. "Okay, so you can change diapers. But that doesn't mean I'm prepared to abdicate my responsibility to Rachel to someone I just met and know very little about."

More than the meaning of her comment, Eric pondered her phrasing, her language. Abdicate? Not a word most people would use in casual conversation. A broad vocabulary could come from many sources. Highly educated parents who used similar language, a habit of reading or being a dedicated student of language. A clue to her past, maybe?

"Point taken," he said, "so...why don't we compromise? I'll stay in the bedroom next to yours and be ready to help if you change your mind, and you understand that I have my own sense of responsibility, which I refuse to ignore."

She tipped her head to the side. "Your responsibility? You mean, as a doctor to a patient?"

He shrugged. "Yeah, sorta like that."

Her mouth compressed in a taut line. "But didn't you say earlier that you left your medical residency to work construction for your uncle?"

"Uh, yeah."

"So, you walked away from your responsibilities as a doctor once before. How am I supposed to believe you won't do the same again with me?"

Chapter Four

Lisa's question nagged Eric the rest of the night. She had a legitimate reason to doubt him. She didn't know much about him, and the little she did know pointed to a quitter, someone who abandoned his hard-earned profession in the eleventh hour of his training. If he could walk away from all the years of study, hundreds of patient cases and significant financial investment, why should she expect him to commit himself to her? To Rachel?

Punching his pillow, he rolled over and stared through the darkness at the dim pattern of striped wallpaper border in his uncle's former bedroom. Like much of the rest of his grandparents' house, the bedroom hadn't been updated in more than twenty-five years—and it showed. Not that outdated wallpaper and curtains mattered to the senior Camerons, who valued memories over style. In truth, Eric rather liked the fact that little changed from year to year in his grandparents' house. For someone whose world had been full of change and upheaval for as long as he could remember, because of his father's military deployment and his parents' divorce, Eric liked the consistency his grandparents and their home provided. He felt anchored here. No wonder the older Camerons' home had been the first place he'd thought to bring Lisa, who clearly needed a safe space.

He rolled to his back to stare at the ceiling, considering

again the bruising Lisa had on her torso. The contusions were not consistent with injuries from a car accident. They suggested a physical beating. Could she have fled an abusive marriage? She wasn't wearing a wedding ring, but not everyone did these days. And she could have removed the ring. Or could have just been living with Rachel's father, or—

A muffled noise, a whimper, filtered to him from the dark hall. He held his breath, listening, trying to determine if Rachel had wakened, if Lisa might need a hand with the baby. When the moan came again, much lower-pitched and more agonized-sounding than a baby's cry, a prickle of alarm nipped his neck.

He tossed back his covers, and after tugging his blue jeans on, he moved to the door of Nanna's old room. He tapped his knuckle on the door quietly, not wanting to wake his grandparents or Rachel. When he got no response, he knocked a little harder. The tapping pushed the door open a crack, such that he could see Lisa in the double bed, her head moving side to side in an agitated "no" motion. She made another strangled sound of distress, and Eric made the choice to wake her.

As he stepped into the room, the lingering scents he'd forever associate with the dear Scottish woman he'd always consider his great-grandmother greeted him—a poignant mix of scented body powder, peppermint candies and mothballs. He quickly pushed aside the pang of grief that struck him, focusing his attention on the young woman thrashing in the bed.

"Lisa?" he whispered, then again louder as he placed a hand on her shoulder. "Wake up. You're safe." He gave her a gentle shake. "Lisa? Wa—"

Her eyes flew open, and she sucked in a sharp breath. Immediately, she scuttled away from his touch, her gaze darting around the unfamiliar room before returning to him. Confusion and fear dented her brow and tugged her mouth in a frown.

He raised both hands, palms toward her, as he crooned. "It's okay. You're safe. You were dreaming."

She took a trembling breath and tugged the sheet up to her chin. "D-dreaming?"

He reached for the small lamp on the bedside stand and clicked it on. She cringed, and they both took a moment to squint and blink as their eyes adjusted to the light. "A bad dream from the sound of it." When the pucker in her brow deepened, he added, "You were sort of...moaning."

She grunted and covered her face with one hand. "I—I'm sorry if I woke you."

"No." He patted her arm, and she flinched away from him.

He heard a rustling from the travel crib, which the older Camerons had kept on hand through the years for frequent babysitting gigs. Perhaps he shouldn't have turned on the lamp, he thought belatedly. He didn't want to wake Rachel unnecessarily, but his priority had been chasing the last cobwebs and shadows away for Lisa. Using the soft light, he surveyed Lisa's posture and read her body language for her mood. Body language, he'd learned, often spoke louder than words.

She was shaking, knees drawn up to her chest, her shoulders hunched as she covered her face and hid her eyes. Classic self-protection. Fear. Avoidance.

"Can you remember what the dream was about?" he asked softly.

She didn't reply right away, but after a couple beats, she lifted her head and glanced at him before turning away. "No. Not really. Just...impressions. I just have this...overall sense of...fear. And—" her voice cracked "—sadness."

Her throat worked as she swallowed. "I have a pit in my stomach. This hard knot of... I don't know. Dread, maybe? Anxiety? I don't know what to call it. And—" she took a shallow breath and released it, the air stuttering from her throat

"—my chest is tight. It's hard...to breathe." Even as she described the symptoms, he noticed her breaths coming quicker.

"I think it's a panic attack. You're starting to hyperventilate." He shifted on the bed to look directly into her eyes. "Lisa, look at me. Hold my gaze and breathe with me. In slowly..." He inhaled, mentally counting to five.

Though her eyes clung to his, her indrawn breath was choppy.

"Good," he said, wanting to encourage her. "Now out for five." He puckered his lips and blew the air out slowly.

She imitated him, and his attention dipped to her pursed lips. Chapped, but a delicate pink and a perfect bow. Her mouth was sexier than anything a beautiful actress had to offer, and so tempting, he had to curl his hand in a fist and remind himself she was off-limits. Lisa was vulnerable and alone and the last person he should be thinking about in sexual terms.

He shoved the impulse down with a tinge of self-reproach and guilt. *Crivvens!*

"What?" Lisa asked, her expression somewhat puzzled.

"Huh?"

"You said something...like 'cravings.'"

"Did I?"

When she nodded, he snorted a short laugh. "Oh. Channeling Nanna apparently."

The obscure humor of his private joke fell flat, and Lisa's breathing grew panicky again.

"Nanna, whose room you're using, sometimes used a Scottish expression—or parts of it. *Jings, crivvens and help ma boab!* I always thought it was...well, so *Nanna*. Spicy and sweet at the same time. And a good alternative, when my parents got on me about the colorful language I leaned into when I was a teenager."

Lisa's bewildered expression didn't ease, and he gave his head a small shake. "Sorry. I'm rambling, aren't I?"

They were silent for a moment, alternately glancing at each other and awkwardly averting their eyes.

Lisa broke the silence first. "What does it mean?"

Eric's eyebrows rose. "Hmm?"

"The Scottish thing your grandmother said." Lisa twisted the sheet around her fingers, and he noted that the distraction of a random Scottish lesson had calmed her breathing a bit.

Score.

"It's a mild curse. An expression that basically means about what you'd think. Sorta like, 'Good grief and heaven help me!'" He flashed a lopsided grin, pleased that she seemed to have largely moved on from whatever terror had filled her dream.

A tremulous twitch of her cheek was as much smile as he got in return.

From the travel crib, Rachel stirred and gave a mewl that quickly rose to a whine. Lisa's eyes widened, reflecting more worry than the circumstances seemed to require. She shoved the blankets down her legs and bicycled her feet to kick them free.

Eric moved out of her way, then followed her across the bedroom to the baby bed. Recalling what his father and stepmother had taught him when his little sister had been born, Eric was about to suggest turning off the light. Perhaps if they tucked Rachel's blanket back around her and gently rubbed the baby's back, she'd drift back to sleep. Before he could make that suggestion, though, Lisa lifted Rachel from the crib. She cuddled Rachel to her shoulder and patted the infant's back firmly. Roused from her slumberous mood, Rachel gave a louder wail.

Eric swallowed the advice he'd intended, telling himself Lisa knew her child's needs and habits better than he did. His part-time babysitting for his sister and brief pediatric rotation did not supplant a mother's on-the-job training and personal experience. And yet...

He watched Lisa bounce Rachel on her shoulder. Lisa's mouth pressed in a taut line, and her forehead creased as she paced the floor, whispering, "Shh. Shh. Don't cry."

A tingle of suspicion chased through him. Why didn't Lisa know how to soothe Rachel? His doubts were followed by a heavy dose of recrimination. Just because Lisa seemed inexperienced and awkward with Rachel didn't mean anything nefarious was going on. Lisa's memory was gone. Maybe the same trauma that had taken her memory had wiped her accumulated bank of baby care tricks. Or simply being out of her element, away from familiar surroundings could have her mothering skills out of sorts. Or her concern with waking Grace and Neil could mean she was trying different tactics to quiet Rachel. Or…any combination of these factors.

Lisa glanced at him. "Would you get a bottle of formula from the refrigerator for me? Maybe she's hungry, and if I take her with me to the kitchen, I'm afraid her crying will wake your grandparents."

Eric hesitated. "Didn't she have a bottle at bedtime?"

Lisa nodded. "Drank the whole thing and had a jar of peas."

"Then it's more likely we woke her up with the light or she's wet. She really shouldn't be hungry." He held out his arms, offering to take Rachel.

Lisa frowned and shook her head. "If she needs a diaper, I'll do it."

She cast her gaze around the dim room until she found the box of diapers and wipes they'd purchased on the way to Cameron Glen that afternoon. She laid the baby on the end of the bed and started completely undressing her instead of just unsnapping the lower half of the pajamas. Again, Eric bit his tongue as he watched Lisa move through the steps of removing one diaper, cleaning Rachel and struggling to get the dry diaper on while Rachel twisted and kicked.

Stepping forward, he took the soiled diaper from the bed—

it was slightly damp but not terribly wet—and bundled it for the diaper pail.

After several attempts, Lisa managed to get the dry diaper fastened in place and began redressing the baby.

"Ya know, my dad and Cait had a special night-light in my sister's nursery for nighttime changes. The brighter lights, even this much," he waved toward the small bedside lamp, "is too stimulating and wakes the baby up. I think I'll ask Cait tomorrow if she still has her old nursery light."

"Okay. Thanks." Lisa finished snapping the long row of fasteners on Rachel's borrowed terry cloth pajamas and lifted the baby in her arms again. Though not crying per se, Rachel wrinkled her nose and fussed before rubbing her eyes with a tiny fist. "I still think she might be hungry." When Eric balked, she tipped her head. "What?"

He sat on the edge of the bed and opened and closed his mouth once before sighing. "I only say this as general information, not as criticism."

Lisa straightened her back and squared her shoulders, clearly already wary and perhaps feeling chastened before he even began. "What?"

"It's just that by six months, a healthy baby—which by all appearances, Rachel is—shouldn't need extra calories before bed to help her sleep through the night. In fact, a lot of experts say that depending on a bottle to soothe an older infant teaches them to use food for comfort and could set up unhealthy habits."

Lisa stared at him, not saying anything, then angled her head to gaze down at Rachel. "So, no bottle at night?"

"Under normal circumstances, no. She seems to be a healthy weight so..." He flipped up a hand. "But I'm also of the opinion there should not be any absolutes in raising children. Just good practices you should strive to make routine as much as possible."

One caramel-blond eyebrow twitched up. "And you're

basing this on all your experience as a father?" Her caustic tone stung.

He took a measured breath and brushed aside the jab. In a calm tone, he said, "Obviously not. But I did a rotation in pediatric medicine, and I have watched every one of my aunts and uncles as they raised a small fleet of babies in the past few years. And I still remember what I learned with my little sister when she was Rachel's age."

Lisa closed her eyes. "Sorry. I know you're trying to help. I just… I should know this stuff, how to take care of my daughter. Why isn't it more obvious to me? Why isn't it like muscle memory?"

He pushed off the bed and crossed to her. He placed a splayed hand on the top of Rachel's head and gave Lisa a reassuring smile. "Give it time. I bet it all comes back in the next few days."

Lisa gave a huff of disagreement. "What was your nanna's word? Criv-something?"

Eric chuckled. "*Jings, crivvens and help ma boab.* Or sometimes simply, *crivvens.*"

"*Crivvens,*" she repeated under her breath. She met his eyes again and asked, "And why did you feel the need to cuss when you said it?" His forehead wrinkled as she scowled. "Something about my nightmare? Something I did?"

Eric rewound his thoughts to the moment earlier, and the image of Lisa's puckered lips, her flushed cheeks and her tousled hair flickered in his mind's eye. He dropped his hand from the baby's warm head and soft peach-fuzz hair to take a long step back.

He cleared his throat, not trusting his voice while those images were so fresh, so tantalizing. "It was…nothing. Never mind." He turned and clicked off the lamp. In the darkness, he faced Lisa again. "I, um…think she's settling down now, so…unless you need me for—" he shrugged "—whatever,

I'll…" He eased toward the door, hitching his thumb toward the hall.

Lisa laid her cheek against Rachel's head and hugged her tighter. The way Lisa pulled her arms in, elbows closer to her body and curled her shoulders in as she clung to Rachel reminded Eric of a frightened child hugging a stuffed animal for comfort. Considering she'd been stripped of so much with the loss of her memory—her home, her livelihood, her family—Lisa's reversion to such an innate response to insecurity didn't surprise him.

She was a case study in Maslow's hierarchy of needs, and her pyramid had been blown to shreds. Someone or something had crushed Lisa's world, crumbled her foundation.

Eric's chest squeezed, and he vowed to do everything in his power to rebuild her sense of safety, provide her shelter, show her a friendship that she could lean on and buoy her self-confidence. He pulled the bedroom door closed as he backed into the hall, carefully avoiding the question of *Why?* behind his determination.

Chapter Five

Lisa stood in the dark bedroom, her heart thudding against her ribs like the warning drumbeat in a horror movie. She could tell herself she was safe here in the Camerons' home, but those mental reassurances did little to ease the coil of anxiety that kept her on edge and taunted her with whispers of an unknown evil. She both wanted to recall her nightmare, hoping for answers, and shy away from dredging up whatever had poisoned her sleep.

She clutched Rachel to her breast. The knowledge that she had to protect this baby from whatever lurked out there, threatening them both, unsettled her. With so much else a blank, the one thing Lisa knew for sure was that danger waited beyond the walls of the Camerons' home. The overriding sense of doom was seated at her core and wound tendrils of fear throughout her soul.

Give it time, Eric had said. But did she have time? What if the threat that haunted her grew more dangerous over time? What if someone was waiting for her, needing her, and her amnesia meant she'd left something important undone? If she was Rachel's mother, did that mean she also had other children out there somewhere? The notion felt hollow. She had no tug of recollection or emotion or instinct in that direction. What did that say?

Rachel wiggled and whimpered, and Lisa swayed her body,

rocking the sweet baby and also taking her own thin solace from the motion. Why couldn't she remember being Rachel's mother?

She was embarrassed by how obvious her unfamiliarity with calming Rachel had been to Eric. Even diapering her had seemed foreign. And yet she felt a deep bond, a powerful love for the infant. Surely that meant Rachel was hers. Didn't it? Amnesia may have stolen her memories of mechanical skills to mothering, but didn't her affection and protectiveness for the baby prove that her heart remembered her child?

Save Rachel...

The light snuffling sounds of her daughter burrowing into the crook of her neck sent bittersweet pangs through her, and Lisa murmured, "We'll be all right, sweetie. I'll keep you safe."

Her own coos of reassurance to Rachel reminded her of the warmth that had filled Eric's kind tone as he calmed her moments ago. His dark eyes had been so full of compassion and given Lisa an anchor to cling to while her nightmare tore at her like storm winds, harsh but invisible.

Whatever other terrible *something* had stolen her memory, she could count Eric as a blessing for spotting her on the side of the highway and coming to her rescue. She could well imagine the cold would have taken her life and Rachel's otherwise. In her numb state of shock, she'd not had the wherewithal to find shelter or seek help. A fugue state, Anya had called it.

Despite the heated bedroom and warm clothes Eric's family had provided, Lisa shivered. Eric had saved her life and her daughter's. She owed him a huge debt of gratitude. And money, thanks to her ER bill. How would she ever repay that?

After a few more minutes of cuddling her daughter, Lisa finally settled Rachel in the travel crib and battled the despondency and empty ache that washed over her without the infant in her arms. Rachel's slow, steady breathing told her that her daughter had fallen back to sleep. She could go back to bed herself and get the rest Eric prescribed.

But...

She glanced to the rumpled covers of the double bed and frowned. Although she needed sleep, she dreaded the idea that more nightmares would find her. In her sleep, she feared that whatever had set her out on that snowy road with just the clothes on her back and Rachel in her arms would catch up to her.

"WELL? YOU SAID you had one! Where is it?" Reggie asked, his tone feral as it boomed from DJ's cell phone.

DJ grimaced as he shifted in the front seat. Even after Donna patched him up, he hurt like hell.

Keep it clean or it could get infected. Then you'll have big problems, Donna had said.

DJ grunted. He already had big problems. Explaining to Reggie what had happened for a start.

"There was trouble." Hell, he didn't want to admit he'd screwed up. He'd thought Vic was in—hook, line and sinker. But the jerk had changed his mind. Had a crisis of conscience or some bull like that. And now DJ was short twenty grand, plus the pills and weed he'd given Vic to win him over.

"Trouble?" Reggie was silent for several seconds. "What kind of trouble?"

His boss's voice was so tight, so low and angry, DJ could imagine the man's narrowed eyes and lethal scowl. If DJ'd been standing in front of Reggie now instead of miles away on his phone, he was sure the man would've inflicted a kind of hurt that made the infection in his current wounds seem like a picnic. A man didn't fail Reggie more than once and live to talk about it.

"I can fix it. I just need a little time." DJ knew he was now on borrowed time. He had to turn this screwup around, or his life wouldn't be worth living.

"How bad is it? Are the cops onto you?" Reggie asked.

"No." He prayed that was true. But he really didn't know where the girl had gone, what she'd told anyone. DJ gritted his teeth and closed his eyes, swimming though the searing pain. Hellfire, what he'd give for something stronger than Advil to kill this pain! But he couldn't afford any downtime, and he knew better than to use any of the product. He saw how fast his customers got addicted. How sorry their lives became, living only for their next hit. Screw that!

"You better hope the cops don't know." DJ heard Reggie's heavy sigh. "Damn it, I got customers waiting. I got a hundred grand on the line. You don't fix this, you not only don't get your cut, you don't get a second chance. You hearing me?"

"Yeah," DJ said. "Loud and clear."

Reggie hung up, and DJ leaned his head back and tried to think. The throbbing in his leg made planning harder than it should have been. It all boiled down to one thing. The girl was a loose end. She could identify him. At this point, he figured he could probably replace the kid, but he had to find the girl.

What had Vic called her? Lila? Lisa? Yeah, Lisa something. That was a start. He'd track down Lisa, and when he did, he'd repay her in spades for the trouble she'd caused.

Chapter Six

The low buzz of a whispered conversation dragged Lisa from a comfortable sleep like an annoying mosquito at her ear. She wanted to swat it away, but the hum of indiscernible voices was no insect. When the murmur finally pierced the veil of sleep, she woke with a gasp of alarm. Someone was there. In the room with her. Hovering over Rachel's crib.

"What are you doing? Get away from her!" she cried, panic shooting through her veins. Protecting Rachel was her only job. Her highest priority. And she'd literally fallen asleep on her watch.

"Lisa, honey, it's okay," said Grace, the older woman wrapped in a fluffy bathrobe and one foam curler in her bangs. "We were just tucking her in for a nap after giving her breakfast and fresh jammies."

"You were sleeping so soundly, we hated to wake you. Clearly your body needed the rest," Eric said. He had a cloth diaper draped over one shoulder and an empty baby bottle in his hand. He waggled the bottle, saying, "She drank every bit."

Tossing back the bedcovers, Lisa stumbled to the crib, nudging her hosts aside and lifting Rachel into her arms.

"Oh, dearest, don't—" Grace protested. "We just got her settled."

Lisa turned her back to them, cuddling Rachel to her racing heart. If something terrible had happened to the baby while she was dead to the world—

Dead to the world...

The phrasing shot fresh waves of horror and shame through Lisa. How could she have failed Rachel so miserably? Failed her duty. Failed—what? Why did the idea that she'd committed some horrible gaff weigh on her so heavily?

Save Rachel...

She drew and released a cleansing breath. Rachel was her responsibility, but she didn't really think the Camerons or Eric posed any danger. Though Rachel was helpless and dependent on Lisa, Grace had more than ample mothering skills. No monsters lurked at the Cameron house. Yet the reassurances did little to alleviate the guilt of having let Rachel down so completely and so early in this...whatever it was. A disaster. An unplanned detour in her life. A sojourn down a dark dead-end alley.

Rachel gave a thin cry, and another prick of guilt lanced Lisa. In her haste to cover her dereliction of duty, she'd caused Rachel to cry, disturbed her from what had apparently been hard-earned rest.

She scrunched her eyes closed and bounced Rachel in her arms, shushing her with soft words. She could feel Eric and Grace watching her, probably judging her. Screwing up her courage, she faced them and opened her eyes. "I'm sorry. When I realized I'd overslept, that I hadn't heard Rachel wake this morning, that someone had entered the room without me knowing..." She shuddered. The last was the scariest proposition—that someone could have snuck in to the room and done any number of evil deeds, including harming her or taking Rachel. She shook her head, trying to rid herself of the jittery feeling crawling through her. "Well, I panicked."

Eric and his grandmother exchanged a glance, and with a small nod, Grace headed toward the door. "I'm making breakfast for everyone. How do you like your eggs, Lisa?"

Lisa considered the question. Surely she could answer a basic question about her preferences. When no answer came immediately to mind, the gravity of her predicament, the vast blankness of her past, sank onto her, weighty and grim. "I, um..."

"Let's all have fried eggs this morning," Eric suggested. "And if a better option occurs to Lisa later, we'll do it that way tomorrow. Sound good?"

Lisa nodded. "That's fine. Thanks."

With a nod of agreement, Grace disappeared into the hall, and Eric faced Lisa with a lopsided smile. "You've got enough brain work to do today without having to make trivial decisions, too."

"Brain work?"

He reached for Rachel, who was still fussing, and Lisa reluctantly allowed him to take the infant. He found the pacifier in the crib and popped it into Rachel's mouth. "We need to start sorting through whatever memories you can call up, try to find something that may be familiar, anything that triggers some recall for you."

Rachel quieted, sucking hard on the pacifier, and Eric laid her in the crib again. He aimed a finger at the crumpled blanket at the foot of the mattress, and Lisa tucked the blanket around Rachel. She gave the baby's mostly bald head a stroke and tried to dig up memories of putting Rachel to bed in a different crib. Nothing came to mind, but she experienced another deep blossoming of love for the child. *Her child.* Rachel had to be her child. Didn't she?

Save Rachel...

"Brain work," she muttered, knowing Eric was right but also dreading what she might dredge up. Once Rachel seemed settled, she donned the bathrobe one of Eric's aunts had contributed to her piecemeal wardrobe and followed him into the kitchen. Tempting aromas of coffee, cinnamon and yeast filled the kitchen, where Grace was cracking eggs into a large frying pan.

Eric headed straight for the coffee maker and took two mugs from the cabinet above. "Want some?"

She nodded eagerly and stepped up beside him, accepting the first pour. She sipped and winced. "Hmm, I think I like sugar in my coffee."

He scooted the sugar bowl to her, and she dumped in a heaping scoop. Tasted the brew again and furrowed her brow. Before she could ask, Eric handed her a small carton of half and half. She added a splash, then another larger one, turning her coffee a light tan shade. She sipped again and sighed in pleasure. "Now that's good."

"All right. One important question answered," Eric said with a grin. "You take your coffee sweet and creamy."

She returned a smile. As small and seemingly trivial as it might be, knowing even this tiny bit about herself felt like progress, and it buoyed her spirits.

She turned to the other end of the counter where a half-full pan of cinnamon rolls sat, waiting. Her stomach growled, and Eric chuckled.

"Help yourself," he said, waving a hand to the sweet treat. "I've already had mine."

She put one of the gooey rolls on a plate and took a seat next to Eric at the small kitchen table. She savored a bite and sighed her bliss. "That's so good. Are these homemade?"

Grace set a plate of eggs in front of Lisa and Eric and chuckled. "Sort of. They're from a local bakery. Do you want any juice with your eggs?"

"No, thank you." Lisa shifted her attention to the platter of eggs, their yolks sunny bulges on top. Eric shoveled two of the fried eggs onto his plate and motioned for her to scoot her plate closer. She did, and he slid two eggs from the serving dish onto her plate. She watched him break his yolks, spilling an orangey puddle across his plate, and her stomach roiled.

She set the cinnamon bun down and frowned as she stared in distaste at Eric's breakfast. The scent of grease and egg filled the air, and a strange sense of discomfort rumbled inside her.

"Lisa?" Eric said, his fork with a runny bite of egg suspended halfway to his mouth. "Something wrong? You look a little green around the gills."

"I think… I must not like fried eggs." She glanced to Grace. "I'm sorry. I—"

"Not a problem." Grace reached around Lisa to take her plate and scrape the eggs back into the frying pan. "I can scramble them a bit, if you want."

Lisa slid a napkin closer and set her cinnamon roll on it, shaking her head. "No, thank you. I—I'm not sure I like any kind of eggs. I—"

"Did you remember something else?" Eric asked, setting his fork down and narrowing his gaze on her. "Did the eggs trigger a memory?"

Lisa licked cinnamon icing from her fingers and cupped her hands around her mug, letting the warm ceramic chase the chill that had settled around her. "I don't know what it was. I just got this weird feeling when you cut into your yolks. The smell of the eggs and grease stirred…something. Not a memory exactly but a sense of…familiarity, maybe? And not a good familiar. More…" She fished for the right word, and when nothing came, she groaned and shook her head. "I don't know. Forget it."

"I know it's frustrating, but you need to follow the leads your subconscious gives you." Eric leaned toward her, his brown eyes growing bright with enthusiasm. "Smell is the sense most closely tied to memory. The smell of eggs or grease is likely bringing something to the surface. It could be an old emotional memory from your childhood or something more recent."

"The whatever-it-was that made me blank out?" she asked, a quiver in her gut.

He shrugged. "Possibly. But not necessarily. The scent of rubber mats and sweat in the gym where I work out reminds me of PE class in high school. I liked PE and was a pretty good athlete. But high school was a rough period for me, so that negative association tends to override the fonder memories of playing basketball with my classmates or doing indoor soccer drills on rainy days."

She nodded. "So eggs could just be a reminder of...something that happened at breakfast time?"

He lifted his shoulder again. "Maybe. I think our goal should be to follow any rabbit trail your brain gives you to see what turns up. Eventually the pieces will start fitting together or lead down a more certain path."

Lisa nodded, and after taking a sip of her coffee, she closed her eyes and tried to discern the odd sense of imbalance she'd experienced when Eric had broken the yolk on his plate and the aroma of frying had hit her nose. Was it the eggs per se, or did the smell conjure an associated bad memory?

An image teased her of dirty breakfast dishes. Lots of dirty breakfast dishes. Many smeared with egg yolk and grease. Was that real or just her trying to force her brain to make a connection?

"Grace, honey?" a male voice called from the back of the house, breaking Lisa's concentration. "I can't find my snow boots. Did you move them?"

Grace flashed a grin as she moved to the door. "I'll be right back." Then called down the hall, "Coming!"

When they were alone in the kitchen, Eric asked, "Anything else come to you?"

Lisa faced Eric, giving him a shake of her head. "Nothing. I don't know what it was. It's...gone now." A partial truth. The hint of recollection had faded, but the odd queasiness still sat in her gut. She pushed her plate away, her appetite gone.

Eric's cell phone rang, and he pulled it from his back pocket to check the screen. "Excuse me, I need to take this."

While he answered the call, she carried her plate to the sink and stared out the window to the backyard, where large white flakes still swirled lazily and icicles dangled from the roofline and deck railing. Large snow-dusted tarps were tepeed inside a chicken wire fence. A garden, she realized, with ground cover protecting plants from the freeze. What sort of plants grew in the winter? she wondered.

She craned her neck to take in the rest of the frozen yard. An A-frame with a bench swing sat on one side next to what appeared to be a terraced flower bed, and beyond the gently sloped yard, the house was surrounded by woods. Tall winter-bare hardwoods stood sentinel beside brushy evergreens. The blanket of snow hadn't been disturbed, and the scene was breathtaking.

"Righto. Thanks for calling," Eric said, and she pivoted to face him.

He put away his phone with a "huh" from his throat. "That's convenient. That was my boss saying not to come in. We were supposed to be framing a house in a new subdivision, but work is postponed due to this weather." He tucked his phone away and raised his mug toward her. "So I'm all yours today to start solving some of the mysteries of who and where your family is."

"And how do we do that if I can't remember anything?" She moved back to her chair and angled it to face him.

"We start with the only clue we have. The name tag and uniform you were wearing when I found you. I'm guessing they're from a restaurant of some sort. Maybe housekeeping at a motel." He arched a dark eyebrow. "Ring any bells?"

Lisa bit her bottom lip and stared down at the wood-grain pattern of the table, trying desperately to conjure any hint of where she'd gotten the name badge and clothing. Her mind not only stayed stubbornly blank, but the effort to recall her past churned inside her, souring her stomach and making her pulse spike. Clearly her brain was not ready for her to know what it was protecting her from. She sighed her dejection and shook her head. "I just...don't know."

"Well, I feel like driving out to various businesses in town to see if anyone remembers you or if you see something that feels familiar is going to be the most productive move, but—" he flipped up a palm "—since the roads are bad thanks to the snow and ice, that's not happening today."

"So, we accomplish nothing because of the weather?" Her tone matched the frustration that balled in her chest.

"Not necessarily." Eric sipped his coffee, clearly meditating on a plan of action. "We could...call around, ask if the businesses have an employee named Lisa and, if they do, ask for a physical description and whether they've seen you in the past twenty-four hours."

Her shoulders drooped. "That'll take forever."

Setting his mug down, he angled his head in inquiry. "You have another idea?"

Lisa grunted. "No." Raking hair back from her face, she sent Eric an apologetic frown. "I'm sorry. I know you're trying to help, and I do appreciate the place to stay, the meals and your concern. I'd probably be dead without you."

Her words caused a chill to creep up her spine.

Save Rachel...

The sense of danger that had nagged her returned, and she wrapped her arms around herself. With effort, she shoved the feeling down.

"Well, I could hardly leave you two on the side of the road to freeze," he said. A crooked smile tugged his cheek and glinted in his chocolate brown eyes. She couldn't help but notice again how handsome he was. Somehow doing so seemed safer, saner today. His cheeks and jaw were chiseled and squared, his nose a narrow, straight blade, his features symmetrical and...almost perfect. But more important, the kindness in his expression burrowed cozily inside her, battling the darker emotions stalking her.

"You could have left me at the hospital. Or taken me to a homeless shelter or…"

"No, I couldn't have." He reached for her hand, drawing it out from the armpit where she'd tucked it, hugging herself, trying to hold herself together. He curled his fingers around hers, their warmth an alluring contrast to her chilly hands. His palms were slightly calloused, a bit dry and chapped. Understandable, considering he'd said he was currently working construction for a living. But she could imagine those same large hands healing patients, tending sick children, performing intricate surgery. He was an intriguing mix of sexy rough edges, intelligence and comforting compassion.

A curiosity about Eric, a need to know more about her savior, washed over her. She wasn't satisfied with the sketchy knowledge and assumptions based on his friendliness and the family's generosity. She wanted to *know* Eric, who and what he was, almost more than she wanted to know who *she* was. What was she supposed to make of this strange pull she felt toward him? Was it just gratitude for his saving her, or was it…more?

The scuffling sound of slippered feet in the hall broke the spell that held her entranced and gazing into his dark eyes. She drew her hand from his. Rallied to her senses, she took a few hasty steps toward the hall. "I should, uh…check on Rachel."

Grace placed a hand on Lisa's forearm, stalling her as she reentered the kitchen. "I just did. She's sleeping." A devilish grin lit the older woman's face before she added, "Like a baby!" Grace chuckled at her own joke.

Lisa mustered a grin, if only to be polite. With her excuse for escape gone, she wound the terry-cloth belt of her robe around her fingers and lingered by the door to the hall, uncertain what to do. Without any idea who she was or where she belonged, her future was as blank as her past. She was adrift in a sea without paddles, or a sail or any navigational maps. And like Pi, she felt as if she had a tiger on her tiny life raft.

Pi?

She frowned, gripping the back of the first chair she reached and puzzling at the odd and random bit of information that had come to her. She braced her arms for support when her knees grew weak. "That's weird."

"What is?" Eric asked. He moved to the counter to refill his coffee but kept darting curious glances her direction.

"I was thinking about feeling alone, and I pictured characters from the novel *The Life of Pi*."

"Oh, I loved that movie! It was so poignant." Grace began handwashing the frying pan she'd used for the eggs.

Eric's focus had narrowed on Lisa, his fresh cup of coffee apparently forgotten. "So, you remember reading *The Life of Pi*? In school? With a book club?"

She shook her head. "Nothing as specific as that. Just… the story, the characters were just…there."

He nodded. "Let's try something. What's five times seven?"

"Thirty-five," she replied confidently.

"What's the capital of Vermont?"

Lisa hesitated. "Uh… Providence?"

Eric pulled a frown. "That's Rhode Island's."

She exhaled and pinched the bridge of her nose as she racked her brain. M-something? She snapped her fingers rapidly as if it could help her raise the factoid from the ether. "Wait… Mont—Mont…pelier!"

"Ding-ding," Eric said grinning. "One more?"

She spread her hands. "Why not?"

"Name the document Lincoln signed that freed the slaves."

"The Emancipation Proclamation," she said, holding up a finger. "But it only freed slaves in the states in rebellion. It took almost three more years and the ratification of the Thirteenth Amendment for slavery to be abolished throughout the United States." She gave a smug nod, then chuckled. "Oh my God! How did I know that?"

"You paid attention in class, apparently," Eric said. "And your reference to *The Life of Pi* hints at another suspicion I had about you."

"Oh?"

"Your language skills and vocabulary tell me you are well-educated or, at least, enjoy reading."

"Huh." Grace twisted at the waist and glanced back at Lisa. "I hadn't realized that. About the Emancipation Proclamation, I mean. I hadn't pieced the timeline together quite like that before. Interesting."

"So, I know history and geography and *The Life of Pi*, but not my own name? How is that possible? That doesn't make sense!" Lisa realized her volume had risen, and she quickly reeled herself in. "Sorry. I didn't mean to shout."

"Honey, if anyone has reason to shout and rail, it's you." Grace sent her a smile as she dried her hands on a towel. "Just...maybe step out on the back porch to do it so you don't wake little Rachel?"

Rounding the end of the table, Eric crossed the floor to her, and taking her by her upper arms, he turned her to face him. His grip was strong but not cruel.

"It makes perfect sense. And it's good news. All the information you learned in school is still right there, on call." He tapped a finger to her forehead. "More evidence that your amnesia wasn't caused by a stroke or seizure or tumor. But it still fits with your previous diagnosis. Knowing mathematics equations doesn't feel threatening the way more personal memories do. Your brain hasn't filtered those facts."

Eric's hands on her biceps steadied her, and she accepted his explanation, more settled now. He had an uncanny way of calming and centering her.

"Now, psychology and neurology were not my areas of specialty before I left medicine." He dropped his hands and stuffed them in his pockets. "I think we should get you appointments with specialists in both fields to continue your treatment."

"I don't know..."

He cocked his head to the side. "You can't solve a problem until you identify it."

She twisted the robe belt tighter. "Yeah, but you may remember the trouble I had at the ER? I don't have...or I don't *know* if I have medical insurance or a way to pay for doctors or shrinks."

He grunted. "Right. That's an issue." He scrubbed a hand on his unshaven jaw, drawing her attention to the masculine shadow of stubble. The light rasp of the short hairs against his callused palm sent a not unpleasant shiver down her back.

"All right. I'll think on it. In the meantime, since the roads aren't good for travel, we'll spend today making those phone calls to local businesses."

"I'll help. And I'm sure Neil will do his part." Grace braced her hands on her hips and cocked her head to one side. "In fact, Lexi has a snow day, so I bet she'd help. And I'll rally Isla and Cait and anyone else who's idle today because of the snowstorm."

Lisa blinked, feeling a bit overwhelmed again. "I don't want to impose on everyone—"

Grace waved a dismissive hand. "Not at all. We'll make it fun for the kids. We can bake cookies and make hot chocolate, and the youngest children can play board games. It's better than having them get cabin fever and spend the day with their noses in their phones!" Grace paused then chuckled. "Oh, well, I guess their ears will still be in their phones, huh? Making calls?"

Affection for the older woman with the joyful spirit and eagerness to help puddled at her core. Had her own mother or grandmother been as loving and available to her? She didn't know. Her family ties were a void in her mind. The tangled knot of anxiety and frustration returned, twisting deep at her core.

She gave Grace a trembling smile. "That sounds nice. Thank you for your help." While she didn't remember her mother, didn't have a family to go home to until she banished the amnesia, she had the Camerons. For today. A temporary home and family for herself and Rachel. She grasped that comforting thought and clung to it. For now, temporary was enough.

Chapter Seven

The Camerons' living room looked like the call center of a low-rate telethon. Eric, his stepmother, his half sister, two aunts, two cousins and both grandparents had gathered to make phone calls and cross businesses off the master checklist as they tried to locate the establishment where she worked. Where they *assumed* she worked. The name tag proved nothing really. She could have stolen the shirt and name badge from someone. Anything was possible.

Lisa was in charge of the main tally sheet of calls made and the results. Some businesses were closed because of the snow and would need to be called again later. Some refused to give information about employees over the phone, even a simple yes or no to the question, "Does someone name Lisa work there?" Meanwhile, the list of "no" responses was adding up, along with Lisa's frustration.

She tapped her pen on the notepad where she was recording responses and let her gaze drift to the window. The large property the family owned, called Cameron Glen, spread before her like a winter wonderland. Snow draped the evergreens and the small rental cabins with blanketed roofs, and tendrils of fireplace smoke were set against a pale blue sky. The snow had stopped falling, but the subfreezing temperatures kept the snow and ice in place. A crystalline layer of ice covered the small fishing pond at the foot of the hill where the senior Camerons lived. The scene was peaceful and—

Beside her, Eric's aunt Emma snapped her fingers loudly, calling the room's attention to her as she spoke on her phone. "Yes, and what is Lisa's last name? Grant? Fantastic. And can you describe Lisa Grant for me? What color hair and eyes? Body type and age?"

A sense of excitement buzzed through Lisa. Or was it dread? Did she want to know who she was if it meant learning the awful thing that had erased her memory and sent her out on the frozen highway in a daze?

But then Emma's hopeful expression fell, and she angled a disappointed frown and head shake toward the room. "No. Sorry. That's not the woman I'm looking for. Thank you." Emma ended the call as a collective groan rose from the others. "Lisa *Grant* is in her fifties and had been at the store earlier this morning."

Lisa flopped back in her chair, slouching as disappointment and frustration washed over her. "This is a waste of y'all's time. I can't ask you to spend endless days randomly calling stores and restaurants and beauty parlors on my behalf."

"Beauty parlors!" Eric snapped his fingers, and his face lit. "Good idea. I hadn't thought of that." Then, cocking his head slightly, he shot a speculative glance at her. "Does something about beauty parlors move the needle for you?"

If possible, she slumped farther into the chair. "No. But Cait called one earlier." She tapped the pad in her lap. "Bella's Cut 'n Clip."

"Oh." Eric buzzed his lips as he exhaled a long slow breath. He shoved to his feet and moved to kneel beside her. "This isn't a waste of time for me. I'm in this until we find your family or, barring that, get you and Rachel safely settled somewhere that you can—I don't know—make a new life?

Or at least get the counseling and medical help you need to move forward."

"That's not your job. You don't have to do any of this!"

"We've been over this. I *want* to do this for you. I can't, in good conscience, walk away until we've figured things out for you, and I know you'll be safe. Provided for. So—" he flashed a charming grin "—you're stuck with me."

She dropped her eyes to her lap, trying to sort out her emotions, which was impossible while gazing into Eric's handsome face and beguiling eyes.

She hated the idea of being a burden to anyone. Heavens, but she wanted to unblock her mind and regain her equilibrium! She had to stand on her own two feet. The idea of relying on anyone for support caused a quaking in her core she couldn't explain.

Was it a clue to who she was? Did her yearning for independence mean she had no family she could count on?

And where was Rachel's father? Did she love him? Was there a man out there waiting for them, worried about them, looking for them? She'd spent hours last night in the dark trying to call up a face, a name, a feeling…anything that would fill in the blank slate. But over and over, the face that came to her was Eric's. His kind eyes, his soothing voice, his warm smile. She returned to that image repeatedly because Eric made her feel…safe.

And why was safety so important to her? Her amnesia was scary, sure. But why did she want Eric to hold her and reassure her the way he held Rachel, calmed her? Why did she get the sense that falling for Eric's charming smile and sweet talk meant she would be giving up something important? How could this kind man and his welcoming, generous family be anything but a blessing for her? But the low hum of uneasiness in her bones couldn't be denied. Nor could the pit of dread or fear or worry that sat heavily in her gut be dismissed.

Down the hall, Rachel whined, and Lisa shot to her feet. Sixteen-year-old Lexi jumped up, as well. "I'll get her."

"No," she returned. "Please. Let me. I...need to hold her. I want to." Though she couldn't verbalize the deep yearning inside her, she needed to be close to Rachel, exploring the bond she felt for her, hoping that something about caring for her baby would lift the fog and start making sense of their situation.

In the guest bedroom, she leaned over the side of the travel crib and lifted her whimpering infant into her arms. She patted Rachel's bottom, and the diaper felt heavy and full, so she carried the baby to the bed. While holding Rachel on her hip, she used her free hand to spread a towel on the bed, where she changed the baby's diaper. Then she dug in an overnight bag that Eric's aunt Isla had brought up with her when she arrived to make calls.

Lisa found a clean set of blue pajamas and dressed Rachel. The terry cloth jammies might have had dinosaurs pictured all over them, but they were clean and fit, and that was all that mattered.

Returning to the living room with Rachel on her hip, Lisa found Isla with her gaze, and when the redhead looked up as if sensing her attention, Isla smiled at them.

"Oh, look at your sweet thing in Joey's pj's!" She climbed off the floor where she sat and hurried over to tickle Rachel's belly. "She looks so cute! I knew there was a reason not to give Joey's clothes away yet. I could feel in my bones that there'd be another Cameron Glen baby needing them."

Lisa considered reminding Isla that Rachel wasn't a "Cameron Glen baby" but bit her tongue, not wanting to sound unappreciative. "Thank you again for bringing them. They're a perfect fit."

Isla hummed and flashed a wry grin. "Which means in five minutes they won't fit. They grow so fast at this stage! Right?"

Lisa opened her mouth and closed it, not knowing how to

respond. How was she supposed to know how rapidly Rachel would grow when she couldn't remember her birth or any other part of her last six months? She settled for an agreeable smile and nod. "I'm going to get her a bottle now."

Eric followed her into the kitchen and helped buckle Rachel in the high chair. He booped Rachel on the nose with one finger and chucked her under the chin once she was strapped in, winning a half grin from the baby. His ease with Rachel was heartening. Lisa could well imagine most bachelors of his age weren't nearly so comfortable around infants, no matter how many small cousins or younger sisters he'd spent time around.

"So, what do you think she'll eat besides a bottle?" he asked, moving to the stash of baby food jars they'd brought in from the store yesterday after leaving the ER. "Pureed bananas are a favorite first food, if I remember right."

"Sure. Sounds fine." She slid the tray of the borrowed high chair in place. "I'm guessing this high chair and the travel crib saw a lot of action in recent years. And I'm guessing Grace loved every minute of it."

Eric selected a jar of bananas, retrieved a tiny plastic spoon and set them on the table next to Lisa. "You'd be right. Lots of babies. Lots of chaos. And lots of love."

Lisa popped open the tiny jar and turned to Rachel, whose attention had homed in on the small jar. She slapped the chair tray and opened her mouth like a bird.

"Someone is hungry," Lisa said, spooning up a bite and feeding it to the eager baby.

"Oh, hey, let's, um..." Eric held up a finger, signaling *wait*. He disappeared down the hall, returning a few moments later with a bib and burp cloth. He snapped the bib around Rachel's neck and handed Lisa the cloth. "Can't forget these or you'll be changing her again."

A strange knot in her chest tightened. She *had* forgotten the bib. Yet it should have been so obvious. She remembered math and Abraham Lincoln, but not a bib when feeding her daughter?

Was Rachel even her daughter? If she wasn't, why did Lisa have the child with her? Was that why caring for her seemed awkward and foreign?

Save Rachel. The imperative niggled, a haunting refrain.

A squawk from Rachel, her little bow lips open and waiting for more lunch, drew Lisa from her momentary daze. She shoved down the nagging doubts and whys and gave Rachel her full attention. The bittersweet bond and affection that told her the baby *must* be hers surged as she spooned puree to Rachel. She marveled at the little girl's smacking lips and bright eyes as she gummed the bananas and let half of them ooze back out of her mouth. Soon bananas were smeared over her cheeks, her hands and the tray.

Eric laughed. "See what I mean about the bib? At this point they don't so much eat lunch as wear it. But she'll get better at it soon."

Isla appeared at the door, her expression hopeful. "Hey, Lisa, I found a hardware store just outside of town that said they had a worker not show up today. He wouldn't give me a name or description, saying he had to protect his employees' privacy, but—" she flapped a hand and wrinkled her nose in query "—do you think you might have worked at a hardware store? The guy said his name was Pete, if that helps."

Lisa sat with the information a moment, trying to see how it felt, if anything tickled her brain. But nothing stirred. She shook her head. "No. Still nothing. Sorry."

Isla shrugged. "Worth a shot. Back to the phones." With a comical swing of her elbows, Isla headed back to the living room.

"Eric," Lisa said, turning to him, a sinking cold in her core. "Who's to say I'm even from Valley Haven? I could live and work anywhere. Asheville. Charlotte. Waynesville. Or *Tennessee!*"

His face sobered. "I know, but we have to start somewhere."

She released her dejection in a weary sigh. "We could spend days, weeks even, calling every business in the state and still not learn anything!"

He pressed his palms flat on the table, his mouth a thin line of frustration. "I know it feels futile and tedious, but it's really all we have to go on at the moment. Unless you've thought of something else to try?"

"What if you run an ad in several regional newspapers with her picture?"

They both turned toward the new voice. Eric's stepmother, who'd asked Lisa to call her Cait, moved from the doorway into the kitchen. She tucked a copper-brown curl behind her ear and raised her eyebrows, inviting reply.

"An ad?" Eric asked.

"With a caption along the lines of 'Do you know this woman? Call…' and then one of our phone numbers. And put it out on several social media platforms and ask for shares. Kinda the reverse of when someone goes missing, but same tactics."

Eric was nodding. "I like that. Good thinking, Cait."

"Speaking of missing persons, have you checked with the police to see if Lisa or Rachel match any missing person reports?"

"Yeah," Eric said. "They did at the hospital yesterday, but it's worth calling the police department and checking again."

A chill crept through Lisa, a foreboding she couldn't explain. "I don't… I mean, I know you're trying to help but… something about the idea…" She swallowed hard, stared at the jar of pureed bananas.

"What?" Eric asked, taking the burp rag from her and wiping Rachel's face.

"I don't like the idea of being so…*exposed* is the only way I know to say it. Ever since you picked me up from the roadside yesterday, I can't shake this…this feeling that something bad, *someone* bad is waiting. Or following me. Or *hunting* me."

Chapter Eight

Eric and Cait exchanged a wary look.

"I know it sounds kooky," Lisa said, "and I can't explain it, but...something or someone scared me. You said so yourself, Eric. Something terrible must have happened, or someone horrible must have threatened me to have put me in such a stunned state and wiped my brain. Isn't that what you said? Why would I want that bad person to know where I was?"

Eric skewed his mouth to one side, his brow furrowed, but he said nothing.

When Rachel slapped the tray and whined, Lisa scooped another bite in the girl's waiting mouth. "I don't mean to be difficult, and I suppose your idea has merit, but... I just wish I could shake this...*feeling*."

Cait arched an eyebrow and sent Eric a knowing grin before moving to the kitchen door. "Isla, can you come here a moment please?"

"Cait, I know what you're thinking," Eric said, his expression skeptical, "but do you really believe—"

"You rang?" Isla rounded the corner from the hall into the kitchen, her blue eyes bright with curiosity and an obvious zest for life.

"Have a seat, sister dear," Cait said, with a lilt in her tone as she pulled the chair next to Lisa out from under the table. She waved Isla to it.

Isla snorted. "Sister dear? Oh, boy. What's going on?"

"Cait, seriously?" Eric grumbled.

"What can it hurt?" Cait returned, then facing her sister said, "Lisa has a *feeling* that something or someone bad might be looking for her."

Lisa stiffened. Frowned. Were they mocking her? It seemed so out of character for this family who'd been so kind and welcoming before now, but something odd was definitely afoot.

Isla tipped her head to one side. "Oh, yeah? And?"

"Well, since we have so little else to go on, I wondered if you…sensed anything. Is your special gift telling you anything?" Cait scrunched her nose and flipped up a hand in question.

Eric groaned.

"What's happening?" Lisa whispered to Eric, her heart thumping.

Cait flapped a hand. "Ignore the skeptic's dismissive grunts. Isla has a sort of sixth sense. She knew before I did when I was pregnant, and she knew, at first sight, when she met her husband that they were soulmates…among other mental feats of wonder and amazement."

Lisa cut a startled look toward Eric's aunt. "Really?"

Isla gave her an embarrassed grin and nodded.

"So, you're like a psychic or something?" Lisa shifted in her chair, a little uneasy with the prospect that Isla could read her mind or tell her things about her life she couldn't remember on her own.

"Not a psychic, no. Nothing quite that dramatic. But I'm what they call an empath. I can easily pick up on others' emotions, and I read subtle signs other folks might ignore. And I sometimes get *feelings* about a situation that I can't explain, but usually turn out to be true."

"When our nephew Ravi was three," Cait added, "all the adults were having lunch together while the kids napped, and she sensed that Ravi was in danger from out of nowhere. We found him playing at the top of the stairs, where he'd managed to get the baby gate unlocked."

The expression that lit Cait's face asked, *Impressive, right?*

"Um, wow," Lisa said, nodding. "That's a handy skill to have."

Cait waggled a finger toward Isla. "So, are you getting anything from Lisa, sis?"

Isla sighed and chuckled. "I've told you it doesn't work like that! I'm not a monkey that can perform on command."

Cait's face fell. "So nothing?"

Isla pivoted on the chair and met Lisa's gaze. "It's worth a shot. Give me your hands."

Not wanting to be rude to Isla, Lisa passed the spoon and baby food jar to Eric. He rolled his eyes, but took over feeding Rachel.

Scooting on her chair toward Isla, Lisa held out her hands and met the strawberry blonde's pale blue eyes. Isla stacked Lisa's hands and sandwiched them between hers, then buffed them. "Well, for starters, your hands are freezing! We can get you a cardigan or sweatshirt if you're cold."

Lisa considered denying she needed more clothes. She was already far too indebted to the Camerons. But she was, in fact, rather chilly. "Uh, yeah. Thanks."

"On it." Cait headed out of the kitchen. "Be right back."

Isla gave Lisa a lopsided smile. "I know this whole situation must feel pretty overwhelming. If this—" she jostled their joined hands "—is uncomfortable for you, we don't have to do it." She leaned close saying under her breath, "And like I said, I'm not a psychic. I don't know what Cait thinks I can do to—"

Isla fell abruptly silent, her brow creasing, and her mouth pulling in a frown.

Lisa's heartbeat stumbled. "What is it?"

Isla blinked rapidly and laughed nervously. "Um, wow. I wasn't expecting that."

"What?" Lisa repeated, trying to pull her hands away.

Isla gripped Lisa's fingers to stop her. "I'm sorry. I've frightened you, and I didn't mean to do that at all. It's just, I am getting some rather strong vibes from you. Give me a moment. I need to sort through them."

"You don't have to do this," Eric said. "Isla, you're putting her on the spot. Don't—"

"Shh," Isla said. "I'm trying to think."

Eric grunted and continued feeding Rachel, who hummed, "Mmm," contentedly with each new bite.

Lisa chewed her bottom lip, not at all sure she wanted to hear what Isla had to say. Or if she even believed in this sort of extrasensory stuff. At least Isla wasn't chanting or asking for locks of her hair to burn.

"Well, I can definitely sense that you're scared. Confused. But that's pretty obvious to all of us. And understandable." Isla looked deep into her eyes, her expression gentle yet probing.

Cait returned with a gray West Point sweatshirt, which she draped around Lisa's shoulders. "Our brother Daryl left this here after Christmas. You're welcome to it. There's no way it fits him anymore. He's gotten so muscular in the Army. What'd I miss?"

"I'm also feeling something beneath your fear. A sadness," Isla said.

"I thought the point was to be helpful. Telling her she's sad only drags her down further, Isla," Eric said, and Cait and Isla shushed him in unison.

"That's not news. I already knew there was sadness in the mix. But can you tell what happened to me? Why I'm sad? What it is I'm blocking?" Lisa asked.

Isla shook her head. "Oh, heavens no, honey. Like I said,

I'm not psychic, and I really don't have any control over what I pick up on."

"Then what's the point of this?" Eric asked, waving the baby spoon. A glob of pureed bananas dripped on his lap. "Crud."

"Shh," the Cameron sisters said.

Lisa cut her glance to Eric in time to see him wipe up the spilled goop and scoop up another bite for Rachel, his own mouth opening slightly as he poked the spoon in the infant's mouth. A wave of warmth flowed through her. His ease with Rachel, his love for his family and his dedication to helping her coalesced in a sweet soup of awe and respect.

"Oh!" Isla said.

Lisa whipped her gaze back to the redhead. "What?"

Isla opened her mouth and cast quick glances to Cait and Eric. "Um…nothing." Scooting her chair back, she moved her hand to Lisa's shoulder. "I'm sorry I couldn't help. Other than to tell you what you already know. But your feelings—fear, sadness—are really all I'm sensing from you."

Isla beat a hasty retreat while sending her sister a strange look.

"I'll, uh…get back to making calls," Cait said, following Isla from the kitchen.

Lisa stared after the sisters, puzzled by their abrupt departure and the unspoken messages flying between them. When they were gone, she said, "That was weird."

"Told ya." Eric gave her a smug look.

"Not the first bit. I don't know how I feel about extrasensory stuff, but…did you see the look she gave your stepmom before they skedaddled?"

Eric stopped scraping out the banana jar to look up at her. "No. What'd I miss?"

Lisa shook her head. "Maybe nothing. Maybe I'm paranoid. Maybe—" She raised a hand to pinch the bridge of her nose, and the West Point sweatshirt slipped off her shoulders. Stooping to gather it from the floor, she had the briefest glimpse of an image in her head. A different shirt on a different floor. And a flash of panic spun through her.

With the sweatshirt clutched in her hand, she sat up, sucking in a sharp breath.

"Lisa?"

She stared hard at the gray shirt, racking her brain for the source of the memory, its meaning. But as quickly as it came, it was gone, leaving only her accelerated heartbeat and shallow breathing in its wake. Was this how it would be for weeks, months to come? Unexpected flashes sneaking out of the ether to scare the tar out of her? The prospect of living on the edge, subject to kamikaze snips that destroyed her peace of mind but offered no valuable insights was daunting. Appalling. How was living in fear of the void, dreading the scary flashbacks, any better than facing the realities of what had happened to her and getting her life back on track?

"Lisa?" Eric repeated louder, and moved his hand to her arm.

She angled her gaze toward him, and dragged up a fleeting smile. The sooner she found whatever memories she'd lost and dealt with them, the sooner she could begin to regain control over her life. "Maybe that idea of placing an ad to see if anyone knows me isn't such a bad idea."

He nodded slowly. "What changed your mind?"

"I just... I need to know who I am. No matter how bad it is, whatever happened... I need to remember."

Chapter Nine

Phone calls continued throughout the afternoon with no success other than eliminating businesses in an ever-growing radius of Valley Haven from contention as Lisa's employer.

The younger members of the telephone team—Lexi, Isla's twelve-year-old daughter, Cece, and Eric's twelve-year-old half sister, Erin—soon resigned their duties in favor of sledding, hot chocolate and video games. Emma was next to quit after she got a phone call that she was needed by her charitable organization to help with an emergency situation.

"Sorry to bail, but a toddler in Winston Salem was snatched from the mother in a grocery store parking lot while she loaded her purchases in the car. I've been asked to go as support and advocate for the family."

Lisa's breath froze in her lungs as she shot Eric's aunt a horrified look. *A toddler was snatched.*

Emma must have felt Lisa's gaze, because she paused in the door and glanced back at her. "It's okay. This baby was taken today. A boy of seventeen months. Completely unrelated to your situation. I'll let Eric explain to you what I do and why. Right now, I must fly." She gave Lisa a warm smile. "Okay?"

Lisa nodded, though it took a few tries to unstick the air from her throat and breathe normally again.

"Do be careful, dear! The roads are so treacherous!" Grace said, giving Emma a tight hug.

"Of course. We're taking Jake's four-wheel-drive. He has snow tires. I'll call when we get in." Emma kissed her mother's cheek and hustled out.

Eric finished the call he was on and moved from the couch to sit next to Lisa at the dining room table where she was still maintaining the master list of calls.

"So, about eleven or twelve years ago, Fenn—Emma's older daughter—was taken by some sex traffickers. They got her back, but the experience motivated them to start a nonprofit that fights sex trafficking and educates teenagers about how sex traffickers operate. Emma also got trained to be an advocate for parents when their children go missing or are stolen. She uses her experience and knowledge to help the parents navigate the crisis and work with law enforcement around the state."

Lisa laid down her pen and pressed both hands to her face. She tried to process what she was learning about Emma and Fenn and the rest of the extended Cameron family today. Her mind reeled. She took a beat, then shook her head. "Your family is…really something. It sounds like y'all have been through all kinds of hell."

Eric grunted and pulled his mouth in a half grin. "You could say that."

"But…you seem to always turn it around, to make something good from it. Nonprofits and marriages and catching killers. I didn't think people as nice as y'all were left in the world."

He lifted a shoulder. "We try to do our part. I don't know that we're all that different than most people. I like to think there's still a lot of good in the world." Eric furrowed his brow as he narrowed his gaze on her. "Where do you think your worldview comes from? Are you remembering people from your past or…?"

She blinked. "I don't know. That is kinda depressing, isn't it? Why should kindness feel so out of the norm?" Lisa wrinkled her nose. "That's not the kind of person I want to be. A pessimist. A Debbie Downer. A Holden Caulfield."

Eric's cheek twitched, and he raised a hand to hide his grin.

"What's funny about that?" she asked.

"Nothing. It's admirable to want to be optimistic. It's just you...did it again."

"Did what?"

"Referenced a literary character. I believe you, ma'am, are a reader. Including the classics."

She slanted a grin at him. "I like that. It feels...right. Comfortable."

"In that case," he said, lacing his fingers with hers, "we'll be sure to go by the library in town as soon as possible. Not only do we want to see if anyone there recognizes you as a patron, but you can pick up some reading material."

His thumb stroked the back of her hand, sending dizzying waves of pleasure through her. She had to swallow before she could speak. "Okay. Sounds good."

"In the meantime, feel free to borrow anything you want from my shelves. And I'm sure my aunts have no shortage of books you could choose from."

The idea of nestling under a warm quilt and reading a good book stirred such an excitement and joy in her, she knew they'd struck on something true and real from her past. She was a reader. More important, she took great comfort in the idea they'd recovered even a tiny piece of her soul, her identity. And it gave her hope.

DJ LIMPED INTO his favorite bar, clutching his injured thigh. His injury hurt like hell. If he wasn't going to use any of the stuff his customers begged him for, he was left with drowning his pain with a legal drug. Bourbon and lots of it.

"What happened to you?" Burt asked from behind the bar, giving him an up-and-down look and frown.

"None of your business. Give me a Jack and keep 'em comin'."

DJ carefully perched on the barstool, his wounded leg stretched out straight below the bar. When Burt slid his drink to him, he downed it in two gulps and shoved the glass back at the bartender. "Another."

This one he drank a bit slower, but not by much. He'd started to feel a bit buzzed, and his pain dulled some by the time he finished his third, which allowed him to think more clearly about his problem. Almost two days had passed, and he was no closer to finding the girl. He'd recovered Vic's phone from the scene of the disaster and found a home address for Lisa in the guy's contacts. DJ had spent the last twenty-two hours watching Lisa's apartment. Waiting. She'd never returned. He couldn't find any other clues in the cell phone hinting where Lisa would have gone. If she was hiding from him, she was doing a damn good job of it.

Grunting his frustration, he turned his attention to the television on the wall. It was tuned to the twenty-four-hour sports channel, where the talking heads were discussing the NFL playoffs. He raised his glass, aiming it toward the TV. "Hey, Burt. Don't the local channels have some news on during the lunch hour?"

The bartender shrugged. "Couldn't say. I keep this set on the sports channel."

"Change it and see."

Burt narrowed a suspicious look on him. "Why?"

DJ glowered at the barkeeper. "Because I want to see the news."

Burt snorted but complied, flipping past soap operas and cartoons and a courtroom drama until he found a local newscast. "Want to know if you've been found out? If the cops are looking for ya?" The bartender turned back toward DJ, a wry grin pulling his mouth to one side.

"Har. Har," DJ said without a morsel of humor. Burt was kidding, but he didn't know how close he was to the truth. He shot the barkeep a middle finger.

Any reply Burt might have made was cut short when the phone beside the cash register rang. Wiping his hands on a towel, Burt moved over to answer the call.

DJ focused on what the local newscast was discussing. The snowstorm, of course. School and business closings.

"Who?" Burt said, "Naw, we don't have no Lisa working here. Sorry, ma'am."

Lisa? The name sent a ripple down his back.

DJ jerked his attention to Burt. "Who was that?"

The bartender flipped up a hand. "Just some lady wanting to know if we had anyone named Lisa working here." He paused and frowned. "Why do you care?"

"I'm looking for someone named Lisa, too. Did this lady say anything else?"

"No. Why are you looking for a Lisa?"

"You got caller ID?" DJ asked, ignoring Burt's question and nodding toward the landline.

"Yeah." Burt walked back to the phone and scrolled the previous calls screen. "No name. Just says Valley Haven, North Carolina. That help you at all?"

DJ tapped his glass on the bar top, demanding a refill. "It just might."

Chapter Ten

After another day of snow and ice on the roads and postponed construction, the sun appeared and quickly thawed out the town. The warmer temperatures left behind mud and all excuses not to return to regular routines. The kids went back to school, and Eric returned to work. The nature of his job, pounding nails and holding two-by-fours for his coworkers as they framed a house, gave his brain ample time to replay every moment he'd spent with Lisa since Monday evening and what little they'd achieved solving the riddles that surrounded her.

By quitting time, he was chilled to the marrow and had come up with nothing new concerning Lisa's situation. He cranked up the heat in his Honda to full blast and pointed his wheels toward home.

As he drove, he continued pondering next steps for Lisa. His plan moving forward involved driving her out to see Valley Haven and surrounding communities, hoping she'd recognize something, and it would trigger a memory for her. A long shot, sure. But calling businesses all over the area, trying to discover where she worked, had been a long shot as well. Right now, long shots were all they had.

Which begged the question—what if they never came up with any answers? What would happen to Lisa and Rachel? Did they find her a job and more permanent lodging here in

Valley Haven? If she got a job, who would watch Rachel? Childcare would eat up a large chunk of what was left of her income after paying rent and food. Diapers were expensive. And—

Eric exhaled and bumped the side of his fist on his steering wheel. Okay, bigger question—why the hell was he planning Lisa's future for her? She'd let him know more than once that she didn't want to be his responsibility. Even if she couldn't remember her past, her future was *hers* to decide.

He grunted his discontent. At this point, he couldn't even make firm plans regarding his own future. Would he ever return to medicine? How long did he plan to work construction? He'd moved to Valley Haven, to Cameron Glen, with the intention of finding his footing again. He'd only planned to take a break, make a new plan. But he still had to deal with his past...

When was he going to deal with the nightmare from that summer eleven years ago so he could get *his* life back on track? Lisa didn't know what had traumatized her. He did. And he'd been avoiding that elephant in the room for so long, he'd elevated avoidance to an art form. Was his fixation on saving Lisa just another ploy to put off dealing with his own crap?

He gritted his teeth, not liking that scenario one bit.

The strobe of emergency lights ahead on the road drew him out of his pondering and focused his attention back on his driving. Though sun and warmer temperatures had melted most of the icy patches, the roads still had sketchy spots. On the narrower, steeper, more twisty mountain roads like the one that led to Cameron Glen, the possibility of skidding off the road held even more dire repercussions. He was on such a road at the moment as he left the worksite, and he slowed as he passed the sheriff's patrol cars and a small volunteer fire department truck.

He rubbernecked as he drove by but saw little. The many

members of the emergency response teams stood at the edge of the road peering down the steep side of the mountain. Single-car wreck? Bear needing relocation? Stranded hiker? Wildfire? He couldn't tell. Could have been any of those things or something more obscure.

After working in the emergency room for a rotation, he knew humans had the capacity to get themselves into crazy situations. He chuckled, remembering some of the crazier cases he'd worked. Full moons. Pay day weekends. Halloween. They all signaled wild times in an ER.

A tug at his core told him he missed working with patients, helping people, healing people. Was that why he'd invested himself so deeply in Lisa's situation? Was he trying to recapture the satisfaction and fulfillment he got practicing medicine?

Thoughts of Lisa waiting back at the Camerons' house stirred a different sort of warmth inside him, one he'd been intentionally shoving down for the last few days. He was attracted to her in a powerful way. Everything about her, from her fine-boned face to her shy smile moved him. He experienced a crackling energy between them and sensed a similar interest from her. And yet...

Rachel.

Didn't the fact that Lisa had a daughter mean she also had a husband or boyfriend? Logic would say *yes*, but why, then, didn't Lisa remember a man in her life? His thoughts cycled again through the unanswered questions, like a dryer tumbling laundry. Around and around. He played with the likelihood that some man was behind her trauma, the injuries on her torso.

A wave of rage filled Eric just at the suggestion of someone abusing Lisa. As he neared Cameron Glen, he shook that tension from his hands and pushed the impotent anger aside.

Another rescue vehicle passed him going the opposite direction, and his thoughts shifted. Emergency vehicles...

car accident. Could they ask the various local police about crashed or abandoned cars? Could Lisa's walking the shoulder of the road be due to her having a car that was wrecked or mechanically broken down? Eager to follow this new avenue, he called his uncle Brody, who was a volunteer with the fire department, from the driveway of his grandparents' house.

"We've answered a lot of calls related to car accidents and stranded vehicles thanks to this weather. What specifically are you looking for?" Brody said. In the background of the connection, Eric heard the squeals and clatter of three active children getting ready for dinner.

Eric gave him an overview of Lisa's situation.

"Oh yeah," Brody said. "Anya told me about you bringing her into the ER."

"If she had a car at some point and left it behind—"

"Right. I see where you're going with this." Then he muttered, "Ravi, put that down and wash your hands for dinner." Back in Eric's ear, Brody finished. "I'll keep my ears open, man. Good luck."

Eric thanked him, disconnected and, encouraged by the new tactic to pursue, he hurried inside. He found Lisa in the living room of his grandparents' house using a borrowed iPad.

"Whatcha up to?" he asked her, stopping by the playpen, where Rachel banged a plastic block against another. He bent to stack a few of the blocks for the baby only to have Rachel knock them down with a gleeful swat.

"Looking for a job," Lisa said.

"What?" He dropped on the couch beside her. "Why?"

"Because it is kinda obvious to me that my memory isn't coming back any time soon—"

"You don't know that."

"—and I can't impose on you and your family forever."

"You're not an imposition."

She gave him a look that said she disagreed. "Before I can

get a place of my own, I need money." She tapped the iPad screen. "Which means I need a job."

He tugged the tablet from her hands and angled his body to face her. "It's still early days. We've barely begun trying to coax out some of your buried memories. Saturday, we can drive into town, visit some popular businesses and see what shakes loose."

She lifted a shoulder. "Okay. But that doesn't change the fact that your grandmother doesn't need me and Rachel underfoot."

He twisted his mouth. "Yeah. I was thinking about that today and wondered…how would you feel about moving in with me? The cabin I'm renting is just across the lake." He aimed his thumb toward the front window where, down the steep hillside from the Cameron's house, a small fishing pond glimmered in the fading daylight. "I've been using the second bedroom as a junk room, but it wouldn't take much to clear it out and set up a futon for me to sleep on. You could stay with me, where I can help with Rachel and be close in case—" He cut himself off.

"In case of trouble," she finished for him. "In case I remember something and flip out. In case whatever horror I left behind catches up to me."

He pressed his mouth in a firm line and exhaled. "Yeah. Something like that."

She buzzed her lips in exasperation. "I do want to get out of Grace's way," she said in a quiet voice. "She's as nice as can be, and I really appreciate everything, but…she's kind of cloying. And she wants to take charge of Rachel. But if Rachel's my daughter, shouldn't caring for her be my job? Don't I need to figure out how this baby care business works?"

If Rachel is my daughter…

He was still musing over the conditional phrasing when Lisa dropped another surprise on him. "And I called a mental health clinic today. They have a counselor there I can talk to at no charge for three visits. My first visit is next Tuesday."

He quirked an eyebrow. "A counselor?"

She shrugged. "Well, I figured rather than spend endless hours looking for someone that knows me, I should go to the source of my problem. I need to try to unblock my memory. I have to figure out what happened to me."

Chapter Eleven

That Saturday, while Lexi watched Rachel, Eric drove Lisa into the small town of Valley Haven to get her impressions and test her recognition.

"It may be a long shot," Eric said as they made their way down the winding road from Cameron Glen to town, "especially since none of the Camerons, who've lived here for generations, recognize you. This town isn't big enough to hide secrets, but we'll give it a try. If nothing sparks here, we can head to Asheville or another of the nearby towns."

Lisa wiped her surprisingly damp palms on her new jeans and nodded. Why did this test of her memory feel so momentous? Was this performance anxiety? She chuckled wryly at herself. She was actually worried about letting Eric down if nothing popped on this cruise through local cities.

Compounding her nerves was the dribble of phone calls that were coming in. The advertisement asking if anyone recognized Lisa's picture ran in the local newspaper for the first time that morning, and the family had begun sharing her picture on social media. Eric had listed his cell phone number as the contact as well as the number of the burner cell phone he'd purchased for Lisa. Though she'd wanted to turn down the burner phone, she knew she needed a contact number to help her get a job, as well as a means to reach Eric or other help in case of an emergency. In case the lurking sense of trouble following her proved real...and caught up to her.

She'd added the phone to the growing list of expenses she intended to pay back...eventually. Somehow.

Lisa scanned the storefronts and quaint homes that lined the streets of Valley Haven as Eric rolled slowly past. She stared hard at the hardware stores, bakeries, funky clothing stores and bistros, digging into the blank pit of her past for any inkling of recognition. Nothing stirred.

But the more of the charming town she saw, the more she longed for a reason to call this community her home. The tree lined streets, refurbished downtown, intriguing local artisan galleries and coffee shops beckoned to her. She *wanted* this sweet town to be her home.

But nothing about it rang familiar.

She was about to give Eric that disappointing news when her burner phone rang.

Heart thumping, she answered with a tentative "Hello?"

"Yeah, this Lisa?" a male voice asked.

She shot Eric an anxious glance and said, "Yes."

"I saw your ad. I don't know you or nothin', but I think you're hot. If you wanted to hook up," he said, his tone leering, "I can help you out with that." He elaborated with some further crude language, and with a gasp of disgust, Lisa jerked the phone away from her ear as if it were a snake that might bite her.

Eric grabbed the phone from her, told the guy off and disconnected the call. "A few crackpots and jerks are to be expected, I guess. But I'm sorry you had to hear that."

A shiver of revulsion shimmied through her, along with another realization. Eric had been nothing but a gentleman from the moment he guided her out of the snowstorm and into the warm front seat of his car. He'd opened doors for her, pulled out chairs for her, shown her kindness and respect and generosity from the start. She knew that men like

Eric weren't extinct, but somehow he seemed like a unicorn to her. What did that say about her past relationships? She hated to think, especially if she was expected to return to that world. A wave of affection for her rescuer swelled in her chest, something deeper and sweeter than the gratitude she'd been feeling. *He's special*, a tiny voice whispered in her mind.

"Well, that's about it," Eric said a few minutes later. "We've pretty much covered all of Valley Haven."

Lisa shrugged. "Pretty much what we expected, considering your family didn't know me."

He acknowledged this with a tip of his head. "Before we move on to the next town or get a bite to eat, let's stop by the police station to see if they've had any new missing person reports or got anything back from the forensics lab on your clothes."

The answer to both, the officer in charge told them, was no. "Our department is small, and we have to farm out our forensic analysis to larger cities. The staggering backlog of cases is a continual source of aggravation."

While the delay and lack of progress on her case was frustrating on one level, Lisa was also secretly pleased for more time to savor with Eric and his loving family. More time to prepare herself for whatever darkness waited behind the screen of her blocked memory.

They ate lunch at a sandwich shop that also offered a variety of tempting pies and cakes for dessert. She gravitated to the red velvet cake and spared a thought to why the rich dessert had called to her over the other temptations. She let each bite of the chocolaty cake and cream cheese icing linger on her tongue, savoring the rich indulgence and waiting for a flash of memory. A birthday party? A grandmother's kitchen? A holiday dinner? But her mind stayed ruthlessly blank.

They drove through the streets of two more small towns and hit the highlights of Asheville and Biltmore Village before heading back to Cameron Glen as the sun sank behind the Smoky Mountains. While popular fast food chains and retail businesses tickled a general sense of familiarity, nothing specific took shape from the ether.

Eric took two calls in response to the advertisement on the drive back to Cameron Glen. One call was a woman offering her psychic abilities…for a price. The second asked if there was a reward for information regarding Lisa's identity.

"Maybe a reward isn't a bad idea," Eric suggested after hanging up with the bounty seeker.

"No, for two reasons," she said, narrowing a stern look on him. "I can't ask you to invest any more of your money in this wild-goose chase, and offering a cash incentive will just bring more termites out of the woodwork, like that guy from earlier."

He groaned. "You're probably right. But let's hang on to the possibility for later if the first run of the ad doesn't pan out."

"First run? How many times do you plan to run the ad?"

He appeared startled by her question. "As long as it takes."

She shook her head. "No. I can't let you throw good money after bad."

He cocked an eyebrow and sent her a lopsided grin. "Well, we're learning you know all the Southern turns of phrase anyway."

She scowled. "I'm serious."

"And I don't feel I'm throwing my money away if it helps you get back on your feet and find your family."

"Still no."

In answer, he only flipped up a palm in concession.

Lisa leaned her head back against the car seat and reflected on the day. "Today was a bust, huh?"

He shot a glance at her. "I don't know. Even process of elimination moves the needle, doesn't it?"

"I suppose. But at this rate, I'll be ready for retirement

before I figure out where I worked, and Rachel will be having her own children before we know who our family is."

He gave her a patient smile and squeezed her knee. "Keep the faith. Something will break soon."

"And if it doesn't?"

He hesitated a beat before shooting a tender look at her. "Then we'll be your family."

Lisa swallowed the lump that knotted her throat. She'd like nothing more than to be forever enfolded with the Camerons. Included in their warm circle. And have a place in Eric's life.

Finding the truth about her past could spoil that wish. But she also couldn't turn her back on the past she'd left behind. As daunting and potentially scary as the truth might be, she owed it to herself, to Rachel to keep searching for answers.

DJ HAD SPENT much of the last few days thinking about Lisa. About Valley Haven. About how to find the girl who could explode his world before she did just that.

And thinking about why she hadn't yet.

If he weren't in so much pain, half drunk most of the time just trying to get through the day without losing his mind, he'd have thought of it sooner. But as it was, the answer only came to him in the middle of the night when he couldn't sleep thanks to the throbbing in his leg. His damned wound was probably infected, and Donna was trying to get him to see a doctor. He was about ready to give in. He didn't want to lose his leg because of that bitch Lisa, who couldn't even remember if she worked at Burt's bar or not. He would not be beaten by anyone so dumb as—

She couldn't remember where she worked? Did that mean…?

DJ rolled to his back and stared at the ceiling. Was he free and clear? Could Lisa have had some kind of blackout where she didn't remember what happened that day? His thoughts spun. He didn't want to make any assumptions about anything and get caught with his butt in the wind.

He rolled his head to look over at Donna. She'd know about stuff like why people forgot things. "Donna." He poked her. "Hey, Donna, wake up."

She grumbled and pulled the blanket higher.

"Donna!" He shook her harder, spoke louder, determined to have answers *now*. "Wake up! It's important."

She finally rolled over and opened her eyes. "What?"

"What makes a person forget stuff, like whole hours of a day or where you work? I mean, besides drinking too much or a drug blackout."

"You mean amnesia?" she asked groggily.

"Yeah, that's the word. Would amnesia make a person forget where they worked? Forget what happened to them one day to the next?"

"Um, yeah. Can we talk about this tomorrow? I'm tired." She tried to roll back over, but he caught her shoulder and shook her again.

"Hang on. Can a person with amnesia remember the stuff they forgot later on?" He winced as he pulled himself to a seated position.

"Come on, DJ. Go back to sleep."

"No! Wake up, damn it! This is important!" He shook her hard, and Donna flinched. "I need to know if someone with amnesia, who forgets something at first, can remember it later. Remember everything later."

Donna rubbed her eyes and sighed. "Nursing school didn't get that deep into things like amnesia. I don't know much about it, but yeah. People remember stuff later all the time. Most amnesia is temporary. Swelling on the brain because of a blow to the head and that sort of thing."

"Damn it!"

"Can we go back to sleep now?"

"How long does it take for them to remember?"

She sat up now and peered at him, squinting in the darkness. "What's this about? Did you forget something?"

"Not me. The bitch who did this to me." He pointed to his leg. "I don't think she's gone to the cops, and I have reason to think she doesn't remember what happened. That she's forgotten about other stuff, too, like where she works."

"I can't say without knowing why she lost her memory. Lots of things can cause temporary memory loss. Like when you get drunk or pass out from drugs."

"What else?"

"Well, some illnesses, like really high fever. Head injury, like I said. Mental health reasons. Lots of stuff."

"And do they always remember later?" he growled, getting impatient.

"It's not black and white. It depends on why they lost their memory."

He fisted a hand in the sheets. "So, she could still remember everything?"

"Yeah," Donna said through a yawn. She rolled back over, muttering, "She probably will. Most amnesia cases are temporary."

Groaning his frustration, DJ flopped back on his pillow. So he had a little time. Maybe. But eventually, Lisa would remember what happened.

His best clue was still Valley Haven. That's where the call to Burt's had come from. How many Lisas could there be trying to remember where they worked?

He clenched his teeth against the throb in his leg and made his plan to drive to Valley Haven in the morning. He'd haunt the streets of the little town until he found her. And he had to find her. Fast. Before she remembered him and what he'd done.

Chapter Twelve

Two weeks later, after the Camerons' weekly Sunday family meal, Lisa joined several of the women in the senior Camerons' living room. They quizzed her on her job search, her meetings with the public health unit's counselor and her progress finding clues to her past.

"We don't mean to pry," Emma said.

"And you don't have to answer anything you don't want to," Cait added.

"It's just that we care about you," Emma said.

"And Rachel," Anya added.

"And because of our love and connection to Eric, we… feel a bit invested," Emma finished.

Lisa, holding a sleeping Rachel on her lap, glanced from one kind face and encouraging smile to another. Rather than feeling their questions were nosy or invasive, she embraced their interest as another example of their support of her, their inclusive and caring natures. She welcomed the interest and warmth she felt from them, soaking it up like a sponge.

Had her own mother cared for her this much? Did she even still have her mother? If so, why hadn't her mother launched a search for her? Two weeks into her search for her past, and the police still had no tips, no missing person reports, no more suggestions where to look. Their newspaper advertisement, seeking someone who might recognize Lisa, had yielded nothing other than requests for reward money, obviously bogus leads and calls from desperate women looking for children who'd been missing for years, even decades.

"No job yet. I've applied at a few places, but when I tell the hiring manager that I don't have references or any idea of my skills or schooling, the job sort of goes...poof."

The women responded with a collective sigh of commiseration.

"I can't blame them," Lisa said. "They're right to be wary about hiring an unknown with a big question mark over her head, no transportation of her own and no childcare for Rachel."

Cait reached for Rachel, wiggling her fingers in a silent request to hold the sleeping baby. "Our offer to watch Rachel stands. I know we can't promise which of us would be available each day, but with a family as big as ours, someone would be free."

Lisa nodded as she eased Rachel in to Cait's arms. "I appreciate that. Truly. Employers are more skeptical about hiring single women with children without assurances of reliable childcare."

Anya placed a hand on Lisa's arm and gave her a sympathizing frown. "I'll check again with the daycare where my kids go. Maybe a spot will open up."

"It's less about the spot and more the means to *pay* for a daycare. The means to pay for *anything*." She blew out a discouraged huff. "I'm racking up quite a debt to Eric, and I've made no breakthroughs with my counselor, Helen. She's focused on helping me cope with the anxiety surrounding my situation. She thinks once my mind feels safe, I'll be more likely to recover tidbits that will let me piece together my past."

"Makes sense to me," Anya said, giving her arm a reassuring squeeze. "I know you want answers *now*. But give it time. Sometimes it's the most unlikely or obscure thing that might shake a memory loose. Like a song or a favorite smell."

"Speaking of favorite smells..." Cait cuddled Rachel close. Closing her eyes, she inhaled deeply. "Oh man, when I smell that sweet scent and hold a cute little bundle like this, it makes me want another baby."

Anya leaned close and peered down at Rachel, whose mouth puckered and blew little bubbles as she slept. "I know. And she's at the perfect age. I love them when they're at this stage especially."

Lisa cocked her head. "What stage is that?"

"Slow enough to catch. Easier to contain. Once they start walking really well..." Anya chuckled and shook her head. She held her long black hair back as she leaned in for another gander at Rachel. "Oh, the mischief they get up to then. It's exhausting chasing after toddlers."

Cait divided a look between Anya and Lisa. "Let's not scare the poor girl, huh?"

Anya pulled an apologetic wince as she cut a side-glance at Lisa. "But then I had three kids under six years old at one time. I'm sure you'll be fine."

Isla, who'd been in the kitchen, strolled into the room carrying two mugs. She handed Lisa a cup of hot chocolate and sipped her own as she sat down beside Cait. "What'd I miss?"

"Just ruminating over the best and worst parts of having a baby." Cait stroked Rachel's cheek with a crooked finger and sighed.

"Oh, I want to play!" Isla licked whipped cream from her top lip and said, "Worst—stretch marks. Distended, raw nipples from breastfeeding. Hemorrhoids. Peeing your pants when you run or laugh or sneeze."

Anya and Cait looked at each other, and the three Cameron women erupted in laughter. Lisa grinned awkwardly, wanting to join the camaraderie but feeling an odd uneasiness instead.

Isla held up a finger and wiped happy tears from her eyelashes. "Best things? Everything else. My goodness I never knew I could love a messy, stinky little person so much!"

Cait inhaled again. "Oh, but this one doesn't stink right now. She smells like baby shampoo and angel kisses."

"Okay, Cait. Stop hogging." Anya held out her arms. "My turn to hold her."

Cait pouted but passed Rachel to Anya, who cooed, "Besides, I saw her first. I took care of you in the ER, didn't I, sweetheart? Yes, I did. And you were such a good girl."

Knowing Rachel was in the best of hands, Lisa rose from the couch and, carrying her hot chocolate with her, she edged past Isla. "Excuse me for a minute. I just…"

She waved a finger toward the door but didn't finish her excuse. The women seemed far too engrossed with Rachel to listen to her, and she really didn't have a reason to leave the room, other than the return of an annoying sense that something was wrong. An edgy sense of discord had plagued her to varying degrees since Eric found her. At times, the feeling was ominous and terrifying. Other times it nagged like a mosquito in her ear. Sometimes, she just felt off-balance, as if her subconscious recognized she was out of her normal environment and routine.

Grace was at the kitchen sink finishing the dishes with three of her grandsons.

"Anything I can do to help?" Lisa asked.

"Just finishing up, thanks. These boys and I make quite a team."

"Can we go play now?" Ravi asked. His dark eyes, so like Anya's, pleaded with Grace.

"Yes," Grace said, ruffling the eleven-year-old's hair. "Your father and uncles took the rest of the kids to Aunt Emma and Uncle Jake's house to play in the yard. Why don't you join them?"

Ravi and Isla's two boys, Brett and Joey, raced out the back door with a cheer and boisterous bumping.

Grace chuckled and turned her attention to Lisa. "Eric went to the Turners' house, as well, if you're looking for him."

Lisa cast a glance back toward the door to the living room. "Rachel—"

"Isn't a problem," Grace interrupted. "If you hurry, you can get the boys to show you the way."

She only hesitated a moment before calling her thanks and rushing out the back door. The afternoon was one of those not uncommon, almost springlike days southern states enjoyed as winter started to give way, often as early as February. The sun beat down, warming Lisa, despite the cooler breeze. She kicked her pace to a jog to keep the scurrying boys in sight as they made their way through the woods and over rolling hills to another corner of the family property. As she ran, she remembered Isla's list of complaints women dealt with after giving birth. She stumbled to a stop, taking a measure of her condition before picking up her pace again. Nope. No problem here. Did that mean...?

"Lisa!" Lexi called out to her from the edge of the yard in front of her. "You can be on our team. You'll bat after my dad."

Lisa watched Anya's husband, Brody, pitch a softball to Lexi, who swung a bat and missed. Scanning the lawn, she looked for Eric but didn't see him.

"He's around in the side yard with Jake," Brody called, clearly reading her mind, as he waited for the kids to retrieve the ball. He aimed a thumb toward a corner of the house, and Lisa made a wide pass around the ball game to search for Eric. Over the cheers and teasing shouts of the ball players, she heard an odd, rhythmic thumping noise in the direction Brody had sent her. She furrowed her brow, curious about the *thunk*, *thunk* that grew louder as she neared the corner of the Turners' home.

She rounded the brick wall and immediately spotted Eric and Jake Turner standing by a stump with split logs spread around their feet. As she watched, Eric raised an axe and brought it down with a mighty swing. *Thunk!*

Like being kicked in the chest, a wave of terror washed through Lisa, another image flashing quickly in her mind's eye. Another axe swinging. Striking. Blood.

She stumbled. Screamed. Dropped to the ground as her knees buckled and her body shook. Curling her fingers in the dead grass and pine straw, she braced her arms as the earth seemed to pitch. She panted shallowly as she grappled for balance, for clarity, for composure. What in the world had just happened? Was she losing her mind? The horrid image came so fast, packed such a punch. Then just as quickly as the flicker of the wakeful nightmare had blinked in her brain, it was gone.

"Lisa!" Eric flew to her side, wrapping her in a hug and framing her face with steady hands. "What happened? Are you all right?"

She opened her mouth to speak but had no voice, no answer. The terrifying, taunting snippet had disappeared without any clues to its source or meaning. She could only numbly shake her head, the grip of the shocking pictures still squeezing her.

"Did you trip? Did something startle you?" He chafed his hands on her arms as if trying to warm her up.

Behind Eric, she saw Jake step close, his brow furrowed in concern. "Can I help? Is she hurt? Should I get Anya?"

More curious eyes peeked around the corner of the house. Brody waved the children back but eased closer with a worried look that matched Jake's.

Eric pitched his voice lower. "Did you remember something?"

Lisa took a deep breath, reluctant to call back whatever she'd seen but knowing she needed clarity. Slowly, she closed her eyes, clutched Eric's shirt. "I think...m-maybe. But... it's gone now."

He nudged her chin up, and she opened her eyes to meet his. As always, his dark eyes calmed her, grounded her.

"Gone? Nothing's there? What triggered it?"

She curled her lips in, her mouth clamped tightly before sighing. "You."

His head snapped back. "Me?"

"Or...the axe." As she said the word, a shiver rippled through her. She lifted a trembling hand to push the hair back from her eyes. "Can we go? I want to get Rachel and... g-go back to your cabin. Please?"

He nodded and brushed a kiss on her forehead. "Of course."

Lisa put her hand in Eric's, and he helped her to her feet. A black dread balled in her gut as they crossed the yard. Was she getting her memory back? Was that terrifying incident a prelude of what awaited her in the coming days? Was that a hint of what her old life was like? If so, she wanted no part of whatever she'd left behind.

DJ CRUISED THROUGH Valley Haven, his eyes scanning faces. He hadn't spent much time with the girl, and he'd been distracted by Vic. Would he recognize her face when he saw her? She'd been blonde. Long hair. He remembered that much. Small. Probably only five foot two at best and skinny. But he was less sure of her face. He cursed and smacked the steering wheel. Roaming the streets of this Podunk town on the off chance of spotting Lisa was a stupid idea. But he had nothing better at the moment. The stakes were way too high if he didn't find her and didn't make sure she couldn't talk. Donna had said folks with amnesia could remember later. Usually did. Lisa's current silence, even if it was from amnesia, could change any day. She could wake up tomorrow with full recall and report everything that had gone down, put the cops on his trail.

So, crapshoot idea or not, he spent every free hour he had searching the small town for a girl he only vaguely remembered. He groaned and rubbed his sore leg. His life sucked. But if the cops found out what he'd done, caught the scent of Reggie's operation, it would suck a whole lot worse.

And so, he had to find Lisa and get rid of her. Like…yesterday.

Chapter Thirteen

Lisa spent the next several days dreading the return of her memory. After the chilling glimpse of what might be locked in her brain, she jumped at shadows and tiptoed through her days. She stayed on high alert, wondering what ordinary or random event might be the next trigger that brought her world crashing down. She withdrew, spending less time away from Eric's cabin, afraid of what she'd see, what she could lose if another flashback or frightening image caught up to her.

Eric was, as always, patient with her but encouraged her daily to walk on the grounds of Cameron Glen and let the signs of the coming spring refresh her soul.

His family visited her from time to time, bringing books, baked goodies and conversation to buoy her spirits. As much as she grew closer and fonder of Eric, she also formed deeper bonds of affection and friendship with his aunts and uncles. With Grace and Neil. The notion of having a big loving family stirred something elemental inside her. Did she have a family in her old life? Did they miss her?

Yet day after day passed, and no one seemed to search for her or answer the social media posts or newspaper ads, and she grew more certain she had no family. Or anyone who cared where she was, anyway. Both notions chafed.

But as February gave way to March and the grays of winter yielded to the greens, pinks and yellows of spring, Lisa began to hope again. She began working odd jobs for the Camerons, giving her a sense of purpose and a chance to chip away at the debt she was accruing. She cleaned the rental cabins, which she could do with Rachel set up in the travel playpen. She assisted Cait with data input in the rental office. She worked with Brody trimming, fertilizing and weeding the landscaping. She filled in a few days answering phones and filing invoices at Turner Construction, Rachel in tow, when the office manager had the flu. All the while, she continued to apply for steady employment without luck.

In early March, she finished her last session with her therapist, Helen, and though she'd not had any miracle breakthroughs, Helen's insights and strategies for coping with her worry and doubts helped quiet her fear. Her three sessions had done so much for her outlook that Neil offered to pay for extra sessions, and she'd humbly accepted, adding it to her growing list for repayment.

Day by day, Eric, Helen and the spring sunshine loosened the grip of her fears. Time gave her perspective and a measure of peace. If nothing bad had happened yet, maybe she was in the clear. Maybe…

Please, God, let me be all right now.

And as one day eased into another, Eric became such a mainstay, such an anchor and bright spot in her life that she gave in to the risky practice of imagining a future with him. She wasn't yet bold enough to give her feelings toward Eric a name or a voice, but the tender ache in her heart, the longing and lust were all there. Every touch of his hand and warm glance fed her growing affection and desperate wish to be more to him.

Anytime her chest would fill with spurts of the joy he brought her, though, a nagging voice would creep out of the shadows to burst her balloon. *You can't move forward until you've settled the past…*

One evening in early March, she studied herself in the

bathroom mirror as she dried off after her shower. The Cameron women's conversation from a few weeks earlier replayed in her mind nagging her again as it had that day. Isla had bemoaned stretch marks and distended nipples and other issues that often came along with pregnancy, childbirth and having a newborn. Lisa had none of the complaints Isla mentioned. While she knew every pregnancy was surely different, the odds that someone as petite as she was wouldn't suffer any of these bodily changes giving birth seemed unlikely.

She was still pondering the discrepancy and circling the inevitable conclusion when she returned to the living room in her pajamas and thick bathrobe, cradling a mug of hot tea in her hands. She sank onto the couch next to Eric and sipped her drink while her thoughts drifted.

Eric said something she was too absorbed in her thoughts to catch, and she blinked at him. "Sorry. What?"

He tugged up his cheek and shook his head. "Nothing important. I said you smelled good, like peaches, and I wondered if it was your shampoo or some other product I was smelling."

"Oh," she said, still too distracted to answer.

He slid closer to her and tugged her earlobe. "Hey. Everything okay? You seem miles away. Or...worried about something."

She inhaled the scent of her herbal tea and gave her head a shake as she angled her body toward him. "I was thinking about some things Cait and your aunts said after Sunday lunch a few weeks back. I might have given it more thought earlier, but that was the same day I had that strange reaction to you splitting firewood."

He tucked her damp hair behind her ear. "What kind of things were Cait and my aunts saying?"

She pulled her bottom lip between her teeth, hesitant to mention such delicate and awkward topics to a man. Sure, he was a doctor, but...

His eyebrow ticked up when she hesitated. "Lisa? What is it?"

"Okay." She cleared her throat, feeling heat unrelated to her hot shower and steaming tea warm her cheeks. "They were talking about things that happen to a woman's body when she has a baby. Stretch marks and other...embarrassing issues."

He puckered his lips and gave a slow nod. "Okay. And...?"

She set her mug aside and clamped her hands in her lap, her eyes down. "I don't have any of the issues they mentioned. I don't have any lasting effects from having a baby, which makes me wonder if...if I did have a baby. If Rachel is mine."

Eric sat back, exhaling and scrubbing a hand down his face. "I see." He scrunched his face as if in deep thought, then with a small cough said, "Every woman's pregnancy is different. Not everyone gets stretch marks."

She nodded. "I get that. But when factored with other things, like my obvious unfamiliarity with caring for a baby when you first found me, it seems like..."

"Are you saying you don't think Rachel is yours?"

Save Rachel.

"I..." She nibbled a fingernail and tilted her head as she angled her gaze to him. "I'm not sure. I've had this...*voice* in my head for weeks telling me to save her. It's not a specific *voice* voice, like a sound I can remember, as much as an imperative that keeps replaying in my head. It's the only thing that I seem to have brought with me from whatever happened. Just 'Save Rachel.'"

He hummed thoughtfully, his mouth still puckered as he mused.

"I know I love her. I know taking care of her means everything to me. But I don't recall the kind of things a mother should. Not her birth. Not rocking her to sleep. Or her first smile. So when you add all the other pregnancy-related stuff that I *don't have* to the mix—" she paused "—why do I have her? And why does the question about why I have her make me feel so…sad?"

"It does?" He leaned forward, narrowing his eyes on her. "That could be your brain giving you a hint. As much as it might hurt to follow that path, it's worth pursuing."

She released a weary sigh. "I guess."

He rubbed her arm. "Spend some time with that feeling and see if anything else comes to you. And mention it to Helen, if you haven't."

She gave a reluctant nod, and after a minute, he opened his arms, a silent invitation for her to scoot closer and be held.

She accepted gladly. Eric's arms were the safe haven she craved every moment of every day. She typically tried to ignore the yearning, knowing she needed to establish her independence, working toward leaving Cameron Glen and resuming her own life, whatever form that took. But in that moment, tucking herself against him and reveling in the warmth of his body and security of his embrace was all she wanted.

While she couldn't make promises or commitments, she could treasure each day she did have with Eric. Even though she couldn't pursue new dreams or desires while so many questions and blanks still tainted her, she could make the most of *now*. Because now was all she truly had.

Chapter Fourteen

One morning in mid-March, Lisa had Rachel contentedly occupied with stacking cups and a teething ring in the playpen while she searched job sites for local openings. The hit-and-miss jobs the Camerons had for her helped her earn money for Rachel's expenses, but she wanted a job that would pay for all her expenses, one that included benefits like health insurance.

Lisa drummed her fingers on the tabletop, groaning as she scanned the empty questionnaire spaces asking for her medical history, past employers and level of education achieved that the job website wanted. She put her head down on her folded arms. How did she find employment with so many blanks about her past?

A sound at the front door yanked her from her deliberations, and she abandoned the job application, glad to have company.

Her spirits lifted further when she found Eric in the living room. "What are you doing here? Playing hooky from work?"

"Not hooky. We're briefly on hold while we wait for the delivery of some drywall materials, so boss man said we could take an early and extended lunch. I just have to be back at the worksite by two."

"How nice!" She called into the den, "Look who's here, Rachel! What do you think? Can you say hi?" Then pivoting on her sock feet to face Eric again, she asked, "Have you eaten yet, or should I make you a sandwich?"

"Actually, I thought we'd go into town today," Eric said, his expression reminding her of a little boy who'd asked for extra desert without really expecting to get it.

She tipped her head, considering. "Why? We've already called most every business and driven streets so many times I could work for the fire department giving directions."

"I meant just for fun."

"Fun?" The notion intrigued her, but...

Any mention of leaving the Cameron Glen grounds always stirred the uncomfortable sense that had plagued her from day one. Somewhere out there, in the real world, her past waited like a crouched tiger, waiting to pounce. The unsettling sense of someone hunting her had faded in recent days but never disappeared.

But when Eric looked at her with so much sweet hope in his eyes, how could she say no?

"I've asked Grandma to watch Squirt so you can have a break. We can drop her off on our way out."

Rachel tired of the teething ring she'd been gumming and threw it out of the playpen. Pulling herself to stand, holding the side railing, she babbled at Eric and waved one chubby hand.

Eric bent to retrieve the teething ring and stroked the top of Rachel's head. "I thought we could get lunch at Ma's Mountain Diner. Maybe explore some of the shops on Main Street?" Eric stuck his hands in his back pockets as he faced Lisa again. "They have some great local artisans and gift shops for tourists. And some really good bakeries for dessert." He paused then added, "Although Ma's has the best apple pie you'll ever eat."

Lisa moved toward the playpen, but Eric held up a staying hand. "Unless I'm mistaken, I believe she asked for me," he said, with a lopsided grin.

Rachel went happily into Eric's arms and patted his cheeks as she giggled. He blew a raspberry against her belly, winning peals of baby laughter from Rachel.

Lisa laughed, too. Who wouldn't, in the face of such bliss and contagious joy? Watching Eric with Rachel, she longed for this life, for Eric to be her forever reality, for a future where she had family and love and protection and—

She shook her head and stopped the thought in its tracks. She had no claim on Eric. The tender feelings she kept leaning into were a dangerous fantasy. How could she give herself to Eric, the way she wanted to, when she didn't know who she was? Did Eric even want her the same way?

As Rachel grabbed his nose with a drooly hand, he asked, "So, what do you say? Is it a date?"

His phrasing caught her off guard, and she blinked. "Um… is it a *date*?"

He hesitated, catching her meaning. "Oh. I didn't mean…" He raised both eyebrows to his hair line. "Or…well, it could be. If you wanted it to be."

Despite his disarming charisma, her deep desire to tell him how much she wanted nothing more than to be his, to have a date today and many more to come, she took a beat. Something fluttered in her gut, telling her they were at a tipping point. Did she pursue her attraction to Eric or draw a line in their relationship not to be crossed?

She glanced down at her hands. No ring. No indentation on her finger where a ring had been worn. No memory of a man in her life. No sense or physical signs that she'd carried Rachel or given birth to her, nursed her. Nothing that held her back from following her heart…other than the giant question marks and circumstantial evidence.

She studied Eric's handsome face, felt the breath-stealing lub-dub in her chest and listened to her heart. "Yes. It's a date."

THE SMALL PARKING lot at Ma's Mountain Diner was full when they arrived, so Eric parked across the street in a vacant lot.

"Does this mean we won't be getting a table anytime soon?" Lisa asked as they crossed the highway hand in hand. "We could go somewhere else to eat."

"Naw. There tends to be an early crowd that arrives around eleven, and they clear out by noon. We're right on time to be part of the second crowd. Things in this town move in pretty established patterns. When I first came to Valley Haven from Charlotte as a teenager for summer break with my dad, I didn't appreciate the nuances of small-town life. But I learned how things work pretty quickly and got into the flow with the rest of the citizenry."

"Small-town life, huh?" She nodded and gave him a side-glance and a grin. "I think I could get used to that."

He bit back the urge to ask her if she got any sense whether she was from a small town or larger metropolis. The relentless questions she grappled with in recent weeks had to be wearing for her. And today was supposed to be fun. A reprieve. *A date.*

His pulse skittered. What did he do with the fact that she'd agreed to call it a date? Of course he'd wanted her to. Didn't that signal she was open to more in their relationship? But more of what?

For years, he'd taken the long view with every relationship he entered. If he had any qualms about the future of the relationship or the repercussions from sexual intimacy with a woman, he tended to err on the side of caution. He might not be a saint, but he'd rather not prove to be a fool with a broken heart. Or worse, a cad who misled and broke a woman's heart. He'd turned down the advances of numerous nurses and fellow medical students in recent years, not wanting to jeopardize his work relationships. And any woman he *did* sleep with had to be fully sober and vocal about her consent.

Given his high standards, then, he was frustrated by his desire to pursue a deeper connection with Lisa. Of course she was beautiful and sweet and had a sense of humor. She displayed an intelligence and quick mind—yes, he saw that irony—that intrigued him. But there were still enough unknowns surrounding her to throw up guardrails and wave a caution flag. He wouldn't seduce another man's wife. He couldn't fall for a woman whose emotions were confused and tangled up in gratitude and fear and far too many unknowns.

And she didn't know his full history. What would she do with that truth when she learned it?

But when she smiled at him, like she was now as he held the door for her to enter the diner, he heard music and had hummingbirds flittering in his chest and all the other sappy stuff that greeting cards said about falling in love.

Whoa! His brain slammed the brakes on hard. *Don't get ahead of yourself, Harkney. It's just lunch at a diner. Don't go sending out wedding invitations yet.*

They were shown to a corner booth, and Eric made a point of sitting across from Lisa, not beside her. He watched her scan the diner with a small dent between her eyebrows. "Everything all right?"

She brightened as she jerked her attention to him. "Sure." A self-deprecating grimace crossed her face, and she sighed. "I know we called Ma's weeks ago, and they said I didn't work here, but I couldn't help searching faces and studying the decor, looking for something familiar. You know?"

He gave the restaurant a quick scan, too. "I can imagine you'll feel that need until your full memory is restored."

"*If* my memory is restored." Dejection weighted her tone as she lifted the plastic-encased menu and started reading.

"*When* it's restored. Have faith."

She tugged her mouth into a lopsided grin. "Besides the appetizer of optimism, what do you recommend?"

He reached over to tap on her menu. "The pork chops are great, but you can't go wrong with anything here. Especially the optimism."

DJ AMBLED OUT of the diner's restroom, sucking at piece of roast beef stuck in his teeth as he headed for the front door. He scanned the dining room one last time as he had every street, store and vehicle for the last two months. The habit had become routine and half-hearted. He grew more lax with his vigilance as time passed without a sighting or any repercussions from the blonde. He knew he couldn't breathe easy yet. He'd be a fool to let his guard down, but every day he didn't find her and no uniforms came knocking at his door, the more he relaxed.

He stopped at the cash register on the way out to take a toothpick from the dispenser when a young couple strolled into the diner. And he froze.

The guy held the door for the woman, and she gazed at him with moony eyes and a smile, her attention fully on her man. But DJ stared intently at her. A prickle of recognition nipped his spine as the couple, their backs to him, walked into the restaurant and chose a table. The blonde lifted her menu, hiding her face for a moment, but DJ lingered, pretending to read the flier listing housing for sale from the stack on the checkout counter.

Finally the blonde put her menu down, and the hint of recognition became a scream of identification.

It was her. He was sure. Finally, he'd found Lisa.

His muscles twitched, eager to act now and tie up that loose end once and for all. But, of course, he couldn't snuff her out in the middle of a crowded restaurant. He gritted his teeth and tore his glare from her. It wouldn't do to have her spot him and slip his snare.

But he wouldn't miss this chance to silence her. He slapped the flier on the counter and stalked out. He strode quickly to Donna's car—he couldn't make his reconnoitering trips in the same vehicle every time—and slumped down in the front seat to wait. And make his plan to strike.

ERIC WAS RELIEVED to see the lunch hour pass with pleasant conversation, gentle teasing and laughter. This was exactly the kind of distraction he'd wanted for Lisa. As the meal and banter continued, he could see the tension in her muscles ease. Her appetite returned, her jaw unclenched, her smile was more ready and her shoulders relaxed from the protective hunch that had characterized her posture these last weeks. Most important, her eyes found the sparkle that reflected an inner happiness.

The only fly in the happy soup had come when a dish had been dropped across the diner, causing a loud clatter. Lisa had flinched, jerking a wide-eyed and wary gaze to the scene. She'd stilled for several seconds, staring across the dining room. After a moment, as conversations around them resumed, she took a deep shuddering breath and seemed to push the incident aside. He made a wisecrack about butter-fingers and told her a story about the disastrous incident of a dropped tray in his college cafeteria during his freshman year. Soon the color returned to her cheeks.

They ordered the locally famous apple pie, and a few minutes later, Lisa licked the last of her dessert from her fork and pushed the plate aside. "I'm so full, I think I'll pop!"

She leaned back in their booth and pressed a hand to her stomach. "But you were right. That was the best apple pie I've ever had." She rolled her eyes and added, "Of course, it's also the *only* apple pie I can remember having, so… there's that."

"Well, even if you could remember other pies, Ma's would still win. I'm sure of it." Eric wiped his mouth on his paper napkin and grinned at Lisa. Something about her sated and blissful expression conjured an image of her in tousled sheets after a round of robust lovemaking. He clenched his hands at his sides and shoved the spike of lust back down. *Don't go there. You'll only drive yourself nuts.*

One step at a time. He couldn't rush her or entertain expectations doomed to leave them both heartbroken if...

"How was everything?" their waitress asked, laying their check on the table and beginning to gather their empty dishes.

"Fantastic," Lisa said.

"As always," Eric added as he handed over his credit card.

Once they'd paid, he took her hand as they strolled out of the diner. "So, do you want to go shopping downtown now or take a walk by the river? I have about forty-five minutes before I have to be back at the worksite."

Lisa chuckled and bumped him with her shoulder as they strolled back to his car. "Don't you think I should get a job before I do any shopping?"

He shrugged. "If you saw something you liked, I could—"

She pulled her hand away, raising it to cut him off. "Nope. Stop right there. I'll already probably be ninety before I finish paying you back for everything you've done so far."

"I wish you'd stop worrying about that." Eric felt a tug at his foot as he reached the curb and glanced down at his shoes. His shoestring had come untied, and he'd stepped on it. Moving back from the street, he crouched to tie it.

He was double-knotting the loops when he heard the squeal of tires and gunning of an engine, like a car peeling off from a stop. Irritated by the idea of a reckless driver, he glanced down the block in time to see an old-model blue sedan race out of the parking lot next door and careen down the road toward them.

He opened his mouth to warn Lisa not to cross yet only to find she'd already started across the road. A hot flash of concern washed over him. "Lisa, look out!"

She'd stopped, clearly having heard and seen the car herself. Quickly, she backpedaled several steps to clear the lane the approaching sedan was in.

But the blue car changed lanes, swerving into the oncoming traffic lane. And barreled straight for Lisa.

Chapter Fifteen

Lisa's heart was already thundering, startled by the careless driver, but when the car veered toward her, her gut swooped. And she froze. Disbelieving. Panicked. Uncertain which way to move.

Time seemed to stretch as she watched the car race toward her. A few seconds felt like minutes as her eyes locked with those of the driver. A man. His glare menacing. Full of hate and intent. He *wanted* to hurt her.

She tensed, bracing for the impact. When she was slammed, though, the blow came from behind. A solid, firm shove that pushed her forward and tumbled her to the pavement. The asphalt bit her elbows, knees and hands. The air whooshed from her lungs. Someone landed on top of her, bumping her face onto the rough road. Hands tugged her shoulders, rolling her just as tires raced past, only inches from her head.

For several stunned seconds, Lisa lay still and silent. Both her rescuer and shock held her immobile—stomach down, her nose smashed into the asphalt. She gasped to suck oxygen into her dazed system. Her brain scrambled to make sense of what had happened. Her heart thrashed as adrenaline flooded her veins.

The weight on top of her shifted away. "Lisa! Are you hurt?"

Eric. Of course, Eric. Once again, he'd saved her life. Risked his own skin to rescue her.

Breathless, she opened her mouth, trying to answer him. The words stuck in her throat.

"Talk to me, Lisa. Did you hit your head? Can you move your arms and legs?"

A groan creaked from her as she rolled to her back. She knew they were in the road, still in danger. *Get up. Move out of the path of traffic.*

Her spirit was willing, but her body was still struggling to function.

Eric stroked a hand down her arm, turned her palms up to examine. "You're pretty scraped up. Do you think anything's broken? How's your head?" He pelted her with questions, and she heard his concern and fear in the quaver in his voice.

More people gathered around them, asking about their condition and offering assistance.

"Did anyone get the license plate?" she heard a woman ask.

"I'm calling the cops," another voice said.

"Lisa?" Eric again, and she focused her attention and her gaze on him. His dark eyes, full of worry, searched hers.

She nodded and blinked. The best she could do at the moment to reassure him. More hands grabbed at her, trying to lift her to her feet.

"Wait! Don't move her till we know if she's got a spinal injury!" a woman called.

Finally, her lungs loosened enough for her to draw a thin breath. She pushed herself to a seated position and rasped for Eric. "I'm o-okay."

Now his arms circled her, hands under her elbows, helping her stand. Her adrenaline-flooded legs wobbled as she limped, Eric beside her, to the parking lot where they'd parked.

"Here ya go, honey." She turned her head to find their waitress from Ma's Mountain Diner handing her a damp towel. "You're bleeding all over. Hands, nose, knees. Poor thing! Can I do anything else to help you clean up? More towels?"

"Thanks," Eric said. "Do you have a first aid kit in the diner? I need disinfectant for these scrapes. And paper napkins or tissues to blot her nose?"

"Should we call an ambulance?" someone asked.

Lisa shook her head, her gaze clinging to Eric's. "No hospital. I already…owe you…for the last time."

"I've called 911! The police are en route," another voice said.

"Oh, darlin'!" The waitress tugged at Eric's arm. "You're bloody, too! Not surprising, the way y'all tumbled on the road. Hang on. I'll be right back with more towels and the first aid kit from the kitchen."

Eric opened the door of his car and helped her sit in the passenger seat, turned sideways, so he could better check the condition of her bloodied knees and scraped hands.

With her initial shock beginning to wane, the sting from her injuries was growing. The sight of the blood stirred a disquiet in her soul, disproportionate to the minor wounds. A clamor of panic swelled inside her, strangling her.

"Hey, hey," Eric said, stroking her face. "Slow, deep breaths. You're okay."

She tried. Really tried. But then the near miss replayed in her mind's eye. The screech of tires. The sun glinting off the bumper barreling toward her.

And the dark glare from the man behind the wheel.

Pinpricks skittered down her back, the whisper of something that felt evil nipped at her, then vanished like smoke in the wind. "He…he meant to hit me."

Eric paused in his ministrations, swabbing gently at her scraped knees. "Um, yeah. I kinda got that impression, too."

"But w-why?"

He sat back on his heels and narrowed his gaze on her. "I was kinda hoping you might know why?"

She blinked and scowled at him. "How would I know?"

He twisted his mouth and shrugged. "Did you recognize the car? The driver?"

Shoving aside the vague sense of evil she couldn't pin down, she shook her head. "Do you think—" She paused and swallowed hard. "Do you think he meant to...*kill* me?"

Eric hesitated, pressing his mouth in a firm line. "We don't know that. There could be any number of explanations. Road rage? Intoxication? Maybe you look like his ex-wife or something?" Though he clearly was trying to allay her panic, the furrow in his brow told her he didn't believe his own reasoning.

Just the same, Lisa tried to take solace from his reassurance and logic. Under normal circumstances, there would be no reason for a stranger to want to run you down and kill you. But her circumstances were not normal. And Eric hadn't seen the malice in the man's eyes as he roared toward her.

She nodded to appease Eric, but the haunting sense of menace clung to her. The nagging darkness that had kept her looking over her shoulder from the day Eric had found her sharpened inside. She knew, deep in her core, that the man had singled her out. Waited for her. And that he *had* been trying to kill her.

Chapter Sixteen

"Good heavens! What happened to you two?" Grace asked, rushing across the Cameron's foyer to inspect them more closely when they returned to Cameron Glen.

"There was a little incident. That's why we're late. We had to give a statement to the police, but—"

"What!"

"—all's well. Nothing for you to worry about." Eric gave his grandmother a placating grin.

Grace frowned at him, then turned to Lisa. "Apparently he thinks I can't handle bad news, but I trust you won't lie to me. What happened?"

Lisa divided a look between Grace and Eric. Heat rushed to her cheeks as she debated what to tell the older woman who Eric clearly wanted to protect from stress and worry. "I, uh, fell while crossing the street."

Grace arched a thin eyebrow and cut her glance to Eric. "Fell? That explains your scrapes, but what about his?"

"Oh, well, he's the reason I fell. He pushed me out of the way of a car I didn't see. We both fell."

Grace's skepticism was obvious, but before she could ask more questions, Eric said, "The important thing is we're both all right. Scrapes will heal. How is Rachel? Did she give you any trouble?"

Grace gave them both an unsatisfied frown, clearly debating whether to press the issue of the troubling incident or let it drop as they wanted. Finally, she sighed and gave them a tight smile. "Rachel was an angel. She ate a good lunch, had a short nap, and now we are playing in the other room." Grace led them into the living room, where Rachel sat on a blanket surrounded by toys.

When Rachel spotted them, she squealed and raised her arms to be picked up by Eric. *Eric*, Lisa thought, not her.

After a flicker of jealousy, a mushy sweetness settled in her chest as she watched him lift the baby into his arms and greet her with a kiss on her nose. The pang of longing Lisa had fought hard in recent days rose again—the fantasy of a permanent home with Eric, raising Rachel together, sharing a future, *sharing a bed*. But mostly her desire was to mean more to him than just his project, a charity case.

She knew he cared on some level. He wouldn't be helping her if he didn't feel *something*. But she wanted that something to be more than platonic. More than compassion-based. He'd called their lunch a date, but what did that mean?

"Okay, Squirt, I have to go." Eric ruffled Rachel's thin cap of hair. "I'm due back at the worksite in ten minutes, and family connection or not, Jake will fire me if I prove unreliable." He turned and handed Rachel off to Lisa.

After an initial whine of disappointment, Rachel nestled her head against Lisa and stuck a thumb in her mouth.

Eric jostled his keys in his hand and gave Lisa a quick smile. "See you tonight." Then lowering his eyebrows, he added, "You're sure you're okay? I hate to leave, considering..."

Oh, how she would have loved for him to stay. How was she going to keep the doubts and demons at bay? The screech of tires hadn't left her ears since the near miss. The evil glare of the driver still hovered too close.

But she couldn't continue to depend on Eric. She had to find a way to distract herself that didn't depend on Eric's presence and protection. She had to start fending for herself, so she nodded and waved him off. "Go. I'm fine, and I do *not* want to be the reason you get fired."

"I can drive you back to our cabin, if you want."

Our cabin? Did he realize his slip? Or did he really think of his home as theirs?

Or was she overthinking this, like most everything else lately? "No. Thanks. I think Rachel and I will walk. I want to show her the newly hatched ducks and the flowers blooming."

He unhooked a key from his ring. "Okay. That's for the front door. Keep everything locked when you're alone."

She gave him a patient smile for the oft repeated and unnecessary reminder. After today's scare, she wanted nothing more than to lock herself inside and bolt every window. "I will."

He stared at her another beat, as if hesitant to leave her, then dropped a quick kiss on her forehead before turning to stride out of the house.

Lisa stared at the space he'd vacated, savoring the damp warmth from his kiss and fighting the empty ache his departure left.

"It's nice to know he feels the same way as you do," Grace said, pulling her out of her musing.

Lisa wrinkled her nose, her pulse tripping. "Pardon?"

"I only mean, unrequited feelings are...tricky. But clearly Eric shares the same fondness for you that you do for him."

"I, uh..."

Grace laughed. "Don't look so surprised. We've known how you feel from almost day one."

Her heart pounded harder. What had Grace seen? Was she that transparent? And had Eric picked up on it, too? "Who is 'we'?"

"Isla was the first to know." She snorted a little laugh. "Of course. She said she sensed it on that snow day when we all gathered here to make phone calls on your behalf. She told

Cait that day, and she told me, Emma and Anya at a family dinner not long after that. Isla could tell right away that you were smitten." Grace smiled. "Not that she had to tell us. It's in your eyes when you look at him."

In her eyes?
We've known...
Eric shares the same fondness...

Lisa's head spun as she drank in this information. On top of the earlier scare, her nerves raw, she wasn't sure how to process it. Did Eric know she had feelings for him? Had she been so busy trying to deny her affection for him that she'd missed something vital?

"And I couldn't be happier for you both. Eric is a dear boy...well, man. I guess I still think about him as the confused teenager he was when we first met," Grace continued, although Lisa only half heard as she reexamined her situation in the new light. Was Eric only helping her because he expected them to have a relationship of some sort? Did he have an ulterior motive?

"But he's come such a long way. Especially in light of the horrible events from the summer his mother was stalked."

Lisa did a double take, her focus now back fully on Grace. "I'm sorry. What did you say? Cait was stalked?"

"Not Cait, dear. Though Cait has had her own trouble with bad men in the past. I meant Jessica. His biological mother. You'll love her when you meet her."

"You said his mother was stalked. That Eric had overcome something from that summer?"

"Well, yes. He was terribly distraught with everything that happened." Grace paused and tilted her head to one side while wrinkling her nose. "Has he told you what happened that summer? It's been about ten—no—closer to eleven years now."

Lisa tried to recall everything she and Eric had discussed. He'd mentioned some pretty horrible things that had befallen the family. His cousin Fenn's kidnapping, a case of arson that destroyed one of the Cameron Glen rental cabins, his uncle and Anya helping catch a serial killer, and a shyster who tried to blackmail the family into selling Cameron Glen. The way the family had rebounded and survived the troubles was a testament to their strength and love for each other. But she couldn't recall anything specific concerning Eric or his mother. A stalker...

She shook her head slowly, a roil of dread building in her gut. "I don't think he has. What happened?"

Grace pressed a hand to her mouth and knitted her brow in consternation. "Oh, I think that must be for Eric to tell you when he's ready. I'm sorry. I've said too much. I only figured he'd have told you."

Lisa shook her head. "I know he gave up medicine rather abruptly a year or two ago. Came back to Valley Haven to work construction from out of the blue. Is it related to that?"

Grace took a breath as if preparing to say more but snapped her mouth closed with a click of teeth. "I think you should ask Eric about it tonight. If he wants to talk about it, he will. If he's not ready to share, then it wouldn't be right for me to talk out of turn." She laid a hand on Lisa's cheek. "But don't fret about it in the meantime, dear. Eric is the trustworthy young man you've come to know. But we all have a past. We all have secrets. Doesn't mean we're bad people. Just humans struggling with all that life can throw at us."

"And it's not like he hasn't put up with more than my fair share of drama and mysteries, huh?" Lisa rolled her eyes.

Grace hooted a laugh. "I suppose you're right about that!"

Startled by Grace's laughter, Rachel roused and whined, rubbing her eyes.

"I should get her back to the cabin for her nap. Thank you again for watching her." Lisa turned to go, her thoughts still whirling with the possibilities of what Eric might have kept from her, what he might have endured that cast a shadow over his life. Reaching the door, she paused. "Oh, I wanted to ask you, do you have a sewing needle and off-white thread? The quilt in the second bedroom at Eric's has a tear that I thought I'd mend."

Grace's gaze widened. "I believe I do. But mending a quilt properly takes a special technique. Not to belittle your sewing skill or willingness to help but…"

When the woman left the sentence dangling, Lisa squared her shoulders. "Thing is, I think I know how to do it. I don't know why, but I have a vague sense of having done a lot of precise needlework. And that quilt and the one in the bedroom here…drew me. Resonated in me. Other than my apparent knowledge of books and literature, it's the only positive thing that has felt familiar to me."

"Well," Eric's grandmother nodded firmly, "in that case, I'll be right back with that needle and thread. And some swatches of fabric for you to noodle around with if you are so inclined?"

"Yes. Thank you." A small bloom of joy swelled inside her, along with gratitude that she'd have something to occupy her hands this afternoon. Far better than dwelling on the face of the man behind the wheel of the car that nearly hit her or worrying about what secret Eric had been keeping from her. Maybe, if her fingers were doing something familiar, her mind would follow. Maybe this interest in the quilts was a sign her brain was finally healing and letting her have a glimpse of the good things in her past.

Once Grace retrieved the requested supplies, Lisa took Rachel back to Eric's cabin and put her down for a nap. She regrouped in the living room with the quilt that needed repair and the needle and thread from Grace. Within a few stitches, it was clear the fresh scrapes on her fingers and hands were going to make the delicate needlework difficult. What's more, she was concerned one of her scrapes might open and leave a smear of blood on the quilt. Instead, she picked a novel off

Eric's shelf—one Eric's father, Matt Harkney, had written—then covered herself with the quilt and settled in to read. She was quickly absorbed by the thriller and lost track of time. Only when she heard Rachel's peeps from the bedroom did she lift her gaze to the clock and realize an hour and a half had passed.

She set the book aside, grateful to Matt that his storytelling had kept her mind off the near accident outside the diner for at least a short time. But as she changed Rachel's diaper, the malevolent glare of the driver who nearly ran her over flashed in her mind again.

She shivered, despite the warm cabin, because the dark glare haunted her. Had she once known the man? The notion that he had been *trying* to hit her, *trying* to hurt her rippled through her again. Was this man the reason she'd had a looming sense of evil chasing her or someone dangerous following her? Was that man at the root of why she'd been out on the roadside, alone?

And if not, why had he targeted her this afternoon?

Lifting Rachel into her arms, she cuddled the baby against her chest, feeling an urgency to keep Rachel close as she returned to the living room.

Save Rachel. Save Rachel. Save Rachel.

The imperative echoed in her head, a panicked heartbeat. A warning.

Fighting for composure, she sat down on the floor with Rachel. Her muscles were stiffening up after her asphalt tumble at lunch, but she occupied herself for the next hour playing with the baby, determined to put aside the uneasy tremor in her gut.

She showed Rachel the colorful blocks, naming the letters on each, and the soft stuffed animals that Eric's family had shared with her. All of the toys went in Rachel's slobbery mouth, a common thing during teething, Cait had said.

Curious, she leaned closer to Rachel and poked an exploratory finger in her mouth. Sure enough, she found a tiny white bud pushing through the girl's bottom gum. "Look at you, getting your first tooth!"

She pressed a kiss to the baby's head and booped her nose. In response, Rachel gazed up at Lisa with wide blinking eyes—and laughed. The sound surprised Lisa. Her first instinct had been that Rachel was coughing or choking, but then the giggle blossomed and bubbled. A warmth Lisa could never have imagined or predicted filled her chest, and she grinned sappily at Rachel. "You're laughing! You silly, sweet girl!"

Of course, now, she had to make Rachel laugh again. What had Rachel found funny? The buzzing noise Lisa made when she tapped the girl's nose? Lisa made a snuffling noise like a pig, and Rachel's angelic peals of laughter rang again. Which roused a belly laugh from Lisa. Which teased more giggles from Rachel. Which led to... Lisa sobbing.

She couldn't say why the tears started flowing, other than an emotional stopper of some sort must have been unplugged. She lifted Rachel onto her lap and rested her cheek against the baby's downy hair. If only she could have this permanently. This cabin. This sweet child. This safety.

And Eric.

He was a key part of the fantasy life she was currently living. But when her memory returned, all of this would disappear like a wisp of smoke caught by a breeze. Just...gone. Because somewhere out there, her real life waited. A whole history that included her own home, her family, likely a job. And Rachel's father. Lisa's gut knotted.

Why, why, *why* couldn't she remember Rachel's father? Had she loved him? Was the driver with the scary dark glare Rachel's father? Was that why he was hunting her?

Those questions continued to taunt her, along with the

comments Grace had made, hinting that Eric had a secret of his own that had shaped his life.

Lost memories. Hidden agendas. Unsolved questions.

Great. The coil of tension was back.

Chapter Seventeen

DJ fumed all the way home over his screwup. He'd had his chance to get rid of Lisa permanently, and he'd failed. Having made such a bold move in front of witnesses had been risky. Maybe even stupid. But he hadn't been able to come up with another way to off the girl on short notice and still make it look like an accident. As it was, the cops would surely be looking for Donna's car. At least he'd smeared mud on the license plate before he'd made his run at Lisa.

When he went back to Valley Haven to look for her, he'd take his truck. And a gun. He couldn't shoot her in public, but the gun would help him force her into the truck, and he'd take her somewhere out of the way.

And how are you going to find her again, now that you've shown your hand?

He couldn't ask around at the diner. The waitstaff had seen what happened, and his asking about Lisa would raise flags. DJ slapped the steering wheel and gritted his teeth. If Lisa had been hiding from him, his blown attempt to run her down had likely scared the little rabbit back underground.

He snarled with frustration. He'd make a few inquiries in Valley Haven later in the week, once the near-miss gossip had cooled down, but he'd focus his attention on the places where he knew Lisa was most likely to return. Her apartment and Vic's house. Eventually she had to go back to one or the other. And he'd be waiting.

"Honey, I'm hooome!" Eric called out in a teasing tone as he shuffled through the door that evening.

"In here," Lisa called back, and he followed the sound of her voice to the kitchen. Rachel was in the high chair, her face—and hair?—smeared with something orange. Carrots maybe?

"Uh, Lisa, you're supposed to feed it to her, not paint her with it," he said lightly.

"Really? Thanks for the tip." She scooped more of the orange glop out of the tiny jar and aimed it at Rachel's mouth. "She's not a fan of carrots. She grabbed the spoon to shove it away earlier and got it on her hand, then rubbed her head and, well, it's been downhill since then."

He pulled out a chair across the table from Lisa and watched the feeding process with an odd fascination. He'd seen plenty of babies fed in his life, even fed them himself to help out. Why did watching Lisa and Rachel feel different? More intimate?

Get over that possessiveness, buddy. Just because he'd been playing house with them for the past few weeks didn't mean they were his to plan a future with. She had a life somewhere else, and his duty was to help her return to it.

Eric sighed. He knew it was true, but the truth depressed the hell out of him. He'd grown deeply fond of Rachel. And Lisa? Geez. He didn't dare name what he felt for her. Better to just squash it before it took root and grew.

"Oh!" Lisa turned to him, her expression brightening. "She has a tooth! Look." She pulled Rachel's bottom lip back to expose her gum and the newly erupted tooth.

"Well, well. Congratulations, Squirt!"

"And," Lisa added with a dramatic pause, "she laughed today!"

"Awesome. Is there a better sound in the world? What got her tickled?"

"I made some funny noise while I was playing with her. Kind of a buzz or snort."

"Snorted?" He curled up his mouth on one side. "Like a pig?"

Lisa shrugged. "Sort of." She faced the baby, wrinkled her nose and snuffled.

Rachel blinked at her and grinned.

Leaving his chair, Eric squatted beside the high chair and boldly imitated a pig. Rachel squealed happily and grabbed his nose with a messy hand, her giggles a balm to Eric's weary soul.

Several minutes of this game and the rest of Rachel's supper later, Eric cleaned the high chair and dish while Lisa gave the baby a bath and dressed her for bed. Simple, common, routine activities that felt so natural, so good to him. He and Lisa made a good team.

With his chores done and a grocery store casserole popped in the oven to heat, Eric settled in the living room. He turned the television on the local news. He'd monitored the stories the local press had covered since finding Lisa, half hoping, half dreading a story would run that directed their search for answers. A missing person case. An arrest that triggered a memory for Lisa. Something. Anything.

Today's incident with the sedan that had almost hit Lisa had stoked his determination to uncover the truth of her past. Only when they knew what they were up against could he fully protect her.

Lisa brought Rachel into the living room and settled the baby into the travel crib to play. She joined him on the couch and glanced at the television. "Anything happen in the world today I should know about?"

He clicked off the TV set. "You mean besides the car that almost ran you down?"

Her mouth pinched, and her brow furrowed. "Yeah, about that..."

He angled his body toward her. "Yeah?"

"I didn't say anything earlier but... I can't shake the sense that I know that guy somehow." She explained how she kept thinking about his dark glare, the intent she saw in his face as he hurtled toward her and the buzz of familiarity she couldn't shake. "I don't know who he is or why his eyes seem familiar but..."

Eric brushed her honey-colored hair from her cheek and tucked it behind her ear. "Are you sure it was the guy, specifically, that seemed familiar and not something about the event, the car, the adrenaline rush and fear that stirred you up?"

She gave him a frustrated look. "I'm not sure about *anything* these days. You know that. Everything is a giant puzzle with no matching pieces. I'm trying to put it together without even knowing what the final picture is supposed to be."

He nodded. "I know."

"But all afternoon, his eyes have haunted me. Shaken me. A lot."

He nodded. "Okay. Well, if this guy is trying to hurt you, then...maybe it's a good thing he's shown his hand."

"A good thing?"

"We know now to be vigilant. Watch for him. We have a basic description of him and his car, as do the police. It's a start."

"I suppose. I just wish I could shake the creepy sensation of his dark eyes watching me. They were so hard and full of malice." She shook her whole body as if trying to shake the man off her skin.

Tugging on her arm, Eric coaxed her closer, wrapping his arms around her as she settled against his chest. Damn it, if she didn't fit perfectly in his arms. Why did she have to feel so right in his embrace when it was so wrong of him to fall for a vulnerable woman? A woman who had a life, a family somewhere else. Waiting for her.

Or did she? Why hadn't her family or Rachel's father filed a missing person report? Why weren't there reports of a baby's disappearance? He'd scanned reports from the entire state, as well as adjoining states. None of the recent reports matched Rachel's or Lisa's description. He was puzzling over that for the hundredth time when Lisa said, "Can I ask you something?"

"Sure. What's up?"

"Well, Grace mentioned something today after you went back to work." Lisa picked at a cuticle and wouldn't look up at him. "She…implied that something big and important had happened to you a while back."

Eric tensed, his pulse stumbling.

"She said your mother was stalked one summer and—"

He pushed Lisa from his arms and stood quickly, his chest tightening. He strode a few steps away and plowed a hand through his hair. "Yeah? And what else did she tell you?"

As soon as the words were out, he realized how gruff his tone sounded. Pinching the bridge of his nose, he turned to face Lisa. She gaped at him with regret and—damn it—apprehension clouding her expression. He exhaled harshly and raised a hand in apology. "Sorry. I didn't mean to bite your head off."

"If I've crossed a line, I'm s—"

"No." He took a long step back toward the couch, both palms facing her to stop her in her tracks. "No. It's not… You didn't know. I just don't…like to talk about…"

"Okay." She gave him a smile that trembled at the corners. Uneasy. Appeasing. Fake. "You don't have to say anything. I only—"

"Lisa." He scrubbed his hands on his thighs before dropping heavily beside her on the couch. "I'm not upset with you for asking. It's just… I haven't really talked to anyone about…"

She dragged a throw pillow onto her lap and clutched it to her belly, an action his counselor had once described as a subconscious self-protective one. As if the pillow were a shield, an extra layer guarding one's vital organs. Or a comforting gesture, like a child clutching one's mother for protection. Or distancing, as if trying to put a wall between herself and something unpleasant.

He gritted his teeth, hating he'd been the reason behind any of those unconscious impulses for her. He angled his body to face her, but also give her a few extra inches of breathing room as he dug into his own emotional baggage to find a starting place. "My grandmother is right. Something did happen several years ago." He took a beat, a slowly inhaled breath. "My mother was stalked a while back. And although some good things came out of the situation—" He flashed Lisa a weak smile and shrugged. "I mean, all the crazy stuff that happened brought my mom and her current husband together. So there's that."

Lisa returned a flicker of a smile and nodded for him to continue, her gaze locked on his, her attention rapt.

He swallowed hard and wiped suddenly damp palms on his jeans. *Just spit it out. Stalling won't change your guilt.*

"But...a lot of bad stuff happened, too. Not just to her and Gage, either. To me."

He stopped himself again, hearing his counselor from years ago telling him the first step to dealing with his feelings, his actions was to take ownership of them. Fisting his hands, he said, "Or rather I did something...awful."

Lisa's brow dipped, and her eyes grew wary.

There just was no way to soften the blow or polish this clod of dirt.

He squared his shoulders and took a deep breath, blurting, "The thing is... I killed a man."

Chapter Eighteen

Lisa's heart jolted, and her face flushed hot then cold in quick succession. She blinked and shook her head as if she'd heard incorrectly. She wasn't sure what she thought Eric was going to tell her, but it sure as heck wasn't *that*. "Wh-what?"

He gave her a slow nod, his mouth a taut line, took a beat. Then another before exhaling and reaching for her.

She couldn't help it. She flinched, backing away from his touch the tiniest bit. But he clearly noticed. A sadness filled his eyes, and he withdrew his hand, curling it again into a fist that he tucked under his armpit. "I know that sounds harsh and all, but there's no point in trying to make it pretty when it's not."

Another strained moment of silence passed before she said, "Who?" at the same time he started, "I wasn't charged—"

They glanced awkwardly at each other, and she waggled a finger. "Go on. I shouldn't have interrupted."

"No, I get it. You have questions. I would." His cheeks puffed out as he exhaled with exaggerated force. "The police called it justifiable homicide, so no charges were filed."

"So self-defense?" she asked, a huge bubble of tension popping in her chest.

"Not precisely but close. It happened the summer I was twenty. The night my mother's stalker tried to kill her. We—my dad and I—heard her scream and hurried to the dock to help her. When we got to the dock—the fish pier down there on the little lake—" He aimed his thumb toward the window, indicating the pond where she and Rachel had fed the ducks earlier in the week.

Her heart lurched. Eric's tragic event had happened here? In Cameron Glen? The notion of such horror happening in this Eden sent a shiver crawling over her skin. Maybe her refuge wasn't as safe as she'd believed.

"When we got there, her stalker was fighting my stepdad, Gage. Gage was injured and struggling for air, so my dad and I were trying to rescue him and Mom and stop the stalker's assault and…"

Lisa frowned as she tried to follow his disjointed account. "Whoa, slow down. Struggling for air?"

He scrubbed a hand on his face, then started his story again.

Eric rewound his account, recalling details of how his mother had been stalked, kidnapped, rescued, then attacked again here at Cameron Glen that night. He described how the attacker and his mother, in their confrontation, had fallen from the end of the fishing pier into the lake, how his mother had nearly drowned as she battled the man who'd stalked her.

"Good grief! How awful!" Lisa said, pressing a hand to her mouth.

"Gage was the first to the scene, and he took on the guy. But the creep was merciless and not above murder. Her stalker played dirty, and when my dad and I arrived, Gage was in the water fighting the stalker but struggling for air. We got my mom out of the lake and were helping her catch her breath after she nearly drowned, when Henry, her stalker, started climbing onto the pier, coming after my mom again—"

Eric closed his eyes, seeing those fateful moments play out again in his mind. The scenario that had haunted him for all these years. Could he have done something different and still rescued Gage and his mother? If he hadn't acted, would the stalker have attacked Eric and his dad next?

"I grabbed one of my mom's crutches—she'd sprained an ankle escaping her stalker that morning—and I cracked it over the guy's head. I knocked him out, and he tumbled into the lake." He paused and pinched the bridge of his nose as tears stung his eyes. "He drowned. Because I got Gage out first."

Acid pooled in his gut, reliving the sights, sounds and smells of that evening as if it were happing all over again. The red-gold reflection of the sunset on the water. The chirp of summer frogs. The fetid scent of decaying vegetation in the pond.

"I jumped in the lake…and helped rescue Gage, but…by the time I found Henry…"

"Oh, Eric."

He shot her a cursory glance but couldn't hold her gaze as he finished. "My dad and I…we dragged Henry up on the dock, but…even the CPR Gage and my dad did couldn't revive him."

The years-old anchor of guilt dragged at him again.

"Hang on," Lisa said. "That's how he died? He drowned, and then you and your fathers tried to revive him with CPR and…" She sighed. "Am I missing something?"

He spread his hands and gave a jerky shrug. "Nope. That's about it."

Her brow furrowed, and she seemed to be puzzling through his account. "Eric, he was trying to kill your loved ones! Your actions saved Gage and your mother. You're not a villain. You're a hero!"

Eric's gut lurched. His head snapped up, and he snarled, "No!" He shoved to his feet and stomped across the floor. At the door to the kitchen, he spun around and aimed a finger at her. "Do you have any idea how tired I am of hearing that?"

She only gaped at him in dismay.

His hands were shaking, and his breathing was ragged. He clenched his jaw and struggled to bring his reaction under control. "A *hero* doesn't take lives."

"You didn't mean for him to die, did you? You just wanted to slow him down, stop his attack. I mean, you pulled him out of the water. Your stepfather gave him CPR. Doesn't that count for anything?"

"How can it? I *meant* to hit him with that crutch. I *meant* to incapacitate him, and my actions led directly to another man's death." He scoffed. "That's hardly heroic."

Her mouth opened and closed. Her brow wrinkled in consternation. "So, you don't like that term, but can't you cut yourself any slack for what happened in light of the circumstances?" She pushed off the couch and crossed the room to him. "Can you honestly say that in the same situation, with your mother's and Gage's lives at risk, you wouldn't do the same thing again?"

He heaved a weighty sigh. "That's the hell of it. Because I absolutely would. I know what I did saved Mom and Gage, but…in the end, I'm still a killer."

Lisa's shoulders sagged. "Oh, Eric. It pains me to hear you say things like that. You're a good person! Can't you forgive yourself after all these years?"

"No! Because Henry is still dead. Nothing can change that. It's a permanent blemish on my soul! No matter how many patients I treated or surgeries I performed, it doesn't change the fact that I *took* a life."

Lisa stiffened. Took a step back as she narrowed a stunned look at him. "Wait a minute. Is that why you left medicine? Why you walked away from your residency?"

Damn. Eric hadn't meant to admit to that, but now that it was out, he scrubbed a hand over his face and jerked a nod. "I couldn't go on feeling like a fraud. I took the Hippocratic oath, for crying out loud! I felt like a pretender, like I was living a lie." He dropped his chin to his chest, his gaze to the hardwood floor. "I still do."

"You're not a fraud! You're the best of men. You've done so much for me and—" Lisa fell abruptly silent. After a moment, he glanced up and found her eyeing him with confusion and suspicion. "Is that what all of this is about?"

He swallowed hard. "All of what?"

She waved a hand vaguely around the cabin. "Me being here. You taking Rachel and me in and sheltering us and feeding us and—" Her voice cracked. "Am I some sort of atonement to you? A shot at redemption? An attempt to balance some scale?"

After the briefest hesitation, he said, "No." But the pause had been long enough to sow doubt.

She stepped back from him, shaking her head. Anger glittered in her eyes. "I told you I don't want to be someone's charity case."

He groaned. "It's not like that. You're not a charity case to me."

"No?" Her tone was heavy with skepticism. "Then you must want something from me. What do you think I can give you? I literally have nothing and no way to repay you." She narrowed her eyes, her expression and tone darkening. "Unless this is about sex. Is that what you want from me?"

"No!" he said quickly, appalled. Maybe too quickly and too appalled. He didn't want her to think she repulsed him…

He raised a hand as he moved toward her. "What I mean is, I'm not after anything, and I *certainly* don't expect you to barter yourself for anything I've done for you."

She gave him a long, considering look before her face relaxed and she nodded. They stood there staring at each other, the echoes of his confession and her wariness palpable, a living thing vibrating in the air between them.

"I stopped to help you and Rachel that day," he said finally, "because it was the right thing to do. No one with a heart could have driven past you and not helped. And then… your situation, your amnesia, your obvious fear and confusion moved something in me. I've done all this for the same reason I went into medicine to begin with, I wanted to help you. I wanted to make a difference…do something good with my life."

She nodded. "I can believe that about the Eric I've come to know."

"But then…" When he paused, she furrowed her brow, once again suspicious. He reached for her hand, pressing it between his, squeezing her fingers. "In recent days, things have…changed for me. I've begun to have…feelings for you."

Lisa's eyes widened. Her mouth formed a little O for a moment, before she clamped her lips closed, drawing the bottom lip between her teeth. "Um…"

"You don't have to say anything. I didn't mean to put you on the spot. I only wanted—"

Her mouth found his in a heartbeat. One second she was staring at him, apparently dazed by his confession, and the next she'd closed the distance between them, captured the back of his head with her free hand and pressed a kiss to his lips that stole his breath.

Groaning his pleasure, Eric dropped her hand to wrap his arms around her. He pulled her snugly against his body, then sank his fingers into the hair at her nape. The thick cascade of her hair was silky against his skin, her lips velvety on his. He reveled in every point of contact between her body and his yet wanted more.

Too soon, she pulled away. He released her, though every fiber of him protested with a hollow ache.

She touched her fingers to her mouth and closed her eyes.

Eric's pulse thumped expectantly as if awaiting a crucial verdict. When she released a sad sigh, his heart sank.

"Eric," she said in a barely audible whisper. Finally, she

raised her eyes to his, tears puddled at her lashes. "I have feelings for you, too, but what if…?"

The first half of her statement spike so much joy and relief in him, that he almost missed the "but," the "what if?"

When she glanced away, not finishing her sentence, he prompted, "What if…?"

She fidgeted with the hem of her shirt, stalling. "What if there's someone else?"

"You mean, like Rachel's father?" Resignation darkened his tone. Of course they had to consider who she might have left behind, who could be waiting for her, what her previous life held. Disappointment and frustration slammed his chest and tensed his muscles. He muttered a word he rarely used but seemed appropriate at the moment.

She touched his arm lightly, and the gentle brush of her fingers scalded him. "I don't remember anyone. I don't even get a vague sense of missing someone like that. But before anything happens between us, I think we should at least lay out the possibility, look at it, together. And if it proves not to hold any water, then…"

"I understand." But his heart twisted at the mere thought of Lisa belonging to anyone else.

"All I can say is I've felt a sadness I can't pin down, but…" She frowned and shook her head. "But I can't really separate it from the general sense of doom or danger and worry that has plagued me all along."

He flexed his fingers and tried to shake out the tension knotted inside him. "That's not really enough to eliminate the possibility there's someone though, huh?"

She folded her arms over her chest as she paced away, then faced him again. "I've tried really hard to remember. If I was involved with someone, wouldn't I remember…*something*?"

He could only shrug. "I don't know. What does Helen say about it?"

"Well, we discussed the possibility that if there was someone, they could be the source of the trauma that caused my amnesia. The bruising I had when you found me would suggest I'd been beaten. So...maybe I can't remember him because I don't want to remember him."

Eric had considered that scenario before as well, and he gritted his teeth, outraged by the suggestion of someone hurting Lisa that way. "If that's the case, he doesn't deserve you or your loyalty. You're better off without him."

She nodded. "I agree with that, but...that's only one explanation."

Eric grunted and tipped his head back, exasperated with the conundrum.

"The good news is," Lisa said, stepping back toward him and holding up her hand, "I'm not wearing a ring of any kind. And there's no indication, no *indentation*, if you will, that I ever did. That says to me that even if there was someone, there was no commitment."

Eric hated the flutter of promise that revelation stirred inside him. He didn't want to build any slim expectation or cling to any false illusions that could rip him apart later. Wasn't it better to be realistic? Practical?

"And," Lisa continued, "if someone were out there waiting for me, why haven't they filed a missing person report? If they cared about me, why aren't they doing anything to find me?"

"Good point." A swell of something like hope filled his chest. The odds were tipping in their favor, and he couldn't deny the surge of anticipation and happiness that rose in him. He wanted her, he allowed his heart to admit. Not just physically but entirely. He wanted her in his life, in his heart, in his future.

Rachel whined, dragging their attention to her as she rubbed her eyes.

"I'll put her to bed now." Lisa scooped the baby into her arms, and Eric followed them to the guest bedroom. After

Lisa had laid Rachel down, he handed her the soft baby blanket draped at the foot of the crib.

"If I'm not her mother, why do I have her?"

"You no longer think she's yours?" he asked, a bit startled by her question.

"Evidence to the contrary has been adding up. But…if I'm not Rachel's mother, why hasn't her real mother come forward looking for her? Why isn't there an Amber Alert or something?"

He dragged a hand down his face and groaned.

"I know, I know! We've been going around and around with the same questions for two months now. It's frustrating and gets us nowhere." She wrapped her hands around the railing of the crib and sighed. "I guess I'm asking…what are we doing? How long am I supposed to stay here without any direction or any answers? I'm in limbo, and my being here keeps you in limbo, too."

He frowned as he faced her. "Are you saying you want to leave?"

Chapter Nineteen

Lisa met Eric's eyes. Even in the dim glow of the nursery night-light, his eyes glimmered with a fierce intensity that burrowed to her core. He'd had the courage to confess his darkest personal battle. Shouldn't she give him the same honesty? "I should. But how do I move forward when I still don't know what's behind me?" she asked, her tone full of frustration.

"What do you *want* to happen?" he asked, and, damn it, his voice had the calm and reason hers did not.

His question rolled through her, plowing down all her what-ifs and maybes. She knew what she wanted. She just hadn't found the inner gumption to voice it. Saying it made it real. Speaking the words left her vulnerable. Expressing her deepest desire risked being dealt her deepest pain.

"Your life is your own, Lisa," he said when she remained quiet, ponderous. "You don't have to wait for something that may happen in a few months, a few years or…may never happen." He covered her hand on the railing with his own. "Living in limbo isn't living. I want you to be happy. Be fulfilled. If you want a different life, go get it. Whatever shape that takes, whatever it is you want from life, fight for it."

The fervor in his voice matched the passion in his expression. Eric, who'd given her far more than shelter and protection these past two months. He'd shared his strength and encouraged her. Shown her a love based on kindness and selflessness. Brought a joy and purpose to her life even, when she had so many questions hovering over her. He gave her hope at a time when her world had felt hopeless.

Yes, she knew what she wanted. But admitting it still seemed dangerous. Scary. Her dream was so fragile. Could she take that next step? Could she trust Eric with her heart?

Rachel snuffled as she drifted off to sleep, and Lisa dropped her gaze to watch the gentle rise and fall of the baby's chest. For several precious moments, she simply watched Rachel sleep. One thought played over and again in her mind. She was so tired of living in fear, being afraid of what she'd forgotten. Afraid of what would happen if she remembered her previous life.

Fear sapped her energy and stole her happiness. Fear held her back. Fear killed her dreams more surely than anything Eric might do or say.

She lifted her gaze to Eric's and turned her hand to lace her fingers with his. "I know what I want. I want *this* life." She leaned close and brushed a kiss on his lips. "And I want you."

LISA'S WORDS, HER raw honesty, her kiss set him on fire. He only paused a moment, staring into her eyes to assess her mood, her sincerity. Her expression held a hint of hesitation, as if waiting for him to reach the same inevitable conclusion—they were meant to be together.

Framing her face with both of his hands, he kissed her back, his mouth slanted across hers and drawing deeply on her sweetness. He conjured every morsel of his strength and willpower to lever back and meet her eyes with a bold and open yearning. "I want this, too. So much. But I cannot... I will not make love to you unless I'm certain it's what you truly want."

She nodded eagerly. "One hundred percent. It's one of the few things I do know absolutely and to my core."

The passion behind her assertion drilled deep into his aching soul, stoking his desire even hotter, his dedication to her more profound. Yet his conscience still tickled, and he whispered, "We have to be as sure as possible that we can do this with a clear conscience and no regrets."

She clearly understood what he was saying and lifted her chin. "I have no proof other than circumstantial evidence, but it all tells me the same thing my heart does. There is no one else. I have no regrets—" she curled her mouth in a half grin "—other than it's taking you so long to kiss me again with all this talk."

He chuckled as he sealed his lips over hers, drawing her hips closer with one hand while his other ran through her hair and settled at her nape.

Lisa draped her arms around his shoulders, her hands clutching his shirt, tugging it until it slipped free of his jeans.

A rustling from the crib brought her head up, her gaze slanting to the sleeping baby next to where they stood.

Eric arched one eyebrow and hitched his head toward the door.

Lisa grinned and held a finger to her lips as she turned to tiptoe out of the room. He caught her hand, bringing her up short and scooped her into his arms. Lisa gave a muted gasp of surprise as he cradled her against his chest and strode purposefully to his own bedroom.

Leaving the door cracked so they could hear Rachel, he carried Lisa to his unmade bed. They tumbled together onto the mattress, limbs tangling and noses bumping as they clambered to undress each other and slake their hunger with kisses and nips and roaming hands.

As eager as he was, Eric made himself take a breath, take a beat, take a mental picture and savor this moment. While not without experience, he'd intentionally limited his sexual encounters, wanting more from a woman than just physical gratification. He longed for connection and a mutual commitment to something beyond just a frenzied coupling. He wanted someone who saw the real Eric—scars, sins and soul—and still believed in him.

Though she'd been understandably reserved and wary at first, he saw the naked trust he'd earned from Lisa whenever he looked into her heavenly blue eyes. More than anything, he wanted to live up to the confidence she placed in him.

Straddling her, he stroked both hands down the length of her torso and over her hips. Her skin was taut and soft, and her subtle curves quietly seductive. "Perfection," he whispered.

She gave a snorting chuckle, her cheeks flushing. "If you say so."

He bent to kiss her nose and trace her cheek with his fingertips. "I do. So there!" In a softer tone, he added, "You are beautiful in so many ways, Lisa. So many ways."

She lowered her gaze, her eyelashes shyly hiding her eyes as she smiled. "You're not so bad yourself, Dr. Harkney." She slanted a coy look up at him and trailed a finger from his shoulder, along his collarbone and down the center of his chest. Her light touch and impish grin that tugged the corner of her mouth sent a thrill through his blood. His anticipation climbed, along with his pulse when her finger continued its trajectory down, lower.

When she wrapped her hand around his sex, his body reacted with a twitch, and he couldn't contain the groan of pleasure. Sparks fired inside him, building as she stroked him. He kissed her neck, nuzzled her breasts and kneaded her flesh from her shoulder to her bottom. When she wiggled against him, wrapping her legs around him so that he lay nestled intimately against her, he tipped her chin up, meeting her languid gaze with his own. "You're sure?"

"Very sure."

He fumbled a condom from his nightstand, sheathed himself and stretched fully along her warm body. Holding her gaze, he guided himself into position. Pushed gently. Moaned from the intensity of sensation. She was so tight. The friction so incredible. He moved his hips slowly, intending to sink farther into her heat.

She hissed, her brow and nose wrinkling quickly as if in pain. He registered her reaction on some level, but his lust urged him on. He rocked his hip forward again and—met resistance.

Her fingers dug into his back, and she winced. And his brain registered what was happening like a light switch being flipped on.

Eric froze, a wash of cold reality spreading through his limbs.

Lisa's breathing was shallow and quick, and she angled a puzzled look at him. "I… Eric?"

He withdrew and rolled to her side. He took a shuddering breath and shifted to face her as he grazed a hand down her cheek.

She gaped at him, her mouth opening and closing as if she couldn't find her voice. Finally she expelled a giant sigh and a wry laugh. "Apparently, I'm a virgin."

"Apparently," he said, his tone gentle.

"Which means…" Her eyes widened as if taking in all the subsequent truths they had to reconcile.

"You're not Rachel's mother." He brushed his thumb across her bottom lip. He tugged her into his arms, folding her into his embrace as they both digested that fact.

"No." She tucked her head under his chin and reached to pull up the blanket wadded beside them. "So that's…interesting."

"It doesn't confirm you have no boyfriend, but…"

She tipped her head back and met his eyes. "Yeah, but it lends more credence to that theory." She kissed him and smiled. "I'm glad. I don't want anyone but you."

"So, it begs the question even more urgently now." He

touched his forehead to hers. "Who are Rachel's parents? Where are Rachel's parents?"

She tensed, her fingers biting into his arms.

Neither of them said anything for long moments, their breath mingling as they held each other and searched each other's face. Finally Lisa wet her lips and broke the silence.

"This…changes everything…and nothing. But tonight, I only want…" She blinked, and he saw the tears that sparkled in her eyes.

"Tell me. Anything."

"Finish what you started. Make love to me, Eric Harkney."

And he did.

Chapter Twenty

DJ parked his truck in his usual spot, where he had a view of Lisa's apartment door. If she came or left home, he'd know it. He only had to be patient. But patience was wearing thin. He'd shown the picture that had been printed in the Valley Haven newspaper of Lisa to a few dozen businesses in the small town where he'd spotted her the week before. No one knew her. Or no one admitted knowing her. Small towns protected their own. When the questions started coming back on him about who he was and what business he had with Lisa, he knew it was time to let the search in Valley Haven rest. For a while.

He still believed that if and when she regained her memory or came out of hiding, she had to come back here.

He sat taller when he saw an older lady approach Lisa's door and knock. Getting no reply, the woman stooped, lifted a cat into her arms and started back the way she came.

DJ hesitated only a moment before climbing out of his truck and approaching the older woman. "Excuse me, do you have a minute? Do you know the girl who lives in F-3?"

THE NEXT WEEKEND, Eric watched the college basketball tournament on television while Lisa puttered with scraps of fabric his grandmother had given her, stitching them together by hand to create intricate designs. Rachel babbled to herself, testing her newfound vocalizations while amusing herself with her stacking cups.

During a commercial break, Eric glanced over at Lisa, feeling a contentment he hadn't known he could feel. Restlessness and regret had been his constant companions so long, he'd come to view them as the norm. He squeezed Lisa's knee, bringing her gaze to his from her needlework. She smiled at him, and a light flush rose in her cheeks. Since their first night of lovemaking, they'd been intimate daily, anxiously waiting for Rachel to nap or fall asleep in the evening.

When persistent shadows flitted across Lisa's face, telling Eric she was thinking about her blank past, the unsettled questions that still lingered, he'd pull her close and whisper, "We'll figure it out. Everything will be fine."

The reassurances were as much for his own benefit as hers.

A knock on his front door pulled Eric from his current contemplation of the turn his life had taken, and he rose to answer the door.

Eric found his father pacing the front porch. "Hey, Dad. What's up?"

His father faced him with a smile that didn't reach his eyes, then stretched his neck to peer past Eric inside the house.

"Is Lisa inside?" Matt asked in a quiet voice.

"She is," Eric answered, matching the low volume without knowing why.

His father hitched his head to the side, silently asking to be followed, and moved off the porch toward a bench under a large walnut tree.

Poking his head back inside the cabin, he called to Lisa, "I'll be right back. My dad wants a word."

Lisa gave a nod, her brow furrowed inquisitively, but said nothing.

As he jogged down the steps to the front yard, Eric noticed the folded newspaper tucked under his father's arm, and a prickle of apprehension crawled through him. Eric liked to tease his novelist father about his stubborn loyalty to a physical newspaper, but combined with his father's serious expression, the presence of the almost-relic newspaper didn't seem humorous to Eric at the moment.

"What is it?" Eric asked as his father sat down on the bench.

"Have you figured anything else out about who Lisa is and what happened to her?" His dad took the paper out from under his arm and held it so tightly the pages crumpled slightly.

"Not much. She's starting to fill in snippets, but—" He stopped short and scowled. "Why don't you just show me what you found?" He waved a finger toward the newspaper. "Isn't that why you're here?"

Matt exhaled a long, weary-sounding sigh through pursed lips. "Right. This is today's paper. I came right over when I saw it."

The newspaper had been folded over several times so that one article on the facing page was prominent. The headline read, "Neighbor's Gruesome Discovery Leads to Search for Missing Child."

Eric's gut somersaulted. He held his breath as he read on.

When Hastings resident Willa Greenburg investigated a bad smell at her nearest neighbor's home earlier this week, no one answered the door, and the 74-year-old homemaker became concerned. Greenburg, who'd recently returned home after spending three months at a rehabilitation center following a fall in December, called the police, requesting a well-being check for her neighbors. When the police entered the home, they discovered the lifeless bodies of homeowners Michelle and Victor Thompson. The condition of the bodies indicated the two had been victims of violence and had been dead for a long time. Due to the isolated location of the Thompsons' home and Greenburg's hospitalization, the deaths had gone undetected for weeks. Greenburg reported to the police that the Thompsons were parents to an infant daughter, who was not found at the scene. Attempts to contact the young couple's next of kin failed, and an APB was issued for the infant, Rachel Thompson.

The article went on, but Eric had read enough. His stomach rebelled, and he had to swallow hard several times and concentrate on calming himself to keep from losing his lunch. He took several slow breaths before he could speak to his father. "Well, that's...awful."

"It's rather damning for Lisa."

Eric whipped his head toward his father, his jaw tight. "Damning?" He gritted his teeth. "You're not suggesting Lisa murdered these people and stole their baby, are you? This happened in Hastings. That's more than forty miles from here."

His father held up a hand to stay his arguments. "Eric, come on. The missing baby's name is Rachel."

"So?" Eric countered, his entire body starting to shake.

"*So?* You can't dismiss that as coincidence."

"Lisa is not a murderer!" Eric snapped, although his brain was scrambling to explain away the tragic and eerily similar revelations reported in the article.

"I didn't say she was," his dad said, his calm in stark contrast to the writhing panic in Eric's veins. "But the circumstances of this case," Matt jabbed a finger to the newspaper, "could certainly explain the mysteries surrounding Lisa's situation. If her Rachel is this Rachel, she's got a lot of explaining to do in regards to how she ended up with the baby. How the parents died."

Eric thrust the paper back at his father, growling a terse

curse word. He shoved to his feet and stalked a few steps before pivoting and marching stiffly back to hover over his father on the bench. "We can't just *assume* because of the similar baby names that this has anything to do with Lisa!"

Even as he defended her innocence, doubts choked him, and the evidence to the contrary twisted knots in his soul. "That woman in there is good and kind and gentle and loving and—" his voice cracked as he shouted at his father "—*not* a killer!"

His father raised a palm, signaling a pause. "I'm not accusing her of anything. Let's take a step back, though, and remember she was covered in blood when you found her. Something terrible happened to her to cause her fugue. We don't know what her part in the big picture is, but...at minimum, we need her to talk to the police in—" Matt glanced at the newspaper again, his finger running down the column of print, tapping the page "—Hastings, where the crime was reported."

Despite the March sun, Eric shivered. A movement in his peripheral vision caught his attention, and he glanced toward the cabin. Lisa had pulled back a curtain and stood at the living room window watching him and his dad.

Matt glanced over his shoulder, followed the path of Eric's gaze and said, "I know you have feelings for her, son. We all like her. But you need to show her this—" he wagged the newspaper "—and be prepared for whatever the fallout might be."

"Fallout?" Eric sent his father a sharp look. "You think she'll be arrested?"

His dad dragged a hand down his face. "I don't want to speculate, but...if her Rachel is this Rachel, she is guilty of kidnapping at a minimum."

He shook his head. "Not if she had the parents' permission to take the baby. Maybe she's their babysitter or a daycare worker, and she kept Rachel safe when the parents didn't show up to collect her from the daycare center. Or maybe she found Rachel abandoned somewhere and took her in out of the goodness of her heart."

His father nodded slowly, his expression grim. "Yeah. But how do either of those scenarios explain her memory loss and obvious trauma? Her nightmares point to something much darker and more sinister."

Sinister...

The word rippled along Eric's nerves, firing sparks that left him jittery and alarm coiling in his gut. "Dad, that car that almost ran over Lisa in town a couple weeks ago..."

His father raised his chin, his eyes narrowing with suspicion. "What about it?"

"What if it was intentional, like Lisa thinks? What if something dark and evil is going on, and the driver was trying to hurt Lisa?" He tried to swallow, his mouth suddenly gone dry. "Or kill her? What if she knows something about the Thompsons' deaths, and someone is trying to silence her?"

His father didn't say anything at first. He stared at the ground for a weighty moment before lifting a troubled gaze to Eric. "I've considered that and several other options before I brought this to you. Most scenarios I've tried to dismiss as an overactive writer's imagination. It's easy enough for me to spin this out in a number of directions. None of them good."

Eric's shoulders sagged, and he dropped heavily onto the bench again, muttering invectives under his breath.

"Which isn't to say that there's not also a reasonable explanation that clears Lisa of all wrongdoing," his father said, though his tone was dubious. When Eric said nothing, his father continued, "Look, Eric... I know you've grown fond of Lisa—"

Eric's head snapped up. "Fond?" He scoffed. "Dad, it's more than fond. She's...special." He grunted again, shaking his head, this time for his own cowardly euphemism. "Special" was too ambiguous and passive to describe Lisa. "She's important to me." He gritted his teeth. Why couldn't he just say the words, give his father the truth?

His dad stayed silent, but the look in his eyes told Eric his father knew what he wasn't ready to admit out loud. He was falling in love with her.

"But you know you can't hide her from the police now that we know this." His dad flapped the newspaper and gave him a sorrowful glance. "You could be charged with something if you don't turn her in. Obstruction. Aiding and abetting. Harboring a fugitive."

Eric shot to his feet. "She's not a criminal! I can't be charged with anything, because she did nothing wrong!"

His father rose to his feet as well. "I hope you're right. But that's not our determination to make. I know it's scary. It's hard sometimes to do the right thing."

"Geez, Dad, I'm not ten! I've made more than a couple of hard decisions in my life. I told the police what I did to Mom's stalker, didn't I?"

"I'm only saying—"

"Protecting Lisa and Rachel *is* the right thing!" He jabbed his index finger toward the cabin. "Now more than ever, I know I have to keep her safe. If the baby in that article is her Rachel, then it only proves that she and the baby could be in danger. The Thompsons were murdered! Their killer could very well be looking for Lisa now!"

His father's jaw tightened. "All the more reason to go to the police. If she's innocent—and I pray that she is—then the police could help her figure out what happened. The information she's blocking could help solve the Thompsons' murders. The cops could protect her from—"

"I'm protecting her!" Eric said, stabbing his chest with his thumb. "I promised not to let anything happen to her. How can I turn her in to the cops if I even suspect they might arrest her?"

"You won't have to."

Eric whirled around.

Lisa stood behind him, her face pale. "I don't want you involved," she said. "I'll turn myself in."

Chapter Twenty-One

Much of the trip to Hastings was made in silence. Eric had already exhausted every argument he had, trying to talk her out of going to the police. But Lisa knew she had to go. The police could have the answers she needed, even if the truth was hard to hear. She refused to live in this limbo any longer. Stuck. Not moving forward, paralyzed by an unknown past. And yet...

More than she feared for her own fate, Lisa feared what would happen to Rachel. If she had any doubts about her choice to turn herself in, they revolved around Rachel. They'd left the baby at Cameron Glen in Grace's expert care, wanting to get a feel for the situation before they handed over the baby. *If* they had to hand over the baby.

Lisa choked down the tears that rose in her throat every time she thought of the real possibility that the authorities could take Rachel away from her. Put her in foster care. Turn Rachel into a helpless case number in an overwhelmed state system.

Save Rachel!

She may not have given birth to Rachel, but Rachel was *hers*. She loved Rachel with a deep, abiding affection and fierce protectiveness. Surely that meant she shared an intimate connection that predated whatever tragedy had put them on that snowy roadside in January. Rachel needed her, and she needed Rachel.

But she also needed to face whatever horrible event had happened in the Thompsons' home. There was a chance the crime had nothing to do with her. But there was also the chance that she could finally know what had happened to her, for better or for worse.

You can't solve a problem until you identify it.

Eric had been right when he told her that so many weeks ago. And she had to solve the riddle of her past, knock down the walls that her brain had erected before she could build a future. With Eric.

She swallowed hard. She hadn't told him he was the prime reason she was doing this—gambling on what the police might tell her in an attempt to win the opportunity to give herself, whole and unanchored, to him.

Out her window, the tender shades of green as the mountains woke to spring should have buoyed her spirits. She wanted to draw strength and hope from the budding trees, the first blossoms poking their heads out from the thawing earth, but the signs of renewal weren't enough to push aside the cold dread that swelled inside her.

They passed a faded billboard that welcomed them to Hastings, and Eric reached across the back seat and took her hand in his. Eric's father had volunteered to drive them, wanting to lend his support and strength. And, ostensibly, because Eric might not be in a good emotional state to drive home should things go sideways for her. Lisa knew she might not be returning to Cameron Glen with Eric and Matt. She could be spending the rest of her life behind bars, if the police had evidence she was the one who'd killed the Thompsons. That she'd stolen Rachel.

She struggled for a breath and pressed a hand to her swirling gut, repeating, *Thompson. Thompson.* Did she want the name to mean something to her, or was she hoping she had no connection to the murdered couple? *Both*, she decided. But so far, the name hadn't stirred any gremlins in her brain, hadn't connected any dots or lifted the obscuring fog.

"Here we are," Matt said unnecessarily as he turned into the parking lot of the small, nondescript brick building.

Lisa heard the parking brake squeak as Matt engaged it, and she stared at the plate glass door, mustering her courage.

"Lisa," Eric whispered, "no matter what happens inside, it changes nothing for me."

She peeled her fingers from his and squared her shoulders. "Yes, it could."

Lisa followed Matt inside the stale-smelling lobby and kept her gaze locked forward on the uniformed female officer at the front desk.

"Can I help you?" the officer asked.

Within seconds, Eric was beside her again, taking her hand and drawing her close. Matt looked toward her, waiting, but her throat closed, and she couldn't find her voice.

When she faltered and Eric only stared at her with worry filling his eyes, Matt cleared his throat and stepped forward. "We believe we might have relevant information regarding the case of the missing child, Rachel Thompson."

She listened numbly as Matt explained why they were there and the events of the day Eric had found her.

The officer sat straighter, eyeing Lisa, then reached for the phone on the desk. "Detective Morris, can you come up front?"

When the officer hung up the phone, she motioned to a row of chairs in the lobby. "You can wait over there. Detective Morris is overseeing that case. He'll be right out."

Lisa walked quickly toward the chairs, grateful for a place to sit, because her legs were shaking so hard, she thought she might crumple.

A few minutes later, a bearded man in a dark brown suit

appeared from the back hall. He gave them a keen scrutiny as he approached, and Lisa wiped her damp palms on her pants.

She rose, somehow, when the man introduced himself as Walter Morris, the lead investigator on the Thompson case. Matt and Eric both shook Morris's hand, and when the detective offered his hand to her, her arm quivered as she extended it. *Good grief!* She had to get a hold of herself! She reeked of guilt and fear. Not the image she wanted to present when her freedom, her life with Eric and Rachel's future were on the line.

Lisa tucked her hands under her armpits, drew a deep breath through her nose, exhaled through her mouth. *Calm down. Just tell the truth. Everything will be fine.*

Matt repeated the explanation for their visit, and the detective's graying eyebrows shot up.

"I see. Well, Ms.—I'm sorry, I didn't catch your last name."

"I don't remember it," she said. "It's just Lisa."

He nodded and motioned toward a side door. "All right. Lisa is good enough for now. If you gentlemen will wait here, I'll talk with Lisa and see if we can sort things out." Facing her, he said, "Come with me." He moved to a keypad beside the door marked Authorized Personnel Only. After punching in a code, he waved a hand for her to precede him. "This way."

Her legs were wooden as she crossed the floor, pausing at the door to look over her shoulder to Eric. His eyes were wide and full of concern and compassion. And something more tender and raw that she didn't dare name.

"You've got this," he mouthed.

With a nod to Eric, she turned and walked into the bowels of the police station. The scent of burned coffee made her stomach roil. The muted conversations of uniformed officers and the clatter of desktop keyboards filtered down the hall as she trailed behind Morris.

He motioned her into a small room with a scarred wooden table and formed plastic chairs. "Have a seat."

She did.

Before he closed the door, he called down the hall, "Grimshaw, will you bring me everything we have on the Thompson case? The whole file. Thanks."

Morris took a seat across from her and gave her a tight-lipped smile. "Well, Lisa. Thank you for coming in today. I'm going to record our conversation for the official record, okay?" He set his phone on the table and tapped the screen. After stating his name and hers, the relevant case number, the date and time, he lifted a gray-eyed gaze to her. "Why don't you start at the beginning and tell me what you know? Then I'll ask my questions, and we'll go from there. Would you like some coffee or water before we start?"

She shook her head, and he waved a hand toward her, inviting her to begin. Hands clamped in her lap, she closed her eyes. "As Matt mentioned, I… I don't have any memory of what happened…b-before Eric stopped to help me. He found me walking on the side of the road in January. The ER doctor said I was in something called a…dissociative fugue. That I had amnesia. Likely because of a trauma or emotional breakdown."

Morris nodded, silently telling her to continue.

"I had no coat and was…" she paused for a breath "…c-covered in blood." *And I was carrying Rachel.* Somehow she wasn't ready to admit that part. Let him hear her circumstances first, so he didn't form any early prejudices against her.

Did cops do that? Weren't they supposed to form their opinions based on the facts?

"Where are those bloody clothes now?" Morris asked.

"The police department in Valley Haven has them, I guess. They came to the emergency room where Eric took us."

"Us? Was someone with you?"

Her heart thudded so hard she felt sure Morris could hear it. Reluctantly, she nodded.

"I'm sorry. You'll need to answer all of my questions out loud, for the recording."

She swallowed. "Yes."

"Who was with you?"

A knock on the door forestalled her reply. Morris answered the door and took the file folder from the officer there. When he'd resettled, he said, "I'm sorry. Please continue. Who was with you?"

"Well, Eric, of course, and...a baby."

Morris narrowed his eyes and lifted his chin. "How old was this baby? A boy or a girl?"

"A girl. About six months at the time, we estimate."

"I see." Morris shuffled through the file and finally slid a photograph across the table to Lisa. "Was it this baby?"

Lisa shifted her attention to the picture of an infant with rosy cheeks and a drooly smile. Her heart squeezed, and tears pricked her eyes. "Yes, sir. That's Rachel."

ERIC PACED THE small lobby, unable to sit still, dying to know what was happening down the hall. He wished he could go into the interview room with Lisa, if only to hold her hand, give her moral support. Being in this small-town police station brought back far too many memories of a night eleven years ago when he'd been the one on the hot seat. He slammed his eyes shut and was instantly back on that fishing dock, hearing the thud of a crutch striking a man on the head. Then later, on the shore with his mother, watching his father and future stepdad giving a dead man CPR. Sitting in an overly air-conditioned interrogation room, shivering with cold and guilt as stern eyes judged him.

"Eric?"

His father's voice yanked him out of the past, and he blinked as he brought his surroundings back into focus.

"You okay, son?"

Eric rubbed his forehead and dropped back into the chair beside his dad. "I guess. It's just... I know what it's like. I remember being interrogated after—" He waved his hand, not wanting to say the name. His dad knew.

"Does that still bother you? I mean, I thought you'd processed it with your counselor and had a come to terms with what happened."

"Yeah, well... I didn't want you and Mom worried about me."

"So, you're saying it does still bother you?"

Eric rubbed his hands on his jeans and sighed. "I'd still be in medicine if it didn't."

"In med—" His father twisted on his chair to face him more directly. "Hang on. I thought you said you left your residency because of burnout. What really happened?"

Scowling, Eric pinched the bridge of his nose. "Can we please not have this discussion now?"

"Depends. If there's something going on, something you haven't told me and your mom, I want to know—I *need* to know what it is. We can help."

Eric shook his head. "I doubt that." Then realizing how harsh his comment probably sounded, he glanced at his father, adding, "That's not to say I don't think you'd try or that you don't care, or..." He blew out a shallow breath. "It's something I have to deal with, something I have to figure out. I'm not your screwup kid anymore that you can fix things for by talking to the principal or putting me on restriction to teach me a lesson."

"You were never a screwup, Eric. You had issues to deal with that no kid ever should, and you acted out. But that does not make you a screwup."

Propping his forearms on his splayed thighs, Eric let his head fall forward as he closed his eyes, trying to shut out the echoes of old pains.

DETECTIVE MORRIS DREW the photograph of Rachel back toward him and slipped it into the file. He pinched and twisted his mouth as if deliberating.

Lisa's stomach whirled, and she looked around for a trash can in case she had to vomit. Which definitely could happen. She squeezed the edges of her seat and watched the detective for some clue of his thoughts. Was he going to arrest her? Demand they turn Rachel over?

"And Rachel is still in your custody at the moment?"

She nodded. "She's safe and happy. The Camerons are watching her today while I'm here. They're good people. They've helped me and Rachel so much since Eric rescued us. They've been like—" *Family.*

Her pulse thumped when the word came to her. It was true. They had been the family she hadn't known she needed. The idea that she'd be losing these people if the detective saw fit to lock her up ripped at her soul. Family…

But Rachel was family, too. She was sure of it. And she would fight for the baby like a mother bear. Even if she wasn't Rachel's biological mother.

Morris nodded slowly, his face still emotionless and meditative. "Does the name Thompson mean anything to you?"

She swallowed hard. Shook her head.

"Aloud, please."

"No, sir. I know it should, if Rachel is really the Thompsons' daughter, but—" tears choked her voice "—it doesn't."

"Victor Thompson? Michelle Thompson? Those names ring any bells?"

"I understand from the newspaper that those are the names of the couple…found in their home." *The murdered couple.* She couldn't make herself say the words. "But the names don't—"

Chelle! No, no, no! God, please, no! Chellie!

Lisa's breath caught as the sound of the horrified wail

rippled through her like an apparition. An echoing scream. A baby crying.

She gasped and braced a hand on the edge of the table when her head spun, and she thought she might pass out.

"Lisa?" Detective Morris unfolded his arms and leaned forward. "Did you think of something? Any snippet could be helpful."

She hunched her shoulders and tucked her hands under her arms, suddenly cold. She shook her head. "No… I—nothing."

Morris grunted a bit and stroked fingers over his gray-threaded brown beard. He drummed his fingers on the file before flipping through the sheets and drawing out another photograph. Two. Three. He slid them over to Lisa, lined them up before her.

"Do these pictures shake anything loose?"

Her gaze moved to the images, and shock punched her in the chest. Nausea. Disgust. Terror.

Crime scene photos. Two bloody bodies lying on the floor. One in a bedroom. One in a living room. Furniture upended. Stains and spatter and gore…

Now she did retch and dash for the trash can. She threw up, and coughed, and threw up again until her stomach was empty. Lightheaded, she spit and wiped her mouth on the back of her hand. She shook from her core. Fear roiled and writhed in her like a provoked snake. A marrow-deep sadness carved her out, leaving her hollow. Raw. Aching.

The crime scene flashed in her mind again, but different this time. It wasn't still images, but a terrible scene playing out in full color.

A discordant howl tore from her as reality crashed in on her, a tidal wave of pain and horror and grief. Chellie was dead. Murdered. Gone.

And she'd been there when it happened.

An animalistic wail ricocheted from somewhere in the heart of the police station. Eric's head snapped up. *Lisa!*

He was instantly on his feet and charging toward the door where Detective Morris had taken her. It was, of course, locked. He banged his fist on the door, shouting, "Let me in! What's going on? Lisa!"

His father grabbed his shoulder. "Eric, you can't—"

He shook off his dad's hand, kept hammering the door. "Hey! Let me in!"

The officer from the front desk materialized at his elbow, shouting sternly, "Sir, you need to sit down! Get back from the door and sit down, or I'll have to take you into custody."

Eric whirled to face the officer. "Lisa needs me! You gotta let me go back there! Didn't you hear that scream?"

"If that was your friend—"

"You know it was!"

"Detective Morris is fully capable of handling the situation and—"

"Handling the *situation*?" Eric stabbed a finger toward the barred door. "Did that sound like he was handling anything? She's terrified! Hurting!" He took a deep breath, his rage and desperation growing. "And she's a traumatized woman, not a *situation*!"

The desk officer squared her shoulders and glared at him, one hand resting on her handcuffs. "Sir, you need step back from that door and *sit down*."

His father wedged himself between Eric and the policewoman. "Let's go, son. Please. Don't make things worse for Lisa by getting yourself arrested."

He could still hear distant sobs and keening behind the door, and everything in him wanted only to go to her, hold her, shield her from whatever horror had caused her to cry out. He flexed and balled his fists, wanting to break through that damn door to reach Lisa. His frustration and worry knotted in his chest. He clenched his jaw so tightly, he thought his back teeth might crack.

But when his father took his arm and pulled him toward the chair he'd just abandoned, Eric stumbled behind him. Sat. Sucked in ragged, angry breaths.

Through his gritted teeth, he said, "I promised her I would protect her. That I would keep her safe."

His father nodded and squeezed Eric's knee. "I understand. And believe it or not, I know how it feels to have the woman you love be in danger or hurting and feel helpless to help her. You do remember that Cait was kidnapped and held at gunpoint that first summer we met, right?"

Eric pinched the bridge of his nose, took a deliberately long, slow breath. "Yeah. Of course I remember." He angled a frown at his father. "But how does that help Lisa?"

His father blinked and opened his mouth. "I... Well, it doesn't. I just wanted you to know I understand your frustration and concern." He gave a short humorless laugh. "I'm not real good at this, I guess."

Eric plowed a hand through his hair. "Sorry. I know you're trying to help."

Matt cleared his throat and said, "Lisa is strong. She'll get through this. She'll be okay."

Eric scowled and weighed his father's assurances. Platitudes. They sounded good, offered as a balm to his worry. But the truth was, whatever had happened to Lisa had already broken her. Her brain had shut down her memory and erected walls to protect her. She was fragile. Her emotions on thin ice. Her memories were a hotbed of demons waiting to ravage her. And the cry he'd heard from behind that locked door had sounded like someone had set the hounds of hell on her.

In truth, Lisa might not get through this, might not be okay, at all.

LISA SAT WITH her knees drawn close to her chest, her chin tucked down and her arms over her head. Rocking. Her breath panting. Her ears ringing. Her mind scrambling both to blot out the gruesome images and drag them out of the dark recess of her amnesia.

Chelle. Oh, no, no, no! Please, don't let my sister be dead!

But the image came again. Her sister, bleeding, weak, hoarse.

"GET RACH...OUT OF *h-here. Save her."*

Lisa cradled her sister against her chest, sobs heaving from deep within her. "You need an ambulance! Where's your phone?" She cast a frantic gaze about and spotted Chelle's cell phone on the floor. Grabbing it with slippery, bloody hands, she tried to stop shaking enough to dial.

"No..." Chelle said, weakly batting at the phone to stop her. "No police. No...ambu—" She dragged in a ragged breath. "They'll take Rachel. Put her...in foster—"

"But you need to go to the hospital!" Lisa tried again to tap in 911.

"Too late..." Her sister swatted at the phone again, and Lisa fumbled it. "Take Rachel. Please. Now."

"Then you have to come with us! Chellie, please, get up. I'll help you walk. We have to go!"

"I can't. I'm not...going to...m-make it."

"Don't say that! I can't lose you!" Lisa could barely see through the tears that puddled and spilled from her eyes. "Please try, Chellie!"

"Save Rachel. For me." Her sister's limp hand lifted to Lisa's cheek, and a glimmer of desperate fire lit Chelle's gaze. "Don't...let them...have her. Promise...me."

"Don't leave me, Chellie!" Lisa shook her head, unable to accept what was playing out before her.

Chelle's hand fell away. Her eyes fixed, and the glimmer of light disappeared.

"No!" Lisa gasped. "No, Chelle, don't go! I'll do anything! Promise anything. Just, please don't die!" She shook her sister, trying to rouse her, and Chelle's head lolled back. "Nooo!"

From the next room, she heard male voices. Vic's and another man's. And across the bedroom, Rachel's high-pitched cry.

Save Rachel...

Nodding, she whispered, "Yes. I promise."

Then letting Chelle's body slip from her grasp, she shoved weakly to her feet and staggered to the bedroom door.

"Lisa?"

A hand touched her back, and she shrank away, scooting as far into the corner as she could. "No! Don't—"

She shuddered as she blinked the brightly lit, largely empty room into focus. Her heart scampered. Her startled gaze darted up to the man hovering over her, and she swallowed the bitter taste in her mouth.

Where was Eric? She wanted Eric, not this man with his hard gray eyes and grizzled beard.

"Tell me what's going on. Did you remember something?" Detective Morris asked.

The image of Chellie's limp and bloodstained body flashed in her mind's eye again. Along with another. A man. More blood. A pained wail. A baby crying...

Lisa clapped her hands over her ears as if she could shut out the sounds echoing in her brain. "Nooo! No, stop! I can't—"

A hand on her arm. Morris.

The man with the neck tattoo grabbed her wrist...

She flinched. Screamed. Curled in a tighter ball.

The images and smells, the sounds and terror were pouring into her brain.

Flooding her. Overwhelming her. Drowning her.

She gasped for breath. Squeezed her eyes shut. Covered her ears. But it wouldn't stop. The pain. The gore. The horror.

"No-no-no-no-no!" she whimpered, praying the tableau unfolding in her head would stop. But it kept coming in fragmented, unordered pieces...

SHE SCRAPED THE *uneaten, runny yolks into the trash and wrinkled her nose at the nasty mess. Her customer had dumped ketchup on his eggs, and the red-and-yellow slurry he'd left on his plate turned her stomach. Gross!*

She set the scraped plate aside as her phone rang, and she dug her cell from her pocket. Chelle. Irritation poked her. Her sister knew not to call her when she was at work.

"This better be an emergency," she told Chelle wryly, without even a greeting. "You know my boss hates it when I take calls while I'm working."

"I need you! Please come!" The strangled and frightened tone of her sister's voice put her immediately on alert.

"Chelle? What's hap—"

"He stabbed me, Lisa. I can't. You have to save Rachel!"

Chapter Twenty-Two

Lisa shook her head, certain she'd heard wrong. "What?"

"Vic's high and t-talking some...crazy thing about selling Rachel...to pay off a guy," her sister said in a rushed and rasping whisper. She could hear her niece crying in the background. "He t-tried to take her from me, and w-when I fought him, he stabbed me."

A bone-deep chill settled over Lisa. She'd known Vic could be violent sometimes, had begged Chelle to leave him, but... he'd stabbed her?

"Chellie, you have to leave! Just...take the baby and go! I'll meet you somewhere, but get out of there!"

"I c-can't," Chelle sobbed. "I think I'm dying. There's so much blood and..."

Tears pooled in Lisa's eyes. "No! You cannot die! Do you hear me?"

"Please hurry! I don't know...how long I can—" Chelle groaned.

"Have you called the police? An ambulance? I can—"

"No! You know that never...helps. And they said...next time they'd...remove Rachel. I can't...you can't call anyone. Please!"

Lisa knew the dire warnings social services had outlined, knew Vic's buddies in the sheriff's office believed him over Chelle. But somehow...

"Oh no! Someone's here." Chelle moaned. *"The guy... that wants to take Rachel...sell her. Please, Lisa...you have to come get her. Hurry! You have to save her!"*

Lisa's head spun, trying to make sense of what her sister was saying. Her options. "I...okay. I'm coming!" A strange sort of shock gripped her, yet she found herself stumbling through the restaurant dining room toward the door.

"Where are you going?" her boss shouted from the cash register. "Get back to work!"

She plowed out the door and into the cold day.

Her boss followed her out onto the sidewalk. "I swear, if you leave now, don't bother coming back! You're fired!"

She climbed in her car without a backward glance. Numb. Chelle needed her, and so she just...went. "Hold on, Chellie! Don't you dare die!"

ERIC HEARD LISA scream again, and he lurched to his feet. He stormed over to the front desk and slapped a palm on the counter. "Do you not hear her? What the hell is going on back there?"

"I'm sure Detective Morris has the situation—"

"Under control?" Eric finished for her, shooting her an incredulous look. He aimed a finger at the locked door. "Does that sound like things are all peachy to you?"

"Sir, you need to—"

"Do not tell me to sit down!"

"—sit down."

"Let me back there! Let me help her! She's clearly terrified!"

"Detective Morris is a trained professional, who—"

"Is scaring the crap out of her right now from the sound of it. Excuse me if I question his ability to deal with her trauma!"

The desk officer sighed and linked her hands across her

stomach. "Just the same. I'm not allowed to permit anyone back there without permission."

"So get permission!" Eric said, leaning so far over the counter he was almost crawling onto the officer's desk.

His father appeared at his side, and Eric gritted his teeth, prepared for his dad to drag him back to his seat.

"Can't you at least check with Detective Morris and see if Eric can be of assistance in comforting Lisa?" His father's tone was surprisingly reasonable. "She's clearly upset, and considering she hasn't been charged with any crime, it seems to me your department wouldn't want to be seen as mistreating a citizen."

The desk officer lifted an eyebrow. Huffed out a sigh. Rocking forward in her chair, she lifted her phone and said, "Hey, Mike. The men who came in with the woman Morris is interviewing are requesting a chance to see her." She nodded. "Yeah, I know. But they can hear her, and they're worried about her. Right. Could you at least check with Morris and see what the situation is? Yeah. Thanks." She hung up the phone and regarded Eric with cool detachment. "Officer Corrigan is checking on the situation. In the meantime—" she aimed her finger at the chairs in the lobby "—please have a seat and wait."

THE SKY WAS *an eerie pale gray. A winter storm was blowing in. Sleet pinged on the windshield, and snowflakes whirled in the wind. Lisa's tires slid once or twice. Black ice. The roads were empty. Abandoned.*

Despite Chelle's pleading not to, she tried to dial 911 with one hand as she drove, but the mountain road to Chelle's had no service. Finally, with a frustrated growl, she threw the phone on the passenger side floor and concentrated on driving faster.

Minutes later she couldn't say how she'd gotten to Chelle's house, a rundown clapboard farmhouse on a rural road, far from anywhere. She'd driven the final miles like an automaton. Using muscle memory to operate her car. Numb with fear and confusion and worry. What would she be walking into? Chelle had said Vic was high. Again. He'd be irrational. Unpredictable. Dangerous.

He'd stabbed Chelle! What the...?

When she sped down her sister's long gravel driveway, she found an unfamiliar truck parked on the lawn.

Oh, no...someone's here. I think it's that guy...who wants to take Rachel...sell her—

Spidery tingles crawled up Lisa's spine. Her heart galloped, and she squeezed the steering wheel hard. She had to get inside. Chelle was in there. Bleeding. Dying. Rachel...

Please hurry!

She shouldered open the car door and stumbled on trembling legs toward the house. Male shouts rang inside. Angry. Scary.

Vic had stabbed Chelle...

Would he come after her, too?

Lisa took a step back from the door and looked around the yard. She needed a weapon or some other means to defend herself and Chelle. A baseball bat? A shovel?

Across the yard, she spied a pile of firewood, where someone had been splitting logs. The axe was still in the stump. Pulse roaring in her ears, she ran across the lawn, her feet slipping as the sky pelted her with sleet. The snow came harder, faster.

She shivered from adrenaline and cold. She'd raced away from work without her coat. Without her purse. Just her phone, her keys...

Please hurry!

Curling fingers already growing stiff from cold around the handle, she pulled the axe free from the stump and hefted it to her shoulder to cross the yard again. Her eyes stung. Tears puddled and froze in her eyes, and she blinked hard to clear her vision.

The sound of the men's arguing and Rachel's crying grew louder as she neared the front door. She stopped on the porch, took a breath for courage and headed inside.

A LOUD POPPING noise and shake of her arm dragged Lisa from her daze, from the horror movie that unspooled in her mind's eye.

The gruff detective crouched beside her, his salt-and-pepper eyebrows knitted together as he gazed at her with something akin to concern. He snapped his fingers in front of her face. "Talk to me, Lisa. Tell me what you remember. You're safe here."

Safe? What did that even mean? Chelle should have been safe in her own home, but Vic had stabbed her. A fresh chill sluiced through her, and grief for her sister dug sharp talons into her heart.

A tapping came on the door before it was opened, and a man in uniform poked his head in.

"What?" Morris asked tersely, glancing over his shoulder and clearly peeved at being interrupted.

"Sorry to disturb you, but the man who came in with your witness is demanding to come back. He heard her shouts and is determined to check on her."

Morris turned from the officer and eyed Lisa. "Are you able to continue, or do you need a moment to compose yourself?"

She hugged her arms tightly around her middle as if she could keep herself from shattering. "I want Eric. Can I see Eric? Please?"

Morris twisted his mouth as if considering her request,

then angling his head toward the door, told the uniformed officer, "Show him back."

The tears that filled her eyes now stemmed from the relief that puddled in her core. Her longing for Eric's arms, Eric's steady presence, Eric's solid strength was a ravenous craving inside her.

Morris stood and held out a hand to her. "May I help you up? Are you ready to return to your chair?"

She cast a glance around her, as if waking from a bad dream and not recognizing her surroundings. The linoleum floor was hard and cold beneath her. The scuff-marred walls of the corner crowded her, and the metal trash can beside her reeked. Wincing, she shoved the trash can with the foul-smelling contents of her stomach away and swiped her mouth with her sleeve. She took a couple unsteady breaths and gave Morris her hand. He hauled her onto trembling legs, and she staggered to the chair she'd abandoned earlier.

The door burst open again, and Eric flew to her. "Lisa, thank God! I heard you scream. What happened?"

She fell against his chest and wrapped her arms around his neck, clinging as if she'd never let go. In turn, he held her with an embrace that nearly suffocated her. If she'd been able to breath in the first place. But her sobs came so hard and fast, she couldn't draw in any oxygen.

He rubbed her back, murmuring to her the way he calmed Rachel. After a moment, he levered back to meet her gaze, drilling her with his own penetrating eyes. "Can you tell me what happened? Are you okay?"

She started to nod, to give the automatic yes that appeased his worry and bought her distance and privacy. But she didn't want to hold Eric at bay any longer. She'd grown to appreciate his attention and the tentative bonds of affection they'd built. And she certainly didn't want to be alone with the stark realities that had crashed down on her just minutes ago.

Lisa curled her fingers into his shirt and shook her head. "No. I'm not okay. I—I remembered."

Chapter Twenty-Three

Lisa's words sucker punched Eric, and his muscles tensed as if readying for the next blow. He studied her wan complexion, her dilated pupils and felt her shudder in his arms. "You… remembered something?"

She closed her eyes for a moment and gave a tiny nod. "Not some. All of it." She leaned her forehead against his, and in a voice that squeaked, strangled by tears, she said, "Chellie is dead."

"Chellie? Who is that?"

"Whoa, whoa…hang on," Morris cut in. "If you're ready to finish your statement, then Mr. Harkney will have to go back out to the waiting room."

Eric shot the other man a disgruntled look. "And if she has recovered her memory and has information about a crime, shouldn't she be offered the chance to have a lawyer present?"

Lisa gasped. "A lawyer?" She divided a panicked look between Eric and Detective Morris. "Am I being arrested? Why—"

The detective shot a hand up. "You aren't under arrest. But you do have the right to a lawyer anytime, especially if you're concerned you may need one once I've heard your story."

Eric stroked her hair and traced her cheekbone with his thumb. "I can call our family lawyer to come, if you want." His gut swooped. "If…you think there's cause."

Anxious curiosity bit him. What exactly had she remembered? Had she walked into the lion's den by coming here?

Lisa curled both lips in, obviously trying to keep her chin from quivering as she battled tears. "I don't...think..." She swallowed hard. "I don't know..."

Eric sat straighter, firmed his resolve but kept his voice gentle. "Why don't I give him a call, just in case. It may not be necessary but...let's just be sure."

She exhaled heavily. Nodded.

Eric pulled out of her embrace, kissed her forehead and slid his cell phone from his pocket. "Would you have my father come back here from the waiting room? I think he has our attorney's number in his phone. And until her lawyer gets here, this interview is on hold."

Morris folded his arms over his chest, huffed a resigned sigh and jerked a nod. "I'll have your father brought back. You can have the room in the meantime."

Once Morris was gone, Eric turned back to Lisa and cupped her face between his hands. "Do you think you can tell me about it?"

She hesitated, and her shaking hands lifted to her mouth. "I—I'm going to have to tell the detective when he comes back. Maybe t-telling you will help me sort it out."

He nodded. "Yeah. Okay." He leaned close again to kiss her temple and pull her into a firm embrace. "Take your time. You're all right. You're safe."

"Chellie is my sister. She's Rachel's mother. She's—" Lisa hiccupped a sob, shaking her head. "She *was* in an abusive marriage, and that day...her husband stabbed her."

Eric muttered a dark curse word, and a rock settled in his stomach.

His father rushed into the room without knocking and slid into the chair across the table from them, reaching for them with an upturned palm. "What's going on? The officer out front said you needed me."

Eric filled his father in on the evolving circumstances and asked him to contact their attorney, Archie Day.

"Of course," his father said, his expression grave. Five minutes later, when his dad got off the phone, he said, "He's on the way as soon as he can finish with the couple in his office. He's in Asheville, and there's construction on the interstate. So it will be a couple hours before he arrives."

Eric felt Lisa sag in his arms. "Thanks, Dad."

"What can I do in the meantime?" his father asked. "How about something with sugar for you, Lisa. A soda, maybe? You look kind of pale."

Lisa cut her eyes toward his dad and shook her head.

"Just some privacy at the moment, Dad," Eric said, his attention locked on her terrified gaze. "Lisa and I need to talk."

ERIC SAID NOTHING as Lisa related her story of getting a panicked call from her sister the day of the snowstorm. She'd been at work at a diner, waiting tables, and left work with such haste and in such a state of panic, she'd left behind everything but the phone in her hand and keys in her pocket. He held her tightly as she told him about arriving at her sister's house and arming herself with an axe before venturing into the active crime scene.

"Vic, Chelle's husband, was arguing with this big guy in the living room," she said, her voice no more than a whisper. "It was heated, and I was able to sneak past them to look for Chelle in the back of the house."

She squeezed her eyes shut, her face crumpling. "Chelle was on the floor in her bedroom. Blood was everywhere. Rachel was in her car seat, covered in her mother's blood. I guess Chelle had put her there, thinking she was going to run, before she collapsed."

"Geez," Eric groaned. "Was your sister dead when you got there?"

Lisa shook her head, her gaze fixed on nothing particular as she stared downward and drew a choppy breath.

LISA DROPPED THE *axe at the bedroom door and raced to Chelle's side. "Chellie! Ohmygodohmygodohmygod!"*

Falling to her knees, she searched for her sister's wounds and pressed her hands to the deep, gaping cut on the side of her torso, then found another on her arm, and another below her ear. More on her leg. Her hands. So much blood.

She snatched a rumpled and discarded sweatshirt from the floor and pressed it to the largest wound at Chelle's waist, moved Chelle's hands to hold it in place. Then shifting her own hands from one smaller cut to another, she tried to staunch the bleeding. There were too many. She didn't have enough hands to cover them all. Tears spilled from her eyes and dripped onto her sister's blood-soaked shirt. "Chelle, listen to me! Don't leave me. I'm gonna get you help! Please don't die!"

Chelle drew a shallow breath and opened her eyes. "Rachel. Take her...and go."

Lisa scooped her sister onto her lap, cradling her close and rocking as she sobbed. "No, no, no! Please Chellie!"

"Get Rach...out of h-here. Save her."

"SO THAT'S WHY you had Rachel with you when I found you," Eric said, drawing Lisa out of the past and back to the small interrogation room.

She nodded. "Chellie died—" her voice cracked "—in my arms."

"What about an ambulance or the police? When did you call them? *Did you* call them?"

Her face crumpled, and she shook her head. "Chelle begged me not to. The cops had been out to their place before...when Vic hurt her. But he went to high school...played baseball with most of the cops in their town, and...they always took his word over hers. Social services came, too... the last time. They threatened to take Rachel away from Chelle if the situation at home didn't change. Chelle was terrified she'd lose Rachel to the state if I called for help of any kind." Lisa's fingers curled more tightly in Eric's shirt as even deeper guilt and grief twisted her countenance. "I didn't call for help! She died because I didn't call for help!"

Eric squeezed her tighter, his heart breaking. "No! Do not blame yourself! Her husband killed her. She bled out from the wounds he inflicted."

"But—"

"You were distraught, and your frightened sister asked you not to involve the cops. You did what you thought she wanted, what she thought was best for Rachel." He swiped at the tears streaming down her face, feeling a welling in his own throat that he choked down. He could grapple with her devastating revelations later. Right now, she needed his strength and his reassurance that she was safe. She needed to know he would protect her, that he was there for her, come what may.

When she pulled back from his embrace and lifted bleary eyes to his, he held his breath. There was more. She didn't have to say it. He saw it in her devastated expression.

He swallowed hard. "Go on."

"I...got Rachel. She was in her carrier...her car seat thing already, but... I buckled her in. I carried her as far as the bedroom door when... Vic and the other guy heard us."

"Shit," Eric muttered.

"Yeah." She exhaled and leaned her forehead against his chest. "Vic yanked the carrier from my hands. Shouting at me."

"LISA, STOP! WHERE *the hell do you think you're going?" Vic screamed, rage reddening his face. His eyes were wild, and he was shaking. Chelle had said he was high. That meant he was also irrational. Volatile.*

Bile churned in her gut.

His hand was bloody—Chelle's blood—and he left red prints on the carrier handle. He still had his hunting knife in his other hand. He aimed it at Lisa as he snarled, "You're not taking my kid anywhere!"

The other man, a tall, burly guy with a tattoo on his neck and a disproportionately large belly, stalked over and extended a hand. "I'll take the kid. I'm done wastin' time with you. My buyer is waiting!"

Buyer? Acid pooled in Lisa's gut. This man really did want to sell the baby.

"What? No!" She tried to grab the carrier back, but Vic blocked her with a beefy arm. Shoved her back.

"C'mon, man!" Tattoo waved his open hand at Vic. "I got twenty grand waiting on me at the pickup. A deal's a deal. Now hand the kid over."

"Maybe I changed my mind." Vic pulled Rachel out of the other man's reach.

Lisa saw her chance. She reached for the baby seat, only to have Vic whirl toward her and aim the knife at her. "Get away from her, or I'll cut you like I did your sniveling sister."

Lisa gasped and held her hands up as if in surrender. "Vic, don't do this. Please let me—"

Before she could finish the sentence, he reared back and planted a foot in her belly, shoving her with a booted kick. She bit her tongue as she crashed into a side table and onto the floor, the impact rattling through her bones. Wind whooshed from her lungs, and she watched, stunned as Vic swung back to face the other man, now pointing the knife at Tattoo. "You ain't taking the baby. I'll get you the money another way."

Tattoo snorted. "Too late for that."

Vic dropped the baby carrier with a thunk *and lunged at Tattoo, swiping with the knife. Tattoo swiftly dodged the blade and reached under his shirt. "You shouldn't've done that, man. Now I'm pissed," he said, pulling out a large black gun.*

Chapter Twenty-Four

Lisa shoved away from Eric, thinking she might be sick again as the memory reverberated in her skull like a gong. She bent at the waist and put her head between her knees, gasping for air.

"Here. Dad brought you this. Take a sip," Eric said. She heard a pop and the telltale hiss of a soda can.

She glanced up to find him holding a Sprite. When had Matt come back with that?

Her stomach roiled at the thought of putting any kind of food or drink in it, but her mouth was dry and Eric was looking at her expectantly. The liquid sloshed as she carried it to her lips for a tentative sip. The fizzy sweetness tickled her tongue, and she tried to focus on it instead of the bitter taste rising in her throat. After another minuscule drink, she shoved the can back toward Eric and raked her fingers through her hair. "Is the lawyer here yet? I just want to be done with this and go home."

"Not yet." Eric scooted his chair closer to hers and opened his arms. "Come here."

She leaned against him, and he tugged at her waist until she sat on his lap, his arm encircling her.

"Remember, I promised to be here for you. Always. And I am. No matter what happens. None of what happened to you changes how I feel for you or my promise to protect you and Rachel."

She angled her face into the crook of his neck, inhaling the comforting scent of his skin. Raw wood, deodorant soap and his natural musk. "You might change your mind...once you've heard it all."

"No. I won't. Because I know your heart. I know how whatever happened affected you, how your deepest, truest self was so moved and horrified by whatever happened that you all but shut down. That defines your character and heart to me more than anything you did or didn't do that day."

She raised her head and levered back to look into his eyes—those beautiful, tranquil eyes that had soothed and reassured her with their warmth and compassion from the day he saved her and Rachel from freezing on the side of the road. In them, now, she saw something else, something she'd tried to deny before but couldn't any longer. Love.

She recognized it because it spoke to an equal feeling that burned inside her, yearning to be released, aching for the right to be freely expressed. Eyes open, she leaned in to brush her lips against his.

A spark lit inside her as she drew back. A hopeful beat as light as the flap of a butterfly's wing. A glimmer in her darkness. Knowing the truth, knowing Rachel was her niece, that she wasn't married, that she was no longer prisoner to the past meant she was free to love Eric. Free to pursue the passion that roared through her blood when she was close to him like this.

Except...was she going to be free once the police heard her whole story or would they lock her in jail?

Swallowing hard, she said, "I need to tell you the rest."

His jaw firmed, and he gave her a small nod. "I'm listening."

LISA FROZE WHEN *the tattooed man pulled his gun. Ice settled in her bones. This situation could go from bad to much,*

much worse in such a short time because of that gun. Still struggling to regain her breath after Vic's kick, Lisa cut a quick glance to the baby carrier. Was this her chance? Rachel cried harder for the jolt when her carrier was dropped, but she seemed unharmed.

Rolling to her hands and knees, Lisa eased to her feet, crouching, staying low, trying not to draw the men's attention.

Vic had the bloody hunting knife aimed at Tattoo, and his other hand raised, palm toward his opponent. "Take it easy, man. We can work something out."

Lisa crept slowly toward the baby carrier, desperate not to be noticed.

"I ain't here to negotiate, and I'm tired of your stallin'. Now, hand over the kid, or I'll pop a cap in your ass!" Tattoo straightened the aim of his weapon.

"All right! All right!" Vic pulled his face in a defeated grimace. "But if I'm gonna give you my kid, I want a cut. I should get half, at least!"

Lisa's breath caught, shocked by Vic's turnabout, his willingness to sell his daughter to save his own miserable hide.

Tattoo laughed darkly. "No."

"Okay. What if—" Vic started.

A loud bang reverberated through the room and something hot and wet splattered on Lisa. She jerked her gaze toward Vic as he crumpled on the floor. Most of his face was missing.

Lisa screamed. Her body shook. Revulsion left her flashing hot and cold, and nausea clutched her belly.

Tattoo spun to face her. "Shut up!" He aimed the gun at her, and survival instinct alone propelled her as the man fired near her. She dropped and rolled, bumping the same flimsy side table, which now toppled onto her. She hazarded another glance in Vic's direction and shuddered. He was most definitely dead. And Chelle was dead. Which meant Rachel...

Oh God, Rachel!

Save Rachel!

Operating purely on adrenaline and purpose, she moved stiffly to her feet, holding her aching side where Vic had kicked her and the table had added its insult. She swayed as she assessed the situation. She was the baby's only defense now. She had to save her. For Chelle.

Tattoo had stooped to lift Rachel's carrier by the blood-splattered handle. He was at least twice her size and had a gun. How the hell was she supposed to stop him from stealing and selling Rachel?

Suppressing the urge to vomit, Lisa dug deep for a courage that made no logical sense. She stepped into Tattoo's path to the front door and grated, "Put her down! You can't have her!"

Scowling at her, as if she were an irritating wasp that kept flying in his face, Tattoo snarled. "Get outta my way, girlie."

He took two long strides toward her. Lisa's knees threatened to buckle, but she lifted her chin. "Give me the baby. She's mine now."

His response was a crude remark. When she remained in his path, he followed Vic's example, raising a foot to her ribs and giving her a solid kick.

As she stumbled and fell to the floor, her hip hit something hard. At first, she ignored the something, *seeing Tattoo stride toward the front door. But as she scrambled to follow him, to give a last effort to save Rachel, the object at her side crystalized. The axe she'd dropped when she spotted Chelle. Fresh adrenaline zinged through her limbs, and she curled her fingers around the axe handle. She scuttled to her feet. Hoisted the axe. Swung.*

Chapter Twenty-Five

Eric's gut swooped and pinpricks chased up his spine. He sat back in his chair, staring at Lisa in shock. "You...killed him?"

Lisa's tears dripped from her lashes, and she swiped a hand under her runny nose. "No. I was...shaking. And the axe was heavy. I'd aimed for his back, but... I hit his arm, I think. His shoulder, maybe. But he stopped. He turned around. Surprised. And pissed off, for sure."

Eric forced a slow breath into his lungs, trying to be patient. Wanting to give Lisa the time she needed to finish her story. "Okay. And then?"

She rubbed her eyes with the pads of her fingers, sighing shakily. "I wanted to swing again, knowing he could just shoot me, and it'd all be over, but—"

"He was still holding Rachel's carrier."

She nodded. "He screamed something at me. I don't even remember what. But I raised the axe. I got ready to swing again and..." She squeezed her eyes more tightly closed. "He put the carrier down. Pulled the gun back out from the waist of his jeans. Used both hands to aim."

Eric clenched his back teeth as ribbons of terror knotted inside him. *She's here. She's whole*, he told himself when dread swamped him, and he waited for Lisa to continue.

She drew a deep breath. Swallowed. "I swung again and hit his hands, the gun. It fired. Into the floor, maybe. But he dropped it." She spoke faster now, in a rush, as if trying to keep up with the images that spun out in her head. "And when he bent to pick up the gun, I swung the axe again. Two hands. And stuck it hard in his thigh. He screamed in pain. Fell over, holding his leg. Cursing a blue streak. I had to step...step over him to get to the door...to Rachel. He grabbed at my foot, tripped me. His blood was on the floor, and my hands slipped in it trying to get away from his grasp. I got loose somehow. Wiped my hands on my clothes and grabbed Rachel's carrier."

Her stricken gaze lifted to his, and she puffed out her cheeks as she exhaled a long breath, her whole body trembling, her face pale. His own limbs shook as he stroked her cheek, squeezed her shoulders and struggled to speak. "That man...with the tattoo is the man who tried to run me down a couple weeks ago."

Eric nodded his understanding, then cupped her chin. "You were...very brave."

She shook her head. "No. I was terrified. Once I had Rachel, I just...ran. I don't think I even buckled her car seat in. I just got in my car and drove as fast as I could down that driveway. I was so, so scared he was going to follow me. Shoot me. Take Rachel. I—" Her voice cracked again. "After that I only remember snippets. Getting on the highway. Leaving town. Trying to get as far away from that house as I could."

"So...what happened to your car? Why were you walking on the side of the road when I found you?" He tucked a wisp of hair behind her ear and dried her cheek with a thumb.

"That part's still foggy. I don't—"

The interview room door opened, and Detective Morris walked in with a man wearing khakis and a golf shirt behind him. "Your lawyer is here. I'll give you two a moment in private to speak before we continue our interview." He directed his attention to Eric then. "You'll have to come with me now."

Lisa's hand clutched at his as he rose from his chair. He

pulled her to her feet and wrapped her in a firm hug. "You're going to be all right. Just tell them what you've told me. I'll be right outside, waiting."

She nodded, her eyes wide and frightened. Leaning close, he kissed her cheek and stepped out of the room.

AFTER A BRIEF meeting with Archie Day, Lisa continued her interview with Detective Morris. Though she was already physically exhausted from the emotional turmoil of having so many frightening and gut-wrenching memories flood her all at once, Morris pushed on relentlessly. As she recounted the tragic events and her actions to the detective, she emphasized the fact that Chelle had asked her to take Rachel, that she was Rachel's closest living relative and that any violence she committed had been to save her own life and protect the baby from being kidnapped and sold on the black market.

She recounted how she'd seen Tattoo recently in Valley Haven, how he had tried to run her down. "I think he wants to kill me. To silence me. I saw everything he did. I heard his plan to sell Rachel."

"And where is the baby now?" Morris asked.

"At home." She hesitated a moment when she realized what she'd said. Cameron Glen might feel like home to her now, but as she'd just painfully recalled, Rachel's home, even Lisa's small apartment were miles from Cameron Glen. "I mean, she's in Valley Haven, where I've been staying since Eric found me. She's with Eric's step-grandparents, Grace and Neil Cameron."

Morris leaned his chair back onto two legs as he tapped a pen on his thigh and studied Lisa. His jaw muscled flexed and bunched as he deliberated. "And you stand by your explanation for not having come forward to the police with any of this information before now? You had eyewitness evidence about two murders and an attempted kidnapping, and your excuse is that you somehow developed amnesia until today?"

Lisa bristled and glanced briefly to Mr. Day. "It's not an excuse. Eric and the ER doctor called my initial shock a dissociative fugue and my memory loss is called psychogenic amnesia. I've voluntarily been in counseling, trying to remember. I'm telling the truth!"

Morris said nothing, continuing to eye her with suspicion.

"I swear to you, I couldn't remember anything specific about what happened until you showed me those horrid pictures. I wanted to remember! I tried hard to remember. You can ask Eric or any of his family."

Archie Day cleared his throat, and with a look, he reminded her she didn't have to convince the detective of anything. She was innocent until the police and the district attorneys proved otherwise.

Morris nodded. "Oh, I will be following up with the ER doctor and state psychologists and the forensic lab and a whole bunch of folks to check your story out." He set the front legs of the chair back down on the floor with a thump. "But my first call will be to child services to do a home visit and background check on you and the Camerons. We have to verify that you are the child's aunt and that the home where you have the missing baby is a safe one."

Lisa sat taller, feeling defensive. "There is no place safer or more loving than the Camerons'. They are the kindest people I've ever known."

"If that proves true following the home inspection and background checks, then I see no reason why the baby can't—"

"Rachel," Lisa interrupted. "The baby has a name. It's Rachel."

Mr. Day touched her arm to stop her. "Lisa, Detective Morris is just doing his job. He and his people just need time to verify everything you've said. That's a good thing, because it will bear out your testimony and clear you of wrongdoing."

She forced herself to take a beat, to shove down the knot

of tangled emotions and fatigue that plagued her. "And until then? What happens now?"

Morris scratched his beard. "While your friend Eric is here, I'd like to talk with him. And before you go, I'd like you to spend some time with our artist to get a rendering of this man with the tattoo on his neck who you say killed your brother-in-law. After that, you are free to go. But—" his gaze darkened with gravity "—make yourself and the ba—Rachel—available to any and all agencies during our follow up investigation. Full cooperation goes a long way."

She nodded. "Yes, sir."

He rose and stuck his head into the hall calling, "Grimshaw, is the artist here yet?"

She heard a muffled reply.

Turning back to her, Morris said, "They're ready for you down the hall. Room six. After you finish with the artist, you're free to go. Thank you for coming in." Morris held the interview room door open.

Lisa balked. "Wait! What am *I* supposed to do about the guy with the tattoo on his neck? I told you he…he tried to kill me! He tried to run me down in Valley Haven a few days ago! How do I know he won't come after me again?"

"We will, of course, be looking for him. Your description will help. But we're a small department. We don't have any type of protection detail for you. Just use common sense, lie low, watch your back, be careful."

Lisa goggled at the man for his litany of unhelpful platitudes. When he tried to leave the room again, she called out, "And what about my sister? Where's her b-body? Can I have a funeral for her and Vic?" Though Vic was responsible for her sister's death, he was Rachel's father, and for her niece's sake, she'd see that Vic got a decent burial.

"When the coroner is finished with them and a complete autopsy report is done, they will be released to the funeral home of your choice." He made a move to leave, then paused and glanced back at her. "Anything else?"

Lisa's head spun, her heart ached, and her gut was raw and wrung out. Was there anything else? She opened her mouth to say no when a new memory came to her. Her heart gave a gentle thump. "One thing. I've remembered my name. It's Lisa Renee Mitchell."

Chapter Twenty-Six

While Eric underwent a round of questioning with Detective Morris, Matt took Lisa to a nearby restaurant, where he ordered her coffee and a sandwich to restore her. She nibbled at the sandwich but was so distracted by her tumbling memories, waves of grief for Chelle, concern for what might happen to Rachel that she had no appetite. Like pulling a plug on a dam, once the crime scene pictures broke the wall to the past, images and facts continued to trickle to the forefront. She wrote many of the facts on her napkin, backing up the tidbits she feared could slip away again.

"My birthday is in October. The fifteenth. I'm twenty-four. I have an apartment in Hendersonville, and I work at a diner called…" She scrunched her eyes closed and pictured the neon sign over the front door of the building. "Greasy Spoon. Or I did. I'm sure I've been replaced by now."

Eric's father nodded as he listened. "This is all good information. I know it must be a relief to have a clearer sense of your identity."

She sighed, choked down another wave of tears and sipped her coffee. "I just wish it didn't come with so much other baggage. Oh, Matt…my sister was murdered by her husband! And I saw Vic get shot. There was so much blood…" She set the coffee mug down hard when her stomach roiled. "No wonder I blocked it out. It was so…horrible." Her voice cracked, and she dabbed at her eyes with her napkin. "Geez, I don't want to start bawling again. It's just...a lot."

"Definitely a lot." Eric's father flattened a hand on the table and lifted a compassionate gaze to her, so like Eric's that her heart squeezed. "Why didn't anyone report your sister or her husband missing sooner? Didn't they have friends or coworkers that would wonder where they were?"

Lisa shook her head. "Chelle used to have friends, but Vic was jealous of her time with them and bullied her into giving them up. He liked having her isolated and all to himself. Especially after he lost his job. He failed a surprise drug test and..." Lisa shook her head. "Chelle quit her job when Rachel was born. She'd always intended to go back to work, but they couldn't afford daycare for Rachel, and she didn't trust Vic with the baby."

"So, no one but you checked up on them?" Matt asked.

"Well, Vic's drug dealer might, I suppose. But they aren't the sort to ask too many questions or call the police, are they?"

Matt's phone rang then, sparing her from further comment.

"Eric's finished at the police station." Matt pushed his chair back from the table. "Do you want a to-go box for your sandwich?"

She glanced down at her untouched food. "I'll take it for Eric. He hasn't eaten."

Thirty minutes later, the trio were back on the road headed home. Eric sat in the back seat with Lisa, and she leaned against him, her head on his shoulder, his arm around her. Road signs passed outside the car, marking the miles, the towns. When she spied a sign with directions to Interstate 26, her pulse thumped.

"Matt?"

"Yes?" Eric's father said.

"Can we...go to Hendersonville on the way back? I want to see my apartment. Maybe get some of my things."

"You can remember how to get there?" Matt asked.

"I guess we'll see. I think I can."

With a nod, Matt took the side road and merged onto the interstate. Within a few minutes, they were navigating the streets of Hendersonville—the shops, the churches, the billboards all familiar to her in an odd, dreamlike way. She knew the place, yet it didn't feel like home anymore. Cameron Glen held that claim. Yet…now that she'd regained her memory, knew who she was and where she lived, how long would she be welcome at Cameron Glen? In truth, other than the late hour and needing to pick up Rachel, she should be returning to her small apartment for good today.

Matt parked where she told him to, and together they walked up the sidewalk to her front door, where a notice of unpaid rent with a deadline for payment before eviction fluttered in the breeze.

Lisa took the notice down and sighed. "I have a week left to pay past-due rent before I'm on the street."

"We can come back tomorrow during business hours to help you get things straightened out if you want," Matt said.

She nodded. "Yeah. Thanks." She turned back to the door but hesitated. "I don't have a key. I haven't had my purse or keys since Eric found me. I—"

She frowned, propping a hand on the door for balance as new memories rolled through her. "I can remember driving away from Chelle's house. With Rachel. I was driving fast. Afraid that Tattoo was coming after me. Wanting to get as far away as possible and…" She clapped a hand to her mouth. "I skidded on the ice. My car went off the road. Down an embankment. I… I don't remember anything after that. It's all just a blank…" She angled her eyes toward Eric. "Until you found me."

Eric and Matt exchanged a look, nodding.

"You were in a fugue state at that point. Too much trauma and bad luck and fright." Eric twisted his mouth, then lifted the woven mat and felt around the top of the doorframe. "No hidden key. Would a neighbor have a spare?"

"Apartment management would," Matt said. "Maybe there's an after-hours phone number posted at the office?"

"Right." As Lisa started back down the sidewalk toward the office, she nearly tripped over a beige cat that charged out of the bushes meowing loudly and winding around her legs. Warmth exploded in her chest as she recognized the cat and squatted to pat the friendly feline. "Peanut!"

"You know this fella?" Matt asked.

"He's mine!" she replied, her voice choked with tears. "Poor Peanut! How could I have forgotten you?"

"Well, look who decided to show up," an irritated female voice said behind them.

The three turned as one and met the glare and hands on hips of an older woman with graying brown hair and a blue housecoat. "Don't know where you've been, but I took it upon myself to feed your kitty and bring him inside when it rained or got cold. Thought you'd moved off and just abandoned him."

Lisa shook her head, scooping Peanut into her arms. "No. Never. I... I'd never—but thank you so much for looking after him. I'll pay you back for the food...when I can. I—"

"Where on earth have you been?" the woman asked.

Lisa opened and closed her mouth. Where to begin? "I was, uh..."

When her words faltered, Eric stepped forward with his hand out to introduce himself to the woman. Matt followed suit.

"Brenda Colfer," the woman returned.

"Lisa and her niece have been staying with us," Eric said.

Lisa swallowed hard. "I was in an accident. I lost my memory until—"

The woman's expression changed from peeved to concerned. "Heaven's sake, child! Are you all right now?"

She nodded and rubbed her cheek on the top of Peanut's head, eliciting a loud purr. "Close enough."

Mrs. Colfer straightened her back and squared her shoulders. "You should know. There was a scruffy-looking dude sniffing around here a few weeks back, looking for you."

A chill raced through Lisa, and she jerked an alarmed gaze at her neighbor. "What?"

Eric stepped closer to Lisa. "Can you describe him?"

Her neighbor wrinkled her nose and looked down as she tried to remember. "White guy. Shaved head. Big dude. Walked with a limp. Black jacket. Oh, and a giant tattoo on one side of his neck."

Lisa's knees buckled, and she might have crumpled if Eric hadn't slipped an arm around her.

"Did he say who he was or what he wanted?" Matt asked.

"Naw. But I didn't get the feeling he was up to anything good. I was hoping he weren't yer boyfriend or nothin'. Smart, pretty gal like you can do way better than that trash." She arched a graying eyebrow and looked Eric up and down, clearly speculating. "Well, glad you're okay. The critter obviously missed you." She nodded her head toward Peanut, who rubbed his head against Lisa's chin.

With that, the woman turned and shuffled back to her apartment.

Several minutes later, after Lisa and Eric called the after-hours number and retrieved a spare key from the super, Lisa opened her door and entered her apartment. A stale, sour scent greeted them. Dirty litter box, unaired rooms, likely rotten food in the refrigerator. Otherwise, the apartment was tidy, and familiarity tickled her.

On a small table in the breakfast nook, a sewing machine was set up, a basket of cloth scraps and a half-finished quilt top beside it. It stirred something inside her to know that even when she'd blocked so much pain and personal history, glimpses of her true self had survived and peeked through the dark curtain.

A large bookshelf drew her attention next, her personal library of beloved stories and gifts from her parents before they'd died in a house fire when she was sixteen.

Before they died...

A shudder raced through her with the returned knowledge. "My parents are dead. Chelle was my only family," she whispered. She stoked her fingers down the spine of a well-read copy of *Pride and Prejudice*. Without opening the book, she could picture the inscription her mother had written on the title page.

"I am determined that only the deepest love will induce me into matrimony."
—Elizabeth Bennet

I pray for you the deepest love and much happiness, my darling Lisa.
Always your champion,
Mom

Lisa's eyes were already watering when her gaze landed on a photograph on the next shelf, one of herself and Chelle, heads together, laughing. She took the photo down and blinked back the rush of tears.

Eric moved up behind her and put a hand on her shoulder. "I'm sorry for your loss. I don't know that I've really said that before now."

She turned and buried her face in his chest, sniffing a bit as she took solace from him and steeled herself for the days ahead. A funeral. Fighting for custody of Rachel. Rebuilding her life.

"I think," Matt said, turning from his examination of her flimsy window locks, "based on what your neighbor said about the guy snooping around here looking for you, that you and Rachel will be safer, at least in the short run, back at Cameron Glen."

As welcome as the invitation was, she felt all the more like an inconvenience now that she knew her identity and where she lived. But knowing Tattoo was out there, hunting her, gave her the shivers. Drawing a deep breath for courage, she shifted her thoughts to what she needed to pack. Spring-weather clothes. Her laptop and bank account information. A couple favorite books.

"Can I bring Peanut with me?" She cast a glance around the apartment and found Peanut sniffing an empty food bowl.

"Done," Eric said, placing a kiss on her forehead. "Why don't you grab a few of your things, and we'll get going."

DJ SPRAWLED IN the recliner at Donna's place, deciding whether he wanted to send her out for tacos or burgers for dinner when a promo for the local news station came on the TV. He'd just tipped his brew up for a pull when the images that flashed on the screen had him choking on his beer.

"Later tonight, we'll bring you the latest on the murders of a local couple and the disappearance of their infant daughter. Police heard from a key witness today and are looking for this man for questioning." A police sketch flashed on the screen. Of him. "We'll have details at eleven."

DJ slammed his beer down on the side table and lowered the footrest with a clunk. He barked a bitter cuss word that brought Donna in from the kitchen.

"What's wrong?" she asked.

"Everything!" He shoved to his feet and stomped toward the front door. "I'm going out. I have to take care of something."

"But—"

He didn't hang around for Donna's protest. He climbed in his truck and gunned the engine. The key witness the news lady mentioned could only be Vic's sister-in-law. The bitch who'd carved his leg with that axe and taken the baby he'd had customers lined up to buy. If she'd come out of hiding and was talking to the cops, would she go by her apartment? One way to know for sure.

He turned down the street and headed for the apartment complex where the sister-in-law lived. Minutes later, he arrived and pulled into the parking lot where he'd spent far too many hours in recent weeks staked out, watching and waiting.

Sure enough, the bitch was there, carrying bags of stuff out of the apartment to a recent model Toyota sedan. Two men were with her. He recognized the younger one as the guy who'd been with her a couple weeks ago in Valley Haven when DJ had screwed up his attempt to run her over. A missed opportunity. And she'd gone back into hiding after that. Until now. Until she'd found the balls to go to the cops about what she saw that day in January.

Now the media was flashing a sketch of him all over everywhere, and the cops would be on him like white on rice in no time. Neighbors talked. The guys at the bar might even roll on him. And Reggie—

DJ slapped the steering wheel, dread bunching inside him. If Reggie saw the news, found out about the police sketch and BOLO on him, he was as good as dead.

But…

DJ sat straighter as the idea crystalized in his mind. If he could find where Lisa was keeping Vic's kid, he could still deliver the baby to Reggie and get off his boss's blacklist. He could solve two problems at once.

As he watched from the far end of the parking lot at the apartment complex, DJ made his plan. He needed to get the hell out of town, out of state even. But before he disappeared, he wanted his pound of flesh. He wanted the baby for Reggie and the cash the baby would bring in. The black market was hotter than ever these days.

He couldn't do much about Lisa while she had the two dudes with her. He'd have to be patient just a little while longer.

He watched them put a final few bags in the trunk, then the girl, with an animal crate in her hand, climbed into the back seat. But no baby. Where was the kid? The sedan backed from the parking space and pulled to the end of the driveway.

Clenching his teeth, DJ cranked his truck's engine again, determination bubbling inside him. When the Toyota pulled out on the highway, DJ followed.

Chapter Twenty-Seven

As tired as she was, as much as she wanted to nap on the drive back to Valley Haven, Lisa couldn't settle her mind, couldn't shove away the horrid images that had returned this afternoon. Archie Day had reassured her he saw nothing in her story that should lead to criminal charges, especially once the ER doctors and her counselor substantiated the medical condition behind her amnesia. But she couldn't help worrying about what would happen to Rachel. About the man with the tattoo who'd already found her once and tried to kill her. And about Eric.

What would happen between them now that she knew her history, remembered her home and had no good excuse to stay at Cameron Glen, imposing on the good graces of the Cameron family any longer? When she left Valley Haven and returned to her life, would he forget her? She knew he cared, but were his feelings...*the deepest love*? Like Elizabeth Bennet, she only wanted a man who loved her with a true, pure, lasting love. Chelle, rest her soul, had married Vic without understanding his true nature, his cruel side and his troubling connections with criminal activity. Chelle had been smitten, swayed by flattery and false promises.

And Lisa had been unable to convince her to break free of the abusive marriage.

Lisa rubbed her arms as a chill tripped through her. Chelle

was gone, but Lisa had Rachel and would do everything in her power to give her niece a good life.

From his carrier, Peanut howled his discontent with being in a car. The plaintive meows echoed the grief in her heart, and she stuck her hand in the carrier to scratch her cat's chin. "I know, boy. Me too."

DJ WEIGHED HIS options. As much as he wanted to run the Toyota off the road and put a bullet in Lisa's head, he had to consider the men with her. And the baby. If the baby wasn't with them, he needed to wait. Let Lisa and the two men lead him to her hiding place.

But he also didn't want to be spotted as he followed them. He hung back as far as he dared, not wanting to lose the Toyota but not wanting the driver to realize he was tailing them. Pretty soon it was clear they were headed back to Valley Haven. From town, the Toyota took a state road up into the foothills. A steep, twisty road that was all the more tricky in the dark.

He watched the brake lights on the Toyota glow just before the sedan left the highway for a private road. He slowed, scanning the side street, looking for a street name. A small wooden sign with a fat arrow and a pine tree read, "Cameron Glen Rental Cabins—Turn here!"

DJ smiled his satisfaction. A rental cabin. So that's where she'd been hiding. He drove on. The men were with Lisa now. But he'd be back.

MATT DROPPED ERIC and Lisa at the senior Camerons' home to get Rachel, promising to put Peanut inside Eric's cabin and start unloading Lisa's other bags from his car. Their intention had been to retrieve Rachel and walk the short distance to Eric's place in time to help with the unloading. Grace and Neil, however, were not so quick to release them. The couple peppered them with concerned questions about what had happened, and when they learned that Lisa had recovered her memory, their inquiries doubled.

Lisa didn't want to go through the whole agonizing story again, but Grace had been so generous in the past months, so helpful with Rachel, she couldn't justify not giving the kind woman at least some answers to settle her worries.

"All of this can wait until tomorrow, surely," Eric said, trying to guide Lisa closer to the front door.

She held up a hand to stay him. "It's all right. I can hit the high points for her."

And so she did, giving them the parts of the story most relevant to them and what was to come. She was Rachel's aunt. Rachel's parents were dead. The state's children's welfare services would be around soon, likely in the morning, to review Rachel's situation and future placement.

Grace and Neil clearly had tons of questions for each new revelation that was made, and Lisa could see the effort it took for them to squelch their understandable curiosity for the short term. Finally, it was Rachel's tired whimper that told Lisa it was time to go, time to put her niece to bed.

Lisa paused on the way out the Camerons' front door and turned back to Grace Cameron. Tears welled in her eyes as she rushed over to embrace the woman who'd cared for her and loved her so unconditionally for the past two months. Knowing now that her parents and grandparents were gone, her only sibling murdered, she treasured the relationship she'd formed with Grace all the more.

"Oh, *m'eudail*. My dearest," Grace said, her voice likewise choked with tears. "Everything will be fine. You'll see."

Stepping back and swiping away the moisture on her eyelashes with her palm, Lisa followed Eric outside. He carried Rachel in her car seat, something Lisa could only do for short distances now that Rachel was growing and gaining weight.

He held her hand as they strolled across the family property, the cool early spring evening quiet and scented with blooming bushes and trees. It struck her how the life she'd found here at Cameron Glen with Eric stood in stark contrast to the cold, haunted vibes that flowed through her when she thought of her past. Even before Chelle's murder and the chaos of that January day, her life had been a struggle. While not a misery, Lisa's life had revolved around working her waitressing job, paying bills and worrying about her sister's bad marriage. Her only joy had come from Peanut, creating quilts to sell at craft fairs and the rare night out with friends.

She blinked now, wondering what her friends, who'd not heard from her in months, must have been thinking. Why hadn't they reported her missing? Had she so often been too busy with work, too unreliable with texting that they hadn't found her lack of communication concerning? She made a silent vow to correct that omission, to not take anyone in her life for granted and be more connected with her friends going forward, no matter what.

"You're awfully quiet. Still thinking about today?" Eric said, drawing her out of her musing.

"In a way. Just looking at all the many dimensions of my life and what's happened. All the changes I have to make."

His brow dipped. "Changes. Right."

He grunted, and his frown deepened. But she wasn't ready to talk about what lay ahead for them. She knew better than to assume anything. Asking Eric to take on all of her baggage, a baby, her traumatic past...she couldn't ask that of him.

And yet...how did she survive the heartbreak of leaving him behind?

Chapter Twenty-Eight

After driving back to town and purchasing a box of ammo for his pistol, DJ returned to the private road where the Toyota had turned in. He shut off his headlights once he reached the first home, a clapboard farmhouse with numerous outbuildings and animals in pens. He narrowed his gaze, studying the vehicles parked in the rutted gravel driveway of this house. Neither was the Toyota. He cruised on.

As he made his way farther up the narrow blacktop road, he found several rustic cabins lining the road, illuminated by the occasional streetlamp and spaced far enough apart to give some privacy to the occupants. In the glow of the road's security lights, he could make out rows of fir trees of varying sizes on the steep hillside behind the cabins. He estimated the value of those trees for cover should he need it, and dismissed them. They seemed too small to hide him.

Driving on, he swept his gaze from one driveway to the next, searching for the Toyota Lisa had been in. He'd just made it around a curve where the road skirted the edge of a large pond with a wooden pier, when he spotted the sedan he was looking for. His grip tightened on the steering wheel, and he made fast calculations about where to leave his truck and how best to approach the cabin without raising suspicion.

He rolled past the larger cabin where the Toyota was parked, trying to see inside. The lights were on, but blinds were pulled. Gritting his teeth, he kept driving until he found a spot where a bushy spruce tree and row of large blooming azaleas hid the dark cabin behind them. Slowing, DJ sized up the cabin, the empty driveway, and made his decision. He parked as far up the driveway and as deep in the shadow cast by the huge spruce as possible and cut his engine.

Gathering the freshly loaded semiautomatic Glock from the passenger seat, he slipped out of his truck, making sure the door didn't *thunk* as it closed. Holding the weapon down and close to his side, he crept back toward the cabin where he'd seen the Toyota sedan. Approaching from the back, he eased up to a window to peer in through the small gap between the sill and the blinds. He spied a preteen girl with auburn hair singing a Taylor Swift song into her hairbrush and posing for her mirror.

DJ snorted his amusement and moved on to the next window. Gazing through the angled slats, he saw a middle-aged couple curled up together on a couch, the woman cradling a wineglass.

"Hey, Butterbean, are you getting ready for bed?" the man shouted, the sound drifting out through the screen door left cracked open on the back deck.

"Yes," came the muted reply.

DJ recognized the dark-haired man as the driver of the Toyota, and his pulse kicked. He craned his head, trying to see the rest of the living room, the kitchen. Where were Lisa and the younger guy? The baby?

As if his thought conjured the sound, he heard the whine of a baby and stilled. The sound hadn't come from inside.

He crouched low and scanned the area until he spotted a couple walking down the blacktop road. The man toted a baby carrier, and the woman's hair glowed gold in the streetlamp. Lisa. And the baby.

He smiled his satisfaction as he scuttled to hide behind the trunk of an old-growth hardwood of some sort while the trio walked past. He followed their progress until they walked up the gravel drive of one of the cabins and climbed the porch steps.

Having located his target, DJ sized up the surrounding property with an eye toward vantage points and escape routes. With so many other cabins and houses close by, he'd have to do the job as quietly as possible. Be as cautious as possible to avoid detection. He hunkered down in a cluster of bushes to wait for the right moment. Maybe when Lisa and the guy were both asleep, when the whole neighborhood was out for the night and no eyes were watching.

He stashed the Glock in the waist of his jeans and settled in to wait.

Chapter Twenty-Nine

The squeak of a floorboard roused Lisa from the light sleep she'd finally achieved after a couple of restless hours. Apparently Eric couldn't sleep, either.

Peanut could. The cat was curled against her legs, dozing soundly.

She peered through slitted eyelids toward the bedroom door looking for Eric. Saw no one. No lights.

Turning carefully to avoid disturbing Peanut, she peeked at the pillow beside her. She knew a brief moment of relief and reassurance. Eric was there. His deep, steadying breathing told her he was sound asleep.

Then the looming shadow pierced her fog. Adrenaline shot through her, sharpening the image before her. A large man, arms extended. A gun aimed at Eric.

She screamed, jacking upright.

Peanut ran.

Eric woke with a jerk, then immediately rolled to the floor. The gun fired, leaving a hole in the pillow where Eric's head had just been.

The gunman shifted his aim toward Lisa, and terror froze her lungs.

"Run!" Eric shouted. "Get Rachel!"

The gun cracked again as she scrambled from the bed. In

her haste, she staggered drunkenly. Another bullet pocked the doorframe as she skittered through.

Save Rachel!

But what about Eric? How could she leave him alone in the room with the gunman? She heard a crash, a grunt, curses. Heart in her throat, she crept back toward the bedroom, keeping her body pressed to the wall out of view. At the open door, she peeked in. Eric was locked in a ferocious wrestling match, his hands clamped around the wrist of his opponent's gun hand. Lisa sucked in a sharp breath. As long as Eric could keep the gun angled away from himself...

From the guest room, she heard Rachel cry, the baby clearly woken by the loud blasts.

Save Rachel! The imperative that had been a drumbeat in her head for the past several weeks echoed again. But a new urgency tugged with equal strength. *Save Eric!*

Deeming Eric to be in more immediate danger, she gathered her wits and her courage to help him. What could she do? How did she stop his assailant?

Edging back inside the bedroom, she slapped the switch to turn on the light. The bright glare stilled the gunman briefly as he glared toward Lisa. When she saw the large black tattoo on his neck, her breath caught. Fear shoved her back a step and made the room tilt. She caught the doorframe to keep from falling. Of course it was Tattoo. Who else wanted to kill her?

Eric flicked a glance at her, his face distorted with pain and worry. He rasped something to her, either "No" or "Go." But with adrenaline-fueled blood whooshing in her ears, she wasn't sure which.

Tattoo delivered an elbow to Eric's gut, and Lisa cringed as if taking the sharp blow herself. Guilt sat like a rock on her heart. She was the reason Tattoo was here, the reason Eric's life was in jeopardy. The realization made her want to wail. To rip her hair out. To throw up. But she couldn't do any of those things now. She had to defend Eric, help him in his struggle for possession of the gun.

She glanced around, searching for a weapon. *Where was that axe now when she needed it?*

She saw nothing useful. A comb, dirty socks, a paperback. Nothing. Noth—

Her breath caught when she spied a large jar of pennies on the top of Eric's dresser. Pressing close to the wall to avoid the grappling men, she sidled across the floor and snatched up the glass jar.

When she turned, Tattoo had Eric in a headlock with an arm across Eric's neck, choking him. Eric's face was growing red, but he held fast to Tattoo's right arm, keeping the gun aimed at the floor.

Lisa looked for an angle to approach, her heart banging. As if understanding her goal, Eric twisted his shoulders sharply, just enough to make Tattoo shift his feet. The man's one sidestep turned the gun's angle away from Lisa and gave her the space she needed to rush forward.

Hoisting the large penny jar with both hands, she brought it down on the back of Tattoo's head. The thug roared in pain, and his knees buckled.

The weight and momentum of swinging the heavy object caused the jar to tumble from her grip. The glass shattered on the floor and pennies spilled across the hardwood.

Eric seized the opportunity. He reared his head backward into Tattoo's nose. The thug, already wobbling from the smack to his head, released Eric as he dropped to his knees. His left hand clutched his offended nose. His right hand still stubbornly clung to his weapon.

Freed from his opponent's hold, Eric stumbled a few steps and also slumped to the floor, gasping in oxygen.

Shaking from her core, Lisa divided her attention between the men, trying to quiet her fear enough to calculate her next move. Down the hall, Rachel's cries reached a sharper level of distress. The baby's shriek matched the frantic terror screaming though Lisa. She wanted to run to Eric, but even as the impulse reached her bare feet, Tattoo lifted his evil glare to her.

"You'll pay for that!" he growled, spittle forming at the corner of his mouth.

When she took a step back, her bare foot slipped on the loose pennies. She grabbed the corner of Eric's dresser to keep from falling. As she fumbled for purchase, a shard of broken glass cut her foot. Although she registered the pain with a whimper, she didn't take her eyes off Tattoo. The man was rising from the floor, his hard eyes narrowed on her.

Tattoo braced the heel of his gun hand on the floor to push up. Lisa's eyes darted to the weapon.

The gun. Of course! Eric had made taking the gun out of the equation his priority, and so should she. But how?

Even as her brain scrambled with that question, Eric rolled to his butt and kicked Tattoo's braced arm, bringing him down again. Both men fumbled for defensive positions, for control of the gun, the pennies and broken glass hampering traction.

Shoving down her qualms, Lisa lunged forward, adding her grappling hands to the battle for the weapon.

"No! Lisa, go!" Eric said, his voice still weak and breathless, but no less urgent.

But she wouldn't. She could not leave Eric at the mercy of this killer. She'd already lost Chelle to violence. How would she live if she abandoned Eric and cost him his life?

In the scrabble of competing hands and arms all vying for the weapon, she realized a better approach was to give Eric a fighting chance. She needed to distract Tattoo. Hamper him.

Sucking in a deep breath, she moved to a crouch and sprung onto Tattoo's back. She wrapped herself around him, clawing at his face, batting his arms, and locking her legs around his waist.

Enraged, he shouted invectives and foul names at her. For a short time, her ploy seemed to be working. Eric gained ground, two hands on the gun to Tattoo's one. With a grunt of effort, he finally pried the weapon from the thug's hand. For a split second, Lisa knew a moment of relief, of hope.

And then the tide shifted. Tattoo reached behind him with one massive hand and grabbed a handful of Lisa's hair. With a shrug and sideways flop, he slammed Lisa to the ground. The air whooshed from her lungs, and a thousand pinpricks of pain seared her scalp as Tattoo used his grip on her hair to jerk her head back. He snatched up one of the larger pieces of broken glass and pressed the jagged edge to her exposed throat. In a terrible heartbeat, the enemy had turned the tables.

ICE SLUICED THROUGH Eric's blood as he watched the large man drag Lisa to her feet. He stared in horror at the sharp edge of broken glass pressed close to her jugular vein. If the man sliced the vital blood vessel, Lisa could bleed out in minutes, even with his attempts to save her.

But he now had possession of the man's pistol. Bleeding cuts on his hands from the broken glass made his hands slick, his grip less than ideal. He aimed the weapon at the man but had no clear shot. Not while the SOB held Lisa in front of him, the glass at her throat.

His opponent twisted his mouth in a gloating grin. "You don't want to do that, man. You might hit your girlfriend."

Eric gritted his teeth, his nostrils flaring as he heaved air into his depleted lungs. "Let her go!"

The goon snorted. "No. Blondie has cost me too much. Tonight is about evening that score."

Lisa's eyes were wide with fright, and tears puddled against her lashes as her blue gaze pleaded silently for help.

Eric scrambled mentally, trying to work out a plan of attack that wouldn't cost Lisa her life. If he had help—

His gut clenched, knowing he needed backup. But the goon stood between him and the door. His phone was on the other side of the room, as well, plugged to the charger. Lisa's cell was down the hall in the kitchen, charging on the counter. He cursed silently. The odds were stacked against him.

Outside help? Had his father or any of the nearby rental guests heard the errant gunshot? Lisa's scream?

He prayed they had, that someone had already called 911. Prayed, too, that his father or another innocent didn't come to the door, putting themselves in the line of fire.

Eric swallowed hard. His throat burned where he'd been choked, but he ignored the pain. He had to focus on saving Lisa.

"Look," he said, trying to sound reasonable despite the fury and fear burning inside him. "I will let you leave, get off the property, no strings, no cops, if you release her to me now. Unharmed."

The man sneered. "I'm not here to negotiate. The girl dies tonight. And the baby comes with me."

A fresh wave of icy horror flashed through Eric. "The baby?"

The thug arched an eyebrow. "Yep. With the right connections, I can get fifty, sixty grand easy for a healthy white baby."

"Don't you lay a finger on Rachel, you pig!" Lisa snarled, her face a mask of rage.

Her captor jerked her head back harder, his fingers tight in her hair. Putting his mouth right by her ear, he grated, "You can shut up. I haven't forgotten the axe you put in my thigh, bitch. For that, I going to make your death slow and painful. Payback."

Eric tensed, his stomach roiling as he stewed over the man's threats. He would not let this man hurt Lisa, steal Rachel, even if it cost him his own life. He eased forward a step, his bare foot making the pennies and broken glass crunch.

The sound brought the man's attention back to Eric. "Drop the gun, or I swear I will cut her."

Eric kept the pistol trained on the thug's head, took another step. "Cut her, and it will be the last thing you ever do. I can make *you* suffer, too, you son of a bitch."

The thug's dark glower morphed into a smug smile. "You don't have the balls. Besides, you don't want to shoot *her* by mistake, now do you?"

Eric's gut churned. No, he did not want to hit Lisa. He clenched his teeth, knowing the loathsome man had him on that point.

Lisa's captor dragged her back several steps. She clawed at his restraining hands, her head at an awkward angle, her feet slipping and stumbling as he backed toward the door.

Eric followed, matching every inch the man moved backward. How the hell did he get Lisa away from this maniac without her getting hurt? Unwilling to take his eyes off Lisa and her assailant for even a fraction of a second to check his step, his bare feet crunched painfully over the pennies and shattered glass.

He tried to play out different tactics in his mind, analyzing the likely outcome of each. Charge the man and try to free Lisa? Shoot toward his leg and pray he didn't hit her? End his pursuit of them and go for his cell phone?

His grip tightened on the gun. In the time it took to call 911 and relay the critical information, the tattooed man could slice Lisa's neck and be out the door with Rachel. *Damn it all!*

Drawing a slow breath, he focused again on finding a way to protect Rachel and rescue Lisa. A knot formed in his chest, twisting hard with apprehension, knowing what he might have to do. To save these two people he'd come to love, he might have to kill a man—for the second time.

LISA DREW IN shallow breaths, afraid to move any more than needed while the sharp edge of glass was pressed to her throat. Her feet already stung from the small cuts on her feet, proof of how little it took for glass shards to ravage skin. And she knew Tattoo's intent was not just a nick. When she was no longer useful as a human shield, he'd cut her. Deeply. A fatal slash of her carotid. In the book she'd read by Matt, Eric's father had detailed such a grisly death, inflicted on one of his characters. A whimper of fear escaped her, dreading such a death for herself.

Tattoo dragged her through the bedroom door into the short hall. Eric stayed with them, the gun aimed at them. Knowing how defending his mother's life had burdened him with guilt, how would he react to shooting Tattoo? Could he pull the trigger? Could she ask him to? Tears pricked her eyes. Couldn't she do something to help herself? Spare Eric? And save Rachel? A tall order.

She swallowed the taste of bile that climbed her throat. *Think, Lisa! Think!*

As Tattoo shuffled backward into the guest room, Lisa darted her gaze to the crib where Rachel stood, clinging to the rail, sobbing. Her niece's cries wrenched inside her. She longed to fly to her and wrap the sweet baby in her arms, soothe her. She'd gladly be a human shield for Rachel if she could break free of Tattoo's deadly grip.

Her captor edged closer to the baby's bed. Confusion filled Rachel's face, along with fear. Rachel had to be wondering who the strange man was and why Lisa hadn't picked her up.

"Please," Lisa begged, "I'll do anything you say. But do not hurt the baby. I'll go with you, but leave her here." She knew the Camerons would love and raise Rachel as surely as she knew she wanted to do the same herself. But she would do what it took to protect her niece as she'd promised Chelle she would.

Tattoo snorted. "You're not in much position to make deals, blondie."

Eric reached the guest room door, filling the space with

his wide shoulders, steady aim and braced stance. "I am in a position to say what happens next. You will not leave this room with that child. I will shoot you first."

As Tattoo sidled up to the crib, he seemed to realize his dilemma. He couldn't both secure Lisa around her waist and hold the sharp glass to her neck if he was going to lift Rachel from the crib. She felt his grip tense, the shard bite her skin. Then his ashy-smelling breath hissed in her ear. "Pick up the baby."

Lisa's pulse tripped. "What?"

"Pick up the baby!" Tattoo gave her a shake, pushing the glass harder against her neck. The answering sting hurt less than the notion of aiding this thug with stealing Rachel.

Lisa balled her hands in the soft fabric of her pajama pants and firmed her resolve. "No."

Her reply clearly startled Tattoo, whose chest vibrated at her back as he growled his discontent. And Eric, whose eyes flashed with concern.

"Let Lisa go! Now!" Eric edged closer, still blocking the door but demonstrating his intention to change the dynamic if Tattoo didn't obey. "And move away from the baby!" Though his voice was hard and demanding, Lisa knew him well enough now to hear the edge of anxiety.

Tattoo shook Lisa again. "Pick up the kid, bitch! I will cut you!"

Rachel's wails tugged at her heart, battling her resolve not to aid the thug who wanted to kidnap her niece. Ice balled in her gut, knowing she could be assuring her imminent death, but she could not, would not comply. "Go to hell!"

With a loud snarl, Tattoo dug the glass into her neck and sliced her throat.

Chapter Thirty

The goon cut Lisa with a vicious swipe of the large shard across her skin, and Eric's heart dropped. In the next instant, her assailant shoved her forward, Lisa stumbling into Eric as she crumpled.

A sound like bees swarming his head buzzed in his ears. Time seemed to stretch as he caught her under her arms and staggered. Dropped the gun. Fell to his knees. Agony ripped through him as he cradled her, watching the bright red blood that oozed down her neck. But a steady, heavy seep, not a spurting, pulsing spray that would indicate the carotid artery had been severed. Thank God! She could still bleed out if he didn't help her. If she didn't get the right medical help ASAP.

In the next instant, a blur of movement snatched his attention back to the thug. Over the precious few seconds that had passed, the goon had grabbed Rachel from the crib and was angling to get through the guest room door—which was no longer blocked since Eric was holding Lisa, scrambling to press his hands, his sleep shirt to the open wound on her throat.

He barked a foul word in frustration, realizing he couldn't stop the man from escaping with the baby and help Lisa at the same time. He had to choose. And fast. The man with the tattoo was already charging into the hall.

"Save... Rachel," Lisa rasped, her eyes wide and her hands clutching at his arms.

A sob of grief, the fear of losing Lisa if he left her now, clogged his throat. But he jerked a nod and moved her hands to her own neck to hold the shirt in place. "Hold that tight and lie still. Try to stay calm, slow your pulse."

Tears leaked onto her wan cheeks. "Eric, I..."

He shook his head. "Don't talk. Save your strength."

With hands slippery with her blood, he fumbled to grab the pistol as he surged to his feet. A fresh wave of adrenaline, fury and purpose propelled him to the hall. The man wasn't at his front door.

Of course. It was locked.

Confused, Eric paused only long enough to determine where Rachel's cries were coming from. The living room? Kitchen?

He rounded the corner from the hall into the kitchen, leading with the pistol. The man was halfway out the window behind the table in the breakfast nook. The window he'd forgotten to close before they went to bed. He shoved aside the self-recriminations he had no time to indulge in. "Stop! I will shoot!"

He immediately knew he couldn't shoot as long as the man held Rachel.

The man only grinned from outside the window as he held Rachel in front of him. "I dare you!"

Frustration clawed at Eric. He had to do something! He had to stop the man from leaving the grounds with Rachel, or she could be lost to them forever.

As he passed the kitchen counter in pursuit, he spotted Lisa's phone and snatched it up. He woke the screen but was met with a number pad. He didn't know her security code, and while he dithered with the phone, Rachel's kidnapper was getting away. He dropped the phone back on the counter with a growl of irritation.

Eric darted to the window and climbed out. The tattooed man was loping across the lawn, strongly favoring his right leg. His awkward gait made him slow.

As Eric sprinted toward the road, a desperation not to fail Lisa, not to allow this horrid man get away nearly choked him. He *had* to stop him! No matter what...

Eric raised the gun and fired.

Chapter Thirty-One

Lisa lay motionless on the floor of the guest room, clutching Eric's shirt to her neck with all her might. It smelled like him. His body wash, his musk, his uniquely *Eric* essence, and the scent stirred an ache inside her. She'd been terrified of losing him, but now she mourned the idea of dying herself and missing out on the life they might have had. Never having the chance to tell him she loved him. Not getting to see Rachel grow into a woman.

She was a little surprised she wasn't dead yet. She thought you died almost instantly when your throat was cut. But she—

A shout and another blast of gunfire rumbled from outside, and she jolted. She wanted so badly to know what was happening, to crawl to the window and look out.

Lie still, Eric had told her.

But how could she lie here doing nothing while he risked his life? How could she not do anything to help him? If she was going to die, to bleed out from the slash on her throat, she wanted her last act, her last moments to be for good. Gathering herself and taking slow breaths to stop the spinning of her head, she rolled to her hands and knees, pushed slowly to her feet. Still clutching the shirt to her neck, she staggered to the hall, toward the front door.

THE GUNFIRE, AIMED at the ground in order to wake his family and elicit help, clearly startled the goon. Surprised by the blast, the man stumbled, nearly falling. Eric gained several more steps on the criminal and shouted, "Stop! Let the baby go!"

When they reached the loose gravel of the driveway, the goon's step faltered again, and Eric made his move. He tossed the gun aside and flung himself onto the man's back. As they toppled, Eric shifted his weight to the side, praying the man fell at an angle that would spare the baby the brunt of the fall. At the last second, he reached around to cradle the back of Rachel's head. He and the thug landed on the ground in a tangle of limbs and loss of breath.

Rachel was scarily silent for a moment, obviously stunned by the fall, but then she sent up a loud wail.

Eric struggled to suck air into his frozen lungs, his eyes tracking both his opponent and Rachel.

Her kidnapper thrust her away as he rolled to engage Eric hand to hand. *Get Rachel!* one voice in his head screamed, while another shouted, *Subdue the thug!*

As the tattooed man righted himself and rose onto his knees over Eric, his choice was made for him. The thug let a fist fly that connected with Eric's chin. Eric planted a foot in the thug's chest to shove him back, but the man caught him by the ankle as he fell back. The goon kept a tight grip on Eric's leg, pinning it to the ground first with his hand, then trapping both of Eric's legs with his knees.

Despite the anchor on his legs, Eric sat up, meeting the other man's grappling hands with a matching strength and deft moves. He jabbed at his opponent's eyes and throat, and when he found the room for an upward arc, he smashed the heel of his hand into the goon's nose.

In return, Eric received much of the same. Pain ricocheted in his skull, his ribs, his arms as he fought off his attacker. The longer he kept the man engaged, the more time he bought his family to arrive, to call police, to come to his aid. What felt like hours, he knew had been only a few critical minutes. But he could feel himself weakening. His legs trapped as they were, gave his opponent an advantage—one he used to wrestle Eric to the ground, wrench him to his stomach and place him in another choke hold. Eric's already raw throat and aching lungs suffered under the abuse of the criminal's strangling grip on his neck and suffocating weight on his back. He dug deep for every morsel of strength, trying to buck the man off, struggling to keep the man's hands from crushing his windpipe.

But the dim edges of his vision told him he was losing consciousness. And if he passed out, he'd lose his life.

LISA WOBBLED ON weak knees, bracing a hand on the wall on her way to the front door. As she passed the decorative mirror in the entryway, she caught a movement in her peripheral vision. Her heart slammed, spooked by the motion. She swallowed hard, and her body sagged, when she realized it was her own reflection. Trembling, she groped to turn on the light.

Stepping to the mirror, she lowered Eric's wadded shirt from her neck and leaned in to examine the gash Tattoo had inflicted. The cut was several inches long, but not nearly as deep as she'd imagined based on the sting. Nearer her shoulder than her chin, more to the right than near the carotid. The wound still seeped blood, but not the copious amounts she'd have expected for a fatal wound. Her heart kicked. The wound was ugly and painful, but...

A sob that hiccupped with relief escaped. She was injured but not dying. Buoyed by fresh resolve, she quickly snatched her winter scarf from the hook by the door and used it to tie Eric's shirt tightly in place over her wound.

She heard more shouts, another gunshot and spun back to the door.

Even after wiping her hands on her nightshirt, her hands

were slippery with blood, but she fumbled the dead bolt and knob lock button and jerked the door open. Stumbling weakly to the porch, she scanned the yard for Eric, for Tattoo, for Rachel. The sight that greeted her was like salt in her flayed soul. "Eric, no!"

The security lamp at the street cast a blue-white light to a spot near the driveway where Tattoo's hulking form hovered over Eric. Tattoo had Eric pinned down, his hands around Eric's throat.

"No!" she screamed, stumbling across the yard as quickly as her weak legs would carry her. "Stop!"

Tattoo only cast her a scowl.

Just beyond the two men but far too close to their fight for Lisa's comfort, Rachel sat on the grass, bawling and shrieking in fear.

Save Rachel!

She beelined for the baby, lifting Rachel and moving her several wavering steps away from the men's combat. As much as she wanted to hold her niece and comfort her, her priority in that moment was Eric. His gasping and sluggish movements told her he was fading. Once again, she needed a weapon. In the darkness she searched the ground for a large rock, a tree branch, *anything* with heft that she could—

Lisa stilled when she glimpsed the light reflecting off the dark metal. Tattoo's gun lay discarded a few feet from the wrestling men. Her breath backed up in her lungs, but she stumbled to it, taking it into her shaking hands. The drying blood was sticky now, but she positioned the weapon between her hands and curled her finger around the trigger.

Her head spun, and she feared she might topple as adrenaline and doubt swamped her. Could she really shoot a man? Did she have a choice? Tattoo was close to killing Eric. She had to do something!

"Let him go," she rasped, her voice far too strangled, too quiet for any impact, "or I'll shoot."

Tattoo didn't even glance at her. Blood streamed from his swollen nose, and his jaw was clenched, teeth bared as he choked Eric.

Lisa pointed the gun at the yard and fired to get Tattoo's attention.

When the man snapped his gaze to her, she aimed the weapon at him. The muzzle wavered. Her blood loss and terror left her arms weak and her hands shaking. If she fired, could she even hit her target? Would she kill Eric by mistake?

Gritting her teeth and mustering all her fury and grief to fuel her, Lisa shouted hoarsely, "Get off him! Or I *will* kill you!"

Tattoo narrowed a wary look, sitting taller as he debated whether to believe her or call her bluff. His dark eyes caught the glow of the streetlight, glinting in a way that sent a chill to her core.

An image flashed in Lisa's mind. Tattoo firing on Vic and her brother-in-law crumpling. The blood, gore and horror of the memory stirred the bile in her gut. This man had nothing but evil intent, cold calculation and malice in his heart. An assurance swept through her that he'd show her, Eric and Rachel no mercy. If she didn't act soon, Eric would die.

Drawing a quavering breath, she squeezed the trigger.

ERIC'S STRENGTH HAD waned significantly, his lungs aching when he'd heard Lisa's voice. She was there, on the lawn. Somehow. The sight of her sparked a small bump in his pulse. A fleeting gasp of energy. But not enough to shake off his attacker.

He'd wanted to warn her away. Wanted to tell her to grab Rachel and run. Wanted to tell her he loved her. But he had so little oxygen left.

He hated that she'd see him go limp. Leave this world. Like she'd seen her sister die. Her brother-in-law murdered.

She'd only just gotten her memory back. What would tonight's trauma do to her?

And then her voice sounded again. Stronger now. Fiercer.

He felt the thug shift, his grip on his throat slacken just a tiny bit.

Then an ear-shattering bang. A gunshot.

The sound sent a bolt of alarm through Eric. *Lisa!*

The weight of the man on his back fell away. His grip on Eric's throat gone.

He heard a roar of male anger. Agony. Cursing.

Eric sucked in a deep gasping breath. Another. His chest heaved as he painfully dragged air through his bruised trachea. His head throbbed and spun.

Mustering strength in his limbs, he rolled away from the bellowing thug. Struggled to his hands and knees. Blinked to bring the scene into focus. The tattooed man lay on his back, clutching his leg, howling in pain.

He followed the sound of Rachel's piercing cry. The baby sat a safe distance away. Obviously terrified. But no obvious injury.

Spots danced in his vision, but he blinked them away. Had he imagined Lisa?

He heard shouts from the road. His father's voice. Jake's.

Twisting at the waist, he searched the dimly lit yard until his gaze stopped on a crumpled heap in the grass. Blond hair. Bloody night shirt.

His gut wrenched as adrenaline spilled into his blood, fueling him. He crawled to her, his arms buckling as he hurried to her side.

"Lis—" The half word was more of an exhale than speech.

She raised wide blue eyes to his, her body trembling, her expression stunned. "I...sh-shot him."

He nodded. As his lungs greedily replenished his body with oxygen, his heart thrashed in his chest and throat ached. But his attention was all for Lisa. "Your neck."

He reached for the tartan scarf she'd tied around her neck, but she grabbed at his hands.

Her fingers were cold, her eyes frantic. "I—I shot him."

His pulse kicked. *Oh, no! No, no, no! Damn it!*

She seemed to be slipping into shock, maybe another fugue. "Lisa!" He coughed and tried again. "Stay…with me," he rasped, his voice growing stronger as he recovered his breath.

His father appeared beside him then, wearing only his pajama pants. "Eric! Are you hurt? What happened? Who is that man?"

"I sh-shot him," Lisa repeated. Her gaze had fixed on the goon, whose shouts had become moans, his body growing stiller.

Eric grabbed her by her shoulders and gave her a small shake. "Listen…to me. Stay…with me. You're safe…now. Help is…coming." He cut a quick glance to his father that silently asked if this was true.

Matt nodded. "Cait's on the phone with 911 now."

Eric hitched his head toward the edge of the yard. "Dad, will you…get the baby? Have Cait or someone…come get her."

His father moved off to follow through on Eric's request, and Eric turned back to Lisa. "Hang on, sweetheart. Help is coming."

"Is…is he dead?" She swayed, clearly weak from blood loss, shock.

A memory flowed through him. A night that still echoed so clearly in his mind, he could still smell the summer honeysuckle and feel the acid bite of panic in his gut. He knew how Lisa's life could be scarred if the goon died from the wound she'd inflicted. And a new resolve fired in his soul.

Eric framed Lisa's face with his hands and stared into her dazed eyes. "He's not dead. And I won't let him die. Just stay with me. Okay? Look! Rachel's here. She's safe."

His father returned quickly with the sobbing baby, holding the tiny girl against his shoulder in a secure and loving embrace.

Lisa blinked, but she continued to look dazed.

"Please, sweetheart. Stay with us. For Rachel." He sighed and glanced to his father. "I need to check on the man she shot." He inclined his head toward Lisa, the gesture asking his father to take care of her until he returned. "Her throat's cut. Keep pressure on the wound."

With that, he rose unsteadily onto his feet and staggered back to the thug. His stepuncle and boss, Jake Turner, was leaning over the injured criminal, his hands on the man's bloody thigh. His boss lifted a grave expression to Eric as he knelt beside them.

"He doesn't look good. His leg's bleeding pretty bad."

As if he'd never left his residency, Eric slipped back into the role for which he'd trained so many years. He shoved aside the fact that this man had tried to kill him, kill Lisa and saw him only as a patient needing emergency care to survive.

Eric waved his boss's hands away from the bleeding hole in his patient's leg and grimaced. "I need more light. I can't see a damn thing!"

Jake's jaw tightened. "I'll get a flashlight."

He sprinted away before Eric could say more. Covering the gushing wound with his own hands, Eric stared down at the thug, whose countenance was twisted in pain and hatred. "I'm going to tend your wound. Cooperate and you might live."

The man curled a lip in a snarl. "That's…second time… that bitch…done this to me."

A flicker of fury blazed in Eric's chest for the slur against Lisa, but with effort he suppressed it, refocusing on his task. "I know you're hurting." His voice was still weak, but he infused it with an air of command and cool control. "But you need to try to slow your breathing. Calm your pulse." He inhaled deeply himself, demonstrating, then released the air, feeling a flow of returning energy. "I'm going to check for an exit wound."

The man's glare was dark, but he gritted his teeth and bobbed his chin.

Wedging one hand under the goon's injured leg, Eric ran his fingers along the underside of his patient's thigh. Finding no evidence of an exit wound, he surmised the bullet was still somewhere in the man's leg. Possibly lodged in his femur. Not good.

As Eric was ripping the man's pant leg for better access to the wound, Jake returned with the large flashlight Eric kept with his construction supplies in the trunk of his Honda and a towel from Eric's gym bag. His boss turned on the flashlight and aimed the beam on the leg wound. Eric cleaned away as much blood as he could in a few swipes and studied the seepage that flowed from the neat bullet hole. The bleed was steady but didn't have the telltale pulsing spurt that indicated an arterial bleed. Not the femoral then. Good. But enough to be concerning.

Muttering a curse word, Eric stacked his hands and pressed hard on the wound, then looked up at Jake. "I need more supplies."

"Name it."

Eric squeezed his eyes shut, trying to clear his head and mentally picture the steps he needed to take. "Clean cotton or gauze to pack the wound. More towels. Gauze will be in the first aid kit over the refrigerator."

With a grim nod, Jake rose and darted away. While he waited for him to return, Eric lifted his hands and remembered a day in the ER during his residency when the lead doctor had instructed him to use his elbow to apply more pressure to a gunshot wound. Shifting, he dug his elbow into his patient's leg. The man screamed in pain then fell silent. Eric prayed the silence meant the thug had passed out and not because he'd died, but he didn't have a free hand to check his patient's pulse.

If the man Lisa shot died…

He shook off that line of thinking as Jake returned with the first aid kit, a couple kitchen towels and some fabric scraps Eric recognized as ones Lisa had been using to quilt. Keeping pressure on the wound, he nodded to the first aid kit. "Open all of the gauze packets. I'll need a lot."

Jake did as instructed, pausing to lift his head and glance toward the road. "I can hear sirens."

Eric raised his head, listening. "They need to hurry. I don't know how much longer he's got."

Once the gauze was ready, he began poking the pads deep in the bullet hole, packing the wound to stem the bleeding. When he'd used all the gauze, he finished with the scraps of fabric. Then, covering the opening with a towel, he leaned hard on the wound with both hands. He frowned at Jake. "That's the best I can do under the circumstances, but…it still may not be enough."

Chapter Thirty-Two

Colored light strobed on the trees, and the murmur of voices surrounded Lisa. She was having trouble focusing, but she fought to stay conscious, Eric's plea echoing in her brain. *Stay with me!*

She held Rachel with as much strength as she could muster, the baby clinging to her with tiny fists twisted in her nightshirt and hair. The baby's wails had quieted to hiccupping whimpers, her head buried against Lisa's chest. She was only vaguely aware of Matt's presence at her side, one hand firmly gripping her shoulder while his other pressed a cloth against the base of her throat. At her other side, Cait huddled close, stroking her back and whispering soft words Lisa tuned out. She kept her gaze down the sloped yard where Eric hunched over Tattoo.

"Up here!" Matt shouted, and Lisa jolted.

A couple of people from the arriving vehicles rushed up the yard. They dropped to a squat in front of her, blocking her view of Eric. Of Tattoo.

She'd shot Tattoo.

Her head spun as she processed that fact again. Had she meant to? Had she had another choice? Her memory of the incident blurred and tangled with images of Chelle dying in her arms, of Vic's head wound as he collapsed on the floor, of a car barreling toward her.

"She was cut, here on her neck," Matt said, his voice sounding like he was under water. "I'm not sure how much blood she's lost, but she's been largely unresponsive for the last few minutes."

"Shock," the man in front of her said, reaching for her.

Lisa stirred, panic fluttering in her chest when Rachel was pulled from her arms. "N-no!"

"It's all right, ma'am. We just want to check the baby for injury. We'll take good care of her."

"R-Rachel…" she rasped as her niece was carried away.

"Let me have a look at you," the man squatting in front of her said. He shone a bright light in her eyes, and she blinked and turned away.

A blanket was draped around her shoulders. The scarf and shirt pressed to her neck were removed and cold wipes swabbed the exposed gash.

Through it all she tried to lean, tried to look around the EMTs for Eric. All she wanted was him. His steadying presence and comforting touch. The warmth and reassurance of his smiling eyes. His calming voice. His—

Hands placed under her elbows eased her to her back. More hands were laid on her as she was moved to a stretcher. Bumped across the lawn. Loaded in an ambulance.

Lisa shook her head, the movement pulling at her cut, but she didn't care. "Eric! Where's Eric?"

"Try to lie still, ma'am." The man to her left put a firm hand on her forehead to quiet her. "Your family will meet you at the hospital." The EMT slapped the wall of the bay, shouting, "All set!"

And the ambulance bounced as they drove away.

ERIC STOOD BACK, spouting his assessment of the goon's condition as the EMTs moved into position to take over his care. "Heavy blood loss, but unlikely damage to the femoral artery. I found no exit wound. Pulse thready. Respiration light but steady."

Jake clapped him on the back as Eric backed up to allow a stretcher to be brought in. "Impressive work, Doc. You probably saved that man's life."

Eric's chest squeezed, and he glanced down at his bloody hands, the red smears all the more glaring and obscene in the headlamps and strobing lights of the emergency vehicles.

"You should be proud of yourself," Jake added. "I sure am."

Eric swallowed, his bruised throat aching. Proud? He sighed. All he was at the moment was numb. With his part in the critical battle for the thug's life past, he felt fatigued to the marrow.

Motion to his right called his attention to the stretcher being rolled toward the open ambulance bay.

Lisa! He staggered across the gravel drive and grassy lawn, attempting to intercept the stretcher. He needed to see her, wanted to know she was all right. But as he neared the ambulance bay, an EMT stuck his arm out, blocking his path. "Stand back, sir."

Eric aimed a bloody finger toward the stretcher. "I just want to—"

The bay doors were slammed shut, cutting him off. The EMT took a step to leave before noticing the blood on Eric's hands. "Are you injured?"

Eric turned up his palms and sighed. "This isn't my blood."

The EMT shined a pen light at Eric then frowned as his gaze took in Eric's red throat and battered face. The flashlight angled lower to his cut feet.

Before the EMT could voice his obvious concerns, Eric said, "I'll have someone take me to the hospital." He signed the form the EMT extended, saying he declined transport, and turned to find a police officer waiting just behind him.

Eric sighed, knowing the night was far from over.

Hours later, after he'd been cleaned up, run through the ER protocol and treated for cuts and other minor injuries, Eric gave his statement to the police. He was careful to word his description of the circumstances so the officer understood that Lisa's firing on the goon was purely in defense and only to save Eric's life.

The patrol officer gave him no clues to what Lisa had said, if anything, and the hospital was likewise guarded giving information on Rachel's or Lisa's condition since he was not family.

"I'm sorry. HIPPA laws prevent me from discussing a patient's condition without permission," his nurse said when she came in with his release forms.

He groaned. "I'm well aware of HIPPA laws. But you can tell her it's me who wants to know. If she asks for me, you can let me back to see her then."

The nurse only gave a sympathetic nod as she took the clipboard back from him. "You're free to go. But...if you hung around the lobby for a little while, it would probably be worth your time."

He found several of the Camerons waiting in the ER lobby. He was swarmed by his adopted family and peppered with questions. What had happened? How badly was he hurt? What had the police said? And on and on.

He gave succinct replies, only enough information to satisfy their concerns, before he launched into his own inquiries. Had they heard any word on Lisa or Rachel? Did they know if the thug had survived?

Neil and Grace exchanged a troubled look that jerked a knot in Eric's gut.

"What? Tell me!"

"We don't know anything about Lisa or the man who attacked you, but...a social worker was here earlier."

Eric tensed. "Rachel..."

Grace nodded, her brow furrowed. "She took Rachel into

state custody while they conduct an investigation of what happened tonight and who her legal guardian would be." She wet her lips before adding, "And whether they deemed her next of kin a safe environment for her."

His heart sank. Lisa's entire mission from the beginning of this nightmare had been to protect Rachel and keep her out of the state system. Lisa would be devastated to know this turn of events.

The doors to the back halls of the ER swung open, and Anya, in her work scrubs, walked swiftly across the room toward her family. "I've been with Lisa, and while I can't divulge anything about her condition, I can tell you she's been admitted. The information desk in the main lobby can tell you which room number."

Eric squeezed Anya's arm. "Thank you." With the rest of the gathered Camerons trailing after him, he headed for the main hospital lobby.

LISA DRIFTED IN and out of alertness. The medicine they'd put in her IV for pain made her so tired. But every unfamiliar sound, every disturbing flashback of the night had her awake again and searching her surroundings for Eric, for Rachel. But they weren't there, and no amount of asking for them changed that. Her voice was slurred, and her head throbbed when she tried to talk, so she eventually quit trying, even when a policeman was allowed into her exam room.

The man's expression was gentle as he interrogated her, but his questions were hard, probing and frightening. She closed her eyes, tears leaking on to her cheeks, and she struggled to bring the events of the night into clear focus.

Finally her nurse, an Indian woman who seemed so familiar, asked the policeman to wait with his questions. Her patient was not in a good condition to answer his queries.

A short while later, new faces appeared at her bedside. The men in scrubs pulled up her guardrails and transferred IV bags before rolling her out of her room and onto an elevator. One of the orderlies grinned and said something about her "overnight accommodations" being ready.

"Eric..." she rasped to these men, but again she went unheard...or ignored.

She'd been left alone in the new room for several minutes before she heard familiar voices at her door. She tried to sit up, but her arm buckled and the stitches at her throat pulled. She flopped back down on her bed and watched, hoping.

When Eric burst into sight, his gaze latching on to hers as he rushed to her side, she gave a sob of relief. He took the hand she lifted, squeezing it and leaning close to kiss her cheek, stroke her hair. "I've been so worried about you," he whispered, moisture filling his bruised and bloodshot eyes. "Tell me you're okay."

She clutched at him and blinked loose tears. "I am now."

He shifted to sit on the edge of her bed, and Lisa gripped his fingers harder. "Don't go. Stay with me! Please."

When he nodded his assurance to her, she allowed her eyes to drift closed. And finally slept.

Chapter Thirty-Three

Lisa was released from the hospital the next day, having received a pint of blood and antibiotics to stave off infection from the gash on her neck. The doctor told her she'd have a scar but that she'd been very lucky the cut had not been deep enough or in a location that had proven imminently life-threatening.

"Still, the pressure you applied to the wound slowed the bleeding and likely saved you from passing out," the doctor said as she scribbled her signature on the release papers.

Lisa glanced at Eric, a chill crawling down her back. If she'd passed out, she realized, Tattoo would have killed Eric. Taken Rachel. And yet...

She was still haunted by the reality that she'd shot a man. While Tattoo—or David John "DJ" Grumbank, according to the policeman who'd come by first thing that morning to interview her—had made it through emergency surgery, he remained in critical condition and could still die.

"Am I being charged for shooting him?" Lisa had asked the policeman, holding her breath.

"Not at this point," he'd replied. "If all the evidence and other witness accounts back up your description of the events, as they have so far, the shooting will be cleared as justifiable."

Knowing that was a relief, but Lisa's primary concern was not her own health or what happened to DJ. She's spent the day agonizing over having failed Chelle, losing Rachel to the system with no guarantee of regaining custody. She'd listened to herself recounting to the policeman the events from January through DJ's attack the night before as if an observer hovering above the room. She knew how bad her case sounded. Would she return Rachel to a woman who'd shot a man or wielded an axe? A woman who'd lost her memory for more than two months? A woman who'd allowed a criminal to nearly kidnap her niece?

The details of the past months were ugly, raw and unfavorable for Lisa. And her heart ached with grief and guilt and disappointment with herself for having let Chelle down.

That afternoon, when Eric drove her back to Cameron Glen, the Camerons' hospitality and comforting kindness was out in force. Someone had even brought Peanut from Eric's cabin to the senior Camerons' home to greet her with soft rubs and a happy purr. Grace had cooked all of Lisa's favorite foods, Eric's aunts offered copious support and optimism, and several of the children brought her artwork intended to cheer her.

"Look at mine, Aunt Lisa! I drew your family. That's you and Eric and Rachel," Joey said, Isla's youngest, pointing out the stick figures under a house and rainbow.

Beside her, Isla caught her breath as if sensing the spear of pain that pierced Lisa's heart. Her family? If only...

Isla reached over and gave Lisa's knee a comforting pat.

While all of their efforts were appreciated, Lisa couldn't shake the funk that had swamped her. How did she get Rachel back? What would happen to Rachel if Child Protective Services ruled she was unfit?

More than anything, she wanted to create a home for Rachel that was safe and loving and stable. A home with Eric. A family...

But how could she plan a life with Eric, knowing she'd always be tainted by the horrors of her past and her guilt over the danger she'd put him and his family in? Eric deserved someone who didn't come with so much baggage. Perhaps he even knew that for himself on some level. He'd never said he loved her. Never talked of a future beyond helping her recover her memory and restore her previous life. On top of everything else she'd lost, would she now lose these cherished people whom she'd come to love? Would she lose Eric? If her history was a predictor, the odds were good.

ERIC SAT ACROSS his grandparents' living room watching his stepfamily envelop Lisa in a sea of kindness and support. He knew the Camerons' love was the best medicine for her at this point, because he'd been on the receiving end of their compassion.

Yet he also saw the lingering shadows in her expression. He recognized the guilt and grief and trauma in her slumped shoulders and haunted eyes, because he'd been in that hellscape once himself. In so many ways, he was still in that dark place. Wasn't that why he'd given up medicine and come to Cameron Glen to get his head straight? How did he help Lisa when he hadn't figured out how to help himself?

Giving Isla a stiff, forced smile, Lisa rose from the couch and wandered out of the living room without saying anything, without meeting Eric's eyes.

When he shoved to his feet to follow her, Cait shot an arm out to stop him. "Give her a few minutes alone, to take a breath, to shed a tear if she needs to. All of this has to be overwhelming at a time she was just grappling with the trauma that had stolen her memory."

He glanced at his stepmother, weighing her advice and slowly sat back down.

Beside Cait, his father rubbed his unshaven chin and cast a worried eye to Eric. "You've been through the wringer yourself. How are you holding up?"

Lifting a hand to his bruised neck and swollen face, Eric

inhaled carefully, appreciating the air in his lungs from a fresh perspective. "I'm fine, all things considered."

His gut twisted, knowing his rescue had come at the cost of Lisa's trauma. He remembered her trancelike expression and the stunned way she'd repeated, "I shot him." A fierce affection and humble gratitude fired in his chest. He swore to do anything in his power to guide Lisa through the coming days and lift her out of the quagmire of tangled feelings.

"If it's any comfort," Jake said, moving to perch on the end of the coffee table in front of Eric, "both Grace and Emma have filed applications to foster Rachel while the court decides what happens next."

Eric nodded. "Thanks. I know Lisa will appreciate that. I hope…"

He didn't bother finishing the sentence. Everyone in the crowded living room knew what he hoped, because they were all praying for the same outcome.

Jake furrowed his brow and rubbed his hands on the legs of his jeans. "Listen, Eric… I—" Jake's cheeks puffed out as he exhaled a large breath, stalling. "I want to talk to you about your job with Turner Construction."

Eric blinked. That was one of the last things he expected Jake to say. "My job?"

His boss, his stepuncle, nodded, his mouth grim. "I don't think construction is where you belong." He raised a hand, forestalling questions. "Not that you haven't done good work. But I saw you rendering aid to that thug last night, the same man who'd tried to kill you and Lisa, and…it said a lot to me."

Eric raised a hand to scrub his face, then winced when he encountered tender flesh. "Jake, I—"

"Let me finish." His uncle cleared his throat. "I gave you a job last year when you came here needing a mental health break. A soft place to land when you'd burnt out. But it would be wrong of me to let you stay indefinitely. I won't be your crutch."

Eric sat taller. His crutch? He opened his mouth to deny the assertion, and Jake aimed a finger at him.

"You belong in medicine. When that man was dying, your instinct was to save him. Just like you didn't think twice about rescuing Lisa and Rachel off that snowy highway, you put healing that man above revenge or anger or hatred. You're a doctor, Eric, not a construction worker."

His father reached over and laid a hand on Eric's back. "I agree. I've seen that truth your whole life."

"I'm not firing you," Jake said, his voice calm. "You'll need income while you make arrangements to go back to medicine, but...you need to move on now."

Eric's pulse hammered in his ears. Go back to medicine? But...

He replayed the images from the night before, remembered how seamlessly he'd kicked into emergency mode, how he'd not needed to debate whether to help DJ Grumbank. He'd just acted.

It is your nature to heal, to help, to fix.

Something swelled then burst in his core. He *had* missed medicine. But hadn't found a way to reconcile his career with his past, with the life he'd taken.

I shot him...

Lisa's quavering voice echoed in his brain. She'd faced the same tragic choice and made the same decision. To save her loved one from a man with deadly intent.

He shoved to his feet. The need to see Lisa, talk to Lisa surged in him.

"Eric?" his father said, his tone full of worry.

He turned his scraped palm toward his father and gave Jake a nod. "I understand. And thank you." With that he strode from the living room in search of Lisa.

Chapter Thirty-Four

Lisa looked up from her contemplation of the spring blossoms in Grace's flowerbed when she heard the squeak of the back screen door. Her heart tripped, as it always did, when she spotted Eric. His handsome face bore evidence to his brutal fight with Tattoo—DJ—and his neck was ringed in bruises. To her, he'd never look handsomer. He approached her with a concerned and questioning tilt to his head.

"Mind if I join you?"

She twitched a cheek, the closest she could come to a smile. "Sure."

He grunted in pain as he lowered himself onto the wrought iron bench next to her and fixed his gaze on the explosion of color around them. "Grace certainly has a green thumb."

"Mmm-hmm." Lisa knew he must have had a reason he'd followed her outside, something to discuss, and she braced herself for bad news. Had DJ died? Had he heard from Child Protective Services? Had he reached the same conclusion she had about the anchor she was around his neck?

To still the tremble in her hands, she clutched them together in her lap and stared at her feet. For long moments, however, he was silent, and the tension inside her grew.

"Just say it," she finally whispered.

"Hmm?"

"Whatever it was that brought you out here. Just...tell me."

She swallowed hard as a sour taste burned the back of her throat. Dread. Regret. Bittersweet longing.

"Jake thinks I should return to medicine. All but fired me, in fact."

Lisa jerked her head up, her startled gaze swinging to Eric's brown eyes. "What?"

"And I think...he's right."

"I..." She took a moment to fit this news into the rearranged puzzle of her life. "That's good." She frowned as she studied the dubious expression creasing his brow. "Isn't it?"

He let his exhalation whistle through his teeth. "It is. I'm just...remembering."

"Remembering what?" she nudged.

He faced her and unclenched her clasped hands, taking them in both of his with a strong and reassuring grip. "I've been where you are right now. Questioning. Struggling. Hurting. I remember how it feels...to take a life in order to save another."

Ice filled her veins. "DJ died?"

Eric squeezed his eyes shut and shook his head. "I meant me. The man I killed. But I saw how upset you were last night. How lost you seem today. And I remember feeling the same way. In some respects, I still do and..."

When he let his voice trail off, she mustered her own honesty for him. "That's part of it. It was...*is* hard to process, but...the thing that's killing me the most is how horribly I failed my sister. She trusted me to protect Rachel, to keep her out of the system, to give her a safe home and... I didn't."

His eyebrows snapped together. "What? You risked your life to save her!"

She shook her head. "No. *You* did. You're the one who chased DJ down when he was fleeing with Rachel. And you were nearly choked to death as a result!"

His mouth firmed, and he squeezed her hands tighter. "Now listen to me! You have done nothing but put that baby's welfare first for the last two months. You saved her from DJ in January and have been devoted to her ever since." He cupped her chin, lifting her head so that his penetrating gaze could burrow into hers. "We fought for her *together* last night. I couldn't have done what I did without you smashing the penny jar on DJ's head or shooting his leg when he was strangling me. Despite your own injury, you were brave and strong. You have nothing to regret!"

"That doesn't help get Rachel back!" she said, her sobs breaking free of the knot in her chest. "The things I've done could cost me custody of her!"

He nodded. "I'm sure when the judge hears the lengths you went to protect her, he'll have no qualms about granting you full custody."

"Even though I shot a man? Hit him with an axe in January? If the things I did prevent me from getting Rachel back—"

He framed her face with both hands now and leaned his forehead against hers. "I know it's hard, not having any control over how Rachel's custody is decided. What you do have control over is how you move forward. Don't stay trapped in a bog of regrets. You have to consider the reason behind your actions—and the result—and forgive yourself."

She pulled away from Eric and looked deep into the eyes that had been such comfort to her in the past several weeks, the windows to the soul of this deeply caring man. Did he hear himself?

Lisa placed a palm on his swollen cheek and whispered, "And what about you? Can you finally forgive yourself for the man who died when you defended your mother?"

HEARING LISA TURN his appeal around on him, surprise like an electric shock zinged through Eric. His mouth opened and shut mutely. He rocked back from her, needing a moment to process her question. Look at it from inside out. For years he'd been told his actions had been justifiable. Not to berate himself. To give himself grace. But he couldn't. But now, wanting the same expiation for Lisa, his own struggle felt different.

Sitting there in his grandmother's yard, surrounded by her blooming garden, he remembered a day some ten years past when he'd sat here with his great-grandmother, Nanna. An ache punched his chest. He missed the dear old woman, her Scottish brogue and blunt form of caring.

Eric Harkney, my dear lad, do not let the events of that terrible day last summer keep you from all the good things your future holds. You saved your mother's life, your stepfather's life. Let that *be your takeaway, and forgive yourself for the rest. Please.*

Her words whispered to him again on the spring breeze, and something deep inside him shifted. A knot he'd been carrying in his soul loosened. A pain he'd buried, trying to ignore the hurt, poured free. He pinched the bridge of his nose as tears stung his eyes.

Lisa draped an arm across his back and rested her head on his shoulder. "Maybe if we both forgive ourselves for our lowest moments, our darkest hours, we can move forward together. Two stronger than one?"

He raised his head and met the blue eyes that had mesmerized him since the day he'd first seen her staggering along the frozen highway. The hope and longing he saw in Lisa's gaze were a balm to his guilt and the release he needed from years of lonely atonement. "I'd like nothing more." He drew a deep breath adding, "Have I told you how much I love you?"

Finally, he saw a smile light her face. "No."

Careful of her stitches, he caught her cheek and pulled her close for a kiss. "I do. I love you with all of my heart, Lisa Mitchell. And I love Rachel as if she were my own."

The mention of Rachel's name dimmed her smile, and he was quick to add, "And together we will get Rachel back.

We'll fight any fight we have to, together, until she is back in our arms."

She threw her arms around his shoulders and held him tightly. "Thank you, Eric. Thank you! How am I ever going to repay you for all the ways you've been there for me?"

"I can think of one."

Lisa levered back and met his lopsided grin with a curious glance. "Eric?"

"Marry me. I love you, and I want us to share a future, build a family together, face down the past together. We *are* stronger as one."

Lisa's face lit with a smile that shamed the spring sun and Grace's budding tulips. "I love you, too, Eric! So much."

She kissed him hard and long, laughing and crying at the same time.

When he paused for a breath, he asked, "Is that a yes?"

She stroked his face. "Definitely a yes!"

Epilogue

Eight months later

Lisa cast her gaze around the crowded judge's chambers at the large and loving family into which she'd married. The entire Cameron clan had turned out for the ceremony today as they had for her and Eric's wedding the month before, and the celebration of Eric's return to medicine the week before that. By the end of the year, he would complete his residency and had a position waiting at a hospital in Asheville.

Even Eric's "uncle" Daryl, the Cameron's adopted son, had returned from his overseas job to share the joyous event today. Her heart swelled as she squeezed her new husband's hand and stretched on her toes to kiss the cheek of the baby in his arms.

"I hate to be anticlimactic in light of the large assembly of guests," the family court judge said with a rueful grin, "but all that is really needed is for the two of you to sign the paperwork, and the adoption will be final."

After weeks of tedious waiting and a full investigation by both the police and Child Protective Services, Lisa was determined to be Rachel's most viable family for assuming custody. Not only did Vic's widowed mother not want the financial burden of raising her granddaughter, the court saw Eric and Lisa's two-parent home, with abundant additional

Cameron family support, as the best home for Rachel. The official adoption process fell into place quickly following the custody ruling.

"We'll create our own pomp," Daryl said, cupping a hand around his mouth as he made a *toot-toot-ta-too* trumpeting sound.

"Works for me!" Lisa said, taking the pen the judge offered her and signing the document on the desk before the judge could change his mind. Turning, she held out the pen to Eric and took Rachel from his arms. "Come here, sweetheart. I'm your mommy now."

Eric signed the papers as well, waving a flourish with his hand as he finished. "Voilà!"

The family cheered and clapped, which prompted Rachel to giggle and clap her chubby hands.

"Back to Cameron Glen for the party!" Neil called, waving everyone out to the courthouse halls. Another cheer went up.

As Lisa and Eric made their way through the clamoring family and eager hands of Rachel's new cousins, Eric paused to reach in his suit jacket pocket for his phone.

"What is it?" Lisa asked when she saw the knit in his brow.

"A text message from Detective Morris. DJ Grumbank was indicted on all charges yesterday and held without bond. Assuming a jury convicts him, which he's confident they will—the evidence is overwhelming—DJ will spend the rest of his life behind bars." He raised a glance to her. "You'll have to testify, you know."

"I know. But he can't hurt me anymore. And as hard as it is to remember what happened, to think about losing Chellie," she reached for his hand, "I can do anything with you at my side."

"Yeah, you can," he returned, grinning proudly.

Lisa exhaled her relief. The news put a period at the end of that dark chapter of her life. Though she'd always miss

Chelle, she could face tomorrow with confidence and all the joy her new husband and daughter bought her.

His expression reflecting the same happiness that bubbled inside her, Eric extended a hand to her. "Shall we go, Mrs. Harkney? Rachel Harkney?"

As Lisa lifted her hand to take Eric's, Rachel leaned away from her and lifted her arms to her new father. "Up, Daddy!"

He blinked. Smiled. And hugged his little girl close. "Up, up and away!"

* * * * *

COMING SOON!

We really hope you enjoyed reading this book.
If you're looking for more romance
be sure to head to the shops when
new books are available on

Thursday 22nd May

To see which titles are coming soon, please visit
millsandboon.co.uk/nextmonth

MILLS & BOON

OUT NOW!

ROMANCE ON DUTY
LOVE IN Action

BRENDA JACKSON   **NICHOLE SEVERN**   **CHARLOTTE HAWKES**

3 BOOKS IN ONE

Available at
millsandboon.co.uk

MILLS & BOON

LET'S TALK
Romance

For exclusive extracts, competitions and special offers, find us online:

- **f** MillsandBoon
- **X** @MillsandBoon
- **◎** @MillsandBoonUK
- **♪** @MillsandBoonUK

Get in touch on 01413 063 232

For all the latest titles coming soon, visit
millsandboon.co.uk/nextmonth